War for the Gulf continues…

ISBN-13: 979-8-9993028-2-3

ISBN-10: 1477123456

Cover design by: Collin Foster https://everythingfeathered.net/

Library of Congress Control Number: 018675309 Printed in the United States of America

Trigger Warnings

If you don't give a shit about triggers, boldly walk right into this war. I'll hold the door for you. I bet you love twisted surprises, don't you?

Trigger Warnings: Please take a moment to go over these if you are unsure about proceeding.

This is an open-door romance. 18+ Adults Only.

Explicit sexual language, Foul language, Descriptive sexual acts, Vulgar language, Murder, Blood, Graphic Violence, Hitting women (NOT by MMCs), Sex trafficking, Abduction, Gun usage, Torture, Family trauma/PTSD, Parental alienation, Parental emotional abuse, Manipulation tactics, Arranged Marriage, Breath play, Edge play, Double Penetration, Stalking, Breaking and Entering, Power dynamics, Touch her and die, Possessive and Obsessive MMCs who are also Cinnamon Rolls inside that tough exterior. MFM, no sword crossing.

This is not an exhaustive list as specific triggers vary widely between each person.

Table of Contents

A word of advice...

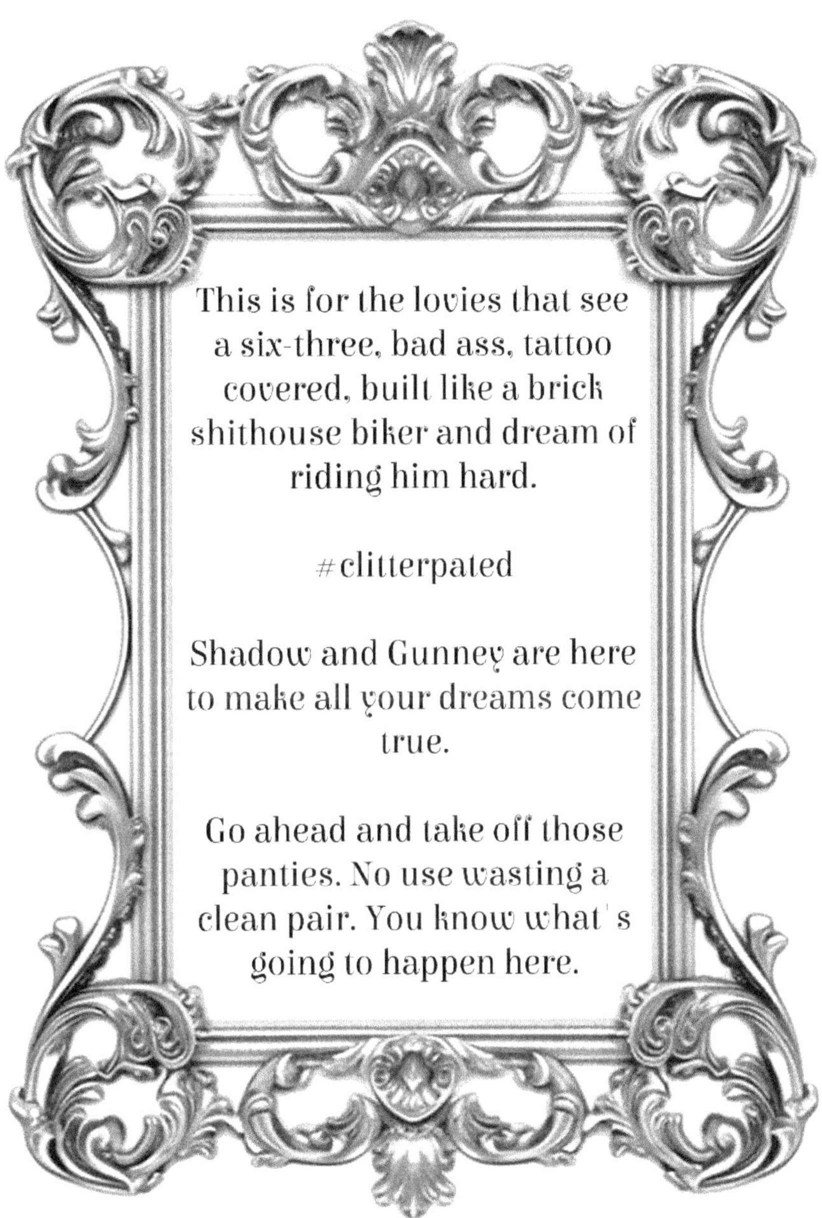
This is for the lovies that see a six-three, bad ass, tattoo covered, built like a brick shithouse biker and dream of riding him hard.

#clitterpated

Shadow and Gunney are here to make all your dreams come true.

Go ahead and take off those panties. No use wasting a clean pair. You know what's going to happen here.

Chapter 1 - Shadow

She thinks she's so fucking cute, trapezing around my best friend's wedding, talking to all the other bikers, flirting with the members, all la-de-fuckin-da. Or as the motorcycle club calls the bikers—associates—who all know damn well they shouldn't even be talking to her thus making me growl under my breath.

This woman gets on my goddamn nerves, man.

Hence the reason we've broken up so many times. And the reason I can't take my eyes off her.

The breakup is her choice, not at all mine. I'd wife her up so fucking fast her head will spin. She's in my blood, under my skin, and I can't shake her. I don't want to. I'm obsessed.

We are currently in the '*off*' stage of our now toxic relationship, and her flouncing around here and there is driving me out of my fucking mind.

Goddamn she looks so beautiful tonight in her bridesmaid dress.

She may hurt my heart, keep me waiting, and act like she hates me, but she still makes my blood boil and my cock hard. And I know her body wants me just as much.

Currently I'm a little pissed at her that it's been two weeks since I've held her.

Now, I must put up with her cold shoulder more often than not, giving me that frosty stare and being an all-around bitch to me, because her best friend married my best friend. And they think we all need to do wedding party bullshit like pictures and taking shots.

They have no idea how much it's slicing my heart. Filet it up on the grill why don'tcha.

Her laughter floats across the clubhouse to my ears and it sets my blood on fire with lust and anger. God, what I wouldn't give to hear her say my name again as she comes. I don't know what it is about Zharia that gets me so riled up. Or the reason I can't stay away from her. There's an undeniable pull that yanks me back to her over and over again.

I know in my heart of hearts; I'm destined to be with her.

I always end up right back in her arms and between her velvety, smooth legs where the best pussy I've ever had resides. Like nothing ever happened.

Take a deep breath, man. At ease, soldier.

Unfortunately, that perfect, succulent pussy is attached to the rest of her that has a razor-sharp tongue and a sassy as fuck mouth that can cut a man down in a heartbeat. I should know, I've been on the receiving end of it more times than I can count.

How do I put it, Zhar can get a little manic if things don't go her way.

This time was all because I wanted to protect her and make a life with her. I had to go and choose a woman who wants no relationships and no strings. And no amount of cajoling and maneuvering on my part will change her mind about being exclusively long term.

She asked how long was long term. When I replied, 'the rest of your life,' because I'm all in, she immediately said nope and shut down the conversation.

She's a commitment-phobe.

But I keep trying. I'll never give up on my woman. She'll be a one-man kinda girl in no time.

Travares saunters up to me half drunk, "Hey man, I thought you were leaving."

I shrug, "Plans fell through. Date had a family emergency," I lie smoothly.

"Good. Let's get trashed together." Travares throws his arm over my shoulders and pulls me over to the table the others are around.

Fuck it, why not.

The old as time cure for heartbreak, get drunk. Nothing could go wrong.

I didn't actually have a date. I just wanted the peace and quiet I've been craving. I'm tired and lonely, if I admit it honestly. I just told everyone that so I could have an excuse to leave at a decent time and not wallow in heartache. I love my best friend, but I don't need to stay the entire reception. Especially if Zharia is here driving me crazy. So, I told everyone I had a date. To have an excuse but also in the hope that it got back to Zhar and makes her jealous.

Unless you can count me going home and playing video games or reading alone as a date—then hey, I'm dating myself and I didn't lie.

His beer breath fans across my face as he tells me, "I see you watching her. You're breaking your own heart, man." He pats me on the chest like that makes his words any better.

Travares is one of the few people I confide in. He's one of my closest friends, besides Danger and Gunney. They know just enough about Zharia and me. Somethings you just want to keep private, especially when your girl doesn't want it public knowledge we are fucking around.

I let him lead me over to the table of my brothers just so I will stop obsessively watching Zharia. Apparently everyone notices. The music is just as loud over here and the table is definitely rowdier than all the others.

Honestly, I'm heartbroken and tired and I knew Danger's wedding was going to be triggering. It reminds me of everything I ever wanted but it doesn't want me back. I'm not enough and I wasn't worth it.

Three shots of whiskey in, I'm having a good time finally laughing and playing Go Fish with Slim, T-Bone, Travares, Gunney, Pierre, Wild Bill and Dobby—because isn't that what grown ass men like to play when they drink. They're ridiculous. It's cutthroat enough and has enough wiggle room for T-Bone and Slim Jim to cheat bigger than shit.

Out of the corner of my eye, I see Zharia heading up the stairs to the apartment up there. Interesting. *Play cool. Wait before you stalk your prey.*

God, I grind my teeth. The urge to chase after her is too strong. I quickly assess the room and the position of people who might follow me following her. I can't have Birdie, Tally or Pierre trying to stop me from stalking their best friend.

The clubhouse is a big warehouse in the Central Business District of New Orleans. The bottom is a wide-open area with pool tables and a fully functioning bar with tables and chairs scattered about. It's always pretty full in here. That's good for business.

Birdie and Danger's wedding happens to be on a special occasion for the club, it's the annual Labor Day Smoke 'n Ride Family Supper. There're a couple hundred people here today. We always hold a charity ride and a giant supper for everyone and their families. This is one tradition that is never skipped or cancelled.

Off to the side of the bar is the industrial kitchen. In the back are the bathrooms, and the back right corner is a sizable office.

There are tables and chairs set up all in the center of the room and up front is a stage. There are pool tables, dart boards and a couple of guys put in a space for axe throwing. Can't forget the one lonely air hockey table but these fuckers are continuously losing the puck.

Zharia's been flitting and flirting about between all of it, everywhere like the social butterfly she is, like she's the fucking hostess on high. Driving me fucking crazy is what she's doing, and I guaran-fuckin-tee she knows and she's rubbing it in my face right now.

Zharia just left the stage area with a purse on her arm. The stage is where I just stood a couple hours earlier, beside my best friend, the Vice President of our motorcycle club—The Southern Devils Society—Mr. Danger, while he married our President's daughter, Birdie, Zharia's best friend.

Upstairs, that's where my girl is headed and I'm about to follow and find out why. It's a very large apartment with ten furnished bedrooms, three bathrooms, and a kitchen. Any time an associate needs a place to hunker down, or they've fallen on hard times, there's a bedroom upstairs to lay their head until they get back on their feet.

The industrial metal stairs are located by the front door and this is where I see Zharia going up, acting like she belongs there, acting like she knows where the fuck she's going. As far as I know, she's never been up there. *Now what the hell does she need up there for?*

"Gentlemen, I need to go see a man about a horse," I say, giving a flippant excuse as to why my half-drunk ass needs to leave the table. I give my cards to Slim, and all the others I had stuffed under my leg. If I can't win, I'm going to do everything in my power not to help anyone else out.

After they grumble a minute about my abandonment, I see Zharia slip through the door at the top like a goddamn shadow. Now, I know there's no one up there currently. One, because I watch everything like a hawk. Second, the rooms aren't for sex for the night and right now, we only have one associate staying at the clubhouse. And I just left the table where Dobby is sitting at.

So, tell me, my vicious little poppet, what's your business in those bedrooms?

I aim to find out as I climb the stairs and slip through the door. The lights are lowered in the downstairs clubhouse area and even if someone did see, I don't care.

The door spills out into the kitchen and the lights are dimmed in here as well. I can smell her perfume in the air, taunting me, luring me to her. I stop to listen, hoping I can hear her movements. I feel her presence up here, like her siren song is calling to me, beckoning me to come find her.

Soon, my love.

I hear fabric rustling down the hallway to the left of the kitchen.

Gotcha, pretty little poppet.

Following the sound, I come to find a bedroom door ajar and the light inside is on. Through the opening I see Zharia standing by the bed in a thong and strapless bra. She's fighting a jumbled mess of a dress it looks like. My cock hardens at the sight of her.

Perfection. She's absolute perfection.

My heart clenches at the sight of her. Fuck, I miss her so bad. It's a bone deep yearning. We had such a good thing going. I thought she was going to be mine forever.

I thought she loved me more than she did…

Pushing open the door, I give a low whistle that startles her, and she squeaks out a half-assed scream with her husky feminine voice—the sultry voice that's going to be the death of me—as she begins shrieking at me.

She whirls around, chest heaving from her fright, "Shadow!!!" Her eyes narrow, "You scared me to death!" she hisses. "What the hell are you doing here?" She holds her clothes to her flushed chest to cover herself, but it doesn't deter me. I love seeing the flush crawl across that brown Indian skin. It makes her look darker, more mysterious and all that more alluring. Her beauty captivates me every time I look at her.

I know exactly what this beauty looks like naked, all five foot eight of her. I've explored every inch, every dip and all those killer curves. She's my chocolate goddess and right now I want to lick her from her head to her tip toes.

Don't get me wrong, Zharia's beautiful and she has this exotic aura about her that sucks you in, but it's like ripping your own skin off to get away from her.

I've tried. I know better than anyone.

We became very close, very quickly and over the course of a few months, she wiggled her way into my heart and took it over. No one has ever made me feel like she has. I'm head over heels in love with her and she knows it. I handed her my heart and soul and I feel like I'm dying without her.

I've never hidden my feelings from her. I made my intentions clear, but she's so stubborn and hard-headed.

Unfortunately, we are in one of those *off* times. This time she's mad because I asked her to move in with me. She started getting heated over being an independent woman, needing her own space and how she doesn't want to settle down right now, and why can't I just keep it how it is. I tried to compromise and told her I would just move in with her then. That set her off even more about losing freedom and her choices and some bullshit about socks on the floor.

It's not enough for me anymore. I don't want to be her kept secret any longer. She's mine and it's about time she fucking gets with the program for once.

Besides, she wants to keep dating other men and I can't have that. 'Keep her options open' she said. Fat load of horseshit. That is not fucking happening.

She wants something casual with me. Said she got too wrapped up in what we had, needed to take a step back, needed to focus on her career as a surgeon.

I was always an afterthought to her career and the long hours she works. Fuck, everything's an afterthought compared to her work life.

So, I stepped back as she wanted. Each time she feels the walls closing in on her, she kicks up a fuss and we spend a few days to a week apart but she's usually right back, right where we left off when she calms down.

While I look my very needy fill of her half naked body, I explain, "I came to check on the upstairs, ya know, because I'm security and imagine my surprise finding you here, practically naked, waiting for me. My lucky day, huh?" I adjust my hard dick through my jeans and situate it in my boxers. This is the reaction I have to her every time I'm around her. I'm a goner, I'm so lost in her.

I don't miss how she licks her lips though. Oh, my baby girl knows exactly what she does to me. And she fucking loves it, thrives on it even. The power she has over me. She relishes it.

Zhar is remembering what my cock tastes like with her eyes diverted to my package and licking her lips. God, can that girl suck a cock. And loves it too!

Zharia is the most passionate lover I've ever been with and she knows deep down, she can't live without me. No one can make her come as hard. No one will love her as hard either, and she needs that. She craves it.

She rolls her eyes at me, "Hardly lucky and I was not waiting on you. Considering we're split up, kindly leave now, I'd like to get dressed and get to my dinner plans that don't involve you." She resumes her fight with the garment.

I see we're still going to be a brat and she's saying shit to piss me off.

It's working.

"Oh? A date?" I grind out. We fucking talked about this shit.

"Yes, if you must know," she huffs out, fighting with the dress again.

"Who the fuck are you going out with?" Immediately she's angered at my heated, possessive words and makes a face. I take a few strides into the room right up to her.

"Whoa! Whoa! I don't want you in here, Shadow." Her angry eyes flash at me as her temper flares. "Get out, goddamn it. It's none of your fucking business." She puts her hands up and backs away. I love it when she plays hard to get. Every fiber in her body is aroused at the nearness of me and she's doing a piss poor job of hiding it.

Zhar is just as twisted as me with her driving need of angsty passion.

See my baby, well she gets mad and it takes a few days to get over it. When she comes back, a good dirty fucking from her Shadow Daddy reminds her of where she belongs. My little bad girl always wants it from me, even when she's telling everyone we're broken up and saying she's over me this time. She doesn't tell me no. Right now, her eyes are betraying her. They're telling me everything I need to know.

She can lie to herself all she wants. She can give herself a headache trying to convince her brain, but I know, I so fucking know, everything about her but that big brain right now is screaming for me to throw her on the bed and have my way with her.

In her eyes I can see the split. One half begging her to allow it, the other half telling her to resist.

She needs to listen to the devil more.

Over me? I scoff in my mind. Yeah, right. She will never be over me. We share this bond that transcends this life. She's not ever going to forget us. She'll have to kill me to keep me from her. She could rip my heart out with her bare hands and I would still love her.

I don't want to live in a place where I don't have her love. I can't exist in a time that doesn't allow me to touch her, smell her, feel her.

My mother was right. When you know, you know. My soul has chosen her and I can't continue without her.

I move into her space, crowding her back towards the bed and her breath catches. Gripping the back of her neck, I pull her close to me, my voice low, lethal and gravelly, "Everything about you is my business, poppet. You're mine. The sooner you get that through your head, the easier this will go on both of us." My lips are so close to her, I can feel her little puffs of aroused pants across my chin. Her breath betrays her every time. I can smell the arousal shifting around her, mingling with her perfume. It's driving me mad.

The harder I push her, the more she melts. Zharia might be a ball buster outside of the bedroom, but she's putty in my hands and loves when I take charge. Her kink is giving up her rigid control of her life and surrendering to the pleasure only I can give her, which feeds her twisted need to be a fucking brat to me. Her love language is seeing how far she can push me. And by fuck, I let her. I love it too.

Because I'm that man for her. She's told me numerous times that no one else can do it as well as me. No one else has pushed beyond her limits and has fully given her what she yearns for…except me, I make her dreams come true.

I pull myself back from her tantalizing scent, her perfume that I love so much, that brings me to my knees. Fuck, I've missed being near her, touching her, damn it, just being in her presence.

"I've missed you so much, Zhar," the break in my voice betraying my restraint. I reach out to touch her.

"No, Shadow. Not this time." Zharia tries to sound determined as she swats my hand but I can tell she's losing that battle. After all, it's only been almost two weeks now since we split the last time. Two dreadful, lonely, quiet weeks where I've basically been stalking her every move. I even snuck in and installed hidden cameras in her house just so I could see her.

She's not herself from what I see. She walks around so sad. So does her cat, Sir Waffles McFluffenstien, that loves me dearly. I miss you too, furball. My black clothes aren't the same without your orange hair all over them.

Then, there's the teensy matter of a small tracker I embedded in her neck. Ehh, one I put there without her consent.

I know that's wrong!

Just hear me out.

One night when I stayed over at her place, I inserted the tracker while she slept peacefully. After what Danger went through with Birdie's kidnapping, I wasn't taking any chances. I'm a high-ranking officer in a nationwide biker club. I'm basically third in command of the biker mafia in the United States. Of course, they'll come after her because of me.

Danger is second in command and his woman was taken. I feel like I'm next. She'll be mad, but it might be the only thing that saves her when the Saints come after her. She'll forgive me eventually.

Better to ask for forgiveness than permission, eh? Am I right? I feel like that's a pretty logical and reasonable excuse to do what I have done.

She felt the sting in her sleep and woke up. I pretended like she was dreaming of the pain, and I wrapped her up in my big arms and she went right back to sleep while I prayed to all the gods it would keep her safe.

She has no idea there's a tracker in her body and I don't plan to tell her. No one knows about it but me.

I know it's a severe violation of her privacy, but I don't give a fuck. That's my woman. My Old Lady. I'll do anything to keep her safe.

Zharia struggles to move away from me, and I grip her long, black hair, pulling just hard enough so I tilt her face up to mine. Her eyes dilate and she sucks in a ragged breath, "Goddammit, Shadow. No."

"Are you sure about that?" I steal her lips in a heated kiss. Her lips part beautifully for me like they're supposed to, just like they're meant to. Slanting my head, I deepen the kiss, lapping and dancing with her tongue, claiming what's mine. Her breath quickens and she moans deep in her chest into my mouth. *I knew you were in there, poppet, you can't resist.*

She doesn't put up a fight when I reach behind her and unclasp her bra and drop it to the floor. She doesn't flinch away when I cup her perfect tits and run my thumbs over those gorgeous peaks.

She definitely doesn't argue when my hand slips inside her thong and I find her wet, wanting and ready for me. The wall she's built between us shatters the moment I circle her clit with a very wet finger.

"I knew you wanted this. You can't deny yourself the pleasure your body seeks. It wants me, Zhar. Let me come home, baby girl."

Her chin wobbles, "No." It sounds so strangled. The conviction wavering.

Zharia can deny it all she wants, but she wants me, just as much as I want her. We can't get away from each other. She's crawled into every cell inside my body, coursing through my veins, the one thought on my mind at all times is her.

For the first time in my life, I'm in love and it's exhilarating. I can't fathom my life without her in it, beside me. I have to get her back.

Working to impress, I deftly circle her stiff clit with my finger, "Do you really mean no? Come on, Zhar, you crave this dick, you know you want it. You never turn it away. It's yours baby, all here for the taking. All yours heart and soul. Lay back and let your Shadow Daddy make you feel good."

Zharia whimpers and her breath turns into pants when I pick up my circular pace. "Yes, baby. Who makes you feel this good?" I tease her while kissing up her neck. I close my eyes and revel in her very essence waiting for her answer.

"You," she pants, barely a whisper.

"I do, that's right. Who's my vicious, sexy poppet?"

"I am," she gasps as I pinch her clit. I pull my hand away, making her whine. I push her back up against the bed, making her sit. I watch as her pretty pussy's so wet and puffy, craving my cock while she scoots back.

With one hand on her sternum, I push her backwards with a little nudge. She hesitantly lays back, but her eyes can't lie to me. Zhar could never hide her love for me. I bet her big brain is misfiring right about now. All the wires are crossing and fighting each other.

Her heart craves me, but her brain won't allow it. Her mind is fighting me, I can see it in her eyes, but her body knows, and her body wants me. Literally dripping its want and need out for me. It knows how good I am to her. It knows what I bring to the table.

Her beautiful long hair fans out around her and her chest and neck are flushed a darker shade. My filthy girl, falling right back in with me. I can never go back to who I was before she entered my life. I am nothing without her.

"That's my perfect girl," I tell her while I pull her wet and sticky thong off. I put it in my pocket and dip my finger back into her warm pussy.

"So wet for me, poppet, always so wet for me. I love how much you want my cock. Tell me the truth Zhar, has there been anyone else here since me?"

"No."

I pull my hands away and say, "Are you lying to me?"

"No, I told you."

I lower myself to my knees and place her thighs on my shoulders. The first lick has her shivering. I kiss across her pussy lips and suck in her sweet bundle of nerves like it's my life's only goal. She jerks and moans and spreads her thighs more.

She runs her hand in my long, silky black hair and murmurs, "I hate that I want you so much."

I chuckle and continue kneading my fingers into her luscious thighs. Her hips lift to press her greedy honeypot into my face harder. *Yes, baby, I want you out of control for me. Let go.*

Her moans grow louder, her hips more frantic.

"Shadow, I'm close, I'm so close," she breathes.

Aaaand that's my cue to stop.

I drop her thighs down onto my hips as I stand up. Grabbing my pants button, I rip the fly open.

"What the fuck?" she sits up on her elbows with the most desperate expression.

"Tell Shadow Daddy which way you want it."

She rolls her eyes then flops back on the bed in a huff and growls out her frustration, "Fucking hell, Shadow." Needing the fix only my body can bring her, she keeps her legs open for me.

While my one hand pulls my cock out, the other wraps around her throat, "Are you still telling me no?" She positively loves when I give her her favorite kind of necklace and when I apply pressure.

Her eyes glaze over, and she lets out a weighted breath, "No, but this is the very last time, I swear to god, so you better make it memorable."

I knew she couldn't resist.

When I find her entrance and rub her wetness around, I shove home, telling her, "This isn't the last time but keep telling yourself that, poppet." The excitement makes my breathing strained. It feels amazing as her pussy gobbles me up. "This tight pussy's mine. Forever. You can never outrun me, I'll find you."

Her breath shudders as her legs lock around me and her arms slide up my biceps, "Shadow, fuck me like only you can. Hurry."

I squeeze her neck gently and place my other thumb strumming her clit while I snap my hips to the rhythm she loves, going deeper into her each thrust. Fuck, she's so tight I can barely pull out, she's gripping me back in, strangling my cock.

The best sounds come from Zharia's wet pussy as I pound away inside her. She gets so wet the skin slapping and slurping almost drive me over the edge.

The bed starts scraping against the floor each thrust. Oh shit, it's moving and I'm chasing her with every push. But I won't fucking stop. I never want to stop fucking her.

I fuck her to remind her who she belongs to.

I fuck her to let her know I'm not going anywhere.

And I fuck her to alleviate my broken, shattered heart.

Zharia rivals the top porn stars for sounds that fall from her mouth when she's getting railed and right now is no different than before. God, I love her moans, and little squeals, the gasps, the loud panting, growls and grunts as she drives me insane. Jesus fuck, all of them. Zhar is a loud lover and I'm fucking here for it. Every time.

"Fuck me like it's the last time, big boy." She says through her pants. She's getting the desired reaction out of me.

I growl at that goddamn gloating mouth and apply more pressure to her throat. Fuck me, she knows how to get me riled up in a nanosecond.

"Be my bad little mouthy cumslut and come for Shadow Daddy," I punctuate between pushes. I make sure to use her favorite dirty, feral word.

I bring out the feral side in her and I have no shame. It turns me the fuck on.

"Fuck, baby girl, you feel incredible. I'm gonna fill you up, you want that, don't you? You want my cum." I'm not playing around with her now; I work her clit harder as I talk to her. Five more strokes is all it takes to set her off keening through her orgasm, shuddering under me. Music to my soul.

Zharia clenches down on my cock so hard, it rips the orgasm from me as I bellow her name. There's no fighting through it. She steals parts of me every time we're together. I empty everything I have into her.

I pull my hand off her throat and squeeze her cheeks together with my hand, puckering her lips like a fish, pulling her face to look up at mine. She tries to catch her breath while she stares me in the eyes, "Who do you belong to?"

She damn near sobs in sorrow, "I can't be yours anymore." Her eyes fill with tears, and it kills me inside when they spill over.

"The fuck you say. You'll always be mine, Zhar. No one will ever come close to me. You'll remember me long after today and think of me every day yet to come. I'll never let you go. Death won't keep me from you. My love for you is never ending. Do you hear me? There's never going to be a day when I don't love you. I'm yours just as much as you are mine."

Her tears run back into her hair as she lays under me and it's alarming. My feisty Indian princess doesn't usually cry, not around me. I'm sure our fights have made her cry her fair share of tears, just as those fights have driven me harder at the gym in silence.

I pull out and bend over top of her, running my hand over her face to wipe the tears away. "Baby..."

Shoving at my chest, "Let me up," she demands, her sad eyes gone hard.

I step back, watching her sit up with hurried movements. I grab her some tissues while she jerks her dress on.

I quickly tuck myself back in and button my jeans up. She's just slipping her heels on when I reach her.

"Zharia."

Throwing her hand out, "No. Just no." She won't even look at me.

"This isn't over between us, and you know it."

After she's done wiping herself she throws the cum covered tissues in my face. She finally does look me in the eye, and I don't like what I see. A sense of finality oozes off her.

"We'll see," is all she says with her determined look. She's in such a hurry to get away from me, she leaves her bridesmaid's dress on the bed. Damn, geez, the bed that's moved halfway across the room with our quick fuck. She's out the door and down the hall before I can stop her, the kitchen door slamming in resolution.

She'll be back. I just have to bide my time. We've been playing this game for the past four months off and on. Zhar always comes back.

The past week since Birdie's wedding has been super busy at work, and I haven't had much downtime. Thank fuck because I'm still mentally berating myself for fucking Shadow when we are broken up.

You're broken up, bitch, get it through your head!! Goddamnit!

How could I be so weak? I knew better. As soon as I did it, the safety sign in my head blinked and lit up: *0 days since you last let Shadow fuck you.* Nice job!

It happens every shitty time. I have *got* to stay away from him, damn. This is getting ridiculous and it's not healthy.

I trust him, he would never hurt me, but he wants so much from me. Much more than I'm comfortable giving. I can't let this continue. Not when I won't just commit to him because of my issues and that's all he wants. I can't be exclusive when he asks for it. I don't want to settle down with one person. Seems like too much of a trap.

He wants babies, and white picket fences. I don't want that right now.

Plus! I love my career. I love being a doctor. I'm focused on that, branching out into specialty and I don't have time for raising kids and wedded bliss. All the things Shadow wants…with me. I want fun, casual. It's the safest bit. I'm already too far down this rabbit hole trying desperately to claw my way out.

Relationships aren't for me no matter how much I love him and I'm trying to reverse the whole falling in love thing.

So far, I believe herding cats is an easier feat.

It makes me shiver to think about being trapped in a marriage. Or even a committed relationship. Shadow wanted us to move in together, but I resisted even though my traitorous heart wanted it. Instead, he would stay at my house as often as possible. We still got in enough quality time together with mine and his crazy work schedules.

He brought up the move in thingy again after I done told him a firm no the last two times he asked. It almost sounded like he was trying to command me to do it this time around. I bristled at the idea and that's the latest reason we've broken up. He pushed too hard; I spooked and dipped. Now, my heart is dying and my brain keeps telling itself to suck it up and get over it, we have more important things to do.

Your girl's just dickmatized. I've spent lots of time bent over or feet up in the horizonal mambo and now I have clouded judgement. But it's not just that, it's snuggling on the couch, laying in his arms or on his chest, watching shows or movies, his sweet gestures reserved just for me, the lazy mornings spent talking about everything we can think of. It's the good morning texts, the nights I spent falling asleep with his arms wrapped around me, it's his scent bringing me so much peace and comfort, it's his mere presence I crave.

But we argue over everything. Jesus. It's toxic as fuck. He tries to control me, and I won't have it. I'm a free spirit, to do as I please, drift in the wind and answer to no one. He isn't about to change that by promising to make me happy or buying me things or wearing me down until I give in.

I'm not for domesticated family life.

I'm for the streets.

I snort to myself. So far from the truth. I'm a spoiled brat. Trust fund baby. But I work really hard! Just so we're clear.

Anyways, this ho can't be a housewife.

Although, I can say the nights are starting to get lonely again and my battery operated boytoy is a very sad substitute for Shadow's thick dick. I cannot afford to let my mind wander down that dark, twisted alley again. It's not a safe space for me.

Obviously. Case in point: Exhibit A—safety sign reading last day fucked Shadow. There should be more time there but I'm a weak woman when it comes to that man.

My life became so wrapped up in him, loving him, being in love with him. Then I snapped out of it and remembered my goals and the promises to myself. Don't get trapped. Be the best doctor I can be. Excel far greater than thought possible.

I'm not giving up my goals for anyone. I've worked too hard on them to give up now.

Next thing you know, you're married with kids dragging you down and all the hopes and dreams you had for yourself go up in smoke so you can be the behind-the-scenes support for a man. Bleh, sounds terrible to me.

Damn it, being apart is torture though. I want all the benefits but none of the work or commitment.

I hate to say it, but I actually went and fell in love. I'm an idiot. Me, the flirt, the secret slut, the woman who feels empowered by her femininity and ability to use men. I fell hard as fuck for a Comanche warrior and bad ass biker. It's for real this time, but it's at the wrong time in my life and that's the tragedy.

I'm almost thirty and my parents are pushing me to settle down, but I want nothing to do with that. I must admit, quick fucks throughout the week with a different guy each time became monotonous and dull to me, but when I got with Shadow, it was just me and him and it was wild, passionate, fun, and wholly scared the shit out of me with how powerful it was. He became my world so quickly.

Sex with him is on another level, the best I ever had. He's exactly what I want in a sexual partner. There's something about him I can't stay away from. It makes me so mad I'm drawn to him so damn much.

The kind of guys I pick aren't looking to settle down either, which is what draws me in. Birdie says I fall for fuckboys, the ones I know want to hit it and quit just like me. I know, it's a bad habit. I freely admit I'm the whole problem here. I know my faults.

Until him. He changed my whole game. He made me break my own rules—I got attached.

My phone vibrates. I reach over to the dresser just to see it's Shadow again. He won't stop texting me and today flowers arrived at the hospital for me. I got home Monday and there were flowers on the island in my house. He broke in and left them there. How twisted is that? How utterly fucked up am I if I secretly loved them yet despised them?

I should never have gotten involved with a biker. Not one like Shadow. It was destined to end up being messy. But fuck me, he's so gorgeous. You know those kinds of guys who are so beautiful to look at but you're afraid to touch them for fear they might not be real? Like AI made them up. Or they belong on the cover of a romance novel.

Shadow is like this. High cheekbones, long jet-black hair like mine, dark mysterious eyes that have the perfect smolder, chiseled jaw sharp enough to shave my legs and muscles for endless days under that smooth bronze skin.

The perfect looking Native American warrior. He stands a dreamy six-three and has the cock to support his attitude problem. And fuck, does he know how to use it. I've never come so hard in my life than I have riding his wicked curved and girthy boy. *Stop! Right now, goddamnit.* Shit on that guy, we are done.

No trap for me, Satan. Eyes on the prize: career, success, freedom.

Smoothing down my dress, I turn to look at it from all angles in my big mirror over my dresser. I really need to get a giant mirror like Birdie's. I wish I had it now so I can see how these shoes go with this floral pattern. Fuck it, I'm already running late and I'm not sure how understanding my parents will be this time.

Grabbing my purse, I'm out the door and flying down the front steps of my four-bedroom shotgun house in Marigny, just outside of the French Quarter New Orleans. I love it here.

I grew up in this city. My parents immigrated thirty-two years ago from India and settled in the city. My dad was a tinkerer of sorts, and when the internet took the world by storm, he was right there in the beginning to launch his company from the ground up with money he had saved. The American dream. I'm not exactly sure what he does. He could make microchips for government weapons for all I know. Now that I think about it, I believe he does do that.

I've never paid attention to the details. That's my brother's job as he's being groomed to take over Davish Logistics.

My dad is one of the leading tech moguls of the world. Like king of the crop. He's a big deal. His products are everywhere. He's almost a billionaire in his own right. Wildly renowned and highly sought after for parties and lavish galas.

My parents indulged me and lavished me with anything I wanted. My brother, Aarav and my sister, Vihana were equally as spoiled, but because I'm the oldest, I paved the way to our parents' outrageous expectations. Because I'm like a super genius. No, really, tested and everything. It's crazy. I don't even know how to explain it. I suck up knowledge like a sponge and I just know everything.

Except how to control my vagina.

My sister and brother were never happy I set the bar that high for them to follow behind me.

I'm in my third year of surgical residency at Hopelove Hospital here in the city and word in the halls is I might be getting offered a permanent spot on the team I'm currently mentoring under. Like this year. Years earlier than expected for a normal-paced student.

"Jesus fuck," I curse the traffic under my breath from the back of the rideshare. I didn't feel like driving myself. Traffic sucks in this city. Like all other cities, am I right?

"Sorry ma'am. As soon as we're past this light we are home free."

"Thank you. It's not your fault." I grind my molars with frustration. I should have left earlier. I wish I could pick up the car and hurl it to the front doors of the restaurant.

I have a lot on my shoulders right now making me edgy. Do not take it out on this kind gentleman who's just doing his job.

I'm a kind person, unless I'm driving, then I'm a motherbeast from the depths of hell with a sailor's potty mouth cursing all of humanity that has the audacity to be out driving when I am.

I sigh and sit back in his stiff as a board back seats.

My parents got lucky tonight my class was cancelled and I was free for their impromptu dinner I was voluntold to come to.

I'm just starting this semester's excelled courses. Last semester of specialized coursework. LAST ONE! Thank fuck! I'm going to graduate way ahead of schedule, like I have done for every school I've ever been to. Schoolwork, great test taking abilities and the ability to recall information at a snap of my fingers helped pave my way to the top of my goals. Smashing each one I reached for. I should be done in a few months, right before Christmas, at the rate I work.

Branching out on my own to practice medicine is the ultimate goal.

My length of time in residency is unprecedented. Usually, you have to last at least five years or more for this to be offered but here I am, killing it in my field and taking on the world in my own way after barely three.

In defense, I started college at fifteen while still taking high school courses at the private school Birdie and I attended.

When I arrive at the restaurant, with my phone ringing from Shadow, I promptly silence my phone because I will not have it buzzing through a dinner like a broken in vibrator. I'm shown to my parents' usual table in a more private area of the restaurant…so they won't be overheard berating me for being a shitty daughter to them.

Great, gloom and doom in a darkened corner. Best place for them to kill my soul just a little bit more.

This is my mom's favorite restaurant that my dad owns, mostly because it's Asian, like her, and it has some of the best food in all of New Orleans.

Together with Dad's Indian heritage and Mom's Asian linage, all of us kids have this dark exotic look to us. My brother and sister are slightly darker than me. In me, our mom's light Asian skin tone washed out and lightened some of the dark Indian skin tone of my father. It's enough to turn heads, such as what I'm doing in this packed restaurant right now.

Or it could be I'm a sexy *biotch* and know it. I'm not conceited, I just know I'm beautiful. Dumb luck because my parents aren't pretty people. Not even close.

"I'm so sorry, work was a little crazy." I try not to sound flippant as I give my excuse. It is what it is. I was helping myself to an orgasm with my magic wand, which technically is work, hard work sometimes. But they don't need to know that. That's between me and BOB.

I sit in the seat the server offers. He snaps my linen napkin like a whip beside me, causing me to flinch slightly and lays it across my lap. I offer a smile and a thank you while he asks for my drink order. Sweet tea will work just fine. I feel it in the air; I need to have my wits about me by the way my parents are sizing me up, so no alcohol. Something's going on. I feel the treachery ooze off of them.

"Zharia, darling, so nice of you to join us on such short notice. I apologize it was last minute, but your father and I have something to discuss with you, and it mustn't wait any longer." *Oh? It mustn't?* I can't stand how uptight my mom always sounds. Years of practice of being a wealthy bitch has paid off for her.

The snack bag of pretzels sitting in my stomach starts to churn, preparing for the worst. *Oh, this definitely isn't good.*

My dad clears his throat, "You're nearing thirty in a few months. It's time to settle down." *Yeah, don't remind me, guy, and excuse you, I just turned twenty-nine…like last year, but still.*

He continues, "You have your career that you wanted so bad, you have the house you begged for." He looks me in my face when he delivers his next heart stopping sentence, "I've arranged for you to marry Gujeet's son, Balaraj Mondal. He will be here later on tonight, and we are having a welcoming

get together for him at the house tomorrow night. You will
have a chance to meet him before your wedding, which will
be in two weeks."

My stomach has dropped out of my asshole. It's rolling
around on the floor by my feet, flopping around because we
have been *GUTTED*…I don't know if I want to poop or puke
at his words.

So, I say the first thing that pops into my head, "No."

"Excuse me, dear?" my mother leans forward and asks.

I clear my throat, "I said no," with a little more force behind
my words, still in shock he said this.

His friend Gujeet is from India and has children our age. He
stayed in India and raised his family there. He is still a farmer
back in the homeland, like my father's family was, and he
and my dad talk often. I secretly think my dad has been
keeping his family afloat for years.

"Zharia," my dad growls under his breath.

I face my dad, hopefully with the scorn I feel written plainly
on my face, "What made you think this was a good idea? It's
not the dark times anymore, frankly this is so dated and
tacky, Dad. Literally, nobody does arranged marriages
anymore." I look between both of them. They're fucking
serious. As a damn heart attack.

This isn't a joke.

My father starts turning red under his dark complexion,
which let's be real, it makes him look like an evil villain
powering up. Beads of sweat appear on his forehead.

Like damn, he's mad mad.

So many thoughts are racing in my head. None of those
thoughts agree with what my parents are saying. Like what
the fuck? I try to be respectful when I seriously want to
scream that question at them. Who fucking does this
anymore?

Seriously. I'm running from marriage and these assholes
are throwing me into the lion's den.

"It's time, Zharia," my dad says with barely contained fury at my insolence.

"I won't do it. You can't make me." What am I? Ten? 'Cause that sounded a little childish coming out, even to me. No wonder these two never take me seriously.

My mom intervenes, "Darling, at least meet the boy. Wait to make any decisions until after you meet him, ok?" my mother offers, trying to keep the peace.

She has a good point. I'm ruffled because they're meddling and still trying to dictate what I do. It's America, I have a right to choose.

"What's in it for me?"

There's always a catch. Everyone knows from reading romance books that arranged marriages are business transactions. There's always something to gain, besides a wife or husband.

My father's gaze holds mine as he says, "I hear from the hospital and your mentor they're going to release you from your residency at the end of the year to allow you to graduate top honors and further your career elsewhere if you choose."

My heart slams into my chest. No one's confirmed anything to me about it yet, but they told my dad???

He continues, "I will give you your own practice. Build you a state-of-the-art modern surgical facility, complete with offices to see patients in. I will fund the start of your new practice. I'll make your dreams come true, Zharia."

Cheese and rice!!!

Just holy fuckoli, ok, breathe. This is not a drill.

He's dangling my goals in front of me. The massive manipulation tactic is noted. I'd be impressed if I weren't so shocked and pissed.

"Fine, I'll meet him but that doesn't mean I'll say yes. Are we clear on that?"

"Yes, dear, that sounds lovely to start with." Mom smiles so wide her eyes disappear into slits.

My dad just grunts while the server comes over to take our orders and just like that, we move on to a different topic with my mom prattling on about redecorating the second living room in their Garden District home, like they just didn't drop a bomb on me.

On my way home in the ride share, I text Birdie,

Me: My parents are trying to marry me off

BirdsTheWord: They been trying that for years lol

Me: No, like legit. It's real now. I'm meeting him tomorrow

BirdsTheWord: OMG you're serious! Like an arranged marriage?

Me: Yep

BirdsTheWord: No, they've gone too far this time

BirdsTheWord: Did you tell them no??

Me: Yes I did but then I agreed to meet him. Tomorrow night. Do you want to go with me?

BirdsTheWord: Is it a date?

Me: No, there's a welcoming party for him at my parents' house

BirdsTheWord: Sure I'll go. Can't be out late, still picking out outfits for my honeymoon day after tomorrow. Dress code? Cocktail dresses?

Me: Chill woman. You have time. Yep, cute ones.

After I make sure the driver is tipped, I bound up the steps and unlock my door. Stepping inside, I immediately know I'm not alone. Those weird heebie jeebies cover my skin as the hair on the back of my neck stands up.

Shadow.

My literal shadow man. Even the boogey man is afraid of him if the stories are true. I've never seen that side of him and I hope I never do.

I turn on the light in the living room and there he sits on my couch, feet on the floor, waiting for me. My two-year-old traitorous long-haired orange cat, Sir Waffles McFluffenstein, sits curled up on his lap. The cat hates everyone, except me, and well, him.

"What are you doing here? Haven't I asked you not to break into my house and stalk me? I distinctly remember asking you not to do that repeatedly." Blowing out a frustrated breath, I slip off my heels and he just continues to sit there staring at me, brushing his hand over Sir Waffles's fur.

Who knew this bad ass biker, Native American warrior, ex-Navy SEAL, was a softie for cats?

"Oook," I breathe under my breath, since he doesn't appear to be answering me. Facing him I ask, "What do you want?"

"You know exactly what I want." At least he finally speaks.

"No. I'm not in the mood for shit tonight. Please leave." It's worth a shot. I'm exasperated with his audacity.

I head into the kitchen to put my leftovers in the fridge. I hear his heavy boots walking across the living room floor, heading my way.

"Another date?"

"Yep," I say straightening back up and shutting the door.

He is right there, behind me, so when I turn around there's really no fighting him off when he grabs my throat and shoves me back into the fridge. His forceful move makes the liquor bottles on top of the fridge rattle.

My fight or fuck reflex kicks in.

Jesus, let it not be fuck this time because I need to fight my instincts.

"Get the fuck off of me, Shadow." I hit at his arm to let me go. He's definitely pissed, and his hand is not letting up.

Shadow leans in to sniff my perfume, running his nose up my neck and then growls, "What did I tell you about going on dates, poppet?"

"We aren't together." I barely get it out before he tightens his vise grip on my neck. Now's when the panic sets in. Not that he'll hurt me, but that I'll cave and give in and fuck him again. He knows the shortcuts to my who-ha.

My little traitorous clit hums in excitement.

Why the fuck is my deranged vagina tingling in the face of this angry Comanche?

Shadow brings his face close to mine. "No more dates. It's time for you to stop fighting this and settle down with me."

Funny you should mention that…

I kick him in the shin and all it does to me is make my toe crack and hurt. I'm pathetic. Like every bit of the self-defense classes he taught me years ago I've forgotten in the face of real danger. Not that I think Shadow will hurt me.

"Shadow, stop, I can't breathe," I wheeze, smacking his hand.

Eyes widening, he loosens his hand necklace on me, running his hand up my neck into the hair at the back of my head to grip me. God, he knows everything I love. He's pulling out all the stops tonight. He is entirely too dangerous for me to be around when I'm alone.

But I must get away from him. I have to take my heart back. I should never have fallen so hard for him. He doesn't let me be me all the time. He wants to control me. And I can't allow that. I don't want to play wife and babysit some man's kids.

Fuckity fuck, why does he have to be so perfect but such an asshole?

His straight black hair falls across his face. He runs his fingers through the strands with his other hand, pulling it off his face and tossing it over his shoulder.

"No more dates, Zharia." He squeezes one last time before he drops his arm.

I run a hand across my neck to soothe my aching muscles, and he finally backs up. I've never been afraid of him but he's getting more unhinged by the day and pushing his fucking luck with me.

I point at him and hiss, "You don't touch me ever again. I'm sick of this shit. Get out before I call the cops." I've never threatened him with the law before and I'm not sure how he'll react but I'm dead serious.

"Zharia," his fists and jaw clench.

"JUST FUCKING GO AWAY!" I practically scream at him. An outburst that's way out of character for me and it shocks him enough that he actually flinches, his eyes flash, going wide but he reluctantly complies.

His face is quickly back to a mask of anger, but he knows I mean business. I've never screamed at him either. I just can't take it anymore. Obviously, it has to be me who draws the boundaries because he clearly has none.

He points in my face, "This isn't over. I love you." But he walks out of the kitchen and out the front door, slamming it and rattling the windows. I take deep gulps of air to steady myself and keep the tears at bay. It does no good as I slide down the front of the fridge while deep, chest wracking sobs gather in my throat.

When we get along, it's great, it's what I envision a partner to be if I wanted one right now, but when we don't see eye to eye on a future life, or he starts getting possessive and controlling; it's absolute hell.

As I sit here and cry, I think of all the good times we've had. Sitting in my living room, intertwined with each other on the couch, watching the ridiculous amount of reality TV I love to watch or my murder documentaries while he gives pointers. Quite frankly, shows he got addicted to because he's all invested now. Ice cream runs, walking around the French Quarter, cozy dinners and dancing in the kitchen while we learn to cook together.

I think about all the amazing motorcycle rides. All the glorious rides with my thighs wrapped around him and him talking to me inside the Bluetooth helmets about everything under the sun. The sunsets right outside of the city limits are to die for.

But I've also noticed he became priority in my mind. My work was being affected because my head wasn't in the game like it should be. This is people's lives at stake. I need complete focus and I couldn't do that with my mind constantly wandering to him and why he couldn't just leave well enough alone.

In such a short time of off-and-on-again dating, he's the first man to make me feel safe, loved and cherished. But he does it in an extreme way that's just too much for me sometimes. The man is extra.

I don't think there's a dimmer on Shadow's feelings meter. He's zero to a thousand every time.

I've known him for years. Maybe not know-known him, but I know who he is as it pertains to security for Birdie's dad. He taught me self-defense in my first few years of college. Even then his hands on my body felt like fire trailing across my skin and made me crave it more.

I've made bedroom eyes at him a time or two, or a hundred, but we've never hooked up. He's always been the handsome, hot as fuck, shadow that follows Birdie and her dad around. And since I'm at most every function with Birdie, he follows me around too.

Danger was always security detail for Birdie. As he should have been as Vice President, most trusted man above all. That man's been in love with her since the first moment he laid eyes on her when we were eighteen and him twenty-eight. I'm thrilled they finally got their heads out of their asses and got together.

That left Shadow a great deal of time to watch me all these years and yes honey, I did bask in his attention the past two years he's been staring non-stop at me. I saw the light come on in his eyes when I started showing him any signs of attraction and flirting with him. He played it off well.

I became more daring with dresses. I watched him right back, always seeing how long he could hold a smoldering stare. Surprisingly, it's a while. His stare is intense and all-consuming and feels like it's setting you on fire internally.

Maybe that's just my blush when he looks at me like that.

I flirted across the rooms with him. I made sure I danced with him at every function. I've made sexually suggestive comments to him and watched him blush on the dance floor.

I've made him adjust himself a time or two with my unabashed comments I got bold enough to whisper to him about 'When are you finally going to fuck me?' or 'I bet you want to know what I have on under this, don't you? I have nothing on, big guy, maybe you could bend me over and find out.'

I have to give it to Shadow, my brazen actions over the past year or two were mighty bold, but he gracefully took everything I said and every bit of flirting I gave to him. His restraint is amazing. I would have bent me over plenty of charity event tables or fucked in broom closets. Fuck, I turned myself on with how shamelessly I flirted with him. I never thought it would happen.

Until we came together one time. Literally.

He actually called my bluff one day. It was like an atomic bomb. No one, nothing, has ever made me feel the way Shadow does. Every time we're together it's explosive like that. And I lost pieces of my heart every time he entered me, touched me, watched me, fucked me in the way my mind and body needed. Told me I was his and whispered to me all the things he loved about me. He quickly became everything to me. I thought I was his everything.

I was wrong. He just wanted to own me. Trap me. Bend me to his will.

And nothing prepared me for what I am right now, a blubbering mess on the kitchen floor with a broken heart.

I just want it to be done. Over. Finished. I can't do this anymore. I don't have time for love. I'm doing the right thing for me. Sitting on my kitchen floor, I decide to give Balaraj a fighting chance. Maybe I'll even marry him anyway. I can always divorce him.

Yes, marriage will make Shadow go away for good. I'm unattainable then. I don't think he would mess with a married woman. Hell, I don't know.

Well, shit. Looks like I'm getting engaged tomorrow.

CHAPTER 3 — ZHARIA

Birdie slides into the ride share next to me in the back seat. A very well-mannered college girl, named Cherry, with long blond hair in a messy bun and glasses, picked me up at my house and then fought the traffic in the Quarter to pick up Birdie at her apartment for an extra $300. She was tickled pink to do it when I asked.

"I had to lie to my husband for you," Birdie grumbles and makes me wince. Cherry clears her throat up front. *Just drive, baby girl.*

"I'm sorry. I didn't want that to happen. Why did you have to lie?"

"He asked what's the occasion and I said it was a small party for one of your father's friends and that you didn't want to be there alone. I sure as shit wasn't going to say it's because we're going to meet your new fiancé for your arranged marriage."

Cherry is full on coughing now.

"Honey, are you ok?" Birdie leans forward and puts her hand on Cherry's shoulder.

"Yes, ma'am, sorry had a tickle in my throat."

"Ok, just checking." She turns to me as I hide the smirk on my face, she says, "Are you up for this? Seriously?" Birdie reaches over and takes my clammy hand.

"Sure, I am," I jokingly chuckle to hopefully cover any shred of my nervousness.

"You don't sound very convincing right now and that worries me." Birdie misses nothing. Fifteen years of close friendship will do that. She's on the same level as my emotional support tumbler; I can't live without either of them.

"Let's just hope he's a nice guy with a huge cock."

Poor Cherry, she's choking again.

We ride in silence for a bit before Birdie starts chatting up our driver. Birdie's holding my hand and patting our joined hands with the other. She's so motherly sometimes. It's cute.

I haven't told Birdie my decision yet, she'll shit a kitten, but walking up to my parents' house seems like a good time as ever.

I stop and half turn to her, "I'm going to marry him, B."

"What? You don't even know him!" Her startled look makes my heart hurt. I know she wants the best for me.

"Shadow broke in again." Birdie gasps. "Last night. I'm never going to get out of this toxic cycle with him unless I do something drastic," I wave absently to my parents' house in front of us. "and this is most definitely drastic."

"I'll have Linx talk to him." Her husband, Danger—or as she calls him Linx for his lesser known government name of

Lincoln—is the bike club's Vice President and second-in-command. He's also Shadow's best friend. He could possibly help but I don't want to seem like a tattle tale and involve them. I especially do not want her going to her daddy who's the President and complain about Shadow, his third-in-command. Of course, I didn't just pick any ole biker, I had to pick one of the important high-ranking ones in a huge motorcycle club that's nationwide.

"Please don't. Actually, I know this puts you in a bad twist, but please don't say anything about me to Danger going forward. I don't want him to know my life anymore. I don't feel comfortable with him knowing what I'm doing either. I don't trust him not to say anything to his best friend." I rub my forehead, "I'm trying to get away from him. Ironic, isn't it? I'm running from marriage with Shadow that has actual love, to marrying a complete stranger to achieve my goals."

"Oh Zhar, I know, and I think this is quite the extreme measure to take to do that. There must be another way," she pleads. "Please don't do this without me talking to Linx."

"My mind's made up, B."

She narrows her eyes, the crease between her eyes growing deeper with concern, "Zhar, what aren't you telling me?" She grabs my hand, "What did your dad offer you in exchange?" Birdie knows how my parents try to buy their children to make them conform to what they want them to be. But my best friend also knows I wouldn't agree to marriage unless I was getting something out of it.

I swallow before I speak, "He offered me every one of my dreams on a platinum platter. My own facility and practice."

She drops my hand about the time her mouth pops open. She covers her mouth with both hands, "Oh god, Zhar. That's a lot. I-I'm not so sure I could pass up that offer either, if we're being honest here."

I place my hand on her arm, "Let's go at least meet him first." I walk up the stairs and hold my hand out for her, wiggling my fingers. She takes my hand, and we walk through the double doors into my parents' sprawling mansion.

There's light jazz music playing when we enter and servers are walking around with bottles of wine or champagne, ready to fill glasses. Looks like a pretentious money-makers gathering. Dick contests are happening between the men as women shrewdly size up the others, wondering which ones are fucking the gardener and if their pool boy is better at eating pussy.

These are the circles my parents want me in. Gross.

I drag Birdie over to the bar. My arrogant parents have a fully stocked bar in the parlor and right now alcohol is needed. I order a glass of sweet red, and Birdie tells him she'll take the same. Second thought, I order two shots of cherry vodka and we down those quickly. After we get our wine glasses, we set off to find my parents. I feel a tiny bit more courageous now.

Heads are already turning to watch us walk through the rooms. We do make a striking pair visually.

We both have very long, waist-length, jet black hair. Birdie's has waves whereas mine is straight as a board. We both decided to wear it down and flowing to our ass cracks. Since we were teenagers we've had this silly competition of who can keep their hair longer than the other.

The only way to see that Birdie has very pale, almost translucent skin, is by her facial coloring, because the rest of her skin is covered in colored tattoos. She is a glorious work of art. I have always envied my friend for her fair skin that sucks up color so well.

My mind mentally pulls up my piece of burnt toast on my wrist and I smile to myself. It's supposed to be a piece of bread with arms and legs and a smile, that has peanut butter smeared on it. Birdie has the other matching piece of bread that has grape jam on it, her favorite. But with my skin tone it looks like burnt toast (go ahead and laugh), something the rest of our friend group gets a laugh out of. It was one of the first pieces Birdie ever did when she started tattooing. I was the only one brave enough to go first out of our Fab Four friend group. Now people clamber and wait for months to get tattooed by her.

Birdie has bright, striking blue eyes compared to my mahogany brown ones. I have a lighter ring of brown, almost caramel in the center around my pupil. My brown eyes are a lighter shade compared to my parents and siblings.

We both like to wear makeup that emphasizes our eyes and lips. Birdie and her whore red lipstick she loves, me and my brazen hussy pink that looks hot as fuck on me.

Birdie and I complement each other well tonight. Birdie's flirty little teal number and my bold pink satin cocktail dress stand out in the crowd of Brads, Chads and Karens. I needed to make a statement.

Beige and pastel women with pearls and men in black jackets stand staring at us as we pass. I don't miss a few sly smiles and eye fucking from men and even some ladies, more than I care to admit. Most of these people know us, watch us grow up.

Our Daddies are some of the most powerful and influential men in the United States.

We arrive at the living room and there stands my parents talking to an older man and woman, and beside them is a super cute Indian boy. Man…cute Indian man…he's a man, Z—with his baby face and dimples.

I slide my eyes over to Birdie beside me, and she raises her eyebrows in response. Out of the side of her mouth she whispers, "At least he's cute." Bingo sister!

I lick my lips and my eyes sparkle, "I need to get him alone." That may have come out a bit breathier than I intended. I'm just shocked he's cute.

Birdie's mouth drops open as her face swings my way, she whispers, "You absolutely will not fuck him right now, Zharia Ishani Davish!"

Now it's my turn to drop my mouth open and look at her, because like I'm seriously offended, "To talk. Jesus Birdie, to have a private conversation. God, I'm not that bad of a whore." I throw my hair over my shoulder and start walking towards my parents. I hear the clickity clack of Birdie's heels behind me as she follows behind, whisper-yelling, "Don't get mad. I'm sorry."

"Oh, here she is!" my mother coos and holds her arms out. I bend down to hug her and cringe at her obnoxiously stinky perfume. I'm sure it's something French and expensive. The woman is barely five feet high and as I crouch down I wonder if she will get shorter as she ages. Mom whispers in my ear, "Thank you, Zharia." This woman doubted I'd even show up.

I rise, steeling my spine and Dad is right there to lean in and kiss my cheek, that's plumped up in a fake smile. *Smile and wave!* Mom hugs Birdie behind me. I pull back to face my destiny.

Or new boy toy.

Trying to see the silver lining.

When I face him head on the first thing I notice is his dark brown eyes and how they almost glitter with excitement. I like them. He has my attention with just his sexy eyes and that grin. I'll give him this, he's a good-looking Indian man and I don't get to meet many of them.

I vaguely hear my father as he says, "Raj, this is my daughter Zharia."

He leans in with his hand extended and says, "Zharia? Am I saying that right?"

I actually blush while slipping my hand into his.

"Sorta. It's Zar-ree-ah."

"Zharia."

"Yes. Perfect."

"I think it's a beautiful name and now I see it matches the lady. Pleasure to meet you."

"Thank you, that's kind. Welcome to New Orleans."

He still has a hold of my hand, and I ask, "Would you like to go somewhere and talk, the two of us?"

My father stops talking to Raj's father and my mom stops chatting up Birdie for all of them to look at me. Like I can't be alone with a man. Oh no, scandalous…

Raj catches himself and says, "Yes, I'd like that very much."

"Great, let's go." Still holding his hand, I drag him towards the back of the house. I'm headed to the patio by the pool.

As we get outside, he looks around the pool area and raises his eyebrows up at me, "Are we going swimming?"

I immediately drop his hand like it's a hot potato because I just now remembered I had a hold of it. *Christ on a stick, get a hold of yourself.*

Don't start with me, this is a little overwhelming, ok!

And I'm out here having an argument with myself in my head.

I give him a strained smile, stamping down the nervous flutters in my gut and say, "No, I just thought we would have some privacy out here, away from the meddling parents. So, we can talk without the stuffiness of in there. Whew, I hate these things."

He lets out a big breath and says, "Thank fuck. You're normal," he chuckles, wiping his forehead.

This makes me genuinely laugh, "Yeah, I am. I think this is all fucking whack. Have you agreed to this arranged marriage?"

I'm super curious to see what's in it for him.

"I agreed to meet you, not marry you. *Yet.*"

I'm shocked, "I agreed to that too!"

He laughs and says, "At least we're both on the same page. Let's start this over, Hi I'm Raj Mondal." He puts his hand back out.

I put my hand back in his and shake his hand, "Hi, I'm Zharia."

We both laugh until I ask him, "What did they promise you if you marry me?"

He clears his throat and says, "Ok, getting right into it. I'm trying to go for my doctorate in computer science, but I want to study in America for it, at Tulane. Between you and me, I need residency to attend and this is how I'm going to get it. It was perfect timing when my father came to me with this harebrained idea. I figured I would get a chance to talk to you and see if you wanted to legally get married but have a roommates kind of relationship."

I'm slightly taken aback at his brilliant idea. "That actually doesn't sound bad. Better than the alternative."

"Which is?" he asks.

"You being a dick."

He throws his head back and laughs. "Yeah, I'm totally not a dick."

I narrow my eyes at him, "Only dicks say they aren't dicks."

He laughs some more, "Fair enough but I'm just a normal average guy who wants to go to college. Maybe we will stay friends, maybe something more. Either way, I'll be good to you and promise I will never hurt you. That's not who I am."

Strangely, I believe him. He seems like a genuinely sweet guy. It's a shame he can't find a girl to love him for him and not just some assigned wife for money. But we all have our price. And I sound like such a prostitute, selling my freedom for a building.

"I hate to bring it up but I'm not abiding by a sexless marriage if we remain friends. I'll be discreet but I'm not agreeing to that part."

"Oh," he waves his other hand, "I'm not holding you to that. It's not fair. Just don't embarrass me please and I'll give you the same respect."

Nodding, I hold out my pinky, "If I agree to this, you promise you'll never hurt me? We can be friends and fuck others?" I have no reason to believe he's not genuine.

He links his pinky with mine with a half-cocked smile and shakes our hands, "I promise I'll never hurt you. I will never lay a hand on you in anger. You have no reason to fear me. Ever. I'll be a friend for you, and we can go off and fuck who we want with discretion if we don't work as a couple."

"I promise I will never hurt you either, Raj. You don't have to fear me abusing you." Our pinkies are still linked and he's still smiling, his pearly whites bright next to his brown skin.

I question him more, "All you need is two years? We either stay together or go separate ways at the end? Do they need to know that though?" I can do that amount of time. Jesus, now I sound like I'm about to go serve hard time.

Dad will have plenty of time to build my facility by his graduation date.

"Yep, more like sixteen to eighteen months," he says as his pinky gets tighter around mine. Even better.

"Ok, we reassess in fifteen months then," I half whisper. "I guess we can let them know now." I pull my hand back after squeezing his pinky and shaking our joined hands.

Raj drops his hand back to his side and clears his thought, "Yeah, we can do that." He puts his hand out to mine to take. I honestly don't know what to do.

"At some point around other people, we are going to have to appear married. I'm going to hold your hand and put my hand on the small of your back, but I would never grope you or make you feel uncomfortable."

I nod absently, "I understand. Thank you. I won't overanalyze it. If it's to keep up appearances, you have my permission then."

"Ok, cool." He pulls his hand back, "All in due time. No one expects us to act that way right off the bat." He cocks his head, "I was really hoping all the way here that no matter what the girl my parents' are setting me up with looked like, or acted like, please let her become a friend."

Ok, this guy knows how to spear a heart.

I smile and say, "I look forward to being friends with you, Raj."

He smiles and nods, "Let's go tell them what they want to hear."

Chapter 4 – Shadow

Even being with the guys at the clubhouse isn't helping my mood. It's been shitty for the past couple of days, since Friday, when I told Zharia no more dates and she screamed at me. I don't know why she insists on pissing me off. Not once has she ever raised her voice to me in anger. I'll admit, it shocked the shit out of me when she did it.

The club hunnies have been trying to cheer me up tonight, but I don't even want to mess with them. There's only one person I want to be with right now and she's hellbent on driving me insane and freezing me out.

I planned on going to see Zharia tonight to get back in her good graces. I miss her something awful. I've given her ample enough time to get over it.

I had thought we would be back together after Danger's wedding, but she made it perfectly clear how she felt a few nights ago with her sharpened claws around my heart.

She could have shot me in the chest, and it still wouldn't have hurt as badly as her screaming at me through tears and acting afraid. Such hatred and sadness came off her. It caught me off guard and slammed me back against the counter away from her. My heart stopped beating for a good five seconds as I registered what had happened. I caused this reaction and I was wholly unprepared.

It struck real fear into my heart. Icy, hot, lightning fast, spreading throughout to my fingertips and toes. I'm really losing her. And I don't know how to get her back.

Raucous laughter circles around me as Travares and Dobby trade 'yo momma' jokes across the bar in the clubhouse. Gunney sits on a stool at the bar talking to Twilla, the clubhouse head Old Lady. I don't even have it in me to drink, so a Coke sits in front of me, ice melting, condensation running down the glass into the napkin. I have that much anxiety now and it's a foreign feeling.

I feel like I'm losing my mind.

I don't normally sweat anything. I have that much confidence in things coming together. I'm a master at facing things head on, spur of the moment, but fuck me if I can't figure out a plan to make Zharia love me again.

Danger asked me to meet him here and now I find myself sitting, waiting on him, debating whether I need liquor or not. I feel like I certainly need to keep my mind sharp.

When my best friend walks in I can tell by the look on his face, the set of his jaw, I'll need the liquor after all. I rise and walk to the bar and arrive there at the same time as he does.

I grip his hand, "Mr. Danger."

He dips his chin and says, "Shadow."

His tone doesn't give me much hope. My gut tells me this isn't about club business. There's a settling sourness in my stomach that tells me this is about Zharia.

Dobby, who's playing bartender right now, slides our bourbons across the bar. Danger picks his up and says, "Let's talk in the office."

Shit.

Deciding his ominous tone calls for liquid courage, I go ahead and accept the drink and follow his lead and take a sip. Glass in hand, I follow him to the back of the clubhouse where the office is located.

Once I close the door and he sits behind the desk, he addresses me then, "We may have a developing problem."

Well, fuck. I just stare at him. *Get on with it, man.*

"Zharia is in New York. Per Birdie's tracker, they are at a wedding gown store. My wife saw fit to turn her phone's location off but forgot about the tracker inside her. Now, I know my lady doesn't need one. I know my brother Pierre sure as fuck don't need a wedding dress, so it's either Zharia or Tally."

Double shit.

Triple shit.

FUCK.

I feel like the wind's been knocked out of me.

I've been deliberately avoiding looking at her tracker. I'm trying so fucking hard to give her the space that she's repeatedly asked for.

"Ok," I blow out a breath and nod. "Ok."

"I just wanted you to be aware. Birdie has been super secretive the past week when she's on the phone. She doesn't normally walk away, leave the room, or fuck, even go outside to talk on the phone. Every time her phone rings she makes damn sure I don't hear the conversation. It's very suspicious."

I chew this new information over in my head. Zharia's parents are loaded. They would have published an engagement announcement. They're traditional like that.

I don't know much about Tally. I know she went to college with Zharia, Pierre and Birdie. They are the Fab Four, as Zharia called them. They've all stayed best friends since they graduated college years ago.

"Do we know if Tally is engaged?" I ask him.

"We do not."

"Ok." I clear my throat, "Do we know if Zharia is engaged?" That rubbed me the wrong way just saying it. Like a thousand needles scraping across my skin. I can't think about her with someone else.

He looks me in the eyes and states, "I have not been told nor have I heard anything about it. The only thing I know is Birdie asked me to keep next Saturday afternoon open." He sits up with his elbows on the desk, "That tells me we have ten days to figure out what's up because I'm sure whatever they're planning is gonna go down that day."

I plop down in the chair opposite him and take another gulp of alcohol. *Try not to panic.* After setting the glass back on the desk, I set my hands on top of my thighs, rubbing the sweat off them. I swear I'm biting down so hard my teeth are going to crack.

"I was going to go over there tonight and see if I could work it out with her." I'm pissed and stunned at the same time. I bring my eyes up to meet his.

"Shadow, I love you man, but maybe she's really done this time. Maybe it's just done."

"It will never be done. She's mine. The sooner she realizes it the faster we can settle down and be happy."

"Are you in love with her that much?"

I look over at the bulletin board on the wall. Anything to make the emotions stop bubbling up. I nod my head slowly, my eyes sliding to meet his, "Yeah, that much." I swallow and can feel the lump in my throat still sitting there, choking me, demanding I release it.

There's no way I'm breaking down in front of him. But I feel that way. I feel like I could cry, but I won't. Bikers don't cry. I haven't cried since I was a teen and my dad died. Before that, I was a nine-year-old child who took a tumble off his bicycle and skinned up his elbows and knees.

But losing Zharia makes me want to drop to my knees and beg, sobbing, screaming to the sky in frustration and loneliness.

Danger nods and purses his lips together, "Ok, brother, alright. If she's your 'One', then I'll do what I can."

I pull my gaze back to his face, "She's my One, Lincoln. She's my everything."

Danger continues to nod, "Shadow, what are you going to do if it's Zharia's wedding? Are you prepared to accept that?"

My hands fist up and I growl, "She's not marrying anybody but me."

Danger holds up his hands in defense, "Alright. I guess I'll keep my ear out and listen. I'll keep you posted."

"Why did we have to meet here to talk about this? Why didn't you just call me from home?"

"I think the penthouse is bugged."

I'm floored by this suspicion, a little shocked and a smattering of amused. No one got around Danger's security. "Who the fuck would bug your place?"

"My wife."

I chuckle, then I flat out laugh. This is totally something ridiculous Birdie would do. "What? No way, man." With that laugh I feel some of my tension easing away.

He frowns and grumbles, "Yes way. She's never altogether forgiven me for inserting that tracker into her, or um, the hidden cameras in her apartment, and I heard her telling Pierre, over the tattoo studio cameras, that she was going to do it to see what I'm doing and saying while working from home since I won't give her access to the camera feeds." He shakes his head like 'see the monster I created,' complete with a shrug. Like he's serious and really put out over this. It's hilarious.

This man's stalking of his wife is a full-time job. Literally, it's his job but I swear to god he would do it for free if asked. I understand his obsession though. I have one of my own over here I'm working on.

Right before they got married, Birdie gave up her French Quarter apartment above her tattoo studio right beside Jackson Square, to her best friend, and Danger's stepbrother, Pierre, so she could live in Danger's penthouse that overlooks the Quarter. Danger has been obsessed with Birdie for years. He ninja'd into her place and set up surveillance cameras everywhere. Where do you think I got the idea from? He can conveniently say it's for her protection since he was/is her bodyguard, but he was so hopelessly in love with her I knew he did it to keep the loneliness at bay.

Of course, he removed them when Pierre and Seven moved in.

This man has been my mentor, my best friend, my brother, and I trust him implicitly. Danger would never lie to me. He would support me if I wanted something bad enough.

"We'll figure this out, brother," Danger promises.

The man sitting across from me is not the same man I've known for eight years. This is a new and improved version of Mr. Danger. Ever since Birdie finally let go and let Danger be her man, he's been on cloud nine. Ain't nobody telling that man shit, he's ruling the world from between his wife's legs.

Then again, if I had to wait ten years for my wife to get with the program and love me back, I would be acting like him too. I'm out of my mind after two weeks.

"I'm suffering from a huge case of wrong time, right person. I can't lose her," I finish with my head shaking. I can't believe we fucked this up so much. I can't even stop to think for a second about her marrying someone else. I feel like my heart is being ripped from my chest just thinking about it.

Danger gets up and walks around the desk, he pulls at my arm making me stand up and he hugs me. Guys need hugs sometimes too, of course I hug him back. My buddy isn't afraid to show his closest people that he loves them and cares about them. It's one of the many reasons he's family by choice to me.

He releases me and steps back, clearing his throat. He pats me on the shoulder, "We'll get you your girl. But you need to figure out how to fix what's fucked up between you two. Do you need to talk it out? I'm not busy the rest of the night. My wife's out sneaking around New York with her feral pack of besties."

I snort because I know what kind of trouble they get into.

I've been Zharia's shadow for years. I run a security detail for Birdie's dad when he is at charity events, dinners and galas. It's my job to get dressed up and stand around, always watching.

Those philanthropic people don't need to know I'm loaded too. A Native American self-made millionaire. Who knew I would be great at investments, stocks using a huge salary from working for Rock.

Almost a year ago, Zhar started flirting with me at these events. It's like my little rabbit finally went from prey to predator and she was testing it out on me.

Little things at first. Smiles, winks, cute coy looks. Her attention was set on me. It progressed. She was actively pursuing me. I noticed.

Goddamn, I noticed. Like a homing beacon switched on, and all I could notice was Zharia. I've always thought she was beautiful, but once her attention was set on me, it's like the whole world became brighter, more colorful and all I could see was her beauty.

She made me stupid.

But Zharia is way out of my league. That's what I thought. She was different from the start. Different from all the other women I had been with. They meant nothing but fun to me, but Zhar was my future, my everything. I knew the second I kissed her for that first time we were destined to be together.

I was like a moth to a flame once I had the green light from her. And I took that green light and ran with it.

Four months ago, we were at a children's fundraiser and Zharia walked up to me bold as brass and took one look at my golden silk tie, lifting it between her fingers, letting the silk slide against her skin and asked, "Is there a height limit for this ride and is it available tonight?" She thoroughly eye-fucked me standing there after delivering her pickup line.

I love a bold woman. I love the ones that know exactly what they want and they go for it with both hands.

It was the first time I actually encouraged her instead of just grinning and shaking my head. Technically, I was working and didn't have time to indulge her like I wanted. Most of the time it's me scowling or the occasional smile and blush with the ole look away. She made butterflies dance in my stomach; they fluttered up to my chest and danced around my heart too. No one had ever made me feel the way Zharia did.

"It depends on who gets to it first," I huskily replied.

"Can it be delivered to my house tonight?" she asked with a sly, coquettish smirk and a soft giggle.

I looked into her gorgeous brown eyes, "That can be arranged."

Her breath hitched, she pulled air through her barely parted, pretty painted pink lips, and her eyes got wider. God, she was a sight. I had her hook, line and sinker. She was mine from that moment on.

She smiled really big and said, "Just warn me ahead of time, big guy."

"I'm warning you now," I informed her. "Be wet and ready."

This made her shake her head and walk away with a ragged breath.

But I wasn't playing. A few hours after that, I was standing outside her four-bedroom shotgun house and I sent her a two word text.

Me: *I'm here.*

The front door flew open a moment later and there stood Zharia in a lace nightgown that left little to the imagination. Especially with the lights on in the house behind her. Her silhouette is beautiful. After her initial shock, she looked up at me and breathed, "You came."

I leaned down and finally captured her lips as I pulled her closer to me, "Not yet, but I will." That's when I fell for her.

I sunk my lips to hers, pushed us back into her house, kicking the door shut and I sweetly stole her breath with one fiery kiss. The rest is history.

She starts feeling like I'm being controlling when I'm trying to help her have a better life. I start doing things for her, but she thinks I'm trying to take away her independence. That I want to own her. She fights me every step of the way.

When she accuses me of being possessive, I admit, I am. I also don't want her with other men. I don't want her to date anyone else. I don't want her to flirt with other guys. I sure as fuck don't want her texting other dudes.

For weeks we were good, then she spooked and put this huge wall between us and started talking about dating other people and keeping things casual and ditching the feelings. I don't want anyone else and nothing I said was changing her mind.

It's like Zharia is allergic to commitment. I've never seen anyone so scared of settling down as she is.

Every fucking time I try to talk to her about this she immediately gets defensive. I've done everything but beg. I'll be damned if I beg her.

Fuck, I miss her so bad though. Begging is starting to sound like a viable option now. Back at my house, I head straight for the shower. My body's on overdrive from wanting her so bad. The longer she's away from me the worse it gets. If thoughts about her aren't stabbing my heart, they're pumping up my dick with memories. Goddamn. I squeeze my fists to survive this wave of grief and longing.

I quickly wash and condition my long, black hair, and wash my body off. I grab Zhar's body wash and slick up my cock thinking about her. The smell drives me wild. I love her scent; I love every bit of feminine products she uses. Her lotion, soap, shampoo, perfume—I'm addicted to them all.

I groan as I grip my cock. Our sex life was out of this world. Our connection is deeper than anything I've ever known. What we had is worth saving. Fuck, I'll even go to couples counseling if it will save us.

I stroke my hard cock to the memory of a sweat covered Zharia straddling my hips, rocking her body, chasing her pleasure. Her gorgeous tits swaying to her movements. Her pants and sounds. I love being inside her. The best pussy I've ever been in. So tight and wet. I loved every second I could show her how much I loved her.

A memory pushes right to the forefront, of her on the bed riding me like that. Her cupping her gorgeous caramel titties in her hands, pinching her nipples. My hands on her plump ass pushing and pulling her on to me, giving her the friction she needs.

The way she sounds when she comes. How hard she rides me and makes herself come using my body. It steals her breath and wracks her body. She loses herself in each orgasm and like the primal animal she is inside, she lets any sounds fly from her mouth each time she comes. Those are my favorite sounds in the world.

Remembering her noises makes the sparks fire down my spine and the familiar fire courses through my body. I throw my other hand up on the tiled wall to support me just as my breath is becoming more ragged with each pump. My grip on my dick is firm while I continue to beat it like it owes me money.

It feels too good to stop or slow down. With my orgasm barreling through me, I squeeze my eyes shut and let out a prolonged groan, letting my cock erupt on my climax. "Fuck, Zharia. Come back to me, baby."

CHAPTER 5 - ZHARIA

I roll my eyes at the three-hundred-and-eleventy-seven-thousand-degree day with a million percent humidity. It's so hot it steals your breath. Why the fuck does it have to be so hot still? It's like Satan sets up shop in the South for half the year and tries to cook all the humans. It's September for fuck's sake, bring on fall, and cooler weather. I guess this is what I get for living in the South on the Gulf. I could have moved anywhere; I shake my head. No, I just had to stay home, in the city that raised me.

I've just left the baker's shop. I ordered a small two-tiered simple wedding cake for next Saturday. There won't be but maybe fifteen people there, including us.

Honestly, I don't want to spend a fortune on a wedding that the union's only going to last less than two years. The only people invited were our immediate families, plus Pierre, Birdie and Danger (who knows nothing about a wedding yet.) Danger will have to come because he will not let Birdie out of his sight since her abduction and our trip to New York…because well, she kinda 'forgot' to mention to him she was going to New York and just boarded her daddy's plane and set off. Of course he was raging pissed. Can't blame the guy.

We all unanimously decided it was best to basically lie to Danger, whereas Birdie is just going to avoid the truth so she doesn't have to lie to her spouse. We aren't telling Danger about the wedding until he's at the church. Birdie said she's going to tell him it's a special event the church is hosting that she really wants to attend. Meh, technically not lying. Creative fibs. Veiled fables.

I would never ask her to bold face lie to her husband. I'm not stepping in between that. That goes against my morals.

I did splurge a little when we went to New York a few days ago and I bought my dress. It was a little more than I wanted it to be, but Birdie said it's ok because this is just the first marriage, I can get a bigger and better dress for my next one.

The wheeze I wheezed when she said that in front of my mother and I saw Mom's disdainful, appalled reaction. It made our Fab Four dissolve into giggles. I'm sure the dress shop's champagne had something to do with it also.

Most brides have an idea of what they want their dress to look like. Then you have me over here asking if I can have pink and simple. We narrowed it down to a simple silk flowy number with a small amount of lace and form fitting. It's like it was made just for me. It passes for the palest pink which is what I wanted. It's good enough for my fake marriage.

…That's in five fucking days. Not freaking out. Not at all. Breathe in.

The constant chant inside my head 'ohmygodohmygodohmygod' sure as hell is not helping.

It helped in this whole stressful process that Tally took over and declared herself the shit show supervisor and out of three dresses she chose, we landed on the one. She knows my tastes, and she also knows the situationship going on in my triangle leading to this moment. Everyone knows now. All the Fab Four is in on my secrets I've kept hidden. Shadow and I were the burning hot tea last night in the hotel suite after dinner.

I had to confide in my friends once we got to New York. I let everything out of the bag. I came clean about how long we'd been sneaking around. How I let everything spiral out of control. How scared I was. How heartbroken I am.

I even apologized to Birdie for having sex at her wedding. I told them how I'm planning a wedding to one man when my heart is locked and loaded for another, and it's completely shattering me. Shadow and I are just too different. I cried and cried the first night there, with my bestest friends huddled around me, trying to console me. All of us cried together at my heartache. We were a hot mess, and the wine certainly didn't help with all the weeping.

True to her word, Birdie didn't try to play both sides. I know Shadow is her man's bestie, but she's made it clear her loyalty lies with me. I never wanted to put her in the middle of this, well, *fuck show* as Tally calls my sham of a marriage. Birdie says if his stalking and breaking and entering keep happening after the wedding, she will go to her dad, and I need to go to the police.

Once we had a good cry, the next day we went around to see some of the sights that Tally was excited to drag us to. She didn't have to drag too hard; I was so down to see some good spots outside of all the touristy hot spots.

The next day was spent shopping and wandering around the city before we flew home that evening.

Tally is a popular fashion designer living in New York full time, like I'm so proud of her, and she just showed at New York Fashion Week. This was her week to decompress and lucky me, it happened to be the week I needed to get a dress. Killing two birds with one stone kinda deal. Seeing her and getting a dress. Memories in the making.

Tally asked if I would be mad if she missed my fake as hell wedding since she was just down there last week for Birdie's very much real wedding and I had to laugh. No, I won't be mad, but I told her she better not miss the opening of my new surgical center. She said it was a deal.

One of the highlights of the trip was Birdie bringing her mini tattoo kit and tattooing on us a number four with a heart and a four-leaf clover. We will always be the Fab Four and nobody can take that away from us. I'm so fortunate that I have three close friends. Some people don't even have one, so I consider myself blessed.

I pull up to my gate that leads into my driveway. I made damn sure I had off street parking when I bought this place. There's never any good parking when you need it. I don't have time for all that shit.

The gate slides back and I pull forward. I hop out of the car as the gate goes back and notice it squeaking. I'll have to put some lubrication on it before it gets worse and Mrs. Fontenot complains. No need to wake the dead over there. For the gamillionth time I wish the houses weren't so close.

Now that I'm down to five days to the wedding I keep getting an urge to tell her there will be a man living here. But as I get out of my SUV, right next to her house mind you, she perches in the window and takes all those thoughts out of my mouth with one sentence, "The man with the loud motorcycle was here earlier."

Thud. Thud. Whoosh. Thud. Thud. Whoosh.

That's my heartbeat in my ears as I try not to pass out.

"He left you something, he said make sure you call him."

My blood is like ice in my veins. What the fuck was he doing here? Fuckity, fuck fuck.

I force a smile at her, "Thank you, Mrs. Fontenot, I'll be sure to call him." I deem now is not the most opportune time to tell her about another man in my life. Or that he's moving in. She already thinks I'm a floozy. I'll give it another few days. She's already a judgey ole biddy. Nosy as all git out.

I go into my house and close the door quickly and make damn sure I lock it. Not like that's ever stopped him any other time. Ob-vi-ously. I don't know how he does it, but it doesn't matter the lock or combination, he still gets in.

He's truly a shadow. It's creepy.

I know she's still watching me through her screened window over there, staring holes into the stucco on the side of my house. I feel the disapproving scowl from inside my house in the dark.

Dusty dried up old woman.

When I flip on the light, I see my narrow island in the kitchen covered in flowers. His saddlebags must have been full to the brim. There's so many. My mouth drops open.

Once I drop my bag, my hands come up to cover my nose and mouth. Holy shit. I walk through the living room and into the kitchen. They're even on the counters. There's a handwritten letter on the island with a white rose sitting on top of it.

I pick it up to read it, my other hand drops to my chest when I see Shadow's, surprisingly good penmanship, signature.

Poppet,

No matter how much you hate me, or are mad at me, I still love you very much, more than anything. You're my everything. My vicious little poppet. I miss you baby. Please call me or let me come home.

I can't hear shit over my heart drumming through my body and my chest gasping for air. Oh god the sobs are coming.

Looking to the ceiling and yelling, "GODDAMNIT!" Fuck you, Mrs. Fontenot, I don't care if you complain.

Why does he have to be so close but so far away from being the perfect man. Gah. Why can't I be normal?

First thing I do is unblock his number.

This is why he's done all this and broken in again. He's trying to get my attention the only way he can. I blocked his number and all contacts in the car on the way to my 'date' after Birdie's wedding AKA the shitty dinner date I had to go meet my parents at.

My hand shakes as I hit speaker phone and let it ring.

"Hello, beautiful. I've been waiting for you." The deep, rugged timbre of his voice sends shivers down my spine. His voice could melt butter. It always makes my clit twitch. I miss his drool worthy voice that makes me weak.

FOCUS! You hate him, don't be a stupid cow! No, I don't. Not even a little. And that's the problem.

"Shadow. Thank you for the flowers but I specifically asked you not to break into my home anymore."

"Baby, I need to talk to you. I'm going out of my mind. Can we please just talk?"

"I don't think that's a good idea."

"It's always a good idea to talk out our issues, however I agree with you, we just can't ever find the right words. Can we try to talk again?" Goddamn it's tempting. My body misses him too.

Triple fuck. *Stop this cockamamie bullshit right meow!* I must hold my ground.

"No, Shadow. There's nothing to talk about."

I feel him bristle across the phone waves. "There's plenty we need to talk about. Tell me what I need to do, I need you back, babe. I'll do anything."

Do not break down now, Zharia!

"No, and don't do this again. Next time I'm calling the cops." I hang up and immediately block his number again.

It would have been so easy to say yes. A big part of me wanted to say yes. The small part of me that's screaming and fighting to say no is getting louder and fighting itself to the surface.

Even if I wanted to go back to him, I couldn't. I'm getting married and the ice-cold bucket of panic splashes over my head. The gut churning, chest wracking silent cries are never ending the closer I get to my wedding date.

This is a lot.

And now with Shadow's call, it's sending me backwards in all my supposed healing Tally's been spouting about and Pierre's insistence about getting over him. God, I miss him so bad. Every fiber in my being misses him.

He became one of my best friends. We hung out every spare minute. I lost myself in him. I had lost my heart to him, but I almost lost my head. My worst mistake I love to regret the most.

Never give a man that much power over you.

I couldn't let him capture me. I'm a free spirit. I bow to no man, I obey no man, and I sure as fuck never want to be under any man's thumb.

I see how my mom is with my dad. She lets him do whatever he pleases. Women, drugs, gambling, you name it. My father is a dirty old rich man that gets his way in everything. As long as it keeps her out of that poverty-stricken village she grew up in, she doesn't give a fuck what that man does.

I'll never put myself in that position. 1) because I have a trust fund, 2) I have my own high paying job and 3) I'd need to trust a man to let him all the way in, like I did with Shadow, and I shan't be doing that shit again any time soon. Bet. Uh huh.

But you let Shadow in and we miss him, a voice slithers through my head.

You know what, fuck you vagina and heart.

Trust him…That I did. I own that. I broke my own heart. A million papercuts on my broken heart later, thinking about how I should have kept him at arm's length; I should have shut him out like all the others.

I was never supposed to fall for him. He was supposed to be a fuck I got out of my system.

But I did, and I fell so fucking hard and deep.

How do other people live through these soul crushing break-ups? I don't feel like I can survive it. Like I'm never going to be the same.

Most of my cries over men are because I have pity parties about how fucked up my taste in men is and why I am the way I am.

There's something inside of me that won't allow me to settle down with just one man. To live with him. To feel suffocated.

He's ruined me for other men though. There is no one quite like him.

Seeing different men is not a commitment to one certain one and it keeps the anxiety away. I don't want to answer to one man the rest of my life. Sounds like a nightmare. My mother would literally lick his toes if my father told her to do it.

I've heard enough yelling and screaming to understand my dad ruled my mother. She told me one time, it wasn't always like this, he was nice and loving at one point. Now he's just a cold, distant asshole.

I want to stay loyal to Shadow and that's the most dangerous thing of all this. *How many times has Shadow called you mine and been super possessive of you?* He's trying to trap you, is what my brain is screaming at me.

Although, Shadow was here so much at my house he practically lived here, and I loved it…when it was good. I see his reference about coming home.

I have to get up off the floor.

Get the fuck up.

Once I stand and grab some tissues, I pick up my phone and call Pierre. I need somewhere to stay. It's glaringly obvious I'm not safe from him here. I just need five days to hide out somewhere. Then I'll come back here because he'll have heard I got married and he'll go away. It will be too late and I'll be free, ironically.

My stomach twists at the thought of not seeing him again. Not hearing his voice. Not feeling his warm touch. There will be nothing. Nothing but a giant gaping hole in my chest where my heart once resided.

A traitorous part of my heart howls her mourning song within my soul. This has to end. I can't be what he wants. What he deserves. He'll get over me quickly enough. Whereas I'll forever hate fate for her timing.

The sick feeling deep inside of me knows I left a piece of my soul with him, and I'll never feel complete again. Sadness throbs with each broken heartbeat. I'm just breaking my own heart again. I can't stop.

Chapter 6 – Shadow

Danger lets me into the room where Zharia is waiting to be walked down the aisle by her father. I couldn't have had this moment with her without my best friend being a sneaky bastard. It's now or never.

Birdie is physically fighting her husband outside the door, in the hallway, to keep me from entering this room. She is putting up a good fight too. Her face is beet red as she growls, claws and hisses at him. It's a huge struggle.

I must hand it to the ladies; they kept her wedding under wraps pretty well. I found out exactly thirty minutes ago…when Danger arrived and all was revealed to him.

Zharia is expected to walk down the aisle in fifteen minutes.

Zhar's face lights up then falls flat when she sees me slip into the room amidst the commotion out in the hallway. That look right there tells me she is doing this against her will. No way would she agree to marriage. I should know. There's only one way…

"What did he promise you? What did he buy you with, Zhar?" I demand quietly through clenched teeth. My jaw locks in anger.

Holy fuck she looks gorgeous though. It should be me, god damn it, it should be me.

"It's none of your fucking business, Shadow. You need to leave."

I lick my lips and take a deep breath, letting it out. *Calmer approach, big guy.* "Zharia, I need to know. I need to know what tipped the scale away from me. You won't marry me, but you'll marry someone else? A fucking stranger?" I can't keep the hurt out of my voice. My heart is bleeding. I can't wrap my head around it.

She sighs and drops my gaze, "He's building me a state-of-the-art surge center that will be all mine to run and work out of. He's fulfilling my ultimate dream."

I'm stunned. This is what she sold out for?

I can barely push the words through my lips, "I would have done that for you."

"Yeah? With what millions?" she scoffs.

"All the ones I have in the bank just sitting there, waiting to spend on the love of my life, on you. I would have built it for you Zhar and anything else you would have asked for. I would've spent every last penny I have to make you happy. Fuck, I would have bought an entire hospital for you if that's what would've made you love me."

She straightens her shoulders while her chin wobbles, "It was never about not loving you; I did plenty of that. It's about the way we have two very different plans for our lives, and the paths don't align. You just weren't right for me. I am not the girl for you."

Jesus fuck. My soul is ripping from my chest. I'm dying. Only dying can cause this much pain. My world is tipping on its axis and I feel like I'm falling into the void.

Strong emotions clog my throat. "No, Zhar, you don't mean that. I'm perfect for you."

"Yes, I do Shadow. Please don't mess this up for me. I only have to stay married for sixteen months and that's plenty of time to get a surge center built and established."

"I can't let you marry him. You're mine, poppet."

"No, I'm not Shadow. Not anymore. You lost the right to call me yours."

I fight hardcore to hold the emotions in. I'm failing. I can already feel the scorching hot tears track down my cheeks. FUCK! Grown men aren't supposed to cry.

They do when the woman who holds the other half of their soul marries another man. She's killing me.

She walks over and wipes my cheeks, "You have to let me go, Shadow. I have to do this. Promise me you won't interfere with my life anymore. Promise you will stay away while I do this. Please."

It's barely a whisper that's leaves me, "I'm begging Zhar, begging, please don't do this, please poppet, goddamnit please." My voice becomes hoarse near the end. I have no shame at this point. None. I'll get on my knees if I have to.

She steps back while her own tears fall, "I don't love you anymore, Shadow. Please leave and never speak to me again." Christ, I can't take anymore. She stands her full five-eight height, chin wobbling, head held up in defiance, tears lacing through her make up. She tries to remain stoic, but her eyes tell the anguish she's feeling. I know she still loves me and that makes this a million times worse.

The cold fingertips of death render my tortured heart a lump of beaten and battered flesh in my chest where it's crushed like a bug. It's like a switch, I shut it off, never to be the same again, never to feel, never to allow another into my heart.

There's no feeling in the world worse than losing the person you're in love with. That you know is the right one. Your other half. The love of your life.

That you know still loves you.

There's no amount of begging that can compete with what her father's offering.

I have to admit defeat and accept the outcome.

With a lot of swallowing, I manage to suppress the sob clawing its way up my throat but not the tears that fall freely down my face. I reach over and lay my hand on her face, I lean down and lightly kiss her damp cheek, "There will never be a day that I don't love you more than my own life. Forever yours, Zhar, even in death. My heart and soul belong to you."

She sobs and I step back, I drop my hand back to my side. My heart seizes as my hand grows cold, her warmth dissipating. The last touch. The last kiss. "You make a beautiful bride. Stunning." Before I can break down and bawl my heart out, I slip back out the door, leaving my bloody heart at her feet, and walking away from the only woman I've ever loved. There will never be another.

CHAPTER 7 — ZHARIA

Fifteen months later

"I'm running late. Surgery ran over and I'm just now leaving the house. Sorry, love," I tell Birdie as I run to my closet and grab my red heels. Once I have them on, I stop by the mirror to check my makeup.

It's a small white lie. Surgery did run over by fifteen minutes but not enough for me to be so late. I actually took too long in the shower fucking myself with a dildo. I needed to get it out of my system before this party while I'm alone.

"I understand but get here soon. The club went all out for the kids this year and Denver can open presents this year." I hear the excitement in her voice.

Danger and Birdie's son, Denver, is their Fourth of July baby. He came into the world red, white, and blue and screaming his little baby lungs out for his momma. At nearly six months old, there's no way that baby is opening his own presents.

Look, I don't know a lot about babies, but he doesn't strike me as having the best dexterity.

The only reason I agreed to go to the annual Christmas party the clubhouse holds is because Birdie begged me to, and I know Shadow won't be there.

She broke it to me gently one night at her and Danger's penthouse for Wine Wednesday—Shadow left the area shortly after my wedding.

He asked Rock for a transfer. He's been overseeing the Mobile, Alabama port. There's been trouble out there with the chapter and then there's the strike of the dock workers. More than a dozen up and moved to Houston to be a Lone Star Saint, the rival club that kidnapped Birdie and Pierre.

They're basically walking right into their deaths when Birdie's dad, Rock, gets his hands on them. From what I've heard, they stole a shipment when their traitorous asses jumped ship.

LSS motorcycle club is scary as fuck. No way in the world I'd ever get involved with one of their members. They sell people. Like steal them and then sell them into sex slavery. Human traffickers. The lowest of the low. Scum of the earth. They don't care about human life, just money. I'm so thankful Birdie and Pierre survived when they were stolen by their now dead President, Grim.

But I hear their new President is a barely sane shitcicle too.

As far as I know, Shadow's been in Mobile the entire time since Birdie's wedding. I've never bumped into him or seen him around here and for that I'm grateful. Sometimes I think I see him, and when I turn around, he's not there. I dream of him at night, like I can smell him near me, but it disappears once I wake up. He comes to me in my dreams and holds me and makes the bad feelings go away.

Sometimes I wake up so sad, even crying. It's been well over a year, and I still can't get over him.

While trying to heal my heart and soul, I've managed to finish my classes, become the specialist surgeon I dreamed of, and I get to practice medicine and the art of surgery every day in my very own facility that opened back in the beginning of summer.

I love my job and my facility. I have amazing employees, and the other doctors are superb surgeons and it's an honor to work with them. We have such a great crew and we're all friends outside of work too.

Lately I feel like all I ever do is work. Granted, I love what I do, but what do I have to show for a life away from working? I have no hobbies to speak of, except reading the books Birdie shoves in my face, but most of them just make me sad. They all have these happy couples, in love, happily ever after. Blah blah bah humbug.

Ya know, it's just everything I shoved away for my goals. Selfish, I was so selfish. Doesn't cause flashbacks at all.

It still hurts. It's never-ending.

As sad as it sounds, I haven't had sex since Shadow. That's a long time for me. I just don't care to. They aren't him. I've been steadily getting through school, then running the facility, and of course doing my actual job of cutting people open.

I stopped caring about a lot of things. I don't go out anymore and I spend most of my time at home.

Instead of taking my Mercedes to the clubhouse, I called Cherry, the perky ride share driver we met on the way to meet my fake real husband for the first time. She has no problem doing private chauffeuring for us.

After Cherry got her first fat tip from us, she gave us her personal number. We use her all the time now. She loves driving us wherever we want because we pay her very well. Traffic in this city sucks, so she earns it. I hate driving around here. Unfortunately, I must drive in it to get to work.

"Hey girl! How you are you doing?" Cherry asks when I slide into the passenger seat. We did away with the backseat shit a long time ago. She gives me a quick, awkward hug over the console, and we start off.

"I'm good. Work keeps me too busy to breathe but I promised Birdie I would come to this Christmas party. Are you busy? Do you want to go?"

She gushes, "Oh no, Z, I have to drive tonight. Need some extra cash for the holidays but thank you for the invite."

I make a mental note to wire an extra five hundred to Cherry after the ride. I watch the scenery drift by and listen to her prattle on about her junior year of college and some guy she's trying to date. I offer appropriate responses, but my heart isn't in it.

I've been stuck in this rut for fifteen months.

It doesn't help that next month I'm filing for divorce.

From my fake real husband, Raj.

It's time.

Chapter 8 – Shadow

I like my hair to be pulled and played with like any normal guy, but this isn't what I mean. Denver has his little baby fist wrapped up in a lock of my hair and he's about to yank it a good one. A laughing Danger is quickly untangling my hair from his son's small hand while I hold him on my hip.

I wouldn't be here if Danger hadn't begged me to be here. It's his son's first Christmas and he wanted his best friends together to celebrate since it's been at least, shit, almost six months since I came back for a visit. I was last here for Denver's birth.

I've been over in Mobile getting that fuckshow under control. I stepped in as interim President until I found a new one and then I started recruiting. We needed a stronger foothold in that city and the last President thought everyone would find their own way magically to the club.

Yeah, I tucked tail and left some time ago. There was no way in hell I was staying here after that day at the church. I had to leave. Call it running or hiding, I don't give a shit. Self-preservation kicked in. It did me good to stay away. I'm not sure if I want to come back, but I've been keeping track of time for the past fifteen months and time is dwindling down until I can win my old lady back.

She said sixteen months.

I didn't forget.

I have to get it right this time. I need my old lady.

That's what she is to me, my old lady. It's a title in the biker world given with esteemed respect and reverence to the lady in your life. That's your best friend, your everything. Old ladies are your ride or die. You don't mess with guys' old ladies. That's how you get your head stomped in.

A commotion at the door draws my attention. There in the flesh, in a pretty little red, curve hugging dress is my vicious little poppet. My life, my love, my everything.

I lose my breath.

You know when you look at someone, and the whole world goes quiet, there's a slight buzz in your head, and all you can hear is your thundering heart while you stare at them in awe; that's the earth moving feelings I'm going through upon seeing her for the first time in all these long grueling months.

God, I missed the sight of her.

Her laugh trickles over to my ears and I damn near swoon on the spot. I didn't realize how much I missed her until this moment.

Danger leans in, "Are you ok, brother?"

I can't take my eyes off her. I nod. It's all I can do.

"At least close your mouth," he urges.

I snap my mouth shut. I've always wondered how I would respond if I saw her again.

When Dreama comes over and gets up in my face to play with Denver, that's when Zharia's eyes find mine and time stands still. Her beautiful smile falters and she looks away to finish laughing at whatever Bam is telling her. I'm immediately jealous of Bam while he's holding her attention.

As soon as she drifts away from Bam, Dobby practically prances up to her with a smile. They begin to talk, and she nods and smiles. I can tell she's not into him, not as interactive as she was with Bam.

Zharia gets stopped two more times on her way to the bar. She smiles at Twilla, the clubhouse head old lady, and I see Twilla hand her a bottle of water. She doesn't drink anymore?

She looks back over to me and meets my eyes. I've never stopped looking at her, my eyes tracking her every move. I've never stopped loving her. Fuck, I've never stopped looking for her in any woman I've been with since. No one compares to my poppet.

Zhar nods her head at me, acknowledging me, all while Dreama is all over me to get to Denver. Fuck. My poppet turns and melds into the crowd of people behind her, dismissing me once again.

Birdie is right in front of me, "I'll take my son now, Shadow," she says, holding her arms out with a forced smile.

"Right, ok, here you go," I hand the chunker over to his momma.

Danger pulls me off to the side. "Are you sure you're ok? You're acting all twitterpated and shit. Like birds are singing around your head and shit. Snap out of it!" He snaps his fingers in my face, and I finally look over at him. "I didn't tell Birdie you were coming. I sure as shit didn't tell her you were coming with a married couple, and the wife is smoking hot. Did you see Zhar's face when she saw Dreama all over you?

That's not gonna be good for your mission to get her back, bro."

"Can't someone just explain to her Demon's the new President I'm training and that's his wife that I'm friends with," hedging him to do it for me.

The light bulb finally clicks in Danger's head, and he replies, "I guess I can do that, bring it up in casual conversation. Or maybe introduce them to her since Dreama won't leave my kid alone…and Birdie is headed Zhar's way with Dreama hot on her heels. Shit, I gotta go."

"I'd appreciate it, brother."

I have one shot, and it has to count, or I'll lose her forever. *Don't fuck it up.*

I should never have come. I should have stayed home. I should have broken my promise to my best friend, my sister, my girly pop.

After watching him with his new woman and her fawning all over my nephew, I had to move as far away as possible. I really can't be around with a cute blond rubbing her tits all over him in front of everyone.

I'm trying not to be a judgey bitch, ok I don't try very hard, but I can see the appeal of her. She is full of smiles and cheerleader curves. She's the typical Playboy stereotype.

Blond, perky, tan. Not someone I thought I'd see him with, but tonight's full of surprises.

As much as I've healed, I have a threshold, and every good bit of healed broken heart I've carefully patched together is now threatening to explode.

I find Gunney, or as I call him, Leo, laughing with Travares, Dobby, Slim Jim (I just adore this old biker), T-Bone and Wild Bill. The table is full of others I've only met in passing, but Slim, T, and Wild Bill are my favorites. They are cranky hilarious old guys who've been around forever. Every time I've been here they trip over themselves to give me the princess treatment. It's cute really.

They've pulled tables together for their clique. I gingerly walk up and sit in the seat beside Leo, which I'm assuming he saved for me. He throws me an eyebrow but doesn't stop talking, telling his story to Slim and T-Bone to his right. He throws his arm around me, not stopping his story, pulling me to his side and I relax a bit. His smell brings me comfort, and I feel the rumble of his deep voice through his ribs that my shoulder leans on.

Leo knows. He knows all about my relationship with Shadow. The good and the bad. He knows how broken my heart was/is.

When Shadow left, I was a wreck. I know, a self-induced wreck. I could have had love at my fingertips, but I chose me. I chose freedom. Quite possibly a choice I regret…to a degree. Torn and confused, a complete mess was an understatement for the state of being I was in when I walked into our local neighborhood grocery store that fateful evening.

I was out of tissues and other food items, so I went out, for like the first time ever looking like a pile of donkey shit. There were no fucks given, alright. I'm minding my own and trying to get things as quickly as possible, but Gunney saw me before I saw him, and we recognized each other.

The first thing he said was, "Who do I need to kill for making you cry?"

He refused to let me pay for my own groceries, or carry them, or put them in my car. He threatened to call Birdie if I didn't let him follow me home so he knew I was safe.

I wasn't in the mood to argue. When he got here, he carried my groceries in. I wasn't sure what to say to him. So, he tried again.

"Who do I need to kill?"

I turned sad eyes to him and replied, "It's ok, it's over, I'll be fine."

Of course that didn't appease him. He ended up staying and cooking me dinner. One half of his family is Italian, and the other half black, so he knows how to cook some really good shit. Like homecooked comfort foods. Hallelujah. I remember telling him he'll make a good wife someday and how funny he thought that was.

We fell into this friendship of ours. Stumbled together on healing journeys. The universe knew I needed him and he landed in my life like a cat-five hurricane. He's one of my best buds now and I wouldn't trade our time for anything. He's helped me heal and he's been a huge part of my life in the past fifteen months.

Besides, only I know that Leo is gay and he was getting over a relationship too. And well the Fab Four knows about Leo's sexual preference. I've talked to them about it. It's his story to tell his brothers if he wants, when he wants; it won't be slipping from my lips.

The best part is seeing how happy Leo is now on his own healing journey.

Leo knew I was hesitant to come here tonight, and he knew why. My night went to complete shit before it even had a chance to suck. I'll just sit here and wait for Birdie to be done and then I'll seek her out far away from Shadow or preferably she'll come to me. I'm for fuck sure not going over there and be closer to him and Bimbo Boobens.

Tsk tsk. Be nice, Zhar.

Slim Jim takes over telling a story and Leo leans down, nudges my hair away from my ear with his nose and whispers, "You look amazing. You ok?" To anyone outside of our bubble, this comes off as an intimate moment between boyfriend and girlfriend. But it's far from the truth. Most everyone here knows we are best friends.

Except Shadow. And maybe Danger.

Tonight it seems Leo wants to prove a point by pulling me closer and looking awfully intimate.

I try not to be a petty person and to walk mostly in the light, but sometimes I want to stop being the bigger person and slash tires. I want to make him jealous since he's flaunting his new woman here. Just wow.

I nod to Leo before taking a gulp of my water. I make sure I'm always drinking only water or something non-alcoholic around him.

He tucks a piece of flyaway tendril behind my ear, but I see his eyes searching the room, as much as he can see from our vantage point. "He's here, isn't he? I haven't left this spot to see. I'm sorry, Z." I feel his lips moving on my cheek, the stubble on his chin brushing my skin and it gives me shivers.

Shivers I shouldn't be having over my platonically gay best friend.

I try soo hard not to have romantic feelings for Leo. I know he's not into girls anymore, but fuck, he's like the perfect man sometimes. It helps he's fucking movie star worthy hotness. No wonder his subscription page has so many people.

Not that I've looked. Or subscribed. Or see him jack off with those perfect washboard abs of his as a background to his nice sized cock. Ok, I looked one time, after he told me about his page and I immediately regretted it. I was instantly wet. Instantly ravenous and horny. God fucking damn, his videos are fire.

Then I tried not to be weird and awkward around him. I will never tell my gay best friend, 'Hey, so like I rubbed one out numerous times to video forty-eight.'

Intimate moments like this, where he looks at me like I'm the only person on the planet and his lips brush anywhere on my body, it gives me goosebumps and I'm not mad about it. Maybe a little sad. I tamper down so many feelings where Leo is concerned. I respect his boundaries though.

I look over at him as a spark of something kindles to life deep down inside me where Leo feelings are shoved. I feel alive, tingly and very aware of where his lips are. I sway into him more involuntarily. He pulls me tighter, moving my chair as close as it can get to his. Pretty soon he will just drag me over to his lap like a caveman if he continues like this. The closer proximity overloads my senses with all things Leo.

The warm leather of his vest mixed with his cologne…

Yep. Those are tingles in my vagina.

Feelings I haven't felt very often with anyone since Shadow stir to life. I have to kill them quick before I moan accidently. He hugs me to him, a comfort I am grateful for right now. There are so many warring emotions inside me going on right now.

I'm all shades of fucked up. I'm a horrible person. I breathe out the flare of heat igniting in me from Leo's touch. Blow that shit out like a birthday candle.

Head in the game, bitch, be aware.

I've thought of this moment—what would it be like to see Shadow in person again?

It sucks, that's what. Sucks big, hairy dirty donkey balls. It's ripping at the scars on my heart. It's like I'm programmed to respond strongly to him. It pokes at the guilt I have, and it pushes at the feelings I've buried deep down. Tonight, in one fell swoop he's choked me with buried emotions by one heated glance.

Remember your power, Z!

It's hard to do when he is walking this way…

"Don't worry, I got you, babe," Leo says and then bites the side of my throat, tickling me, causing me to jerk and throw my head back and making me laugh. That's when Shadow arrives at the end of the table, beside me.

Birdie is hot on his tail and arrives just seconds after him with a big smile on her face. He only had time to open his mouth before she showed up. I can tell by the worry and tension in her eyes she did not know Shadow would be here tonight and she's really nervous about how this is going to play out.

I'm sure her husband planned this surprise and good for him, it's his best friend and he has every right to be here. It's his club, I'm just a visitor. But Birdie is just as blindsided as I am, I can tell.

Maybe leaving and avoiding any drama that might happen is the best thing. I'm the outsider.

That idea is blown to shit when Birdie, with her baby in her arms, hip checks Shadow out of the way to pull me out of Leo's arms and into her with one arm.

I wrap my arms around both her and Denver and stand up as she's latched onto me. Her shaky whisper reaches only my ears, "I had no idea, I'm so sorry."

I pat her on the back to let her know I'm not mad. By this point in our friendship, we can communicate with eye movements and hand twitches.

She pulls back and loudly says, "I'm so happy you could make it, I wasn't sure with your busy schedule," she leans out around me and winks at Leo, "Or if he was going to be hogging your time again. Either way, I'm so glad you're here."

In my peripheral, I see the jaw clenching Shadow is doing and I know he's mad. He could spit venom right now and Leo's getting the first hit.

I recognize his jealousy. His hard stare is on me and it's making me more uncomfortable. I feel my cheeks heating up and my nipples hardening. Thank goodness for padded bras, right?

One minute I'm getting worked up with arousal, next minute I'm getting worked up with anxiety. Obviously, we've both moved on. I can tell from that little scene being played out when I walked into the building. Let him think Gunney is mine, I give zero fucks what he thinks.

Although, I bet my vibrator collection he would leave her for me if I went back to him.

Denver reaches out for his Auntie Z, and I scoop him up in my arms while he smiles his little dimpled baby smile ear to ear. I smile and snuggle him, loving his baby smell, cooing at him and making him giggle. Of course that makes me smile harder at him. He helps settle my nerves. I would die for this kid. Once I settle him in my arms, I tickle under his chin and make eyes at the little boy who stole my heart.

Kids aren't so bad I guess. Denver won me over.

This is the perfect time for Dipshit Debbie to show up, right at Shadow's side. Being all cutesy and shit.

Danger and another man are making their way here too. Danger looks nervous and pissed at the same time. *I hope it ain't at me 'cause I didn't do shit!* I'm over here minding my own for damn sure. He needs to tell his bestie to cool it and get out of my space.

Thankfully Shadow's moved behind Birdie a couple steps. Her hip check worked. But this woman, needling her way in, playing with Denver....Lord, grant me grace.

Birdie, oblivious to what I saw earlier, pulls Dipshit Debbie up beside her and says, "Dreama," —of fucking course her name is Dreama—Dipshit Dreama, I was so close. "This is my best friend Zharia, Zhar this is Dreama. She's visiting from Mobile." Danger puts his hand on Birdie's shoulder and says something to her I can't quite hear.

Being a gracious lady with a southern upbringing, I look at Dreama and nod, the most forced smile cracks my face. I muster up some kind of decorum and sweetness before I say, "Nice to meet you, Dreama."

Dreama sticks a finger in Denver's hand and smiles at him. "I'm hoping with this trip I can convince my husband to have a baby finally."

They got married?

My stomach tightens up. Married. I think I'm going to throw up. *Don't you dare look at him.* Too late, my eyes flit over to him and back quickly. He looks petrified but pissed.

"That would be nice for you, I'm sure." What else am I supposed to say? Sure, I hope you have a baby with my ex-boyfriend I think I'm still in love with. This is difficult enough. *What the fuck did I do for this bullshit, karma? You gotta lotta nerve, man.*

My chest is seizing inside. I can't control my racing heart.

My assigned, slacker guardian angel must be in the back room snorting coke off a club hunny's tits again because nothing is saving me from drowning in a few seconds.

I feel it coming on. I've reached my threshold and I'm super pissed I'm allowing myself to have these reactions.

Birdie turns back to us and doesn't look happy. I look in Birdie's eyes and I know she can see my fight or flight kicking into overdrive. With all these 'get the fuck out of here' vibes flooding off of me I don't know how anyone can miss it.

At about that time my hero and chosen guardian angel steps up behind me, pulling me back against his front, resting his chin on my head, he wraps his arms around me to play with Denver. I let out a sigh. God, I love Leo.

If I didn't know better, I would say Leo has a small streak of petty running through his drop-dead gorgeous body too.

Birdie jumps into action and reaches for Denver and gives me another apologetic glance, "I need to go get his gifts ready. Zharia, can you come help me please?"

Leo's arms stay wrapped around me and I notice Shadow's jaw working in frustration. He's trying so hard not to say anything.

Dreama pipes up, "I can help too."

I internally roll my eyes. God damn this woman's baby fever is about to explode her damn ovaries.

"Thank you, Dreama, but I'd like to speak to Zhar for a minute, alone, catch up."

Dreama slaps at the air in front of her and says, "Of course. Have fun ladies." She steps back and goes to the guy standing with Danger. He throws an arm over her and says something in her ear that makes her smile really big.

Interesting.

In order to follow Birdie, I have to walk right by Shadow. Birdie keeps walking to the back where the giant Christmas tree is, hightailing away from the drama. I lean back and whisper in Leo's ear, "Be good."

He grins and says, "Never, gorgeous." I tap his broad, muscular chest and walk away. Towards Shadow. *Just walk, you can do this.*

I look at him as I go to pass him. His arm jerks out and his fingers enclose on my upper arm, effectively bringing me to a halt. On reflex, I try to yank out of his grasp, but he pulls me to him.

"Shadow," I say in warning.

"Zhar, please," he says where only I can hear. He sounds so broken.

Immediately Leo is up, rounding the table and grabbing Shadow by the throat. Violent things happen quickly around me. Chairs fall backwards, men stop talking, and the air stands still.

"Fuck you, man," Shadow yells at Leo, while he still won't drop my arm. More tables and chairs are being overturned as they scuffle. Shadow still won't stop gripping my arm and is dragging me with him, in the middle of the altercation. "So, you just gonna swoop in and steal my old lady, is that how it's played now, *friend*?"

Leo puts pressure on Shadow's wrist to release his hand while he still has his throat gripped. "Drop your fuckin' hand off of her before I break it, Shadow," he growls. I'm pushed backwards by Leo which stretches Shadow's arm out, to hopefully get him to stop touching me and let me go.

Shadow finally drops my arm and Leo won't let him go yet. "And yeah, it's like that. She's mine now so you can fuck right off, *brother*." Leo shoves a very shocked me behind him with his other hand and never takes the other one from Shadow's body.

Being the nosy ass I am, I lean out around him to see what's going on.

"Get your fucking hands off me." Shadow tries to jerk Leo's hand off of him. Leo releases his throat but grabs his vest. Shadow is fuming. Both of them are built similar, it would be a close call if this comes to blows. Danger slides by me to get to Shadow and he gets between them and raises his voice, "Woah! Stop! Take a deep breath. At ease, guys."

Leo releases Shadow's leather vest, but not before he pushes him against the table one final time, then turns around and rubs the hair out of my face. Resting his hands lightly on my face, tilting my chin up to his worried face, he asks, "You ok?"

I nod, even though I want to cry, I bravely nod, chin wobbling. He thumbs away the tear that's daring enough to fall. He nods back at me because he knows how difficult this is for me.

"I know, princess, I know." Leo's soothing voice washes over me. "Do you want to go home? I'll take you wherever you want to go. Say the word."

I hear Danger telling Shadow to get his ass in the office right fucking now. My mind is reeling. This is like a goddamn nightmare crawled through the window, like it snuck into reality and spilled drama everywhere.

"No, I promised Birdie," barely loud enough to hear. He pulls me to his chest and wraps his arms around me.

"When it gets too much, I'll take my princess back home to her ivory castle and feed her copious amounts of ice cream and rub her aching feet from these gorgeous hooker heels, ok?"

My lips twitch. "Ok."

Just like that, Leo makes everything better.

Birdie tried everything she could to help Denver 'open presents' but he just wasn't interested. Next year, I told her. I can't wait to see his little baby fingers rip at the paper and hear his squeals of happiness. Holidays are forever changed because of him, in the best way possible.

I must admit, sometimes little Denny gives me some unreal baby fever. And sometimes I be wanting to indulge in it, but I always snap back to my senses and maintain my avoidance of all things domesticated for me. I don't think I would make a good mom and I'm too self-absorbed to be a good, attentive wife, let alone a mother. I know my faults.

Once Denver 'opens' his presents and Shadow stays across the room with Dreama and the other man, Leo comes over and puts his arm around my shoulders, "You about ready now? I want you out of the same room as him. No more of his bullshit."

My lips press into a thin line, and I nod, "Yeah, it's about time to go. Let me say goodbye to my bestie."

I beeline straight for Birdie so I can get the fuck out of here. I'm getting really fucking tired of Shadow staring a hole into me. I keep feeling my skin heat up. I know exactly where his eyes are on me. I've had years of practice with this.

This right here, all of this, is exactly what I was afraid of happening. I weave through the crowded tables with a purpose, coming to a stop by Birdie who is still sitting by the tree with Denver knocked out in a pack-n-play, sleeping peacefully.

"Hey sis, I'm going to go now. It was fun watching Denver's first Christmas. Thanks for the invite."

Birdie stands up and throws her arms around me, speaking to me where I can only hear, "I'm so sorry. I'm so mad at my husband. It's shady and I don't like it."

"Don't let my issues come between you two. I'm just happy I had Leo close by," I say releasing her.

"That guy never leaves your side while you're here. It's too bad, ya know."

I roll my eyes. I know what she's thinking. It's something along the lines of my thoughts tonight. "He tells me it's his duty as alternate best friend to keep bad things away from me so I can live with sunshine and bubbles, because that's what I deserve," I half-heartedly laugh, mainly because he's done exactly that in the past fifteen months.

"I hate to see you go, but I completely understand, hon. Talk tomorrow?"

I nod my head and say, "Yep."

Birdie hugs me again and when I step back, I see Shadow coming this way. "Jesus fuck," I mutter. "Here he comes, eleven o'clock behind you."

"I'm not putting up with his shit," she murmurs.

When he steps up, he nods to her, "Birdie," he turns his gaze on me, "Zharia, could I have a moment with you?"

Before I can answer, Birdie pipes up, "No, you may not. Now, I've tried everything to stay out of this and remain neutral but if you have something to say to her, after she's repeatedly for years asked you to stay away, you can just say it right here with me present. I don't trust you alone with her."

"You're fucking with me, right? I would never hurt her."

"I beg to differ, I just saw you manhandle her in front of everyone." Birdie crosses her arms over her chest, juts her chin out, and cocks a hip. The attitude has come out, along with her claws.

Shadow's muscle in his jaw works in his frustration. He takes a deep breath, "I just wanted to apologize for my actions. I didn't mean to hurt you or scare you, I just wanted to talk to you, as a friend I guess."

"We aren't friends, Shadow, we are nothing and I prefer it that way. If you'll excuse me, Leo is waiting on me." I walk away, trying my hardest to keep my head up.

I walk because I am weak and my traitorous body wants him, my betraying heart beats rapidly from his closeness and it's so happy to be near him again. I have to get away before I start crying or throw myself at him. That irresistible pull is still there. That magnetic charge still sparks.

Two steps later, "Gunney? Really?" Said in the tone I expected from his jealousy.

Don't turn around!

Don't do it!

I stop in my tracks; fuck this, I do turn around. "Yes, Gunney. Leo treats me like a queen and lets me be me and expects nothing from me in return. I wouldn't trade him for the world."

Before he can say anything, I walk away to keep my petty, smartass mouth shut. Any further commentary and I can't be held responsible for it.

I get back to Leo, and he hands me my purse. I see him look over my head towards Shadow, and my eyes follow Leo's gaze. Shadow's face is set in a hard stare, looking right at Leo. Then his gaze drops to me and softens. I see sadness take over his features. *No, I can't.* I grab Leo's arm and pull him to me. I'm going home and I can't wait.

"I'll follow you home, Z." Leo takes my hand and leads me out of the clubhouse.

CHAPTER 10 – GUNNEY

Shadow has some big fucking balls to pull what he just did. I stew all the way to Zhar's. Like where does he get off?

She was doing really great. It was a thought in the past and she moved on. She's happy. She smiles again. I like to think I have something to do with that.

Zharia has my heart. I may be mainly attracted to guys, but she owns me, and I want her. So help me god, I want her so fucking bad. She's the first woman to make my heart skip a beat, the first woman to turn my head, the first pussy I dream of tasting.

I've had a lot of conflicted feelings in the past year, but I've fallen more and more in love with her. That I know for sure.

How do I go from wanting guys to wanting one girl? This specific one and only one.

And I do want her. Any way I can have her.

Sure, I fooled around with girls in high school and even tried with a few when I first went into the Army. It seemed like I was just doing something that was expected of me as a man, but that wasn't what I wanted at all. It had no umph to it, no spark, no fire.

Sure, I thought girls were pretty but I wasn't as sexually attracted to them as a young guy should have been. Now men…that's where I felt stirrings in my cock.

I was in my late teens before I truly realized and accepted, I'm gay. My eyes tracked the guys in the locker rooms; my gaze lingered a little too long on guys and I fantasized about them a little too much.

Nowadays I fantasize about her.

I fantasize about her so many ways. Nothing safe and wholesome like a best friend would think, only filthy things I want to do to her.

There's never been a right time to tell her. Maybe with Shadow sniffing around, it's the perfect time to speak up.

To lay claim to her.

I'm just scared of what she'll say, and I really don't want to lose her as a friend. Our relationship is so good. She's a wonderful woman, beyond beautiful, and the smartest, sharpest, and wittiest person I've ever met.

It's a special treat to be in her inner circle. Without her friendship, I would never have had the courage to start seeing a counselor for my PTSD and nightmares. I spent six years active-duty Army. Right after I turned eighteen I was shipped off to basic training. I'm in my last year of on call duty.

I met her when I was only two weeks sober and it was after a bad breakup with the guy I was seeing. Her unwavering support has held me up in some of my darkest times.

We've sufficiently trauma bonded.

I would die for this woman.

I'm still waiting on the right time to let my sexuality be known to the club. It's not that I'm ashamed; I'm concerned with how they'll react and treat me. And maybe now it won't matter.

Hanging out with Zharia as I do usually quells some of the questions I get about where's my old lady and when am I getting one. I'm sure tonight laid a lot of people's minds to rest about where we stand. I all but bit her neck and pissed on her to assert my dominance.

But bikers aren't supposed to be gay. They expect me to be with Zhar. There are a few guys in the club that think like that, the 'old school' ones; bigots and they don't give a shit who they offend. Not all of them have tact. They don't do that shit around me, Danger, Shadow and Travares. They know we will be pissed over hearing ignorant shit spew from their mouths.

As leaders we aim to weed out any comments like that. We don't want it in our club.

When we got home tonight, ha, home, even my brain recognized this place as home since I spend so much time here. When we got back to her house, I went into her bathroom and started her a hot bath. I didn't bother with all the containers and bottles she has. She can do that shit. I never know what combo she wants.

I'm chilling on the couch with the TV on. I'm nervous. I don't think she knows the magnitude of what I did back at the clubhouse. I don't know if she understands the ramifications of defending her in the clubhouse and basically declaring her as my old lady.

I don't want to burst her happy bubble right now. She's sitting in the bath, having a good soak and I hear her humming. I can tell her moods by the songs she hums.

When she's really happy, she hums upbeat tunes, her favorite being the main song from her favorite cartoon.

When she's sad, she barely hums, and it's always low and quiet.

But right now, she's humming a soothing melody. Her favorite, which is a good sign. It's the same melody every time when she feels safe, and content. She hums it around me a lot. It's definitely my favorite to hear coming out of her—Once Upon a Dream from Sleeping Beauty.

I hear her sultry voice start singing the lyrics and my heart rate speeds up.

She only sings if she's really relaxed, feels loved, safe and she lets go. Singing is rare.

I'm pretty sure the anti-anxiety pills the doctor prescribed her are helping too. I made sure she took it before I shut the bathroom door.

It makes my heart happy to hear her in the bathroom right now. I know that makes me sound like a creeper. Take it how you want.

To quote her favorite movie she's made me watch a hundred times by now, 'They say if you dream a thing more than once, it's sure to come true.'

And I've dreamed of her so many times. I could only hope my wish would come true.

Zhar has stolen my heart and I'm not at all upset about it. I'm not sitting here questioning my sexuality with her. I'm just going where my heart and head lead me.

Eh, maybe my dick is also leading us around too.

Chapter 11 – Shadow

What. THE. Fuck. is happening??

Danger drags me back to the office after I grabbed Zharia.

"Are you out of your fucking mind?" he hisses at me, pointer finger in my face.

"Yes, goddamnit! I tried to tell you this!" I retort.

"Dude, you can't fucking do that. Birdie's going to kill me."

My chest heaves, trying to suck in air. "Why didn't you tell me about Gunney?" My voice has gone hoarse and I feel like the room is spinning. Why didn't Gunney tell me? Each time I've reached out to him he's never said anything about Zharia and him, not once.

His eyes go wide whereas mine shoot daggers at his face. He throws his arms out, "For fuck's sake, last I knew they were just friends. I didn't know! They've been friends since a couple of weeks after you left. She spends all her time with him. They're thick as thieves."

"They sure looked like they were real cozy as only *friends*, Lincoln."

"Hey man, I don't keep up with Zharia. Birdie stopped telling me anything about her since before Zhar got married."

"About that. Where's her husband?"

"Oh, that guy. Probably out fucking his boyfriend. Life's a lot different here than in India for him. They lead two separate lives, that I do know. They're basically roommates and married just for the benefits. That's it. She can do whatever she wants. She's getting divorced here soon."

"I know. Why do you think I'm back at this time."

Finally getting my breathing under control, I realize I don't have to fight her husband then. One less altercation I have to cause.

So, she is keeping her word about the sixteen months. That will take care of him, now I just have to get rid of Gunney, an unexpected twist. By the looks of it, Zharia is firmly attached to him. If I off him, she will suffer, therefore, he still lives and breathes.

Plus, he's one of my brothers. I can't just take him out.

"She saw me. She saw when Dreama was all over me, rubbing her tits on me. Zhar probably thinks I'm with her. I wanted to tell her I'm not. That's why I grabbed her arm. I wanted to tell her I'm not with Dreama in that capacity. I saw it in her eyes, Linc, I had to clear it up." I look at the ceiling and exhale loudly.

"Well, you went about it a shit way."

"Yeah. I'm an idiot, I know."

"I can't have you go near her again. I'm in enough trouble as it is. Don't make me get mean, please Shadow."

I hear him, but I don't know if I can listen.

I can't stop staring. She's been my sinful obsession for almost the past two years. Not a day goes by I don't think of her. Right now, my whole person is being pulled to her. We've always been two stars circling each other, and when we come together it's like an explosion. I'm tired of waiting. I want my universe and stars back.

She finally leaves Gunney's side and goes over to Birdie. I head that way, not even caring what Danger said. I have to talk to her.

Talking to her went to complete shit earlier…and this time too.

The worst thing happened; I lost her further. She wanted nothing to do with talking to me either time. I'm not the one who shit on us, she is. Why the fuck is she so mad at me?

After Zhar walks away, Birdie looks at me and hisses, "Don't ever touch her without her permission again, do I make myself clear?"

"Very."

Birdie turns to walk off and I stop her, "Wait, please." Birdie, hearing the pleading in my tone, stops and turns back to me as I watch Gunney hold her hand and they slip through the door, leaving together. It damn near breaks me. I reach up and rub my chest because it physically hurts me. It fucking hurts.

My voice is rough when I ask Birdie, "What did I do so wrong?" My voice cracks with emotion. "What did I do so bad?" I turn my desperate eyes to her. I am desperate, I need to know what I did. I need her back. She's my life. I gave her time and space, what more do I have to do? We were so good together.

And now he has her.

He has what's mine.

I thought it was bad watching her get married, but this is a thousand times worse. One of my brothers has what should be mine. How can I be mad at Gunney? I can't. I'm not mad; I'm jealous. She'll always be mine.

"I'm sorry, Shadow. You tried to tame her, and she wasn't ready."

"Is she ready now?"

"I don't know."

"What else can I do, Birdie? She's my everything. How can I get her back? Please, Birdie. I don't know how to fix it."

Birdie takes her time answering, looking me in the eye the whole time. I feel her eyes searching around in my mind, testing, seeing if I'm genuine. She must find what she's looking for because she sighs and softly says, "Shadow, I say this in love, you can be a little much for her. It's your possessive nature and I totally get that it's a biker thing, but you want kids and marriage. I know Zhar, she has never wanted those things. Doing what she loves, medicine, has always been more important to her. She never wants to quit to raise kids and be a man's sidekick. She doesn't want to sacrifice her goals and accomplishments to play house."

I pinch the bridge of my nose and will away the tears gathering behind my eyes. *Jesus fuck, man.* "I never said that." I look at Birdie and I must look like hell. She lays her hand on my arm. "I was possessive because I didn't want her dating other men when she was with me. She led me on to think we were a couple. We were dating. Regardless if she told the Fab Four, to me we were dating, in a relationship, it was real for me. I'm so far deep in love with her I'm on the other side of the planet." I put my hand up to my forehead and then run it down my face. I look back at Birdie, "And yeah, I want all that but I'm happy to sacrifice that to keep her, I was willing to give it up to be with her. She would never listen. I never wanted to hold her back. I don't care what it takes, as long as I get to have her again. I miss her so fucking bad."

I quickly look away and take a deep cleansing breath. *You will not fucking cry here. Suck it the fuck up.*

"Shadow, I don't know what to say. Um, maybe this is all stuff Zharia needs to hear." She stirs hope inside me. When I look back at Birdie, all I see is compassion and concern, "How about I talk to her? Would it be ok to repeat some of this conversation to her?"

I half smile at her with relief, "Yeah, tell her whatever you need to. I'll be eternally grateful, Birdie." I pull her in for a hug. She is still my sis-in-law and I love her. I know she only wants the best for both of us.

"I never wanted you in the middle of any of this but thank you."

I release her and she steps back. She smiles and says, "In the great immortal words of the master Eminem, you only get one shot, this opportunity only comes once in a lifetime. Don't fuck up."

Spooky how I thought the same thing.

Leo is in the kitchen when I come out of my bedroom with my satin pajamas set on. I checked the shorts, at least my ass isn't hanging out. It's only Leo and he's not into women anyways. I know he's not staring at my booty.

However, Leo is shirtless, standing at the counter with his back to me in a pair of basketball shorts, and that alone is enough to make my toes curl. Ho-ly FUCK. *He's your bestie! Stop staring! Bestie! Bestie! Bestie!*

My bestie might be gay, but I'm most definitely not and I appreciate his manly rock-solid body. I notice everything. Sometimes I wish...

He's a good-looking man, it's hard not to stare. He's tall, broad shoulders, muscles for days and y'all, when he's dressed like this, *chef's kiss*. I quickly bring my eyes up to the top of his head.

Not doing anything bad here. Just me looking at my *friend*. I'm cool, everything's cool.

I try not to swoon. Leo's beautiful. He's half black, half white, with the most gorgeous hazel eyes you can get lost in and this panty melting perpetual five o'clock shadow. His smile is to die for and makes my heart flip over every time he bestows it on me. I feel like I'm the center of his universe when he smiles at me. He's built like a brick shithouse and has tattoos all over him making him fit the bill for a biker. But he's the most adorable, carefree snuggle buddy a girl could ask for.

He's perfect and he absolutely knows it.

And he flaunts it religiously on his subscription page. Leo is a thirst trap and gets paid lots of money to show off his body and all the things it can do…without putting his face out there. He said his mom would disown him if she was still alive. Of course, he said it jokingly but I think there might be some underlying truth to that.

Sometimes his site makes me jealous. Like any other nosy ass hot-blooded woman with a vagina, I may have looked at his videos…but I've tried hard not to notice how hot and sexy he is all.the.fricking.time. It's been a struggle since I saw his videos.

But I can't cross that line. I don't want to. I value him too much to ruin what we have with sex and those other types of emotions.

Although, sometimes when I'm really hard up and it's been a while since I masturbated, it's damn near torturous to be around him. Those are the times I say my brain is misfiring because there's no way he's into me and I'm working myself up for no reason.

Like right now, his muscular back flexes as he moves, his nice ass is filling out the backside of those basketball shorts, tapering into muscular legs. He's barefoot and even his feet are sexy and masculine. There's nothing about him that doesn't scream sex.

Look at the top of his goddamn head, Z.

"Hey, Leo."

He turns with a heart pitter pattering smile and coos, "Ahh, there's my Indian princess, feel better?"

"Yes, I do. Thank you very much."

"Anytime." He jerks a thumb behind him to the counter, "I made snacks. Your favorite."

This lights up my face. He's so considerate and I love how he takes care of me. He hands me a bowl of cookies 'n cream ice cream with hot fudge and Spanish peanuts. He knows the way into my good graces.

"Thank you, Leo. Do you want to sit on the couch with me?"

He smiles and says, "Absolutely," bringing his bowl with him to sit beside me. He sits in his spot, at the end and I take my place in the middle.

He winks at me when he asks, "So what are we watching?"

I love the smile he gives me all the time. Like it's reserved just for me. His smiles are just breathtaking and I feel my cheeks flame. I'll be sad when he does find a boyfriend. He won't have as much time for me and our fun, calm, cozy hang out nights will turn back into cold, lonely nights for me. Sometimes I feel like I'm holding him back. Like if he wasn't so wrapped up in me he could be out there treating some guy like this. It makes me feel so guilty.

Then a fiery streak of jealousy runs through me when I think of him with someone else. It's happened a few times lately, this flash of heat. It's a mixture of emotions and the strongest one is jealousy floating to the top. Maybe I am the most selfish person I know. I can't keep him here with me, locked up in this house, but I don't want him let loose out there in the wild where a guy could snatch him up.

I'm an awful person.

"Where did you go? What are you thinking about so hard over there?"

I blink and realize I've been staring off into space, letting my ice cream melt. *You are going to have to bring up the hard subject. It has to be dealt with. Take a bite first.*

After I swallow my bite of creamy heaven, I summon the courage to speak my truth, "I was thinking I'm standing in your way of finding true love. You could be sitting in your own living room, eating ice cream with your boyfriend or husband instead of spending so much time with me," I finish quietly, taking another bite.

Gods of the ice cream, let me be brave. Another bite.

I watch him set his spoon down slowly back into the bowl. The clang of metal against the glass bowl sounds so much louder in here with those words dropped between us.

He swallows and sits up, putting his bowl on the coffee table. I know he's thinking hard. He's going through how to tell me it's time he moves on. A small sob wants to break free from my chest when I think about losing him.

Leo sits back and turns his body to me. "Funny you should say that, I, uhh," oh god, here it comes, "Umm, I am interested in someone." Boom. It's really out there now.

I can't stop the tears from welling in my eyes. He's going to leave me.

I take a deep shaky breath, willing my eyes to dry up. "Ok. That's good. I'm happy for you." Fake smile. Give him the Miss America smile sans the wave. I want to vomit. He needs to do this. I've become too attached. Too dependent. Rip the Band-aid off.

"Yeah, I'm really nervous to tell her."

Before I stop myself, my smile falls flat and the unfiltered, confused expression pops out of my mouth, "What? Her? Wait, what..." A her? I could have had him before?

I put my ice cream on the coffee table and scoot around to face him because this is seriously important. He's sitting there all smiles but he may be trying to fool me to get a rise out of me, but I can see his underlying nervousness. I suppose he is coming out to me as bisexual now. Go with it. Don't make it awkward. Yeah, right.

"When do I get to meet her?" *Be happy for him, bestie.* Even though I'm pretty jealous it's a woman right now.

"That's the thing, you already know her."

I can't stop my eyes from bugging out. I need to school my facial reactions better.

He doesn't miss the confused as fuck look I know I have. Instead, he seems to be enjoying this. He must really like her. When the fuck does he have any time to get involved with someone? *Be a big girl and suck it up, Zharia.*

"Oh, ok. Well, that's cool but I don't really feel like playing a guessing game right now. Can you just tell me? Pleeease?" I give him the biggest and fakest smile while I jerk his arm, batting my eyes. Hoping he doesn't see my warring emotions. Still trying to get with the idea of him being with someone else and a woman, to boot.

"I'm interested in you, Zharia. Only you."

A ton of bricks just landed on my head and stole my life's breath. I'm dead. Splat. Me?

ME?

Oh my god.

CHAPTER 13 - GUNNEY

Zhar's mouth pops open in shock. "What do you mean? What are you saying?" Her perplexed, bewildered look presses on my nervousness. Her eyes have gone twitchy. I'm fighting to remain calm here. *Please let her handle this well.* This is Z, this is my girl, she can handle anything thrown at her.

"I mean, I want you. I'm wrapped up in you. I want more than this," I lift my hand in a back-and-forth motion between us. "Surprise, apparently I'm bi, and only for you. I want only you, my Indian princess. I'm in love with you and want to be your boyfriend, more than friends. If you'll have me. If not, I'm still your bestie."

She closes her mouth, then opens her mouth to speak. Then she closes it and tries again. She kinda looks like a fish out of water, and I imagine that's how she feels right now, going by the look on her face.

"Zhar?" I reach for her hand and she allows me to touch her. "Breathe, babe." I lean over and lovingly cup the side of her face. She looks about three seconds from running. I tell her, "Take a deep breath, baby," in a low husky tone that washes over her and instantly calms her. She closes her eyes and her dark lashes flutter on the tops of her cheeks.

When she slowly opens them again she's more centered, grounded into the here and now. Less shock and awe, calmer and more levelheaded. Not as much *what the fuck*.

"I don't know what to say," she says softly and bites her plump bottom lip. It's adorable when she does that.

I rub part of her bottom lip with my thumb, looking into her beautiful brown eyes, "You don't have to say anything. I just needed it out there. I need you to know I love you, and it encompasses more than just friendship for me. I'm in love with you, Zharia Davish and I want you to be mine."

Her mouth pops open and she goes to say something but no words come out. Slowly, I lower my lips to hers, softly at first. She sighs into my lips BUT doesn't pull away, she engages.

Ohmygod it's working.

I gently prod her lips open with my tongue and she parts her sweet, juicy lips for me, our tongues meeting in the middle. I wrap my other arm around her waist and pull her to my lap to straddle me, deepening the kiss. She slides willingly.

Our breaths pick up and mingle together. My blood is on fire. I pull her down harder onto my thickening cock that's trapped in these thin shorts. I know she can feel me.

Zharia moans and I feel her body relax deeper into my arms. A lot of tension easing off her and she starts grinding back on me. Gingerly at first but I'll take it.

I tilt her head using her hair, just a light tug, and it makes her shiver. I felt it going through her body that's pressed up against me now, my hands rubbing her back. Her hands come up to my cheeks and she holds me to her, her touch light. At least she's not pulling away yet. Win-win for me.

I nip her bottom lip and slide my tongue against hers. This kiss is probably the best I've ever had. Slow, sensual, building to something more. Fuck, I want her so bad right now. I need her. I never want this to end.

Maybe because I'm so far gone for her.

Maybe because I want to be all in with this woman.

Maybe I can convince her with one kiss. This is my shot. I'm shooting to the moon!

My arms pull her harder down on my dick to grind. We're out of breath. Neither of us breaking this sexy as fuck toe curling kiss though. She slides her sexy body willingly against my big, lanky one. The body that's been waiting for this. Dying for this. Yes! Yes!

I know she has to feel how hard I am. All for her. I have no underwear on under these shorts and it is noticeable. Precum leaks from my tip onto my inner thigh and her movements smear it around.

We're a clash of lips, tongues, hands roaming everywhere. She's so responsive and willing. I keep going further with her. As much as she'll allow.

Sliding my calloused hand to the nape of her neck, palming her head, making sure to wrap my fingers in her hair, I gently tug. Enough that it pops her lips off mine but I quickly go for her neck, nipping, licking making her moan louder.

Smelling her soap on her skin this close makes my cock jump even harder. I love how she smells when she gets out of the shower. It's very feminine.

"Leo," she moans breathlessly, head thrown back and it only spurs me on. Goddamn, the sound of my name falling from her pouty lips all husky, laced with arousal and lust, drives me crazy. I'm fucking crazy for this girl.

"Zharia…I've waited so long." My breath makes its way across her skin causing her to shiver.

It's the sound of her panting and my heavy breathing, along with the caress of lips on her skin that echo in the silent living room as I continue my seduction. I can feel her frantic heartbeat under my lips as they trail across her throat and my fingers make their way up her flimsy shorts.

"Stop."

That broken word spoken so quietly makes me halt in place, not moving a muscle. I blink and slowly suck in a breath. I thought this was going good? I slowly pull my lips off her neck, set my arms on the couch beside me and sit back, looking at her. I refuse to push her. She says stop, we stop.

Zharia tries to catch her breath while she pulls her arms from around my neck and leans back away from me.

Her voice is shaky, "I need a minute. I don't want to jump into anything that could destroy us. I like us. I love and adore *us*. Can I think about this? I don't want this to be a heat of the moment kinda thing. I want to think and be in the right headspace. I don't feel like I can do that right now for a fair shot." She lifts her hands and runs her palms down the stubble on my cheeks. It scratches her hands and she groans, then drops her hands like she realizes what she's doing. "I don't want to rush into this. I mean, I just found out you're in love with me. I've suppressed so many feelings and emotions where you're concerned I have to slowly open that door in my heart back up and see where I'm at. I don't know if this is a good idea right now and if I lose you it will kill me. Does that make sense?"

"Yes, it does, absolutely it does. I'm not offended, maybe a little blue balled but not upset with your decision," I say with a cheeky grin and a chuckle that makes her smile.

"Good, because I'm super tired and it's past my bedtime and I want to go to bed. I may need to go rub one out though."

Laying my head back against the couch, I groan, "Fuck. I'd love to see that."

"Not tonight, Leo. Give me some time."

"Of course, love. Anything you want."

Now onto the next problem. This is going to get tricky, I usually sleep with her, in her big king-sized bed, with her fluffy, down comforter and butter soft sheets. She's always said she feels safer when I'm in there with her. Of course, I have to oblige. Of course, it's become torture.

"Where do you want me to sleep, Zhar? You want me to go home? It's whatever you want me to do; it's however you feel most comfortable." I want to give her an out if she needs one. I don't want to back her into a corner or expect too much from her at once. The fact she wants to think about it is making my heart sing. She didn't outright reject me and my declared feelings.

"Would you mind sleeping out here? Like in the spare?" Not going to lie, I can't say my feelings aren't a little hurt but if space and time is what she wants that's what I'm going to give her. But I'm not going to let her wait long. I'm not pulling a Danger, waiting ten years on his old lady to come around. Fuck that shit. I'm not saint like material like he is.

I can't stay in limbo that long. I want her now, but I will play the long game.

She walks in her room and closes the door after telling me goodnight. I need a cold shower. That was super intense and all I want to do is waltz into her room and spread her out under me across *our* bed. I want to make her scream my name as she falls apart riding my cock.

I decided to take a shower in the bathroom downstairs, the furthest away from her room. I make my way there with my duffle bag that has my clothes and soap. I don't want to brush my teeth, effectively cleaning out the taste of her sweetness, but I do. I want to hold on to her as much as possible. Especially if I don't know if I ruined what we have between us.

The water feels so good running over my muscular body. I wish it was her hands, tickling my skin, rubbing the day away. Every time she touches me I get a thrill zapping through my body. To have her spread across my lap was a dream come true. I'll forever remember our first kiss. It was fucking hot as hell. Lots of chili peppers rating.

Just remembering it makes my cock twitch and come back to life. Yeah, I'm excited and nervous, and I think I have a good shot, but *fuucckk,* her soft body pressed up against me, her sultry moans falling from her mouth set fire to my blood. God they sounded so sexy. I can't wait to hear her moaning while I'm inside her. The best part is her calling my name when she comes. I can't wait to hear that first time it happens. My heart might actually shatter because it's so full.

For now, I'll stroke my cock and dream of the day I get to be buried in her pussy and lost in her moans.

I have to have some kind of release. Taking my shower gel, I use it to slick up my cock and give it a firm tug. I bite my lip at the shiver it gives me. My cock's ready. It wants her so bad. I felt the heat radiating off her through our clothes. I bet she has the hottest, wettest pussy I've ever seen…not that I've seen a lot.

I know enough to figure it out. I'm pretty sure I remember how to make a girl come. I should probably watch some videos to brush up, ya know, for research purposes. I laugh to myself as I stroke my cock.

Sounds of skin across skin fill the acoustics of the shower stall. I glide my hand over my rock hard dick and speed up the process. This is where it gets good. I widen my stance and put one hand up on the shower wall. The water hits the lower half of my back behind me, rivulets of water running down my ball sack tickling me.

There's precum dripping down in a long string from the slit in my crown to the floor of the shower as I fuck my hand harder. Fuck, the arousal courses through my body. I'm so close already. I always feel this close when I'm around her now. I push my hips forward, tightening my ass muscles and grip my dick in a firmer hold.

"Fuck, Zhar," I moan into the stall, jacking myself closer. "Goddamn, I can't wait to be balls deep inside of you with your pussy wrapped around me," I pant to the steam gathering inside the shower.

One last thought of our hot, sweet kiss lingers before I explode into my hand, cum shooting out onto the wall as I grunt through my orgasm, softly chanting her name over and over.

She's it for me. No one else has ever gotten me like her. She's my one and I intend to fight for her.

I lay my phone down for the hundredth time. Mindlessly scrolling social media just for the distraction, as I lay on the couch in the living room, has been my pastime for the last few hours while I can't sleep. I updated my subscription site and posted a few pics. I take another shirtless selfie laying here and post it on my social media with the caption, *'Is anyone else out there awake at 3AM?'* I still can't sleep from the turn of events a few hours ago. Maybe I need a snack. Grandma always said snacks help everything. I *am* a growing man, after all.

I wander my way over to the kitchen. Zharia's little house is interesting. It's a unique shotgun house with an upstairs and a downstairs. There are two bedrooms downstairs, a bathroom, a small living room and a laundry room that has French doors leading to a porch outside on the ground level.

Upstairs is the main living room, kitchen, dining room, two more bedrooms and two bathrooms. The house is silent except for me gulping down sweet tea straight out of the jug from the fridge. Once I'm done, I put it back, grab a few cheese sticks and close the door.

I stand there, leaning against the counter for a while, chewing cheese and trying not to think about how much I want to be in there with her right now. How she should be wrapped up in my arms, sighing in contentment and finally relaxing her mind that stays whirling all the time.

I should have told Shadow about my relationship with Zhar. He was my friend before he left. We stayed in contact. I just never felt it was a good time to tell him when he would call or text me. I knew Zharia wouldn't have wanted me to say anything to him anyways.

Shadow did a fucking number on her and here I am asking for the same thing. I knew it was a risk. A big one. She might turn and hightail it away from me too.

It's a risk I'm willing to take. But I think she's ready. I know she is. I put no expectations on her like he did. I don't ask for the American dream with her, I just want it to be our dream, together, however we make it. I would never ask her to give up herself to be with me.

We've had so many talks about what we want in a partner that I know I'm exactly what she's looking for.

I know she's going to be worried about the age difference. There's four years between us, with me being younger than her almost thirty-two years. This might be a factor for her.

Oh, and the fact that I'm basically a hired assassin and gunman for a billionaire shipping mogul. Or the fact I'm the pornstar of my own subscription page with over a million followers.

Also, throw in she's married and her parents would never approve of her being with me. It's a great mix of things against me. Fabulous.

The sound of the floor creaking in this old house pulls me out of my musings, instantly alert. There's one place in the whole house where that specific wooden groan comes from. It's right in front of Zhar's bedroom door.

I never heard the door open and her come out. I would have heard it. I'm sure of it. That spot only creaks when it's stepped on.

I reach up on the top of the fridge and into the basket laying up there, I pull out my revolver I have stashed without her knowledge. I peek around the kitchen wall, glancing further back in the house and see a silhouette in front of her white closed door. The door opens and they start walking through. I know that body frame so similar to mine.

God. Damn. It.

Motherfuck.

Deadly quiet, I sneak up behind the man and level my gun at the back of his head, cocking the hammer back which echoes into the quiet house. "Give me one good reason, Shadow."

He puts his hands up in surrender mode. "I mean no harm, Gunney."

I whisper, "I'm going to move back and let you get the fuck out of her room and shut the fucking door. I won't hesitate to keep her safe and happy and right now you're pretty high on the shit list." I back up further into the hallway as he tiptoes softly out of the room, still aiming the gun at my brother. Once the door clicks shut, and the floor stops groaning, in a hushed voice I tell him, "Go to the living room and sit the fuck down."

Jesus. He really is a Shadow. This means he got around the security system…a-fuckin-gain. I have no idea how he does it, then just walks through the deadbolted door like there's no alarm or digital keypad on it. Whatever way he does it, this shit has to stop now.

Zharia has lived in peace for the past year and a half and I'm not about to let this obsessive asshole ruin it for her.

He stands in the living room and turns around to face me with his hands still up. "Gunney I just wanted to see her, that's all. I swear I wasn't going to hurt her or even wake her up. I just had to see her, smell her, be in her presence. Please man, you don't know what it's like."

"Actually, I do. I know what it's like to want those things from her, be so close, but yet so far away. But you can't keep breaking in here, man. No more. This is exactly the kind of shit she's fed up with and it pisses her off to no end. Do you even care how paranoid it makes her? Fuck man, just stop, dude, stop."

I slowly slide the hammer back into place and turn the safety back on. Zharia isn't hip to guns in the house but she understands the necessity so allows me some grace with mine.

Good thing too because shit like this keeps happening.

I look over at him, point to the couch and tell him, "Sit the fuck down and then you're going to tell me what the shit happened tonight."

Shadow clears his throat, my body facing him from the comfy chair beside the couch that I slid into. This way I have a clear visual of the hallway and her closed door.

Zhar's house is weird and if she comes out here, we're had. He could possibly meld back into the couch and duck to keep from being seen.

Her house is old school seventies or eighties style is my best guess. Her kitchen is open concept but has a kick wall around it facing the living room, this is where the sink is, and the entrance is on the side with the hallway. This wall is what the couch sits up against. It's like this weird picture window looking out over the living room. I make fun and tell her it's like an old school diner. So, when I fix dinner I tell her *order up* through the window.

With his elbows on his knees, he looks at me, so lost and admits, "I don't even know where to start."

"Let's start with why you were there tonight and why you felt it was ok to try and snatch her in front of everyone."

His eyes are so sad in the dim living room light. He nods and replies, "Danger asked me to be there for Denver's first club Christmas. All I wanted was to talk to Zhar. Gunney, listen brother, I still don't even know what I really did wrong. She just refused to see me or talk to me one day after telling me she didn't love me anymore. We were madly in love until one day we weren't. I never stopped."

"Are you looking for closure?" I ask him point-blank.

"No, I'm looking to get my old lady back."

Fuck. I knew it. It's like a punch to the gut. This definitely puts a wrench into my plans now. I kinda knew this was going to happen one day. I knew he'd never give up. Last night proved it.

"Why now?"

"The time limit she told me about at her wedding is almost up next month. She'll have done what she told me she needed to do, what prevented her from committing to me in the first place was her career, and I'm here to get her back after waiting patiently." He lays it out to me. I have to give it to him, he has balls. For all he knows, we could be a couple. To come in here, not knowing if I live here or not, just to see her while she slept, that's audacity.

That's some powerful love and obsession.

I remember the week after Zharia got married, he still hadn't left yet, Shadow was a bear to work with. Straight up asshole. His mood was so erratic, he was sullen and a thick black cloud surrounded him. It wasn't until I became friends with Zharia that I pieced it together. I've always wondered about his side of that last conversation in the church's back room at her wedding.

I've met Zharia's husband plenty of times. She's friendly with him and they get along well. You can tell they weren't love interests for each other right off the bat just meeting him. For one, she helped him come out of the closet and helped him find himself and gave him the support to be gay in a world where he'll be disowned for it. She lent him the bravery he needed to come out and find his boyfriend. He practically lives at his house now, rarely coming back here. Most every night Zhar and I have privacy.

"What happened at the church in that last conversation? I want your side."

Chapter 14 – Shadow

    I'm at a loss as to how everything came to this point. It's been the loneliest year and a half of my life and I just want it to end. I don't think I can take anymore.

    "I begged her. I begged so hard for her not to marry him. Honestly, I cried, man. As much as that makes me sound like a pussy, I cried and I begged. Why wouldn't she marry me? I was going to give her the world on a silver platter. She killed me the day she married a stranger instead of me. Ripped my heart out and spit on it. Why wasn't I good enough? What the fuck did I do wrong?" I put my hands in my hair and hang my head.

Gunney and I were somewhat close before this but I still don't want to cry in front of him. Jesus fuck, why am I so emotional? Like get.your.shit.together.

I continue in a voice filled with emotions because I can't stop them, and at this point, do I really wanna? I have no choice but to let this out, it's festering inside me, eating me alive. Gunney was one of my brothers before I left but he didn't know about Zhar. No one did. It's how she wanted it.

Fuck being stoic, it's not gotten me anywhere so far. Desperate men need to do desperate things.

And I am desperate.

"She told me what he bought her for." I can't help but roll my tongue inside my cheek to keep from bashing her dad. "I'm thrilled for her. I truly am. I wish I could have stood by and watched her build her dream right by her side. I'm proud of her. I never wanted to take that dream from her. I wanted whatever she wanted, with one exception, no more dating other men, she was mine. She never liked that idea, she rebelled against it. I never understood why. We were in love, I practically lived here, we spent all our time together. There was never a day I didn't see her. You have to know how addictive she is." I look at Gunney and I know he understands. There's just something about her.

He still has a neutral face but he's watching me for any signs of deceit.

He taps his chin like he's lost in thought, "Ok." I keep watching him. I know why Zharia fell for Gunney. He's a great guy, good looking, caring, and gentle with her. I could tell how much she trusts him and how well he treats her from seeing them together at the party.

Gunney is a sweetheart and doesn't run through women. Always has a smile, charismatic, fun and by the looks of them cuddled up together earlier tonight, she feels hella safe with him.

If it's not me, I'm glad it's him. He'll treat her right.

"I never wanted her to walk away from her career and give it up to be a mom and wife. Never would I have asked that of her. She wouldn't listen. She always took me daydreaming about a normal life with kids, a mortgage, and a dog as me trying to tie her down. God, it made her so damn mad. I would try repeatedly to ask why not be with me and she shut me down each time I brought up the question or idea. Until one day she just froze me out and then got bribed to marry a fucking stranger."

He leans forward and mimics my position, with his elbows on his knees and Gunney says, "I think this is a huge issue of miscommunication and her stubborn bullheadedness."

I can't help but snort, "Ya think, man?" I shake my head, "I need her to know this. I know it's not over between us. She's mine and I have never stopped loving her once."

His eyes narrow at me and he gets a deadly glint in them, "I hope you don't think I'm just going to hand her over to you, because that's not happening. I'm half black, not half stupid. I know what your end game is and I'm definitely going to stand in the way. I'm also going to decide whether you get to talk to her or not. It's taken her this long to heal. You have no idea what she's been through over you. What pieces I've picked up, how hard I got them to stick back together to make her whole again."

This shit makes me mad, but fair enough. I get it.

"She's a workaholic and drives her body to the brink of exhaustion to bury her emotions. Her mind is full of regrets and she's always so sad. I've just now gotten her to a point she can be happy and live again." He scoots closer to the edge of his seat, stressing his point, "Do you know she hasn't dated or fucked anyone since she got married? Since she let you go? Since you."

This blows me away. Not Zharia, not fun, good time Zhar— who refused to give up a carefree, fun-loving life for me. That's nothing like the girl I knew before we got together. I've

watched her for years go through men just because she
could, then settle her heart on me. Only to give me up.

Wait, what about him?

"I might be convinced to share her with you, but I sure as
fuck am not walking away, Shadow. I love her more than
anything. She'll have to shove me out the door at gunpoint
before I'll leave her alone. Probably not even then."

Imagine that. He really does get it. "Now you see where I'm
at, brother. I never stopped loving her, not even for a
second," I say softly.

"Leo?"

Zharia's sweet, sleepy as fuck voice calls for Gunney from
deeper in the house. I hear her feet shuffling down the
hallway coming towards us. Fuckity fuck. Gunney's eyes
clash with mine and his face gives away nothing but a hard
clenched jaw telling me to keep my mouth shut. He knows
this is not good. Panic rises up instantly. If she sees me
here…but I want to see her. I want to talk to her. I want her
to hear me.

"Yeah, princess, I'm coming." Gunney is up out of his seat
in a flash, coming round it to meet her at the edge of the
kitchen entrance. He moved with a quickness. If she moves
into the living room another step she will be able to see me
sitting on the couch.

"Baby, what're you doing up?" Leo asks her in a hushed
tone.

"I was having a bad dream and then you weren't there to
hold me."

Her words stab me in the heart, twisting slowly, and I
almost can't breathe. That should be me comforting her. It
should be me she runs to in the middle of the night. I should
be the one to keep her safe.

"What was this one? Tell me about it. Let's get it out of that
beautiful head of yours so you can go back to sleep." I watch
his arms go around her. I'm right on the edge of her vision. If

he moves to the right or she leans out just a smidge more then I'm seen and all hell and fury will break loose. I ever so slowly move back out of her sight more and just listen. I try to flatten myself against the couch.

Her sleepy voice says, "I was in the church again, in that dreadful room. Shadow was there." This perks up my ears. She dreams of me, yet calls them nightmares? She continues, practically a whisper, "I stabbed him again, in the heart, with the big knife and blood coated my hands and splashed all over my white dress. I watched the light die in his eyes for the thousandth time. I can't stand it. Make it stop." Zhar starts lightly crying.

"He's not dead. You didn't kill him. It's only a dream." He looks over at me while she has her head buried in his chest. His eyes are hard and I suddenly understand part of what he's been doing for her. I didn't know she took our parting this hard.

"But I did," she cries through her tears. "You didn't see him that day. I did. I killed his soul so I could chase my dream. I killed him, Leo. But I had to let him go to chase his own dreams and it killed me. I killed myself that day too, Leo, you don't understand. You don't want something like this. Someone so broken. So hollow. You should leave." Her voice sounds so anguished, so strangled and exhausted. She has guilt over how she treated me.

"Hey, hey. Look here, I love you, all of you. Every last little thing. Let me get you back to bed. I'll stay in there this time. You sure you want me back in there?"

"Yes. I can't be without you right now."

My heart breaks all over again. I've truly lost her. This is the worst feeling in the world. I feel like I'm on an emotional precipice and there's no way I can stop the fallout. A thousand memories of her flood my mind and I damn near stagger.

Gunney picks her up, wrapping her legs around him and I hear her deep sigh. He looks over at me and I get the meaning—see myself out immediately. He talks to her softly as his footfalls move further away from me and I finally hear her bedroom door close quietly. The bedroom I've made love to her in countless times. That soft click echoes in my head.

I pray to whatever god that it's not a finality.

CHAPTER 15 – GUNNEY

"In turn, they didn't give up. They've been gathering forces and plotting. Their new president conducted a raid on the Mobile port while Shadow was here visiting with the new president, Demon. There were significant hits to the port and we barely hung on to dock workers. We lost three lives and Rock is out for blood," Danger tells us.

"Good, those fuckers need exterminated," Gas Pedal Fred says.

We're at a debriefing for the restricted part of the club that specializes in killing people more so than just riding bikes and doing fundraisers.

We kill people for money. More importantly, the Lone Star Saints members who are trafficking in flesh. They run the largest sex trafficking ring across a few countries. Our goal is to stop them. We have the numbers and manpower but per Rock we have to do things legally…for now. Which means Rock is trying to find a way around legal, by definition.

I happen to be an excellent shot, near and far, and have had extensive combat training from my years in the Army Special Forces. It's come in handy here in the club and doing our missions. It's also helped make me fourth-in-command.

Since the passing of Gnat, the Secretary position opened up and Rock just promoted me to the position. I was shocked when he offered. I believe in the mission and the purpose of this club and that's why I accepted. It's never been about titles or levels for me, he knows and values that.

"It must be noted that about a dozen Lone Star Saints have been seen around the greater New Orleans area. I don't have to tell you what this means."

"Shoot on sight!" Bam hoots.

Rock holds up his hands, "We aren't trying to catch a charge. Be mindful of your surroundings. Make sure you check in often with the people you love. We aren't sure what the play is for their presence."

Knowing Bam, he really would shoot on sight. His road name should've been Crazy Ass. As secretary, I make sure I write down Bam's comment as I chuckle to myself.

"If we can't kill 'em, what are we doing then?" Slim Jim asks.

"Ask them to play Go Fish, you old fucker," Bam yells.

The group of guys burst out laughing. Slim and his cheating ass loves playing Go Fish at the clubhouse. They've managed to monetize the game and he'll win the kitty a time or two with his cheating and gloat about it. No one tries to prove his cheating, it's just common knowledge the old man cheats.

Danger's smirk says he's trying hard not to laugh. One of us needs to be serious. I see it's Danger's turn tonight. "We detain. Without drawing attention, grab them and bring them to the warehouse on the next street over. You are all familiar with the dungeon, I don't need to remind you. Text me, Gunney, or Travares if you see one. They have no business here but to steal our kids and women. Be alert. That's all I have for you gentlemen." Danger holds his hand up and says, "Oh, one last thing, Shadow will be back in a week, permanently." His eyes cut over to me. There are so many unspoken things being said right now.

Once everyone leaves, I move to the front of the clubhouse where the stage is, where Danger is gathering up his notes.

"Hey Danger, I wanted to apologize for the disrespect."

He stands up and looks at me. He's basically the same size as me, which means he's a built motherfucker.

"Is that what it was? I thought it was protecting your old lady? That's what you said she was and she didn't contest it."

"It's complicated."

"Yeah, I bet it is for you and her."

I'm not going to act like I understand what that meant. Fuck it, he needs to know. "Shadow broke into her house that night. I was sleeping there and thought he was an intruder and pulled my revolver on him." Danger changes his stance to face me with his hand on his hips taking in what I'm saying. "That's the exact kind of shit she's mad about. Tell your boy to stop doing it, he's lucky I recognized his scent and body outline."

While I said all that, I could see Danger's eyes narrow and his jaw work. I don't know if it's my veiled threat or because Shadow keeps on his bullshit behind Danger's back after being told repeatedly to knock it off.

Danger rubs his forehead. "He's not ok right now, as I'm sure you can understand. I know that doesn't excuse it. I'll talk to him. Thanks for bringing it to my attention."

"No problem. You know, after hearing both sides, I think this is just a big misunderstanding and they both suck at communicating, stubborn as all hell. I think I can convince her to talk to him, but if he keeps breaking in at night, he's liable to get shot, since I'm there most every night." I make sure that threat isn't veiled.

Back at my townhouse, I'm doing laundry and cleaning up. Not like it's been getting dirty. I practically live at Zhar's and now I'm not so sure that will still happen since the shit show that happened two nights ago.

We woke up the next morning and she asked me to stay at my place until she calls me. I haven't heard from her, except for a few random texts. I spooked her. I came on too strong. I just know it.

Sounds to me like she did the same thing to Shadow. If I believe his side. Suddenly, I understand him a lot better. I couldn't imagine not having her in my life. The past two and a half days have been hell. Yeah, I'm pretty sure I'm addicted to the girl and I'm in a helluva withdrawal period.

I clearly understand Shadow's obsession.

Speaking of, what the hell am I going to do about Shadow? He'll be back soon and he doesn't intend to stay away. He made that perfectly clear.

I made it clear I wasn't going anywhere, yet here I sit on my own couch, eating Cool Ranch Doritos like my world's not at a standstill currently.

I turn on my TV to some re-runs of The Office and let the background noise settle over me.

My mind still drifts back to Shadow. No wonder he's stark raving mad now. Almost three days and I'm ready to pull my hair out. I can't imagine going damn near sixteen months. Fuck. I'm going to be him soon if she doesn't call me.

And I haven't even slept with her yet.

I thought about calling Birdie to ask how Zhar was but I know how protective Birdie is of Z. Since we all have Birdie's number in case anything ever happens to Danger, I text her:

Me: Hey B! I was wondering if you would tell me how Zharia's doing. It's killing me to give her space. I miss her.

I stare at it for a minute and then remind myself that she's a new mom of a baby and she's probably busy with Denver. I set my phone down and hear the dryer buzzer going off.

I go grab my clothes and then start folding them and my text notification goes off. I snatch it up off the table so fast I almost sending it sailing over my shoulder.

Birdie LaFleur: She's fine. A little shook up, confused but she's ok.

Me: I'm worried.

Me: I fucked up, didn't I? I asked for the same thing Shadow asked for and she shut him out. I don't want to lose her. She's everything to me.

I don't need to ask if she knows. I know Zharia would have told her Fab Four by now. She learned her lesson about not venting about Shadow. Her heartbreak blindsided the friend group. They had no idea it was that serious. No one did. She kept Shadow a secret from everyone.

Birdie LaFleur: Have faith Gunney <smiley face emoji> I think you're going to be getting a phone call soon

Me: *fingers crossed

Me: I miss her something terrible

I guess I just sit here and wait for my phone call.

CHAPTER 16 — ZHARIA

He grabs my arm and my first instinct is to pull out of his grasp, but he's my surgery patient and he's a little drugged up. He's gruff and rough around the edges. Reminds me of some of the older bikers at the clubhouse. I don't recognize him from there, or the man that's been here with him. They could be brothers in their sixties or early seventies or just friends or lovers. I have no clue who they are.

"Yes, Mr. Callahan?"

"I was wondering if a pretty thing like you would want to move to Texas with me?"

I chuckle and let him down easy, "No sir, my life is here and I love it a lot. Who else would take care of people and cut them open? Is there anything else I can get you before you're released from my care?"

"No ma'am. I think you would like Texas, give it some thought."

"Sure, Mr. Callahan. Have a safe trip back home."

I leave the room and think about the offer. I might have done that two years ago before everything and the creation of my facility but my place is here now. I don't think this place can run without me. I have my hands in a little bit of everything, plus normal duties of being a doctor.

I stop at the nurse's desk and let them know Mr. Callahan, with the bullet wound, is ready for departure. I have absolute faith that my staff can handle patient care and paperwork without me so I head to my office.

I had to report the bullet wound to the authorities and let them investigate. I just patch up the patients and hope for the best. Mr. Callahan said he was minding his business (sure, aren't they all) and out of the blue a car drove by and shot at him and a few friends standing in front of a notoriously rowdy biker bar at the sus hour of three AM. Yeah, if that doesn't sound fishy.

Not here to judge. I'm here to perform life saving measures and make people feel better when Hopelove's ER is over capacity. It was just my luck to be the on-call surgeon last night from my one night a week we have to sign up for after hour duty to cover the hospital. Been here since three-thirty AM and I've already put in my eight hours.

Ha! Eight hour workdays, what are those? I snort to myself.

I check my emails but my mind keeps dragging my focus away to the same subject I've been incessantly thinking about—Leo.

I miss him so much.

I didn't think I'd have such withdrawals from him but here I am, pining over him like a twitterpated girl in love. It's hard, ya know, to go from thinking your best friend is gay, unattainable, the safe bet…to he's in love with you.

A woman.

Very much not a man. Not even in passing.

I realized last night this is not the way to handle it. I can't just go radio silent and not give answers. I also realized I do love him. He's my best friend and if I look further down, I'm low key in love with him too.

Last night, I let the suppressed emotions I have concerning Leo loose. I opened Pandora's box and now I'm even more confused but the shining fact is he truly is perfect for me. We've practically lived together for months. The only thing between us that is not happening as a couple is anything sexual. We never crossed that line.

Until the other night.

It's no secret to him that I find him attractive. I would tell him often to boost his ego and confidence but it's seriously true. He really is gorgeous, almost too pretty to look at. And he has over a million paying subscribers to show for it.

Leo has the same beauty as Shadow that pulled me in—dark eyes, dark hair, dark humor. They're both gorgeous in a dark, lethal way.

My heart knocks in my chest at the thought of Shadow. The Christmas party threw me for a loop. I thought I had gotten over him and buried my feelings but I was very mistaken. All it did was open the floodgates again.

I still love Shadow. I never stopped. He's my one that slipped away. If only he would not have pushed or wanted what he wanted, when he wanted it. I can't fault him for that. But our future plans didn't align, and regardless how I feel about him, I can't choose a life of servitude to a man. I'm not marriage material, or at least I wasn't at the time.

Now that I've found out who Dipshit Dreama really is and that Shadow's single still, it has really weighed on me. Clearly Shadow has shown an interest in me still. Knowing who she is, and reading the situation again, I can see how scared Shadow was thinking that I thought Dreama and him were together.

Birdie said from her secretly gathered intel—whatever that means—she overheard Danger talking to who she assumed was Shadow, 'I can confirm she thought Dreama was your wife and she wanted to convince you to have a baby.' She said there was a pause, and then said 'Yeah, well I couldn't very well set her straight before you acted like an idiot and grabbed her. I still can't believe you did that, man. That had to have been rough for her. I feel like such an asshole now. And then you went and made it even worse, dick.'

At least they both recognize.

I'm now over thirty years old. At some point I need to get it together and find a personal life. I mean I did to a degree with Shadow and now Leo. Not everything should be about work. That concept is starting to grow on me. I want more time for a life outside of a sterile building and Wine Wednesdays.

If only I could have them both and Shadow and Leo's future aligns with mine. It would be the perfect situation for me. A girl can dream, right?

After a few hours of doing paperwork in my office, I pull out my phone and find mine and Leo's messaging thread.

Me: Hey! First, I want to apologize for my radio silence. Thank you for giving me time and space. You can imagine how confused I am. I don't want you to think I'm abandoning you.

Me: Second, I'd like you to come over tonight. I'd like to see you. I miss you. About 7 sound good? I'll feed you <smiling emoji> <kissy face emoji>

Next, I message Birdie and let her know what I've decided since she was insistent about knowing.

Me: I did it. I messaged Leo. I asked him to come over tonight. I miss him so bad. I want him, I want to have a relationship. I want everything he has to offer.

BirdsTheWord: Good. I think you're ready too.

BirdsTheWord: You know I gotta ask – What about Shadow?

Me: IDK. You said it was a misunderstanding but it's too late. I did what I did. I can't take it back. I doubt he would forgive me. God. Can't I just have both? <purple heart emoji>

BirdsTheWord: That sounds like a you problem LOL I imagine neither will go for that but hey, it doesn't hurt to ask, right? Definitely bring it up to him before committing completely to Gunney <winky face emoji> I'm happy for you.

I set my phone down and realize it's after three in the afternoon. Twelve-hour day and still going. The overflow from the hospital has taken its toll. There's been an uptick in violence in the city. We've taken in patients needing surgery on an emergency basis, such as Mr. Callahan.

Not to mention the emergency room at Hopelove is overflowing with flu cases. Tis the season. Christmas is in a few days. Winter, even though it's not as cold down here, still brings out the germs.

I let my nurses know I'm leaving for the day and head to my office.

My phone dings with a notification and when I pick it up. I see it's Leo.

My butterflies ignite and flutter about my core. I know he has to miss me as much as I miss him. My bed's been so lonely, the couch too big without his long body and the nights suck ass without him there to talk to and joke around with. I miss my best friend.

Don't even get me started on how many times I've masturbated to my 'best friend' since he told me he wants me and I felt his hard cock under my ass while sitting on his lap with his tongue down my throat. I thought I would test out my brain and see how receptive it was to the fantasies of fucking him. I allowed myself to dream.

By the leg shaking, breath stealing orgasms I've given myself, I'd say my pussy is agreeable.

Very agreeable.

Just me over here counting down the minutes until I get to see him and tell him I want to give it a go with him.

I'm nervous and excited.

CHAPTER 17 – GUNNEY

I don't see Zharia's car when I pull up at six-forty-five. Which is odd. Maybe she had to run out or got detained at work. Both reasons are plausible. I let myself in since I know the combination to her lock and plus, I've done it a hundred times before.

"Zhar?" I call when I get in the door and have it relocked. Silence greets me. Ok.

"Zharia? Are you here?" No answer.

This is not good. Zhar never misses an appointment or date. She's meticulous about that stuff.

I walk back to her bedroom thinking maybe she's asleep. Maybe her car's in the shop. She's not in there and her bed is still made up from this morning. She's picky about that too.

I search the entire house and I don't find her. I walk next door over to Mrs. Fontenot's house and rap on the door enough for the old broad to hear me. She comes to the door and starts smiling as she says hello. For an old biddy she sure doesn't mind staring me up and down. I'm sure she'd wolf whistle me every chance she got if she wasn't such a bible bending southern lady.

"Hi Mrs. Fontenot, I was wondering if you had seen or heard Zharia come home today."

"No chile, I haven't. You know I watch out my window and I can tell these things." Yes, I know how nosy you are. "I'm always watching out for her. This day and age, you never know what's going to happen."

"Yes ma'am, and I appreciate you keeping an eye on my girl." This makes her raise her eyebrows. I've met Mrs. Fontenot a few times but only as Zhar's friend. I'm sure the old lady sees me coming and going to a married woman's house and knows I spend the nights there, practically living there.

"Well, I appreciate it. I'm just going to hang out and wait on her. Thanks!"

Before she can delay me, I start bounding down the stairs and whipping out my phone. I call Zharia, no answer. I text instead and wait for an answer. In the meantime, I call Birdie.

"Hello Gunney, what's wrong?"

Birdie is a little paranoid. I imagine I would be too if a year and a half ago the rival biker gang over in Texas kidnapped me and tried to sell me into sex slavery. Birdie ended up killing their president and from the word around the clubhouse, they replaced him with a guy named Panhead Pete, who's equally as dumb as the old prez.

That doesn't even sound close to a leader's name. So far, he's been quiet. We know he's secretly building back numbers. He's expanded further north and encroaching into Arkansas and Oklahoma, two of Rock's territories. Panhead is amassing numbers and we aren't sure what for.

The Lone Star Saints were almost wiped off the map when Rock and Danger went on the rescue mission but the other half of the Houston based club stayed behind, not participating in their little kidnapping mission that didn't end well. Every LSS member there died that night. Their numbers took a huge hit but they still rule the entire state of Texas, New Mexico and good chunk of Arizona. They've grown exponentially in the past five years.

A good majority of us feel that the Saints are gearing up for something big, especially if members have been seen around New Orleans. We have a mole planted in their upper divisions but even he doesn't know what's planned. It's a sit and wait game, much like the military. Hurry up and wait.

"Have you seen or heard from Zhar? I was supposed to meet her at her house at seven and it's long after that. I've been waiting at her house for her the past half hour or so. Mrs. Fontenot says she's not been home yet. Did she let you know she was running late? I've not heard from her. This is strange."

"Shit. I agree, this is not like her. She never misses where she's supposed to be. Let me check my phone." I hear her hands shuffling on the speaker and after a few moments, she comes back, "I don't have anything from her since noon today."

"I guess I can wait here for a while. If she's not here by eight I'm going to her hospital to look for her."

"Gunney, please let me know. I'll join the hunt with you. For the time being sit tight, I'll call her too and see if I can find her."

"Thanks, Birdie."

  After I disconnect with Birdie I still feel anxious. I can't shake the feeling something is wrong. I have fifteen more minutes. I use them to text and call Zharia.
  I swear to god if LSS stole my princess I will kill every single one of them vigilante style.

Chapter 18 – Shadow

Fuck yeah. Tomorrow is the big day. I'm moving back to Louisiana, closer to my baby girl. The time has come.

Finishing up here a few days early has allowed time to come home earlier than planned. I can't wait to be home. Alabama is not my ideal place to call home but it worked for me in the interim. I miss the feel of my city and that Mississippi River is calling me back.

There have been some really great moments here, but for the most part it's been lonely. No one, no woman especially, appeals to me if they aren't Zharia, so having a relationship here was out of the equation. I'd push myself to find an easy club hunny to bury myself in occasionally but it was no use and not often. I can count on one hand the number of times

I've had sex since coming here. It was just a means to get off whenever I did. They were always her in my mind. I'm ruined, absolutely wrecked. I can't get her out of my system and maybe now I have a shot when I get back.

…If I can push Gunney out of the picture. Although, I distinctly remember him saying something about sharing her. And Zharia does like to date numerous men at a time, well she did before, she might just go for being shared. That opens up a whole new can of worms. I've never even thought about sharing her with someone else. She's mine.

But now, she's his too. That's the conundrum.

It will give me something to think about on the drive home.

That's a tomorrow's thought. I just completely handed off the books to the Treasurer, President and Secretary I have appointed here in Mobile. Things are running smoothly now and I can finally go home. The pull of the Crescent City and Zhar are calling me back.

The attack from LSS we sustained was not enough to unravel our operations. It was a drop in the bucket compared to daily activities, but lives were lost. Families are grieving and that is what hits hardest, the most out of everything stolen from us. It's the lives we lost.

LSS made off with a few pallets of merch AKA illegal guns and drugs, spilled some blood, and tore out of here like banshees. Very sloppy all the way through their mission.

It's almost eleven, past time for me to be asleep for my drive tomorrow. I'm starting out early in the morning to make the two-hour drive so I can get settled at my apartment I've owned the entire time I've been gone. I know it will be clean and fresh because I pay people to upkeep it for me since I've been gone.

I have to report to Rock's house by noon and I have a lot to get sorted when I arrive back in town. No rest for the wicked.

My phone rings and I pick it up to see it's Danger…at this hour, this can't be good.

"Hey, brother, what's up?"

"Tell me you implanted a tracker like Birdie's into Zharia."

Uhh, I don't know if I want to admit to that. Birdie will kill me for sure, Danger might. My gut twists and I know something is really wrong. I can tell by the tone of his voice.

"What's happened?"

"Don't deflect. I need to know. Zhar is missing. She didn't show up at home and when she didn't, Gunney went to the hospital to find her. Her car is still locked in the staff parking garage at her facility. We found her phone and her purse under the car. Nothing on the cameras, they were disabled."

The more he talks the louder the roaring in my ears gets. My Zharia is missing.

"Fuck. What time did she leave her shift?"

"A few nurses said she left about four. They said she was excited to get home and had a big night at home planned with her boyfriend." The knife twists in my chest. "Mrs. Fontenot told Gunney that she never came home. When Gunney got there nothing was out of place, her car wasn't there and there's was no entries on the alarm system to indicate she came into the house since she left at three-thirty this morning."

I stand up and pull my vest off the back of the seat. Good thing everything's already packed and in my truck because it looks like I'm leaving now.

"Let me tell Demon I'm leaving now. I'll be there in two hours, maybe less."

"Shadow, about the tracker, did you do it?"

"Can I plead the fifth and just go directly to her?"

"That's the confirmation I needed. Tell me her location as soon as you find it."

"I deleted the app, so I need to go find it again and redownload it. I'm on my way."

Danger disconnects and as I swing through the clubhouse I tell the guys goodbye and let Demon know I'm heading out tonight, emergency back home.

I hop in my truck and turn myself west. While I'm driving I download the tracker app and it starts searching. It appears to be having issues locating her.

Shadow Daddy is on his way Zhar, hang tight, babe.

Holy fuck my head hurts. I try to crack my eyes open and they are like sandpaper and stay shut. My mouth tastes awful and it's dry as a bone. Christ, what the fuck is going on?

There's light flickering from somewhere and it's ticking at my throbbing head through my closed eyelids. There's a slight chill to the air, it's damp and musty, underground like a basement, but that doesn't make sense. People don't normally have basements in Louisiana.

My eyes fly open because I'm not where I'm supposed to be and I don't know how I got here. Panic is rushing in. I'm supposed to be with Leo. I'm supposed to be telling him I love him, I was going to say yes.

This is definitely not my house.

I push past the throbbing in my head to focus my eyes on my surroundings. I'm lying on a hard surface, in a room with concrete walls, no windows and one single bulb hanging in the middle of the ceiling, throwing around stark light with the occasional flicker in the small room. I lift my arm to grip my head and that's when I realize I have chains on, complete with leather cuffs. Panic—cold, brutal and shocking races through my body. I can't get enough air. Please panic attack, please don't happen. Leo's not here to save me. My eyes instantly tear up when I realize Leo isn't here.

My chest constricts.

Breathe, Zhar!

I try to sit up through the grogginess and the pots and pans banging in my head. Did I hit my head? Am I drugged? I look down and see I still have my scrubs on and my sneakers. The room has essentially nothing in it. It's a prison and I'm the prisoner.

Finally, getting myself upright and my feet on the floor, I take in my surroundings a bit more. Nausea slams into my gut. There's a metal door that has no window. There's light coming in from under the door and I can make out someone standing in front of the door.

I yell, "HELLO! ANYONE THERE?"

I see the shadow of feet move away. I sigh and use my assessing doctor's brain to run down all the data I've collected about the situation. I have to focus on me right now and evaluate my being. I'm scared, panicky, my heart is pounding out of my chest from fear. My head pounds, which leads me to think they either hit me in the head or drugged me.

I lift my hands to see if I can feel my skull and see if there's any bumps or cuts. I don't find any painful spots, feel no blood, and I decide they must have drugged me. All of this means I have no idea how long it's been.

I could be anywhere.

My heart rate jumps up when the sound of jangling keys outside the door happens. The metal door starts rattling open and there is a man in jeans and a leather vest coming in with another man in tactical gear and what looks like a big bad ass long gun that I want no part of.

Another man stands just in the doorway. I recognize him.

"Mr. Callahan?"

He has the audacity to leer at me and gives me a wretched smile. Eww. Did he steal me from the facility? He was at my hospital facility and got discharged today. Granted, if it's still today.

Asshole in the vest goes, "Good morning, Dr. Davish. So nice of you to finally join us. I thinks they may have given you a tad too much sauce, sweetheart," he chuckles like it's a great joke. "But you're awake now and we can get down to business." Wonderful, I've been kidnapped by a condescending asshole.

I just stare at this slimy weasel. His aura smells worse than a camel's ball sack. His chakras need to be aligned with a baseball bat. Something tells me this is their leader.

My slow ass brain is starting to catch up. Mr. Callahan, who is now the biggest cocksucker I've ever met, set me up to get kidnapped. Rude motherfucker.

I'm feeling murdery.

Peace be damned, these horrible men stole me. I'm utterly terrified now. Mr. Callahan asked me to come to Texas. I know the reputation of the Lone Star Saints based there. Are these men part of that club?

Through my racing thoughts, I say nothing.

"My name is Panhead, or your beautiful mouth can call me Pete. I am the esteemed President of the Lone Star Saints, at your service," he says in a slow Texas drawl with an exaggerated bow. Guess that answers that question. Alright. Shit's just gotten real. This man is a loon; you can see it in his crazy squirrelly eyes. *The eyes never lie, Chico.* Sure, let's think about Scarface right now in times of peril.

I know what happened to Birdie when these fuckers took her. She hasn't come right out and said it, but I think my best friend's a murderer. Good for her. We don't judge; she had reasons.

I was told no *man* killed Grim. The rest of the Fab Four surmised Birdie killed him. As much as I want details, she can't give them. All she said was the threat had been eliminated. She's been sworn to secrecy by her godfather-esque biker mafia dad. Sorry, motorcycle *club* dad.

My eyes stay glued to his face with a keen peripheral view of the doorway, waiting on any movement.

"You see, we find ourselves needing a doctor on staff. Butters over here took a shine to ya yesterday and he had the great idea to relocate you to our facility. Welcome to your new life, doctor."

"What new life?" I ask the head dickhead in charge.

"Now, Zharia, we just went over this. Surely you remember. It happened like five minutes ago." He may feign amused but there's an underlying warning there and he's not putting up with stupid questions from me.

"Am I allowed to leave this room? What do you mean facility? Where am I?"

He stands hunched over with his arms folded across his chest, he has the most condescending look on his face, "Of course you'll get to leave this room. I'm not bringing members in here to get operated on." He laughs like that's the most absurd idea.

"Can I see this facility?"

"All in due time, Doc. Enjoy your time in your luxury accommodations. I'll send a hot plate for you to eat. I know you must be starving. After all, you missed dinner." He chuckles like being hungry is amusing. This fucking guy. Wow, I don't think I've ever met a bigger dick.

He turns to leave and I say, "Wait! What am I supposed to do about using the bathroom? I really need to go."

"Yes, well, I'll have Romulus take you." The big tactical looking man with the gun nods. "Any time you need the little girls' room, just knock on the door. One of my guards will always be out here, just in case you need them for anything." Ok, veiled words much? I clearly heard—guards all the time so don't even think about escaping.

"What am I supposed to fill my time with?" I work so hard at schooling my face to look bored as fuck despite my fear. I don't want to show him how afraid I am. Sickos like him thrive on it. It's gets their rocks off.

"I've always heard doctors are some of the tiredest people in the world, darlin'. Maybe catch up on your sleep until we need you. Don't worry, you won't be bothered, no one but Hercules or Romulus will be allowed in here." With that he leaves the room and the lone man with a Kevlar vest and plenty of guns is left with another guy dressed like him.

"Romulus?" I lift an arched eyebrow at him.

He moves across the room and undoes the cuffs, letting them fall to the sides, "Let's go."

He smells like fresh laundry and it makes me homesick.

He grabs my upper arm and hauls me to my feet and I try not to sway, but I end up falling into him. Wow, he has a really hard arm.

Romulus rights me and sets me back on my feet with a grunt. I get a little better footing and he starts dragging me from the room. I have to quickly get my bearings and wake my body the fuck up.

I'm led into a brightly lit hallway and turn left, a few more steps and Romulus shoves open a door to the right. Inside is a stark white full bathroom, shower, sink, and toilet. Thank fuck!

"We'll be right out here." He shuts the door and I'm left alone in this bathroom with no escape.

I know Leo is looking for me by now. I know he's called Birdie. There are people looking for me as I stand here. They would want me to be brave.

I bite my lip and steady my wobbling chin. I take a deep, ragged breath, in through my nose, out of my mouth. Inhale good shit, exhale bad shit.

To the hundreds of my dad's Hindu gods and goddesses, I offer up a big prayer, please let them find me soon.

CHAPTER 20 – GUNNEY

Homebase has been set up at Zharia's house. We want to be here if she comes home. Someone we trust is always here. We've been here damn near a week. My baby's been missing that long.

I can't tell you how rough this week has been.

I can't tell you how bad my PTSD is trying to rear its ugly head because she's gone.

I need her. I can't live without her. I'm always on edge now, on the verge of tears. I want to drop to my knees and scream at least a thousand times a day.

I've accepted there's another man here helping find her, acting like a maniac. A man who had her first and he's still in love with her and is planning on actively pursuing her away from me.

Danger called Shadow and of course, he came running. I'm not going to be ungrateful for more help but damn it.

We learned he put a tracker in Zharia, without her permission, which made Birdie verbally assault him until he almost yelled back.

Shadow almost roared that this might be the only way we ever find her. Danger was there with a warning look to make sure Shadow didn't get any louder with his wife.

That didn't stop me. I grabbed him up and shoved him up against the wall, knocking a picture off the wall and tipping over a dish on the sideboard. I expressed my displeasure at him flagrantly invading her privacy. Danger pulled me back but I let Shadow know I was grateful for what he'd done, but it will never excuse the blatant invasion of her privacy. Body autonomy is a joke to him.

He has a good point though, this might be the only way, hence the reason I'm not as upset as I should be but I still got my two cents in on him. Zharia's going to be furious but if that tracker ever works and we get her back, I'm sure she'll be willing to forgive him. Maybe. If she hadn't disappeared, I would be pissed that he did it without her knowledge and beat his ass, but right now that's the only thing giving us hope.

Trying to be the bigger person here is killing me.

It's complicated. That's my brother. He was one of my close friends before he left. I'm so conflicted about his presence and involvement. I'm conflicted about my feelings towards him now. I heard shit from him from time to time while he was gone, but I never divulged my relationship with his ex to him.

I look around the living room and see everyone that loves Zhar, sitting around eating a meal together after another grueling day looking for her. I fixed supper and everyone met up here to regroup and check in for the day. We've been running pretty steadily. Twenty-four hours a day we have people out scouring for her.

I feel like part of my soul is missing. It's enough to almost make me pick up a bottle and drown.

Almost.

But I won't. I can't. I promised my princess.

I have to cope in a different way. I have to put to use the stress management lessons from the counseling Zharia's been making me go to the past year. So, I just be over here sober as can be, man, humming Once Upon a Dream and cooking for everyone that's looking for my girl, baking muffins for breakfast and other Betty Crocker shit like that. I'm rage-baking. Stress-cooking. It keeps me from screaming and destroying shit. You know how it is.

I made Shadow butter the French bread and put it in the oven even though he grumbled.

The first time he was here with everyone, he looked really uncomfortable. I found amusement in that. He's not my rival, he's my brother in arms and I got love for him as one of my closest friends, but it was nice to see him squirm just a bit. The man is not untouchable.

I've been out of my mind this week. I've barely slept and ate. I spend all my free time here at her house when I'm not out questioning people. I sleep in her bed, surrounded by her scent, praying she's ok and I can find her soon.

Thankfully, Zharia's living room is big enough to host this many people in her house at one time. I'm standing in the kitchen pulling the last batch of garlic bread out of the oven while Danger starts an unofficial church meeting, with guests. Technically, Birdie should not be here for this but she's refusing to be shut out of the search for her best friend. Her dad has called a truce and is allowing her to attend these debriefings. She's been behaving *most* of the time.

Danger starts talking, "I don't need to remind anyone that it's been a week. We've had a lot of false sightings. Apparently everyone thinks all Indian girls look the same." He rolls his eyes and continues, "We also don't have any hits on the tracker. We have deduced they are using a signal jammer wherever she is being held. We do not want to think of the alternative—they found the device and cut it out of her, destroying it." Birdie gasps. "This is the same tracker I implanted in my wife and we found her no problem. A jammer is the only logical explanation we can come up with."

Rock nods to Danger and clears his throat, "We don't have a reason to believe Zharia is dead, and we will search until we find her." Birdie's shoulders shake in silent cries against her sleeping son.

"Rock," I hate how my voice cracks, "I want to take a moment to thank all of you for your efforts in finding her. I appreciate you."

Slim Jim, standing next to me, rubs between my shoulder blades and pulls me into a hug, "We'll find your old lady, son, have faith."

I clapped him on the back one last time and pull away. I tell him, and the rest of the room, "She's Shadow's old lady too."

You could have heard a pin drop at my declaration. Birdie's eyes go from me, to Shadow, who's standing next to her husband across the room from me, then back to me. I meet her eyes and give a 'Who gives a shit right now' look. I shrug, hopefully reminding her—he loves her just as much as I do.

Slim walks across the room and gives Shadow a hug too and says, "We'll find her. Your old lady will be back in your arms before you know it."

Now Birdie is giving me the 'What the fuck' look with her nose scrunched up. I swear, I wish Slim would just shut up. He means well, but damn, he has no tact and he is the very worst secret keeper. A raging fucking gossip, he is. That's why he's useful now.

Slim, T-Bone, and Travares have been bouncing all over the city, in and out of bars, asking around, showing Zhar's pics about, making sure word is spread far and wide.

Without these gossipmongers we wouldn't have the network of people that we do.

Through the old guys and their charisma, we have three lawyers on retainers ready to help the club whenever, two solid hackers besides Travares who love digging up the shit we ask for, and there's numerous eyes and ears scattered all over the greater New Orleans area. These guys have people all over the state. They know how to get people to open up and tell their stories, then convince them to do good things with a motorcycle club. They wiggle their way in as a friend and that's how they hook them. Next thing you know, they want to do things for the nice old men with plenty of cool stories.

Per Zharia's parents, we had to involve the cops. As soon as Zhar was confirmed missing, Birdie called her parents late in the evening and a police report was filed. The cops came here and I was waiting outside for them with Birdie and Danger and Bryan, one of the lawyers. We never deal with the police without a lawyer riding around in our back pocket.

Her house was cleared as a crime scene and the cops main focus is the hospital Zhar runs. We can clearly see her walking across the hospital, from camera to camera, making her way to the garage. We see her walking in the garage, heading up a ramp, putting her phone in her scrubs pocket. This is where she goes out of view.

We found her car, her phone—cracked all to hell—lying by the driver's side door. We did not tell the police about the phone or that we are currently looking through it nor did we divulge we already had one of our men reviewing the CCTV feed, searching for Zharia or any other thing helpful.

Of fucking course, the camera that covers the other side of that ramp didn't work and had been tampered with. This told us that this was planned. This is not a random carjacking gone wrong in this dangerous city.

Zharia is meticulous about her building security. No way that thing was broken and not fixed immediately.

Zharia was targeted.

They had a plan.

Was she targeted for her involvement with the Southern Devils Society? Or from the facility? A disgruntled patient or past employee? Hey, stranger shit has happened. We look at all of them.

After everyone left, Shadow stuck around, helped clean up, and now he's sitting next to me on Zhar's porch while he drinks a beer. We've been pretty quiet, but I can tell something's on his mind.

"Spit it out," I tell him without looking over at him. I'm tired of him hemming and hawing around.

"Were you serious about sharing her?" he tentatively asks.

Now I do look over at him. I study his face, seeing no judgement, "Yes, if she'll go for it. But only with you, no one else, ever."

"Why?"

I cock my head, really looking at him then, "I will do anything to make her happy. After the past fifteen months, she needs happiness, she deserves it. I take every opportunity to make her smile and I love it when it happens. Some days are easier than others. My main goal is to keep her happy. I think you in her life, AFTER a big discussion, might benefit her. I think she wants you in her life as much as wants to deny it and fight it. She misses you, bro. Hell, I missed you."

"God, I miss you guys too. It's been so lonely. But if you think she would go for this, I'm all in. I mean, I've shared girls before with other brothers, but that was just sex, just a threesome, it wasn't a full-on fucking relationship, man. I don't know how to feel about sharing an old lady." He shakes his head like he can't fathom the idea.

"Well, it depends on her. I do truly think y'all's problem is lack of communication." I watch him very closely for this next part, "I think she still loves you."

His eyes go big and then he narrows them, "Are you fucking with me right now?"

I chuckle and say, "Naw man, I don't need to lie. It doesn't help me out one bit to say it. Actually, it kinda fucks me over to admit that to you." I put my hand up before he can say anything, "I see it, ok, I've been here since the week you left. I can see it in her eyes and in the way she guards herself and holds herself back now. It's there, as much as she tries to hide it, I know it's there. And that's why it took her three days to call me once I told her I love her and I want to be with her as a committed boyfriend."

"Fuck. When was this?"

"I was supposed to be meeting her here to discuss our relationship the night she disappeared. I made my move three nights before that, after you accosted her at the Christmas party."

"Hey, man…"

I hold my hand up to silence him again. "She didn't outright reject me, but I could tell, something in the way she kissed me, I felt in my heart that I wasn't going to be enough for her. As much as that hurts me to admit, I strongly feel that way. That's what got me to thinking about this whole sharing thing. What if both of us together is enough for her? What if she didn't have to choose?"

He slouches back in the chair, an ankle resting on his knee. We still size each other up, until he quietly says, "I know I should leave her alone, but I can't. I've tried so hard. It's like a piece of my soul is missing."

"I understand that feeling. I feel the same way right now. I'm dying inside. When she gets back I think I can convince her to talk to you, but only if you're rational and calm with her. You better learn how to talk to her before you do. One sign of aggression and I'll haul your ass out of the house myself. I'm willing to let her make up her own mind. If she chooses you, I'll respect that. If she chooses me, you'll have to respect that decision and walk away. But if she chooses both, like I think she will, then we build a life together, all three of us. Then we live happily ever after like her favorite Disney movie and shit." I rather like the last idea best as I'd still be in her life and she's happy and whole. That's what it's about.

Shadow's eyes narrow and he blows out a pent-up breath, "If we all build a life together, are you expecting me to fuck you too? I don't know how you swing but I don't."

I snort then laugh, "Naw, man, you ain't fucking me, you're not my type. I can fuck her with you, but we ain't gonna be a thing. I love you like a brother but not like that."

He nods, contemplating my words, "Copy that. I don't want to fuck you either, no offense, I just prefer pussy. Her pussy to be more specific." He relaxes enough to huff out a soft laugh and it puts me more at ease.

"I do want to disclose this first. I've been gay the past ten years. I thought I was completely gay, until I fell in love with Zhar and then hey, what do ya know, I want pussy too. Not just any pussy, only hers. It was a shock to her that I wanted her."

"You know, I had my thoughts but said nothing. I figured if you wanted me to know you woulda told me."

"The club doesn't know. I didn't know how they would react to it. I've kept it to myself, although I think Zharia told Birdie who told Danger."

"Well, your secret is safe with me, bro. Do your thing. Don't give a shit what the others in the club think. Live your life authentically. Fuck the haters."

"I appreciate that. You know…at first she's going to be mad as hell that you're here." I sit back in my chair and take a long pull of my orange pop. That's the Yankee coming out in me. Even after a few years down here in the south I refuse to call it Coke or soda.

It's pop.

You can take a guy out of Ohio, but the Buckeye inside never dies. Midwest born and bred, Southern by choice.

"I know." Shadow sits back in his seat and looks out over the quiet street. There's a dog barking, it smells like someone's cooking steaks on the grill, there're kids riding bikes down the street and Sir Waffles, Zharia's baby, sits in the window behind us, tail swooshing slowly, reigning over his domain through glass. He's too prissy to actually come outside. Zharia would die if he got lost.

It's not a busy, loud neighborhood that she lives in, quite the opposite. It's peaceful, there is not a lot of traffic and neighbors take care of each other. Neighbors that we have already interviewed and no one saw anything at her house. This tells me they were after her personally, not anything materialistic.

"We'll find her, brother. I have to keep believing that. We have to keep faith that she'll be found. It's why I wake up in the mornings. I won't rest easy until she's back with us. I refuse to believe she's dead." I almost let the emotions take over on that last word. I'm so lost without her.

"Fuck," Shadow presses his fingers to his eyes and takes a deep, cleansing breath. *I'm almost crying right there with you, buddy.*

Chapter 21 – Shadow

"Take about a dozen men and scope out Lake Charles area. Ask around. That's the area they took Birdie to so maybe they went back there. Start breaking out serious threats to find her. Someone's bound to talk. We just need one good lead. Whoever has her is keeping her off our radar. I have a strong suspicion it's Lone Star Saints. This kind of shit reeks of their stench. We can't just roll up and start killing everyone to find her," he holds up a finger, "…yet. But I'm not opposed to that if we can get a good enough lead on where she's being held."

T-Bone raises his hand, "If we do get a lead while in Lake Charles, do you want us acting on it or calling you in for backup and waiting for your arrival?"

Danger scratches at his few days' growth beard, mulling over T-Bone's question. Even Danger looks as rough as the rest of us. This search is taking its toll.

Rock speaks up before Danger can answer, "We can most likely scope out the place and make an executive decision. We won't know until we're there."

"True," Dobby speaks up, he's usually so quiet, "When are we going to Houston?" I'm still not sure about this squirrelly guy but he does everything we ask with no complaints and earned his patch fair and square.

"I'm trying to avoid that but we aren't removing that option for the future," Rock says. Dobby nods and the rest of the group nods with him. We are out for blood.

They stole one of ours. We want her back.

I shift my weight to my other hip as I sit on the couch holding a sleeping Denver. Sometimes I just want to hold a baby. Babies fascinate me. I like to think I'll make a good father one day…possibly. I had a great one to learn from until he died when I was seventeen.

Birdie stands up and you can tell she's trying hard not to lose it, "Again, I want to tell each of you thank you from the bottom of my heart. She's my sister and I won't stop until she's found. Thank you for going above and beyond for her safe return. I realize it's New Year's Eve," Christmas and New Year's just doesn't sit right with any of us with this looming black cloud over us and her absence, "and I know there are other places you'd rather be, not to mention the clubhouse is having a party tonight. I want you to know I won't be upset if you stop searching and take some much needed time for yourselves. I actually encourage it tonight. Party for me."

"Aww, Miss Birdie, I couldn't think about drinking and partying knowing that pretty girl is out there, scared to death and not knowing what's happening to her." Slim continues to shake his head, disagreeing with her. Others join in to side with Slim.

Birdie's face softens as she sits back down in the overstuffed chair. Tears well in her eyes while she cuddles Sir Waffles Fluffenstein, who we can tell misses his momma so much, "Thank you Slim, you are such a kind soul, but please, for me, for Zharia, take some time for yourself." Slim dips his chin at her and winks.

Rock claps his hands and says, "That's all for the debriefing we have. As always, I appreciate your work."

The fifteen people who are active players in the search party funnel out of the house to head wherever. Rock says, "Shadow, Gunney, a word, please."

After I hand Denver off back to his momma, Rock leads us to the back of the house where the spare bedroom is located and when we enter he closes the door. He looks over us and his eyes take on a concerned gleam. "You two have put in a lot of man hours searching for her. Maybe you should take a night off." Gunney takes a breath to argue. Rock lifts his hand, halting Gunney, "Matter of fact, fuck maybe, I'm ordering it. You're coming to the clubhouse."

I open my mouth to disagree and he cuts me off, "This is not negotiable, Shadow. You two are exhausted and it shows. I need you both at your best and right now, you're running on energy drinks and spite."

"I'm sleep deprived but I'm still alive and I don't want to rest until she's back home," Gunney states.

"Guys, I get it. I was a fucking mess when Birdie was kidnapped. But I'm watching you two wilt away. Take tonight. Get your head straight. Shit, come to the clubhouse with your brothers. You need to lean on them for support. I'm sure the others not in the search party would like to see you. Lend their support. People are worried for you guys." Rock switches his weight to his other leg and rubs his bearded chin, "I know you both love her and I just hope this doesn't cause problems between you two. I'd hate to see a friendship, a brotherhood, ruined over a woman."

My teeth grind, "She's not just any woman."

"I didn't say she was, Shadow. I know Zharia is special. I've watched her grow from a gangly teenager to the beautiful, intelligent woman she is today. Trust me when I say, my heart hurts too. I look at her as another daughter. I want her found just as much as anyone else. We'll get through this guys, have faith." Rock reaches over to crush me to him and then he reaches over to hug Gunney too. It almost makes me choke up.

Gunney and I end up at the clubhouse later like we were voluntold to do. We aren't in the mood to party or be around fun and frivolity, but Rock had a good point. We are the top five, the upper echelon, and certain things are expected of us. Not to mention they are having the top five give speeches to the brotherhood for the coming year. Leadership basically gets on stage and tells everyone we wish them a happy and prosperous year in fancy words.

Sometimes I forget I'm in the top five. There's Rock then Danger, me, Gunney and last is Travares.

I have nothing prepared.

Kinda feeling like I don't give a fuck.

"Shadow! Come sit down, man. You're glaring at all the pretty ladies and starting to bring the vibe down," Slim Jim yells over to me.

"No," I grumble back to him.

"No?"

"No is a complete sentence, I didn't stutter," I bite back.

I watch Slim Jim walk over to where I stand at the bar. He sets his wrinkled, calloused hand on my shoulder, "I know it's hard, son, I want you to know we are all feeling part of your pain. Share the load. You don't have to bear it all on your own. You and Gunney are doing everything you can do. Come sit with your brothers, son."

His soft, gentle voice soothes me and it's hard to argue with the old man. His voice washes over me like a balm to my hurting soul. There's no amount of praying, hoping, or wishing that I haven't done already. Hell, I've even started praying to different gods of other religions. Need to cover all the bases, I don't discriminate.

I know Slim means well. I know he's just looking out for us. I can't hold it against him. He's one of the most levelheaded of the bunch. Slim is part of the Elder Counsel and his specialty is counseling young pups who are having a rough time.

I must be his new project.

Sometimes one of us hardened dogs need a fatherly talkin' to from him. He's one of the best in that position and an invaluable associate to the club. Always has genuine words of wisdom and his compassion is on point.

"I'm sorry, Slim. I shouldn't be here." I swallow the Coke I'm drinking to keep me from hollering like a fool or screaming out my frustrations. I opted not to drink in case I had to take off quickly if we got a lead.

Plus, Gunney confided in me his journey to recovery. Out of respect and solidarity, I'm not drinking either. I commend him for his resilience and strength. It has to be hard being here around it all and being under as much stress as we are.

"It's ok, Shadow. It's ok not to be ok all the time, bud. No one's going to hold it against you. This is a serious and traumatic experience for you. We will get our vengeance soon. Sometimes patience then violence is the answer."

I grin, "For a guy who speaks fluent bullshit, you have a way with pretty words of advice, old man."

He winks at me and replies, "I must warn you; my inner child is a little shit and wants to make a flippant comment about that, but I'm not going to do that to you right now, it's not the proper time." The mischievous sparkle in the old man's eyes has me smiling. I really like Slim.

"There you go. Good to see a smile grace your face finally. Now come sit. Gunney is just as grumpy as you are, so be miserable together at a table full of brothers."

Slim turns and moseys back to the table where it's gotten louder and more laughter fills the clubhouse.

There's a good number of people here tonight and it's a good atmosphere. I'm trying not to bring the vibe down but fuck, it's so hard. I want to break things, light something on fire, fucking spill blood. But whose?

I hope the people who have my girl fuck up. I just need them to fuck up just once and have that little dot appear on my tracking map. I have that notification set on the highest setting to notify me. It will sound like a bomb warning going off. There will be no mistaking it.

"Hey Shadow, welcome to the table!" Bam gets up and gestures to his seat, "Have a seat, brother."

I nod to him and tell him thanks then sit down. I see these fuckers are still playing Uno. I guess it's better than the Go Fish they usually play. They must have three decks put together. Bam still has his cards in his hand, hunched over hiding them from the others.

I see they are making good use of their spare time.

"You want dealt in?" T-Bone asks me.

"No, man, I'm good. I just want to sit and watch for now."

"Suit yourself." He leans in close to me and says for only my ears, "We've all teamed up to put the probie in the hole." He gets a good laugh at that. The older guys can be pretty ruthless to the probies—our probates, the ones trying to gain an initiation, still in their probationary period. I guess the old timers earned the right to do a little razing.

That's when I notice the new guy, Patches, hanging out with a shit ton of cards at the opposite end of the table from me. They've buried him with cards. He's not coming back from that shit. I cover my mouth and chuckle to myself and T-Bone says, "That's more like it, kid." He gives me an approving grin.

I see Gunny sitting down by Patches and Slim and neither one of them looks like they're going to be winning this either. I know better than to play with these older guys. They are shameless cheaters and when you call them out, they deny and lie, snickering the whole time.

Gunney looks about as thrilled as I feel. At least he's engaging, which is more than I've done tonight. I've been a shit friend. A shit brother since I got back, but I have a really good fucking reason to be a moody dick right now and they all have been giving me some grace.

I can't be a dick to the only family I have left here, even if it's not blood. My cousin that moved here with me almost nine years ago, took off about three years ago, moved back to the rez with the rest of our family in Oklahoma.

I've been a shit son too. Fuck. I need to call my mom.

I tap T-Bone on the shoulder and say, "Be right back, gotta call my mom." T-Bone nods and goes back to cheating. Before you defend his old ass, he is, I saw his hand. And the damn cards stuck under his leg

The phone rings and then I hear my mother's precious voice, "Teddy Bear, it's so good to hear from you."

"Hey, Mom. Sorry I haven't checked in."

"What's wrong? You've got a tone. What's happened?"

So, I tell her about Zharia going missing. My mom knows all about her and our history, she's listened to me on bunches of calls piss and moan about losing her. You could go so far as to say I'm a momma's boy and my mom is like my best friend.

I tell her about the search efforts and about all the leads we've chased down. I tell her about how the cops in New Orleans are useless and it's a good thing we are doing our own investigation.

Then I tell my mom how I feel deep inside me. I profess my love of a woman who's in a dangerous situation.

I'm man enough to admit, as I walked slow circles in the parking lot, kicking gravel, I cried to my mom while I poured my heart out, lovesick and heartbroken.

CHAPTER 22 – ZHARIA

Who knew a vicious biker club would need a doctor so much? What the fuck are these people doing out there? Not me thinking we're in a war zone but here I am, patching up guys left and right. I have no idea what time it is, what day it is, or how long I've been here. Somedays I feel like I lay my head down and just get to sleep and they are waking me up with jangling keys at the door to go dig a bullet out or sew up some gashes.

I have no idea where we are that people are constantly getting this hurt like this all the time. Been wondering if I'm still in New Orleans with the number of gunshots wounds I've tended to. Not saying I stay super busy because I do have downtime. I have no idea how long it really is but I do have time to think.

I can tell you the times they let me sit in my room alone, with absolutely nothing to do, I've had plenty of time to re-evaluate my life.

I've done some serious, down and dirty soul searching. Nothing like stripping your emotions bare and looking at your character under a microscope. I've had plenty of time to figure out why I am the way I am.

I've thought a lot about Shadow and how I still feel about him. Regret lives in my heart. I still feel like I had to take the deal to achieve my highest good. I would have wilted being a wife and mom.

At least that's what I thought at the time.

Now not so much, I frown.

There are co-workers I have talked to at my hospital, ladies that have children and still maintain a stellar career. I had so many questions about working through pregnancy and how they balance work and life. I always got the same answer: get a partner that helps carry the load and stress and makes it a team effort.

Shadow would be a good dad honestly. He was so intense with his feelings about me, but when he mentioned children, his face lit up every time. How could I deny him the chance to be a dad? I had to let him go so he could chase his own dream.

I overly flip my hair and flutter my lashes, mocking Dipshit Dreama.

Stop being a mean girl. We don't do this. You know now they weren't together.

But my chest aches whenever I think of him and her together, even knowing what I know now. It aches to think of him with anyone. I thought at the time his life had moved on so smoothly without me and here I am stuck. That's what it looked like. Seeing them together was the worst. I've never felt inferior to anyone, and I wasn't about to let her make me feel like that, but goddamn if I didn't feel less.

Birdie assured me per secret Danger intel Shadow has been single the entire time he's been gone.

But so have I and it's confusing people. Maybe I'm not enough for someone else.

Like I need another thing I need to think about—why I feel that when I know I'm more than enough. My brain is lying to me again.

He was supposed to be moving back soon. Because I know him, I know how he is, he's out there looking for me regardless of who doesn't like it. He'll never stop. I know because I saw it in his eyes standing next to her. Shadow is still deeply in love with me. I don't know what I did to deserve his devotion but sometimes it overwhelms me.

I have to be honest with myself; I'm still in love with him.

The realization washed over me as a relief, able to admit it, finally free to release that.

That's not fair to Leo though. I've also come to realize I'm in love with him too. I softly and slowly fell for him and kept those feelings trapped and shoved down because I knew there wasn't any hope for a relationship. He's a big part of the reason I haven't dated again.

He surprised me with his declaration and I had to dig through a year and a half of suppressed feelings to see if I could give him the love he deserves in return. I had to visually plot in my head our future together and then decide if I would want that for my own path I'm already on. I pray I get a chance to tell him I would love to be his girlfriend. We have to move on at some point, right?

Unless, like I said to Birdie, why can't I have both.

I can't stop thinking about Leo's heated kiss with his hands and lips all over my body. I wanted him so bad at that moment. I often dream about what it would have been like if I hadn't stopped him.

I think I'm ready for a relationship in general, but more specifically with Leo. I chased my dreams. I made them happen and I feel like I have the energy and attention to dedicate to a relationship now. I feel like I've grown in the time Shadow's been gone and the quality time I've spent with Gunney means the world to me.

Now, I feel like I have to make a choice. That is if I ever fucking get out of here. They don't seem to be eager to let me go any time soon.

Thankfully, not one of them has tried to grope me or assault me. I was terrified they would chain me to the wall and all take turns. I know their reputation, how they handle females. They have no regard for her feelings, for her pain. They are the sickest of the sickos. Not one of these men have tried to talk to me, they don't answer when I ask questions. Only the guy bringing me food and watching me eat has the decency to treat me like I exist.

Hercules is his name. He is tasked with bringing me food, babysitting while I eat it, and making sure I actually do eat. He also makes sure I don't steal utensils to make a weapon to use against them. He comes in and we've struck up a friendship of sorts. We talk and he's a really interesting kid. He makes my day feel normal-ish.

I say kid because he feels like that to my old ass. He's nineteen. Smart, nice, and almost as scared as me.

It makes my skin crawl to be here. At any minute one of the guards may bust in here and drag me next door to treat someone. It's becoming one big blur. Day in and day out I have blood on my hands of people I'd like to kill myself, but I know if I lose one, I'm a dead girl.

Fear keeps me sharp and so far, I've made no mistakes. I'm also trying to see if I can see anything in the hallway every time I'm dragged out of the room. They are quick to move me, jerking me around where I can barely focus on my surroundings.

I think I'm going crazy in here.

Think about something positive right now or the panic will take over again! My mind switches from fear to all the good moments I've had with Leo the past year and a half. He was such a welcome gift to my life. At the time I was so lost and so was he. We both saved each other and grew into better people with the other's support.

It was easy to fall in love with him. It was hard to suppress it.

I think about all the times I was happy with him. We did so many fun things in our time together. We may have saved each other and there's a bond between us no one can break.

I'm so proud of him for not drinking. I hope and pray he didn't pick up a bottle while I've been gone. I can't blame him if he does. I spent the two weeks after Shadow left, before I met up with Leo that fateful day in the grocery store, mostly drunk off my ass to numb the pain, holed up in my house with the 'flu.' So much so that Raj threatened to call my parents. He called Birdie instead.

Yeah, I had the lovesick flu. More like shriveling up inside.

I had just gotten married only two short weeks before I met Leo in that store. Leo really walked into a shit show. He tried to leave when I told him I was married, giving his sincere apology for overstepping my husband's role, but once I explained to him the arrangement, he was all too happy to become my bestest bud.

Only he's not that anymore.

I don't know what he is to me except someone that loves me and that I love back. He's someone I miss terribly and I long to be held in his arms. I guess he's my boyfriend at this point, he just doesn't know yet.

Because I never got the chance to tell him everything.

If I make it out of here the first thing I'm doing is telling both of my men that I love them. They deserve to know, for whatever it's worth.

I'd be a lying bitch if I said I hadn't thought about what it would be like to be fucked by both of them at the same time. That's become my new ultimate fantasy to think about while I'm here.

I've got it all planned out in my head. It plays on repeat.

Hey, I have a lot of time on my hands to think about this sort of stuff. You can hear about it too. I mean, it's some really good things I've never tried.

I have this one fantasy where I'm doggy style and Leo is balls deep fucking my pussy, thumb in my ass and Shadow has his big cock shoved into my mouth, railing the back of my throat. Their thrusting syncs up and I'm a fucking mess. Leo wraps my hair around his fist and yanks back, telling Shadow, "Now you can go deeper inside our princess's throat." I'm so stuffed full of cock I can't see straight. They make me gag and drool all over myself and my tears stream down my cheeks, but I love every degrading second of it.

Shadow's right. I am a filthy girl.

That's the number one fantasy getting me off within two minutes in the shower.

The other is where they're both shoved into my pussy and ass at the same time. That one is a huge fantasy. I want Leo beneath me and Shadow behind me. I miss Shadow's filthy mouth. I wonder if Leo has a potty mouth too. I love some good filthy talk while being fucked.

Unfortunately, with the constant adrenaline pumping through my veins from anxiety and fear, I've not been able to diddle like I want to in here so I can relieve the heaviness in my loins my imagination has created. I get excited but yet I'm still terrified. Last thing I need is one of these horrible men walking in while my fingers are knuckle deep in my vagina and they see it as an invitation. Or, oh god, smell my arousal when they walk into this small room. *Yuck*. I throw up a little in my mouth.

The shower is the only safe space. There's a lock on the door. I know it's not going to stop someone from coming in, especially those brutes out there, but it gives me a false sense of safety. It's just enough of a false feeling to get the job done quickly.

I think it's nighttime. My body thinks it is anyways. I try to settle down on this hard as hell prison cot they have for me, at least the blanket is soft. I was pleasantly surprised I got a soft cotton blanket and a nice pillow. It's made sleep more restful given the circumstances.

This is one of those times I feel like I've been in here for hours. These are the times I have time to think, time to wonder what's happening out there. Wondering how Birdie is coping without me. She has to be out of her mind, Tally and Pierre too. I know I was when I heard she had been taken. Tally and Pierre must be heartbroken at my disappearance. I miss my life and all the people I love.

Gunney. My Leo. I know he won't give up looking for me. I've analyzed all of our interactions. I should have seen it earlier. He shouldn't have had to tell me. I thought it was a friendship kind of love but when I look back, I recognize it for what it is.

Isn't it just so pretty to think all along there was some invisible string tying him to me.

He's looked at me like that for some time now. He hid it in plain sight and I was too self-absorbed to see it.

God damn it.

Old habits die hard, I guess.

I know I've looked at him like that in return plenty of times but I make sure my features are schooled right back in the friend zone as soon as I realize I'm doing it. I'm not his type. I don't have a penis. And now I guess my special lady parts are something he wants.

The same man who told me he's not into pink tacos.

This is wild.

What if he doesn't really like my pink taco? He prefers hot dogs after all? He only thinks he wants me.

We've talked about our pasts extensively. He's mentioned before his failed attempts are being attracted to females. He said he finds them pretty and cute, but as for dating and wanting to fuck one, he's never had the urge to do either.

Do I believe I'm the first woman he's fallen for? Yes, I do. If anything, Leo is genuine and honest; he would never lie to me.

I can't wait to wrap my arms around him while he holds me. I can't wait to smell his cologne and the unique scent that is him, the scent that soothes me and makes every bad thing disappear. Ever smelled a man that excited and relaxed you at the same time? The way I fall under his spell when I smell it on him is ridiculous. Goddamn it smells so good.

Look, I've had my heart skip a beat a time or ten when I've gotten a good whiff of his cologne. Bit my cheek to remind me we don't eat friends too. Friend's cum is not food.

I think about how when we sit on the couch and he holds me to his side while we watch a movie, his warm body under me, chest rising and falling. That is the best time to let his scent and aura overcome me. I always close my eyes, letting it fill me up.

I miss that. I miss being so close to him. I miss how he makes me feel safe and cherished. With just a few words from my Leo, I'm a blushing virgin when he starts telling me how beautiful I am and to stop comparing myself to other women. One time I asked him why I couldn't have an ass like Beyonce. He told me he would kill for my ass and it was perfect the way it is. Then he smacked me on the ass and as I felt it jiggle, he said, "See, perfect."

I see that comment in a completely different light now. Along with a bunch more interactions. Leo is an undercover flirt. It's all clear to me now. He wasn't just a gay best friend.

And lordy, does he know how to kiss. He stole my breath with our heated kiss on my couch. Which seems like it was so long ago now.

I wouldn't mind accepting a kiss like that again. Lay it on me, big guy. It was exhilarating. I was so wet, so hot, throbbing to take him inside me, ready to throw caution to the wind. My body had fire in my veins and I wanted to rip my clothes off and let him spear me with his cock right then and there. I've thought about it so many times.

This is one of my favorite fantasies about what should have happened that night:

Our tongues clashing, he unbuttons my pajama top and slides it down my arms, exposing my handful of breasts to him. Leo leans forward and captures one of my nipples in his mouth. He moans low in his chest, almost a growl. I love all the sounds a man makes when he's aroused. And aroused he is if his hard cock under me is any indication.

It's always a small triumph to a woman who turns a man on with barely trying.

He releases my nipple and kisses his way to the other one, leaving a trail of shivers in his wake from his short beard. His intensity sparks my core. He swirls his tongue, making my nipple bud up in his mouth. The sensations he sends through my body are familiar and have a label now, love not lust.

He stands me up in front of him and finishes undressing me. He pulls away and I'm out of breath.

"Just let me look at you, beautiful. My god, you're glorious."

My cheeks warm at his praise and I love how it makes me feel. Clit twitching, I can only think of how good it's going to feel with him inside me. No, I need him inside me. Like it's my last breath.

There's so much that needed to be said after that kiss, but in my mind right now, I imagine what it would have been like if I'd never have said stop.

In my daydream, *he slowly peels my satin sleeping shorts down my tan legs, taking my panties with them. I'm bare before him. Naked and horny. Wanting him so bad I clench my thighs to get some type of relief. I can feel how wet I am and I don't feel like hiding from him.*

"You're gorgeous, baby, my beautiful princess. You want to sit on my cock and bounce those gorgeous titties in my mouth?"

I bite my lip and nod. Fuck yes, please.

"Use your words, beautiful."

"Yes, more than anything." It's been so long since I've had sex. I was almost worried I would never be horny ever again until Leo turned me on and jolted me out of the frame of mind I'd been in for too long. I'm like a born-again virgin.

He pulls his thick cock out of his basketball shorts and grips it at the base. I pull the memory of his size off the videos I watched. Not too big, not too small. I see the bead of precum gathering on the crown and my mouth waters to lick it off of him.

Gripping his cock, watching me with a lethal grin, he takes his thumb and swirls it around his head. It's so shiny and it calls to my tongue who's dying to wrap around it. I can almost feel it on my tongue now if I try hard enough.

"You want this, princess?"

"Please, Leo."

"I love when you say my name. I want to hear it when I make you come."

I'm ready to drop to my knees and open for him when he crooks his finger and says, "Come sit on your throne, princess."

My breath quickens and my heart skips a beat. I push aside all the racing thoughts that this is my best friend. He's supposed to be like a brother to me. We aren't supposed to be doing this. But if I'm honest, it feels sooo right. So dirty and taboo. It feels like I'm finally coming home.

Something is lifting in my chest every time I think of us together like this. It brings forth all the feelings I wasn't ready to deal with and now that I make myself wet with these fantasies I want to take another shower.

Through my mind, *I make my way over to the couch and set my knees on either side of his hips. My heart is pounding out of my chest. There's no use trying to get my breathing under control, it's just not happening.*

He uses one hand to rub his cock over my wetness. The top of his dick prods at my entrance. He uses the other hand to grip the back of my neck, pulling me down so his lips are on mine. I can't help the guttural moan that comes out of me.

He groans, "Goddamn, I've wanted this for so long." He gets in place at my slick opening, as he gently says, "Now sit, princess."

I slowly lower myself on to his cock, reveling in the delicious burn of the stretch, letting my head fall back with a contented sigh. I let out a low moan as I slide down further and hit bottom. He latches onto one of my nipples while his hands grip my as—

Keys rattle outside the door snapping me back to reality. Worst timing ever.

This only means one thing. I have to go to work.

Pete walks in with a sly smile. I wasn't expecting him. Usually, it's a guard and another member escorting me next door. This must be a special social call. How fucking lovely for me.

Yay, visitors. Hope they don't mind the lack of furnishings or cleanliness. Inwardly, I roll my eyes.

Pete's almost jovial. Am I dreaming? This is scary now. Nothing good can come of this dumbass being joyful.

He plasters a leering smile across his ugly face, "Imagine how surprised I was to find out how useful you are now, not just as a doctor."

No, this viper is not a dream. The heebie jeebies that plague me every time I'm in his presence start crawling across my skin. Something's not right.

"In what capacity?" I ask, not really wanting to play his game.

"Collateral."

What the fuck does that mean? Confusion furrows my brow. I'm sure he sees it.

"You are my ticket to a negotiation. To winning this stupid war over the Gulf. Word on the street is your two men are combing every hidden, dark corner for you." Two? Shadow and Leo working together? "Your best friend's daddy is combing the entire state. All of them looking for you. So, imagine how surprised I was to learn you weren't just any ole doctor, you were special and connected. Even your parents are important. Butters really lucked into you at that hospital. We hit the jackpot when we relocated you."

You mean stole me, jackass.

Christ he looks like an evil gremlin. At least that's how my brain sees him now. You know, the ones you feed after midnight and they turn into evil bastards, yeah, that's him, the evilest of the bastards.

So far, I take from this impromptu conversation: Leo and Shadow are looking for me, even after I didn't speak to him for a few days. Even after I broke one of their hearts.

I didn't want to test mine and Leo's relationship so soon or like this, but it does warm my heart he's looking. I sigh in relief. Someone is looking for me and knowing Leo, he will never stop. Shadow won't either.

"I must admit, this is a rather serendipitous outcome. Low and behold, you are our ticket to owning ports, young lady. They'll give anything to get you back I reckon, even Lake Charles and his dirty little secret from the US government, the Havana port. Texas ports aren't enough anymore, even though Houston is the busiest port on the Gulf; I want more and you're going to get it for me." The entire time Pete has spoken he's been pacing back and forth in my little prison cell, thinking and gloating.

I doubt Rock will give up a port just for me, let alone two. I've always been friendly with Birdie's dad but even I know he's a shrewd businessman and I'm just, well me, his daughter's best friend, big whoop.

And besides, what idiot limits themselves when they have a bargaining tool. Just ask for everything, that's the ceiling you want to start negotiations at, but whatever. I'm not telling this psycho how to be insane.

"I'm sending word to Rock soon and we will see if he's willing to negotiate for your safe return." He's practically giddy with the thought of getting a port for his nefarious dealings. God, I hate these guys. I wish the Southern Devils Society would just wipe them off the Earth. Saints, my brown ass.

I continue to sit on the bed just staring at him. I've learned in god knows how long I've been here already, in that amount of time to just keep quiet. In the beginning I tried to get them to let me go but it was useless. They think I can help and save every member that comes in here. I'm not sure what they are expecting but I'm not a fucking miracle worker, and when I said so much the other day, I got a backhand to the face by Pete when I was told if he doesn't live, I die. Now, my goddamn lip is split and my cheek is so sore.

Come to find out that was his third-in-command bleeding out from a stab wound.

What little bit I've seen of this place seems like a concrete building with rooms. I'm in one that opens up to a hallway. Right next to my room to the right is a door that leads into a bigger room for surgeries or treating patients. Windowless too. It has a drain on the tiled floor and I shudder to think this might have been some type of torture chamber before it became my surge unit. The walls here seem to be finished and painted a stark white. Reminds me of what hell would look like for me. Oh, imagine that…I'm already in hell.

They've stocked it fairly well for medical supplies. I've been able to take care of what seems like dozens of people and I've not had any issues like running out of supplies. Not sure where they got most of the equipment and I have decided I'm not asking. The less I know about these criminals the better.

"I'll keep you posted, Doc. In the meantime, I'll have Hercules bring you something special to eat, befitting of your station in life, madam."

Yes! I get information from Hercules if I turn on the charm. He loves it. Maybe he has a little crush on me. I think he actually feels sorry for me. Unlike the others who are indifferent to me and don't give a flying fuck.

Also, whoever gave him that nickname was a cruel son of a bitch with a wicked sense of humor. Hercules is about five-seven, I'm technically about an inch or so taller than him. He's skinny. There's no way he could take me in a fight, not since Shadow and Danger formally trained Birdie and I in our first year of college. I could break this man like a twig.

A sharp pain pierces my heart, knowing those lessons are where my crush on Shadow developed.

My problem is even though I can take him, can I take the big guys that hang out outside my door? And where the fuck is the exit? I'd never make it and he never comes in here with any weapons on him…that I know of. Maybe he does have a weapon and that's why he's always leaning up against the far wall.

However, his greatest asset to me is his knowledge and his loose tongue.

Pete turns and leaves me in here alone again. Now I just wait for Hercules-the-Mighty-Small to bring me whatever is chef's special and tell me things I need to know. For starters, how long I have been here. I need to demand answers.

I'm going to be trained like a Pavlovian dog with the sound of these fucking keys—it's either food or fight for someone's life.

More keys jingle at the door and a zip of excitement zaps through me. I rub my hands together like an evil villain. A super nervous villain but one, nonetheless.

Hercules has been the one to bring me my food every day, every time. I finally wore him down many meals ago to talk to me. Who knew he was such a whore for gossiping, one of my favorite past times to listen to.

He told me on the first couple of meals he has orders to stay here while I eat and watch me because I'm not to be trusted with the utensils. So, he sits, and waits, and watches. And I ask questions to listen to him talk.

Me—Where are we?

Hercules—Near the state line.

What state?

Me—Is this a far drive from your apartment, you said in Houston, yeah?

Hercules—Maybe an hour. An hour which way? Closest to New Orleans?

A few meals later.

Me—Where are you from? Tell me a little something about yourself. Where did you grow up?

Hercules—I grew up around Detroit.

Me—I bet this is different from back home, huh?

Hercules—Yeah, being by the gulf like this sucks because of the bugs and humidity. Makes my hair frizz too much.

By powers of deduction, I've learned I'm somewhere between Houston and Lake Charles, I'm guessing Beaumont.

Another conversation comes back to me,

Me—I wish I could call my mom and tell her I'm ok. I know she's so worried. (I really hammed it up.) *Would you let me use your phone for a quick call?*

Hercules—I'm sorry, even if I wanted to, I can't. There are jammers all over the building, no reception for anything except Panhead's weird satellite phone.

Ok, that was depressing news. So much for trying to make a call from this place.

My heart races as I set eyes on Hercules with my tray. I don't even care what it is. So far, they've fed me decently and I can't complain. They don't feed me normal meals such as breakfast food. It's a mix of entrees for like lunch or dinner. As an OCD person who has to eat breakfast foods for breakfast before anything else for the day, no matter the time of day, it has really been fucking with me. Nothing in this compound feels right to me.

It's exhausting existing here. I imagine burning the place down on a regular basis. Dancing around the building naked with a torch. Very heathen of me.

I smile brightly at Hercules and turn on the charm. I might be a little hurt when the Southern Devils kill him. Maybe I can save him. Talk to SDS on his behalf.

"Hey, Zhar." He returns my smile.

"Hi, Hercules."

"I was told to make up something special for you," He lifts off the lid over the plate, "I fixed you baked rosemary chicken, sweetened glazed baby carrots, a baked potato with cheese, butter and shallots. Oh, and I remembered, cookies 'n cream ice cream for dessert, your favorite."

I'm touched he remembered, but not enough to let it derail my plan.

"Thank you so much, Hercules," eyelashes batting at him coyly and smiling like a supermodel. He sets the tray on the cot in front of me, nervous, as usual. I don't have a table to eat at. Barbarians. I've been eating on my bed sitting crisscross applesauce while he leans up against the wall by the door.

"How are you doing today?"

He grins at me, flattered that I care to ask. I know how to stroke a man's ego. Just because I haven't used my feminine wiles in a while doesn't mean I forgot how to use them. And honey, I've been using them on this man.

I was born to flirt.

"I'm good. Tired but I'm hanging in there."

I fake a small pout, "Aww. Is there anything I can help with?" I ask him then plaster on my prettiest smile, "I like to think we moved on to friends now, Hercules. Do you want to be my friend in here?"

"Yes ma'am, we're friends. I'm like your best friend in here." He blushes and smiles. I've got him. YES!

"I'm happy to have someone I can trust in here. I'm still so scared, Herc. It's the unknown. Like I don't even know how long I've been here. Do you know how confusing and sad it is to not know time? Like what's the date even?"

"It's January fifth."

Oh god! I've been here nearly two and a half weeks. Two fucking weeks. I try not to let my panic show. Instead, I smile softly at him again, "Thank you. I hadn't realized we've been friends for over two weeks."

"Yes ma'am. I have something special planned for Three King's Day tomorrow. I remember you saying you always celebrated it with your best friend's family and you were really sad to miss it this year," he sheepishly tells me.

I place my hand on my heart, "Oh, Hercules, I'm so touched. Thank you for the kind gesture. I can't wait to see my surprise."

I eat more of my food and stop to tell him, "This is an excellent meal. I love it." I'm not lying, it really is good. It should be since he's an aspiring chef.

This makes him blush and look away. Well, I can't see his blush on his dark skin, but I imagine it for my own dramatic purposes. I'm putting on a good show here.

He still has peach fuzz for fuck's sake but he's an easy target. Gangly, dorky, outcast, low self-esteem—yeah, he's perfect to fall for any woman who gives him a smidgen of attention.

And I'm slathering him with attention every time he walks in here.

He doesn't like to talk about his life too much, whereas I'm over here rambling on and on about my life, but I'm going to push some personal questions at him and see if he answers.

"Do you have any other job besides cooking for me?" I love these carrots. They are made just like Birdie's dad's cook makes them for Thanksgiving dinner. I wasn't lying when I said I've been fed good. It helps I've made the cook fall in lust with me.

"No, I'm a college kid. Going to culinary school. I'm in my last year." Bingo! No fucking wonder this food has been so good, he's trained not just beginning his education.

"I must say, Hercules, this has been some of the best food I've ever had and I'm honored to be served your food every meal."

Flattery will get you everywhere with him.

He clears his throat, standing there awkwardly, "Thank you," he squeaks out.

"No, thank you. I was starving." I really was. I never know when they will bring me one meal to the next.

"Can you tell me what time it is, please?"

"I'm not supposed to."

"Please? My mind is so confused, Herc." Batting of lashes, pouty lip in place. "Will you set it right for me? Help me get my bearings, honey. Only you can help me understand how time works in here." *Back off a little*. I might be laying it on too thick.

He looks at his watch and mutters, "It's eleven at night."

Holy fuck, I'm eating close to midnight. I would never eat this late. I believe my body still recognizes to some degree when nighttime comes by how tired I am. I'm normally in bed by now. Five-thirty in the morning comes early. Doctor life. Good to know my circadian rhythm hasn't been knocked askew yet.

I make a show of stretching my arms over my head and jutting out my tits, then I yawn, "No wonder I'm so tired." I put my arms back down and settle in to eat my ice cream. I sigh and drop my shoulders, making my tits bounce. "Have I told you how much I love your cooking? It's some of the best I've ever had. My parents have a Michelin star chef in their kitchen and this is still better than his."

His smile is worth gold, crinkling his eyes and showing pearly whites. Hmm, yes, he likes praise. Good to know.

"Do you know if they plan to keep me in here all the time? Is this my life now?" I give him puppy dog eyes to get any details I can weasel out of him.

He shifts his body weight off the wall and onto the other leg. He crosses his arms in front of him and sighs, "I don't know, Zhar. They don't tell me shit. I'm just the cook. None of this is what I signed up for. I can't get out of it. They told me I was spending too long in here and I was talking to you too much. I'm not even sure what I can say to you anymore."

"Why not? What do you mean?" I breathe, enraptured by his words.

He shakes his head and his jaw clenches, "I didn't know they did any of this. Like this shit is for the movies, right? So, how the hell did I get mixed up in this?" Hercules starts pacing, getting agitated. "Panhead's threatened all our families and we believe it. He's insane. He has proof he's watching them. I can't put my grandma and sister into this mess, so I do what I'm told. It's been a huge regret, joining these fuckers."

Through my shock, I stand up and cross over to him and place my hand on his arm. "I'm so sorry. Hercules, what is your real name? Can I know that?"

He looks into my eyes and I notice his are more a yellow-green hazel. "My name is Shawn."

"Shawn, thank you for taking care of me and I'm going to give you some advice, even if I go hungry. Run. My boyfriends are coming for me and they will spare no one."

His smile drops. He stands up fully, "What do you mean? The ones you've been talking about?"

"Yes, remember, my boyfriends are third and fourth in command in the Southern Devils Society. My best friend since childhood is Rock's daughter. They're coming, I know it. I can feel it. They won't let me go. They are going to annihilate every one of you when they get here. And they will find me, make no mistake. I need you to leave and not come back. Get yourself out of here. I'll be fine."

Shawn runs his fingers through his curly hair and blows out a breath, "Holy shit Zharia, I can't just leave you."

"Yes, you can! And you will. They let you leave here, right?"

"Yeah, I'm the one who goes to the grocery store, other than that, I live here right now. Panhead won't let me leave but I didn't really mind since I was on break from school. I have to get back soon to Houston because classes start back up in two days. I can't just quit. I worked too hard for my scholarship."

"Great! Leave now." I try shoving him towards the door.

He plants his feet, "Zharia I can't leave, it's the middle of the night." Good point.

"Tomorrow, as soon as you can. Promise me."

"They'll kill me if they find me."

"Run to New Orleans. As a matter of fact, don't call the police, call a man named Jaques Chavanet, Shadow Baer or Lincoln LaFleur. Repeat those names to me so I know you have them."

"I've heard of these men, who hasn't. They're famous. Like nationwide famous. I know how much weight they carry."

"Then you know what's coming for you. Call them Shawn, please. Tell them I'm here. Then get as far away as you can. Rock will harbor you and take you in once I explain to him what happened. Finish school in NOLA."

He acts like he's thinking it over. I shot my shot. It's up to him now. Please tell me all this flirting has paid off.

"I—"

The door swings open—this fucking door is the bane of my shitty existence, always opening at the most inopportune goddamn times—the guard gestures for Shawn to leave. He looks away from me and picks up the tray, walking out of the room. He doesn't turn back to look at me. The door swings shut with a slam.

Once again I'm left in silence, but I'm closer. So much closer.

They're coming…

CHAPTER 24 – GUNNEY

It's been eighteen days since my girl disappeared. Eighteen motherfucking days of pure hell. No one knows what to say anymore. There's nothing to say, unless someone shouts 'I found her.'

The one thing we do know is that the Lone Star Saints have her. Somewhere. Their leader, Panhead, sent a message to Rock asking for a trade. He will give Zharia back for control of the Havanna and Lake Charles ports.

This is why we were thinking he's in Lake Charles. He would be stupid enough to set up shop in our territory like he's the big dick in charge.

This idiot has more nuts than a fruitcake. Brave fucker too. Or he's certifiably insane.

Right now, he's holding all the cards.

That leads to where I am. Shadow and I came to Lake Charles with a small group of guys to search around before heading further into Texas. We're poking the wasp's nest but we don't give a fuck.

Both me and Shadow are bone weary and exhausted. We aren't sitting around waiting. We have hit the streets in all the neighboring towns. Now we sit at a big-name brand steak house in Lake Charles where Shadow and I have killed three baskets of rolls. Goddamn they're so good.

"Why do you think the tracker isn't working still the closer we get to Texas?" I ask him quietly from across the table. "You still think they have her stationed in one place with a jammer?"

We have to be careful of who hears us at the surrounding tables. You never know if there's some LSS infiltrating Lake Charles since it's so close to their territory. We know they are around but still best to keep our conversation private.

"Has to be some type of cell phone jammer. I've never known it not to work. The signal is being interrupted somehow. I just need it to slip up for two seconds and it will find her." Shadow looks around the room, trying to see if he can pick out any Lone Star Saints members here. I know he wants to beat the shit out of every one of them and I have to keep him in check. "I have a very loud alarm set for the app if she ever comes on radar. We aren't going to miss it. Even in here."

For as calm, cool, and calculated as Shadow is, Zharia's disappearance has derailed some of his control. He's a little bit more on edge and snappy. Same as I. Same as a lot of us.

We are meeting the chapter president in about two hours at their clubhouse here. The Lake Charles chapter president is a good guy. He's constantly recruiting and keeping his associates in line. His numbers are up and order is maintained. This port and the city are a profitable one and he and his guys reap the rewards. There's no way Tank is allowing anything to happen in his city that feeds his men. He shuts down squabbles between SDS and LSS all the time.

"Have you stopped to think maybe this isn't LSS? It's some random kidnapping and Panhead is lying about having her? I mean, it's not going to be unheard of in our city. It's one of the most dangerous. He's bound to have heard of her disappearance and our search." The thought has occurred to me numerous times this might not be LSS. Lord knows any Saint I've met has been a fucking liar.

"I have thought of that. Why haven't they asked for a ransom then? They're money hungry sons-a-bitches. Why just keep her like this? It makes no sense. Why didn't he make his demands sooner? Those bastards gave Rock an ultimatum within the hour of snatching Birdie from Danger."

True. The Saints sent a link to a live camera feed of Birdie and Pierre in captivity. They did not use a jammer at that time and that's how we knew where she was. Her tracker worked. Panhead Pete must have learned a lesson from that jacked up kidnapping Grim died for. The jammer is a precaution.

By now, he has to know we're coming and we plan to kill him. If not, he's about to learn more life lessons.

"I'm tired, Shadow, so tired."

"Me too, man."

"We can't stop though. I try not to think about her out there, alone, being held against her will. I've imagined the worst. My mind is punishing me," I tell him.

"I got the same thoughts, brother. I wouldn't admit it to anyone else, but I'm starting to get scared for her. We have to keep faith we'll find her. No matter what. We love her too much to just give up. I'll understand if you want to."

"Fuck no I don't want to. I want her safe back in my arms," I say, "As I'm sure you do too."

He nods while cutting his steak, "Then we keep going."

Tank leads this meeting like a natural. He was a good choice to pull up through the ranks. Travares and Danger did well in training him to handle these situations. Both of them have stellar leadership training from where they were in Delta Force in the Army and they saw his potential and led him to his position now. I guess Army guys aren't so bad. At least they're not Air Force. I say this as an ex-Navy SEAL who still believes the Navy is superior. Don't even get me started on the insane Marines I've known.

"Alright men, we come together at this special church meeting to go over the disappearance of the old lady of these gentlemen. I introduce Shadow and Gunney from the homebase New Orleans chapter. They are your upper leadership, top five, and the Saints stole their old lady. I'm going to turn it over to them and they will bring you up to speed. Gentlemen," Tank moves away from the center of the speaking area, gesturing for us to take the center stage and lead.

"Hello, brothers. I'm Shadow," he jerks a thumb over to me, "This is Gunney. Our girlfriend Doctor Zharia Davish disappeared eighteen days ago from the hospital she works at and owns. She's a prestigious surgeon and they picked her up in the parking garage of her facility. She's on camera walking up the ramp. On the other side of the ramp, the camera was tampered with and rendered useless. We aren't sure who took her, but we have a strong suspicion of it being LSS. As you will remember, it was almost two years ago they stole Rock's daughter, Birdie. Zharia is Birdie's best friend since childhood. We don't know if they knew the connection before taking her or the connection is the reason she was taken."

A voice from somewhere in the middle of the room speaks up, "So why don't we storm their clubhouse and kill them all?"

I'm for it. Let's spill some fucking blood. Sounds of approval circulate in the room, calls for violence, answers of death to all.

Danger's voice slams to the forefront of my mind, *"Don't kill anyone until I get there."*

I hold up a hand to stop the bloodlust, "While I agree with the sentiment, Rock does not want us to storm their clubhouse until we have one hundred and ten percent proof it was them. We aren't sure their president isn't lying, you know how they are," I say.

"What do you need from us?" another brother asks.

"We need people scouring the area. Any abandoned buildings, any factories, any abandoned looking houses. Pretend to sell Girl Scout cookies or whatever you can do to get an in, just get a feel for these places. We need people beating the streets and ears to the ground. Any rumors we can come up with and follow up as a lead. Whatever we can drum up," Shadow tells them.

"Do you have any pics of her?" another associate says loudly.

"Yes we brought a few. Zharia is thirty-two years old, about five-eight, one hundred and fifty pounds, Indian-Asian descent, very long, waist length black hair, brown eyes, one tattoo on her wrist of a piece of bread with arms and legs. She was last seen wearing purple scrubs with white sneakers." Shadow holds up a few pictures and starts handing them out while I talk. "Please pass them around and get a good look. We have a few more to take with you to show people. Any help you can give us we are grateful for."

Tank speaks up, "We will give as much assistance as we can. I imagine y'all are out of your minds with stress and worry." He looks out across the big room to all the men sitting there, "As I would imagine any one of us would feel if our old ladies came up missing." A chorus of men agreeing sounds off in the clubhouse. Tank looks back at us, "We stand with you, brothers."

"We appreciate that," Shadow says, his gruff voice full of emotion but he's trying to keep it together, not showing weakness. I've been around him for so long now, I can tell his voice is packed with feelings of loss, anxiety and stress. We've done great at keeping it together, but we are fragile now, about to break. We've already broken down in front of each other, and the other comforted the upset one. This has gone on for too long. How much is one human supposed to take?

Whatever we're going through, she's going through worse, so we push on.

I refuse to feel sorry for myself when she's out there and they are doing god knows what, and she's suffering at their hands.

There's no rest for the wicked and we are out for blood.

Once church has been concluded, Shadow and I head out to a few of the local shithole bars to ask around. We get to one and you can tell from the vibe this is a rough place to be. Not worried. Shadow and I are some rough motherfuckers that can handle themselves. The other guys should be worried.

We show around her pic to the handful of people at this dingy bar when a new guy walks in. He doesn't wear a vest with a cut but we can tell he's a biker. Member? We don't know.

I walk up to him, "Hey man, could you look at this picture and tell me if you've seen her or heard anything about her?"

He scoffs at me and says, "No, now get the fuck outta my way."

He makes to walk by me, and Shadow comes up to block his way, "You can just look and tell us or we can make you look. Choose wisely, easy or hard way?"

The man actually laughs and says, "I'd like to see you try."

This guy is either stupid or doesn't care he's about to get his ass beat. We are wearing our cuts and he can clearly see we are part of the Southern Devils Society.

"Did you lose your piece of pussy?"

That is the remark that snaps Shadow's patience. Quick as lightning, Shadow reaches out and punches his face, staggering the loud mouth fucker back against the pool table, almost knocking the guy to the floor.

The bartender yells, "Take it outside boys," then cocks a gun.

I grab Shadow's elbow and tell him, "He's not worth it. Let's hit the next one."

Shadow sizes up the guy when he stands back up again and knocks his shoulder as he passes by. Tank asked us not to kill anyone or cause too many violent waves in his area. This is the only reason we are walking away. Respect.

"Fuck you. I hope you end up with a life of bad sex," Shadow curses him. That's a horrible curse to get stuck with. Brilliant.

On to the next bar. It's a bit more of a crowd and seedier. We walk in and people stop to look at us. The past few days we've been putting it out there that Southern Devils Society is at your backdoor and we don't give a fuck how you feel about it. I've only gotten to beat up two LSS members.

A few people will speak to us at the bar. They graciously looked at Zharia's pictures and took our calling cards to call us with any information, day or night.

I'd call this crowd half-friendly and half-aggressive. Once we run out of people to talk to we head out the door. The street isn't quiet and it seems to be a busy strip of restaurants and bars. We've hit every single one of them. It's time to call it a night.

We hang a right between the buildings, to the back of the parking lot. When we round the corner there's three guys from inside. I assume they have something to say and want to launch a formal complaint about our presence.

Since I'm standing behind Shadow I make sure they can't see me reach for my piece under my cut, tucked into my waistband. Shadow isn't as lucky to pull his, but have no fear, I got him covered. I slip my hand up under his vest and grab his piece too, holding them both in one hand. At some point I'm passing one off, either to my other hand or into his.

"Howdy, boys," the smallest of the bunch says. No wonder he travels with the two idiots behind him. This guy is Zharia's size. From what I've heard from both Shadow and Zharia, Zhar is a pretty good scrapper. She could take this guy. I bet my pinky on it.

Neither of us gives him a response.

"It seems you ain't welcome here."

"Says who?" Shadows asks nonchalantly. I hear the pissed off tone though. We don't have the time nor energy for these stupid fuckers.

"LSS."

"Is that so?" Shadow nods his head, "Tell ya what, you tell us where our girlfriend is and we'll let you live."

The three morons laugh at that like it's hilarious. When they aren't looking, I shove Shadow's gun into his hand and reach up behind him, under his vest, and get his other, smaller gun. No use racking on these boys, one's already in the chamber. That's how we roll.

"You got middle. Ready whenever you are number three."

"Now," is the smooth response I receive from Shadow. Simultaneously we lift arms and train each one on a different idiot. Shadow has his almost to the forehead of little man.

"It seems you are on the wrong side of the line. This is SDS territory and we are on a mission tonight to exterminate as many as we can, unless they tell us where our girlfriend is. So, what will it be?" Shadow cocks his revolver. The click reverberates through the quiet parking lot, echoing off buildings.

One of the larger beer bellied guys puts his hands up and says, "Wait! I don't want no trouble."

"That's what most men with guns in their faces say," Shadow taunts them.

"Fuck you, Indian. You think you can come into our house and throw your dicks around and just throw us out? The fuck that's happening." Little man thinks he has the upper hand.

"Shut up, Kyle, you're gonna get us killed," Tweedle Idiot says.

"Shadow, sir, on behalf of myself and my four babies at home with my wife, I don't know nothing about your old lady. I've never seen her or heard anything about her. Please let me go home to my family." Tweedle Dipshit looks like he's about to cry and shit himself at the same time.

I'm playing backup, this is Shadow's show. He technically trumps me in club hierarchy and I'm letting him handle this. He needs some fun, lately he's been a bear to be around. Killing fools is a passion of his.

"You're lucky I'm in love and understand. You, go." Shadow nods him on, "Get the fuck outta here and turn in your patch. You're getting lucky tonight."

The man runs I tell ya. He throws himself into his truck and it roars to life. He's quick to step on the gas and get the hell out of Dodge. Smart man.

Tweedle Idiot thinks he's smooth reaching behind his back.

"I wouldn't do that if I were you," Shadow taunts him some more.

Little Shit spits at Shadow's feet, "For what you did to Grim, fuck you both. I hope Panhead's done raped and killed her."

Right in sync triggers are pulled. Stupid men drop dead. All is quiet again. All that's left is gun smoke and 2 corpses. All in a night's work.

Shadow turns around and claps me on the shoulder, "Thanks, man."

I stare back at his intense gaze and shrug, "That's what brothers are for."

He puts his guns back in his holsters and says, "Come on. I'm hungry and tired."

The way he kisses me so hard and deep makes me think his tongue's caressing the tops of my lungs. Either way, my chest flutters and my butterflies are frantic with excitement. His sexy breathless voice asks me, "Do you want to start by laying on your back or bending over? The choice is yours tonight, baby girl. Let me worship you."

This dream feels so familiar. Almost as if I've been here before. I feel all the emotions—sad, loss, happiness, arousal, love.

"On my back so I can see how lost you are for me. Let me see that face when I make you come squeezing this tight pussy."

"Fuck, Zharia, that delicious mouth."

Shadow picks me up off the couch in his living room and carries me to his huge bed, kissing and nuzzling my neck. There's plenty of room to play in here. He can toss me around and I still wouldn't find the edge.

We quickly strip our clothes off. His eyes roam my body hungrily and I feel fire lighting my skin from where his gaze touches me. I show him my nakedness with pride.

I've never been one to be ashamed of my body or try to hide it from a partner.

Shadow's hands roam all over my body, and I shiver from his touch. "Please," I ask, no I beg, for him to ease the fire erupting inside me.

"Does my pretty pussy want me that bad?"

"Yes," my own breathless voice answers him. Lava runs through my veins now. I may want to see him lost for me, but I'm just as lost for him.

I run my hands up his muscular forearms and love every piece of hair that tickles my palms. He lays above me, staring lovingly into my eyes. "Zharia," he whispers as he enters me slowly, stretching me, my wetness guiding his way home.

Every time he slides into me, the butterflies in my body scream with happiness and flutter about down to every last extremity. I positively vibrate with love for him.

And that terrifies me.

Then his hands are all over me soothing the fear, one tangled in my hair, where he rests on his elbow, the other gripping my hip as he traps my leg against him. My knee rests on his ribs so he can get deeper. Our breaths mingle and he still looks me in the eyes like I'm the center of his universe.

What I see there makes my heart soar, but it makes me so, so sad. We are two different stars heading on the opposite trajectory. We just happened to have met in passing and together we shine brightly for a brief moment in time, soon to part and be back on our own paths.

However fun this may be, it isn't lasting. But he's staring at me like it is for him.

"Zharia, fuck," him saying my name makes me whimper. Shadow slips his arm under my knee and pushes my leg up, making me cry out and press my head back into the pillow.

Shadow takes this opportunity to bite the side of my neck, claiming me in his animalistic way. The pain makes my pussy quiver around him. I fucking love it. He kisses up my neck onto my face, all the while growling low.

"Shadow, you feel so good."

His lips crash on mine as he steals my breath kissing me, snapping his hips to the rhythm I love so well and moaning into my mouth. I fucking love his sounds too.

He pulls back and drops my leg, only to sit back on his heels, spreading my thick thighs further apart. He circles my engorged clit with his deft fingers. Suddenly, he slides his strong arms under me and lifts me up to straddle him while he leans back.

"Fuck me Zhar, ride my body and take your pleasure, poppet, I'm yours," his lips drag up my chest and neck.

I do as I'm told and I lower as far as I can go on his cock making us both moan. I rock my hips and grind down on him. Shadow's arms are locked around me, one hand drifts down to my bottom dangerously low and I feel one of his fingers work their way into my ass.

My head comes down to his, forehead to forehead, breathing in his air and our combined pants the only sound in the room. "Do it, finger fuck my ass while I ride your cock."

"Fuck, poppet." A few thrusts of his finger in my ass and I'm set off, spiraling up and over the clouds. "Shadow," I cry out, "Fuck, oh my god."

He lets my pussy pulsate around him before I'm pulling his climax out of him. His arms get tighter and his raspy voice calls to me as he comes inside me, "Zharia, my poppet, fuck babe."

Both out of breath, chests heaving, his hands come up to my cheeks as he pulls my face away from his, "Zharia Ishani, I lov—"

The door swings open suddenly—FUCKING DOOR, banging into the wall and a clearly distraught Pete walks in with blood splattered on his dress shirt. I'm immediately sitting up on the makeshift bed once I grasp how he looks. My hair is disheveled, my face flush from my sex dream and eyes bleary. I'm sure I'm a hot mess. My memory dream fades away like smoke in the wind.

"I need your help, Zharia," his rough voice says.

In all this time, Pete has never been the one to come gather me for surgeries and lead me over to their treatment room. I'm alarmed to say the least. This isn't his usual taunting tone. Something is seriously wrong.

I stand up and wipe my sweaty palms down my sides. My groin feels heavy from the memory dream and I desperately try to shake its after effects. My weight shifts from foot to foot. "O-ok. What do you need?"

I'm always so nervous because I know at any minute they could hit me, kill me, rape me or sell me. These guys don't fuck around and I'm not trying to get more trauma or die today. No *FAFO* for me, thanks.

"We have a patient incoming. I need them treated as the number one VIP and just know if they die, you die."

I try to swallow over the lump in my throat. "Who is it?"

"My wife," Pete croaks out.

My heart slams against my ribs. I never expected that to come out of his mouth. Pete is a family man yet deals in flesh? What a sick bastard.

"Ok." I nod. "How long until she's here?"

"Ten minutes."

"Why isn't she going to a real hospital?"

"Hospitals ask too many questions. They'll immediately think I've done it. Besides you can handle it."

"What happened?" I almost dread finding out. I rub my eyes and gather my tangled hair up in the extra thick hair ties they supplied me with.

"She's a security guard at a copper wire manufacturing warehouse at night. She was going for a walk-about for her security check points and was attacked by some low life scum trying to steal copper from the company. The other guard found her and called me. He's abandoned post to bring her here. I'm glad they didn't take her." Seriously rich coming from this guy.

Karma is my girlfriend and she's very much real. I'm alive here witnessing her eternal glory.

"What time is it?" My head feels swimmy, like I've not gotten enough sleep and I'm damn near loopy. I swear on all that's holy I only get to sleep a few hours at a time and it's beginning to wear on me. It reminds me of Birdie telling me that's what motherhood is like. She calls it the No Sleep Elite Club.

"It's two in the morning."

Midnights have become my afternoons. Time is not real.

I can only nod. No wonder I feel rough. I've only been asleep like two hours. "Can you give me any more information about the attack? Like what injuries she's sustained?"

He almost growls with frustration. "I was told she was hit in the face, her eye, cheek and nose." He stops pacing and puts his hand to his forehead, "And she's been shot. In the stomach and left for dead."

Holy fucking Christ.

The full realization of the severity of the situation is washing over me like a bucket of ice-cold water. There's a huge margin for error, a giant possibility of her dying. I need a miracle on my side. If I have at least one guardian angel on my side, please let them be sober right now because I really need all the help I can get. This shit is insane. This is Hollywood movie bullshit.

Zharia, how did your life end in this way. This lady has a high probability of dying.

"Ok." I rub my palms down my thighs again. My nerves are showing. "Alright, can you take to me to prepare the surgery room, please?"

He nods in anguish and heads to the door. Speaking over his shoulder to the handful of guards surrounding the outside of the door, "Make sure she has everything she needs and is ready. I'll be in the bay waiting."

I guess it's show time.

"She needs blood and antibiotics and I need more lidocaine or something stronger. You're going to have to let me go or she's not going to make it."

It's been the argument the past five desperately needed minutes. Minutes I do not have to spare. We are talking about Panhead Pete's wife. She's in bad shape. She needs blood in a bad way and there's none here.

But there's a blood bank .4 miles away a guard said. It won't take but a couple of minutes to get there and a few more back.

"Look Pete, you're running out of time here. I have to get the blood and antibiotics into her or we're going to lose her. Let me go, I beg you. Keep as many guards with me as you want so I don't run, but if you keep fucking around, she's going to die on this table."

"FUCK!" Pete screams while gripping his head with his blood stained hands. He takes in a few shuddering breaths. His bloodshot eyes meet mine, "Go, but you have fifteen minutes. Everyone in the hall, take her to New Horizons and get her in there. I don't care how. Now go," he barks.

I waste no time hustling out of the surgery room. As soon as I'm out in the hallway, my eyes clash with Shawn's. I see he didn't leave like I advised him to. It's his life I guess.

The guards file out in front of me and my anxiety is on high alert, head on a swivel, taking in my surroundings. This is the first time I've seen the facility.

It's like an old office building. A large urgent care maybe. It's weird. It truly is a mini hospital. I'm in awe looking around, so much so, that I run into the back of the guard in front of me and squeak out a 'sorry.'

Once the doors open they throw me in a big black SUV. Why do gangsters always have to own a blacked-out SUV? Is there some requirement?

It literally took two minutes to get here. It took another minute to pick the lock and boom; I'm in my element. I quickly get to work finding what I need me. Thank fuck, Pete's wife had a Red Cross card in her wallet where she's a regular donor and it has her blood type on it. See, those things are actually helpful in emergencies.

Chapter 27 – Shadow

   The shrill noise sounding like a freight train jolts me from my sleep. WAKE UP BEAR! I'm in our shared hotel room. My phone's going off, sounds like cops are chasing it the way it's screaming.

   I pick it up and my bleary eyes search for the notifications. There's a red one and I see it's the tracker.

   Blue dot. There's a fucking blue dot! A blue dot moves on the screen! Holy fuck.

   "**GUNNEY**!! Wake up!" I jump out of bed to a groaning Gunney. I move over to his bed on his side of the room wearing just a pair of boxer briefs. I don't give a fuck. At this point we've made peace between us and just accepted the nakedness.

My heart is pounding out of my chest. Fire is zooming through my veins.

"What's happening?" he asks sleepily.

I turn the phone around to face him. Blinking a few good times, his eyes go wide and his face lights up when he sees the blue dot. "Holy fuck, it's her," he breathes out like the wind has been knocked out of him. "She's alive. It's her!"

"Call Danger. Hurry." I run from his bed back over to mine by the bathroom. I start throwing on clothes, then dashing to the bathroom to brush my teeth and splash water on my face. I actually had a shot of whiskey last night at the Lake Charles club house with the guys who have been helping us the past couple of days. I still taste the nacky stuff.

It was enough to give me this awful taste in my mouth. We came back to the hotel room and just passed out from exhaustion. We've only slept for a few hours.

We're supposed to head back home tomorrow.

Or is it today?

It's 2:06 AM. She's currently moving on the screen. They're probably moving her because they know we've gotten too close. "She's moving!" I yell out at Gunney while his phone rings to Danger.

I hear Gunney from the other side of the room with the speakerphone on, he's slightly breathless, in disbelief. "Danger, we got her. We got the signal. There's a blue dot and it's moving." This is the first good lead. It's a fucking relief, a fucking godsend.

Danger's rough sleepy voice says, "Fuck. Where is she?" I hear the blankets rustling and Birdie's soft voice, "What is it, Linx?"

I'm already pulling up the app on my laptop to pinpoint the location and get this info over to Travares. He's our number one resident hacker on the team. The best in the nation.

There's not much that nosy fucker can't find out or crack into like a stealth ninja with a keyboard. I know he's still up. Man hardly ever sleeps, he's one of those sleepless elite people minus the kids. I send the coordinates over to him in email and text him it's an emergency.

He answers immediately and says he's on it. We need to know exact location. He's going to pull street cameras, building cameras, any info to have eyes on her.

I hear Danger mumble to Birdie that it's club business, he's gotta take this call. I hear what I assume is his bedroom door closing with a faint click and then he whisper-yells, "Are you fucking serious?"

"Yeah, boss, I swear to god on my life."

I walk back into the room and say, "Beaumont Texas is where she's at. It's an hour away."

"Shadow, now don't even fucking think about it. You're going to wait until I get there."

"Negative."

"Motherfuck! Yes you will." Danger rants into the phone. "You two are not enough to go into a nest of rats with guns. It's a suicide mission and you fucking know it. Let me pull together some men and I'll be there as soon as I can. Let Tank know to wake up some men." He blows air through his lips and sounds like a raging bull. I know Danger is trying to get his bearings too. This news is a lot to take in.

"I'm not waiting. What if she needs us?" I can't *not* run to her. It chokes me up to think about her alone out there afraid.

"You're no good to her dead, brother. I need you to stand down until the cavalry comes. Give me four hours then we will go kill every last one of them." Danger uses his stern voice first and when that doesn't get through, he uses his compassionate voice.

"We need to move on this right now," I press.

"Shadow, no dude. I can't lose my best friend, don't do it. I know, but you have to be smart about it. Waiting for a plan of action is the smartest move."

"What if they take her back to where the jammer is? We'll never find her then." My voice cracks in heartache. My breath sits like acid in my chest at the thought of losing her again.

"I'm giving you a direct order, Shadow Theodore Baer."

Fuck he just government named me. Lots of people think Shadow is my road name, but it is indeed my actual name from my Comanche mother and father. "If you choose to disobey and don't get yourself killed, I'll have no choice but to take your patch. She's been alive this long, give me four hours, brother. I love you; I don't want to see you die when backup is on the way. Your choice, man. I'll be there in three and a half hours the soonest. I'll wake up the calvary." Danger doesn't threaten. I know he'll do it if I survive the ambush.

"Fine," I whisper before disconnecting.

CHAPTER 28 – ZHARIA

The past few hours I've sat in this room, bedside to Pete's wife, Bonnie, I've really thought about how I'm going to escape. Tonight was the prime opportunity and I didn't take it.

I don't know if it was stupid or smart. I can't outrun bullets. I may think I'm Superwoman most days but sadly I am not invincible and bulletproof. They wouldn't have hesitated to shoot me if I ran.

I sat in the backseat between two heavy duty guys I didn't feel brave enough to tangle with. When we reached the blood bank that happened to be a blood collection and containment lab, I also saw there was an urgent care next to it. This is perfect.

"I need into both these buildings," I told any one of these rabid ninjas that was listening.

We screeched into the parking lot, coming to a halt so quick it had me jerking forward in the seat, plastering my chest on the vinyl of the seat in front of me. Jesus Christ people. I still have to live through this ride.

I was roughly yanked out of the oversized SUV and thrown to another guy who was just equally as giant and scary as all the rest of the guys in tactical gear. I longingly looked around at my surroundings. *If I could just run and get away…*

"Don't even think about it," one of the black clad guards said to me before he pulled down his balaclava and the others followed the action.

"Are you like the shit show supervisor?" I sarcastically asked. My sarcasm is my natural defense against the less intelligent…such as these fine, upstanding citizens.

He just grunted and moved forward, and I'm pushed right behind him, giving me no choice but to follow.

"I take that as yes," I mumbled.

We looked like we were on some undercover mission, doing a little B&E, creeping through buildings on some reenactment of Mission Impossible. My life has turned into some cheesy action flick.

I was trying hard to stay calm. They were decked out in tactical gear, carrying many loaded firearms and knives looking all bad ass and shit...Then there's me, in a pair of hideous orange scrubs that's one size too big and my socks and Crocs. I lovingly refer to it as my prison attire.

At least I got provided clothes, right? Most victims don't even get that. I should consider myself a lucky hostage. Master has given Zharia a sock. Yay! I wish it worked that way.

After they gained access to the lab, I saw flashlight beams bouncing around everywhere as they searched the building. I hoped they didn't have to kill anyone. I didn't need that on my conscience too.

I creeped behind the militia men in front of me. There were a few behind me bringing up the rear. I remember trying hard not to clutch my pearls figuratively as my heart was beating out of my asshole just knowing I'm committing so many felonies and can lose my license.

I don't know if I can face that humiliation.

Sure, lose my life, no problem.

Lose my license to practice medicine—end of the freaking world for me.

There was a time in my life when I had thought that would have been the worst thing to ever happen to me. I went to school for a long time for that licensing.

I've come to learn during my time in my imprisonment, losing Leo, Shadow, Denver, the Fab Four, Sir Waffles; that's the worst thing in the world that would ever happen to me. I feel like I've lost all of them already. I'm still here fighting, fam.

There was a door in front of us that had a coded entry. Ninja number five whipped out some techy stuff and next thing I knew he's opening the door and they are ushering me in.

I wanted to say my dad made that thingamabobber. I recognized Dad's company logo on it. Idiots.

My heart leapt into my throat when I fully realized I was in the blood storage room. Bingo! One of the faceless guards, ninja number three or some shit, appeared beside me with a bag held open. I grabbed at least five bags of Bonnie's blood type and nodded, "We're good, I need next door now."

I followed the guard with the bag of blood out of the room. He led me straight to the front door we came in through and he didn't stop, but escorted me next door to the urgent care, where another ninja was waiting, holding open the door.

It's going to be such a shame when SDS comes to kill them.

Other ninjas were stationed around waiting for me. One waved me to a room near the back of the building. When I arrived, I realized it was like a storage closet full of samples of pharmaceuticals. I truly have my pick of the litter at this point. Only way I would have been more blessed is if it were an actual pharmacy.

Once again, an open bag appeared waiting beside me. I didn't delay; I found a few antibiotic IV bags to toss in the bag. I grabbed antibiotic ointment and anything else I thought I'd need.

We came back here just as fast and jerky as the first ride. I'm yanked back out of the SUV and hauled back into the building that looks like a vacant urgent care or doctor's office. It's cold and dark and it was raining. Even though it's January it's still humid. I'm still by the Gulf. It's a two-story building they are dragging me into. Looks like a doctor's office but yet an urgent care on the inside. This explains so much. I bet I'm staying in the janitor's closet. It's all coming together.

After she was given the blood and started on the IV antibiotic drip, her vitals picked up significantly, which made me very happy. I was able to operate on her and get her stable. It was touch and go there for a while but I didn't want to say anything. I was determined to keep myself alive by keeping her alive.

I have Bonnie on a good amount of painkillers. She's been sleeping for the past few hours. I'd hate to be her when she wakes up. She took a beat down. I still think she should be in the actual hospital but I stopped recommending that about the sixth time I was ignored.

My head propped in my hand starts to wobble again. I'm exhausted and falling asleep in the chair. I don't know how much more my body can tolerate before I pass out one day and don't wake up. I've never been run so ragged, even working the emergency room during a full moon. This place is like the Fourth of July on a full moon with endless beer on meth.

Pete comes into the make-shift hospital room and stops before me. He has his hands behind his back. "I'd like to thank you for saving my Bonnie."

Looking up at him, I numbly nod, "You're welcome." It's better when I pretend to be sincere.

In all honesty, Pete hasn't been a horrible captor to me. I've been fed, clothed, I can shower whenever I want. I'm just locked up in a guarded room and punished with sleep deprivation. It could always be worse.

Remember to be a grateful hostage, Zharia.

"Rock was given an ultimatum that ended an hour ago. He replied at 2:23 this morning with 'Fuck You.'"

My heart drops. I'm emotionally wrecked by that. I think of Rock as another father. I knew he would never give up a port for me, but to actually hear I'm not worth it is a gut wrencher.

I press my lips in a line and nod grimly, willing my eyes not to tear up. *Do not show this asshole anything. Don't let him know he's gotten to you.*

"Of course, this means we keep you and fortunately for you, you get to stay alive as we ransom your parents next. It would be sacrilege to kill such a brilliant mind."

Yes, I'm grateful for living but this is seriously no way to exist. I'm like the living dead now. What a glorious existence I have going for me. But I'm alive so it's all cool.

Jesus fuck, my thoughts are depressing.

This is the part where I wish I had a tracker like Birdie's. Danger found her within a few hours because of it. I'm not sure how long I've been here but I do know it's been well over two and a half weeks at this point.

"Do you have any requests for your stay with us?" Pete eyeballs me for an answer.

"Yes, I have one…let me go." And just for good measure I add on a curt little, "Please" at the end.

He has the audacity to laugh at me. To my face. Rude. "That's not happening, princess." Eww, when he says it it's foul. Do not taint my nickname, asshole. "See we also realized you are the heiress to a billion-dollar tech empire. Your daddy's loaded. We have already sent the ransom request to your parents for three hundred million dollars. Their deadline is tonight at midnight." He looks at his watch dramatically, just to be a smart ass I presume. "That leaves them roughly eighteen hours to decide if you're worth it." This tells me it's six in the morning, thank you very much. I don't know what day but I know time right now and that means I've been up all night again. "If Rock won't give me ports, I'll get the money another way. Thank you for your continued efforts towards our success." A horrible, wicked, deranged smile follows up his venomous speech.

I hate this man with every fiber of my being. I hope they kill him first.

Yet he still continues, "I am heading out for a meeting and you may go sleep some while my wife sleeps and recovers. You did good today, Doc. I appreciate you. Just for that, I'll have Hercules fix you something special. Do you like chocolate?"

My eyes narrow, "Yes."

"Good it's settled. Go take a shower, you smell like a construction worker from your life saving efforts. Then you can eat and go to bed. Someone will wake you if Bonnie needs something. Can't have our star doctor be too exhausted to treat my Bonnie."

A guard opens the door and Pete leaves me to the beeping silence of the room once again.

I learned three things from that pompous conversation, Shawn is still here, and my parents are aware of my disappearance and it's six AM.

We'll see how much my parents like me.

CHAPTER 29 – GUNNEY

The hotel conference room is a good place to hold this meeting of the Southern Devils Society associates who came with Danger and the ones from the Lake Charles chapter here with Tank. They arrived twenty minutes ago with about forty men and a fuck ton of firearms.

I guess there's no limit on them when you're the arms dealer.

They came on bikes, trikes, trucks, and cars. The cavalry has arrived just in time because I don't think I can keep Shadow calm much longer. Not that he's anywhere near calm anyways.

We both have been pacing the floor, wearing a hole in the ugly hotel carpet. We've drank enough coffee to make a cruise ship fly. We're slightly wired and jumpy. The jitters are becoming a problem but we'll need it if we're going to get through this. I'd punch myself in the face if I thought it would help. I keep reminding myself we are almost at the end of this ordeal.

"Good morning, gentlemen."

Grumpy choruses lift up from the men gathered, replying to Danger so early in the morning. These men were woken up in the middle of the night, dragged out of bed, and drove three hours to come on this mission.

"We have to make this quick. Travares has pinpointed where Zharia was last seen on the tracker then matched it up to vehicles driving in the vicinity at that time and the surroundings. We came up with two oversized blacked out SUVs barreling down the city streets off the traffic cams."

We figured whoever has her was making a quick trip. She was only on the tracker for like twelve minutes. Which was enough for Travares to run a query on places around the area.

"It's an abandoned doctor's office with an upstairs apartment. We have tapped into the traffic cams surrounding the area and have seen the SUVs heading to the back of that building. We cannot confirm she was in the SUVs, but by how fast the dot was moving on the screen, it's safe to say she was in one of those vehicles and that was the destination point for her. They took her out to a blood bank and an urgent care. It's safe to assume she is treating patients and she needed blood."

Shadow and I got all intel from Danger while he drove here at breakneck speed across the state. Birdie threw a massive fit about being excluded. I had no doubt she would. She made him promise the very minute he had her to safety he'd call her.

I thought for sure he would have fueled up the jet but he had a good point, he said he could have been halfway here by the time the flight crew got there and the plane was cross checked for takeoff.

We are so close I can smell her perfume. Because, crazy as it sounds, Shadow and I brought her perfume so we could smell it and feel close to her. I guess we are just sentimental and romantic like that.

The plan is to get Zharia, then me and Shadow immediately hit the road and get her back to New Orleans. We want her as far away as possible from these sick fucks. It's going to be a long drive and I just pray she's up for it.

Unfortunately, we have no way to know how she is physically, or mentally, at this point. We are all just hoping for the best. All we know is she's alive and by the heart rate that was being reported by the tracker, she was in a highly stressful situation. I mean, being with those assholes is stressful enough.

"Shadow and Gunney are taking point on getting to Zharia and bringing her out. They will disappear with her ASAP but we are killing every last one of them who tries to stop us. It's shoot on sight, men. Any questions?"

"No but it's about damn time we push back on these motherfuckers. I say while we're here we storm Houston and get rid of them once and for all. Getting Zharia is the main objective though," Bam says to the room and receives some cheers for that idea.

"As much as I would love to do that, we are under orders from Rock to accomplish this mission and only this one," Danger points out.

"What if there are other women and children held captive there? Are we to just leave them?"

"Absolutely not. We are taking them with us, getting them to safety. Travares and Joker are responsible for getting them to the safehouse outside the city. Just like any ole mission, we get in, get people, kill all in our path, get out. Any more questions?"

Shadow has been leaning up against a wall and I can see his jaw working with his anger and feel the rage seething off of him. His fists keep clenching as he tries his damndest to maintain some semblance of control. *I feel ya, brother.*

No one speaks up with questions, so Danger claps his hands and joyfully says, "Let's go hunting, boys." Guys start filing out of the conference room to the waiting vehicles in the parking lot.

Danger walks over to Shadow and me and in a low tone says, "Get her and get the fuck out. I'll see you in New Orleans." He shakes our hands and hugs us, then he's walking out of the room too.

"Ready?" I ask Shadow.

"I'm beyond ready. Let's go get our woman." He claps me on the back, pulling me with him out of the room.

Every man who joins the SDS taskforce gets a firearm and a Kevlar vest. All the men are standing around in the parking lot getting theirs on and doing a weapons check. Mine's already on, so is Shadow's. We are locked and loaded. I make sure my lucky pin is on the soft part of my vest. It says, 'Your Worst Nightmare,' the other lucky pin is on the opposite side. It's a replica of my favorite gun, an M-4, which I have nestled in my hands.

Bam walks up with a plastic grocery bag and a feral smile; Travares follows up behind him. I swear Bam's legit crazy. Fun to hang out with, but don't piss him off. This outta be good. "Brothers, I come bearing gifts." He does a little dance as he hands the plastic grocery bag to Shadow with a dramatic, over-the-top bow, "I present flash bangs." He winks and giggles…like a schoolgirl. I watch him practically skip over to the truck he's riding in.

Who the fuck carries explosives in a grocery bag? With a fucking hole in the bottom to boot. Bam, that's who. That guy is a mess.

Travares grips my hand and pulls me in for a hug and a back slap. He does the same to Shadow then hands us our earpieces, quiet as usual while on a mission. He's our invisible man, our eyes in the back of our heads. He salutes and goes back to the truck where he'll wait with his laptop while we storm the Saints hideout.

Travares can be an odd duck. He's a techie with a brain that runs on a hundred different tabs open at a time. I've never met a smarter guy. The shit he does is like magic.

Shadow shrugs and starts loading up his vest and tactical pockets with the surprise flash bangs and extra ammo, then hands the bag over for me to do the same thing. Once we are properly armed to the teeth, I check my watch again, while Shadow looks at the app.

He looks up and shakes his head. Well, that fucking sucks. They have her back where the jammer is but this time, we have a really good idea where she's at. We are going to the office building first and surrounding the entire block.

"It's six-forty-six, let's roll. We have an hour's drive." We climb into the SUV and head West towards our girl. *Just hang in there, baby, we're coming.*

I know it's early but she'll be awake.

"Hey, Teddy Bear," her sleepy voice says. If I know my mom, she's sitting at her breakfast nook having her coffee with French Vanilla creamer and two Sweet 'n Lows, working her seek and find word puzzle.

"Hey, Mom."

Gunney looks over at me sharply. I know he didn't expect to hear that when I placed the phone up to my ear. Momma's boy, remember?

"There's worry in your voice and I can feel something swirling in the atmosphere." I knew my mom would pick up on my state of mind immediately. She's always had that special knack. I guess that's what it takes to be a good mom, you develop a great sixth sense.

"We think we found Zharia and we are on our way there now," I tell her quietly.

"Oh honey, that's good news. I'm so happy for you." Moms always know the right words to say and make their kids feel better. "I'm sure she'll be happy to see you, Teddy, don't fret."

"Mom, I'm sure she'll be happy to see anyone at this point," I mumble. Don't get me wrong, I know she'll be ecstatic to see us, but there's still this anchor in my heart, drowning me, wanting to be near her, touch her, allowed to love her freely again and the constant fear she'll reject me. I'm missing half my soul. I'll just be happy with her being safe, and happy with Gunney if that's what she wants. I will accept that, grudgingly.

The closer I've grown to Gunney I can clearly see how much he loves and cares for her.

I clear my throat, "I just called to tell you I love you and let you know about Zhar. I'll call when I can."

"Oh, I love you too, Teddy Bear. Bring your girl home. I pray for the best possible outcome, *wasape*." I love when she calls me Bear in our native tongue. Only she says it with so much love and respect.

When I get off the phone with my mom, I look over at Gunney and ask, "Do you need to call anyone?"

"No, I'm good, bro. Everyone that matters to me is in on this mission." Gunney is quiet for a few minutes, I don't miss the hurt in his eyes or the way he looks at me, but he follows up with, "I think it's cool you're close with your mom. Mine died when I was five and I never got to know her. I've heard plenty of stories from my dad before he died a few years ago, but I have no memories of her. I have vague impressions of what I think she was like, ya know, like I've matrixed her out of all the stories I've heard and made her into this person in my mind. I just think it's beautiful you called her before this."

"Thanks, man. My mom is my world, besides Zhar. She knows everything, even about you."

"Aww, you told your momma about me? Are we official now? Did you post it on the Book of Face?" Gunney continues to grin while he drives us.

"No, dick, I don't even have social media. It's a waste of time."

"You'd be surprised how entertaining it can be. Especially the breakup drama, the cheating partners, the pics of food that looks like dog shit, the pics of kids and pets. I quite enjoy my social media, specifically the funny dog and cat videos. Although, I must say there's a certain rapper that is positively hilarious to follow with his posts digging on another rapper. It's content gold and not at all wholesome," he laughs.

When he puts it all that way, social media doesn't sound like the devil.

While we drive, Gunney taps his finger to the metal music of Bad Omens streaming on the radio. I don't mind his music choice, it's better than when Zharia tried to make me like country so she could go line dancing as a fleeting hobby. Thank fuck that only lasted five days.

"I know Zhar has one but she hardly ever posts on it, at least that's what she told me like two years ago," I say.

"Yeah, she does. Only time she posts is when her or her facility wins any awards or she goes to some charity function and takes a selfie to show how gorgeous she is. Which is not very often anymore, I mean her going out, not how she looks. She declines those events now, says there's nothing interesting at them and they are boring with nothing to do. She hates hob-knobbing with those people."

She doesn't go anymore? She went all the time. And nothing interesting there? She used to spend so much time focused on watching me and making eyes at me that it was never boring. Does she not go because I'm not there? I would have thought she'd be pleased to go to a function without me hovering and undressing her with my eyes. Those things were always hard to attend with a semi stiffy while she was around.

"However, I think the boring part is because you aren't there." And that's what I thought. He looks over at me in the dark but I can make out his serious features from the dash lights, his carefree smile gone, "She misses you, ya know. She did what she thought was best for her at the time. Was it selfish? Fuck yeah it was, but I've listened to her hash this out in her head for the better part of a year and a half now. She regrets what she did but she's also satisfied. I've told her repeatedly, it's ok to feel like shit after making the right decision for yourself, even if you regret it." Gunney has no idea the feelings he's stirring up in me. Then again, maybe he does.

I still sit here quietly taking in all he has to offer about her. There hasn't been a day that I haven't wondered if she regretted how she ended things with me and if she ever missed me. Because I miss her with every fiber of my being. There was never an ending for me, just this never-ending abyss of love that has nowhere to go, so I still cling to her and wish upon every fucking star she will come back to me.

Gunney and I have talked about what was between Zharia and me, and through his viewpoint, I do see some things differently. I also understand more about the dynamics of her parents and why she felt the way she did.

I guess I didn't reassure her enough that I wasn't trying to trap her or suffocate her. I thought I had explained to her I wanted her to be free and mine, but in the end, she still left me for what she perceived as her freedom.

Gunney explained how scared she was about her feelings. She said they were too strong and were choking her and she felt suffocated by how intense I was. The wanting to date other men, he said it was all a front to keep her from feeling trapped. Her reasoning was if she saw other people she could tread water with her sea of emotions.

Per Gunney, it did not work for her.

"She'll be happy to see you, because it's *you*. She's far from over you. Trust me, bro. I should know, I've been living in your literal shadow this whole time." Gunney nods in the dim light and smiles, "She might be mad at first, but our girl will come around. Wait and see."

If only we could all be as positive as Gunney. I bet he even folds his underwear.

CHAPTER 31 – ZHARIA

I reckon I should be grateful for clean panties, even if they are granny panties in a size too big. I know I have a fat ass, but this just makes me feel worse about it. *Stop complaining.*

I declined to wash my hair in the shower because, one—it's too much work, and two—it takes forever to dry and I don't want to go to sleep with a head full of wet hair.

The shower is the only time I get me time.

They've allowed me some cheap soap, shampoo and conditioner, one single blade razor that leaves burn marks, and shaving cream. I'm not ashamed to say I've used that cheapy razor to keep my body hair tame, but the first time, it gave me hella bumps in my bikini line. I long for the days of getting waxed.

Every few showers, I hide behind the curtain with the water running and run my fingers through my lower lips until I find my aching clit. I circle quickly and jumpstart my brain into a steamy fantasy I've cooked up with my guys, either of them tag teaming me or solo. Both of them inside of me somehow usually does the trick. I've never come so fast in my life, which is what I needed anyways. God, I feel like Jell-O now. Stick a fork in me.

Once again, I do not want them to catch me and think it's an open invitation. Fuck that. Eww, shudder. So, I finish everything up quickly.

Once I'm dried off and dressed—I'd give my pinky away right now for some Q-tips and lotion—I shuffle back to my prison cell. Exhaustion is eating away at my soul but I'm hungry, and if the loud ass growling coming from my abdomen is any indication, I could eat my weight in carbs at this point.

Oh god, Tito's shrimp fettuccine alfredo.

French Quarter beignets.

Ophelia's smoked salmon and broccoli with cheese.

Alfredo's Pizza.

I'm only torturing myself here. Shawn's been good to me.

I make a mental note to ask Shawn-that's-still-here if I can have pizza. I should have asked sooner.

About the time I start to lay down, the fucking keys on the other side of the door start jingling. Of course they do. I want to scream. There's no rest for doctors.

What now?

Shawn, who I see is still around, walks in and he's carrying a tray for me. Oh, thank fuck to the goddess Dolly Parton and any other bright human beings full of grace, luck and butter, I get to eat.

"Hi, Shawn. How are you?"

"I'm fine, Zharia." He gives me no indication of any emotions behind his words. He could be talking to the rubber on his shoe for all the reaction he has at seeing me. I, on the other hand, have not seen him in what I would guess is over a day. Someone else brought my food and it was most definitely lacking that certain familiar Bam! that Shawn's food has. The man knows his way around a spice rack. Points in his favor.

"I appreciate the food."

"I fixed you something special as requested. I made beignets, and iced cinnamon French toast with orange juice and milk. I didn't bring you coffee since Panhead said you were going to sleep right after eating." You can tell Shawn doesn't have too much experience interacting with women, especially pretty women, but he's gotten better around me with our one-sided meals. He looks me in the eyes, but he's quick not to look for too long, always looking away. He's not always been this way around me but today there's a little edge to him.

I take a seat on my cot and start wolfing down the beignets. "What would you like to talk about today, Shawn?" Powdered sugar puffs off my lips like smoke as I talk.

"I finally looked you up while I was at the grocery store," he says. So, this is where we're going today. "It's the only place I get signal. I wasn't aware you're a billionaire." He shifts his weight from side to side, as if he's nervous. Like he can't believe that amount of worth.

"I'm not a billionaire; my parents are. I'm a doctor."

"Yeah, but doctors still make a lot of money. I saw pictures of you online at rich bitch functions. You are definitely out of our league here." He says it almost accusatory, like I had a choice how much money my parents have or how much I get paid.

Well, technically I did have a choice in my pay because I own the business, but what he doesn't know is I slashed my yearly salary so I could pay my staff more than typical hospital pay. I made sure the rewards were great if they left the stability of the hospital or their previous jobs and came and tried out this new adventure with me.

This first year is shaping up to be a very profitable one and I was preparing to give my people a yearly bonus the day after I was taken. It would have been given before Christmas. I feel awful about that. They were counting on me, I promised them. I hope I didn't ruin Christmas for anyone.

"It's not about money, Shawn."

"Only people who have money to blow say it's not about money. Life revolves around money, Zharia. Some of us can barely afford to eat or have a place to live. You expect someone to rent a place on ten dollars an hour? Everything is insane nowadays. Yes, it is about money and for those of us that are always grinding, always hustling, it will never be enough, even if we have a billion dollars." Shawn does finally look me in the eyes as he says his piece with conviction.

I'm about to fuck this up or get out of here but I'm shooting my shot, "I'll give you a million dollars to help me escape."

He scoffs at me, "It's not that simple. You are heavily guarded. This place is always crawling with Saints. There's no way to get you out without being noticed. I'm sorry, as much as I could use the money, I can't." He genuinely looks dejected so I know he isn't blowing smoke up my ass.

"Can you at least give me a gun? Just in case of emergencies?" I beg him.

"I really shouldn't. You're gonna get me killed. I can see the headline now, 'Black guy killed by Indian girl, by his own gun.'" He actually grins at me. Finally! Something real.

I smile back at him, "What if I promise not to shoot you with your own gun? Would you give me one then?"

"The answer is still no," he says shaking his head sadly.

"We can always say I took it from you if they find it."

I can see him contemplating it. I can see the cogs and wheels working in his brain. He wants to do it, but he's also terrified. I switch tactics trying to glean as much info out of him as I can.

"What day is it?"

"Thursday. January ninth." Ok. I've been here nineteen days. It's almost hopeless at this point but I still try my hardest to keep that flame alive. *They're coming for me.*

"Thank you, Shawn. Have you given anymore thought to leaving and fleeing to New Orleans?" I quirk an eyebrow at him while I chew my glorious French toast. This is amazing stuff right here. Orgasmic even. I wish I could cook like this.

Don't tell Leo, but these are levels better than his.

"Sorta. I mean, it's a nice offer but I'm sure they'd rather kill me on sight than help me."

"No, no! They won't," I urge him. *Breathe in, breathe out.* In helping himself, he helps me. "They will be excited to learn where I am and reward you." I try to dazzle him with a brilliant smile making sure there is emphasis on the word *reward*.

"I can't do that Zhar, it would be breaking my oath." And my smile dies just like that.

Now he's ruffling my feathers, "Fuck your oath. So, you would rather help them hold me hostage and wear me down, than let me out and have both of our freedoms? That's fucked up, Shawn. Tell me, what if it was your mother being held here? Your sister, girlfriend, best friend? Would you still tell someone no you won't help them get out of this prison." I have to take a deep breath and center myself. My voice was starting to raise a few octaves in my desperation.

More breathing. Stop seeing red. Reel him back in.

"Look, he's threatened—"

Suddenly there's a loud explosion and the building rocks. Outside my door men are yelling and it sounds like chaos as gunfire erupts. I can hear screams loudly through the closed door.

Shawn looks at me with terror in his eyes. I smile, Cheshire style lighting up my face, all my teeth on display. I must look like a maniac because Shawn's terror just escalates the louder the noises from outside come through the door.

I look him dead in the eye, I take a deep breath and exhale, wiggling my fingers, "Finally. They're here Shawn and they've come for me. I suggest if you want to live you give me your gun and get behind me." He still doesn't move. "Now! Move it!" I bark at him.

I hold out my hand.

More men yelling, more gun fire, something else blows up. I feel like dancing around like a sugar plum fairy I'm so giddy. It sounds like absolute annihilation beyond that door. Good. I hope they all die. Rotten to the core men who don't deserve to breathe the same air as women.

"I can't, Zharia," he practically whispers to me.

"Do you want to live?" I yell at him, jolting him out of his panic.

"Yes!"

"Then give me your *fucking* gun!" I yell at him. "They'll kill you otherwise."

He reaches behind him and pulls a PP-22 out of his waistband and shoves it at me. Not what I was expecting, but I can work with it. Twenty-twos can cause enough damage. It's a gun; it'll do.

I check the chamber as I tell him, "Get the fuck behind me and don't you dare fucking try anything with any Devil that walks through that door. I can only save you so much before they don't give a fuck about my words and kill you. They won't lose sleep about putting a bullet between your eyes." I take a fighting stance, gun raised and poised at the ready, trying to get prepared for whatever comes through the door.

I shake my unoccupied hand out, wiggling my fingers. I'm exhilarated. I feel like I'm about to go rounds with Mike Tyson. Whooo! I imagine this is what an adrenaline shot feels like.

Shawn, like the good boy he is, gets behind me. I stand facing the door, one in the chamber, waiting like a good angel of death. Shadow and Leo would be so proud of me right now.

I have Shawn backed into the corner that's diagonal from the doorway, me covering his body. It's not like he's much bigger than me. His ragged breathing belies his fear.

Loud gunshots are heard right outside the door. I'm not stupid enough to try to escape through that unlocked door right now. I know everyone out there is distracted but there's a hail of bullets whizzing everywhere and thankfully, I'm in a concrete box where no strays are going to get me.

They'll tear this place apart. They'll find me, I just need to stay put. I'm so excited I could pee my pants right now.

They're here!

There's a single shot and what sounds like a body hitting the floor. Then quietness. My guess is the guard outside the door is down and dead. *Fuck off in hell, Romulus.* That's my hope anyways. That guy was a dick and I caught him more than once giving me looks, ya know, *those looks.* Creeped me out. I can't say I wasn't afraid he would try to rape me when no one was around.

On the other hand here, is it strange that I'm slightly aroused from all this excitement and danger? Like I'm positively vibrating with joy at seeing who walks through that door. Feral. Ravenous to see me men.

Without warning, the door swings wide and bounces off the wall with a loud crack.

Our eyes lock. Leo! Seeing him kicks me in the gut. I'm running before I even think about it. I jump into Leo's arms right after he moves his gun. I wrap my gun toting hand around his neck, my legs around his waist as I sob, "Oh my god, Leo. Oh, Leo." I can't help it; I can't stop shaking.

He holds me close, as close as he can get, wrapping me tightly up in his muscular arms and breathes into my neck, "My princess. Fuck, am I glad to see you. Are you ok, baby?"

I lean back and kiss him, not once but twice and once more for good measure. I nod while kissing him. The exhaustion is overwhelming but the excitement over seeing him, the soul churning relief is thrumming through me and I can finally relax for the first time in nineteen days. The happy tears flow freely.

"We have to go, baby." He eases me off him, setting me back on the ground, "Trust me, I don't want to let go of you either." As soon as my feet hit the floor and his arms are free, two things happen. Gunney points his gun at Shawn and I lunge in front of him, "No, no, we take him with us. Please, Leo, he's just a kid."

"No."

I look beside Leo and just now realize Shadow is standing in the doorway. I launch myself at him too and hug him as tight as I can. I'm thrilled to see him. To see both of them together. Both of the men I love.

Shadow wraps his arms around me. Fiercely, tight enough I have difficulty breathing, and I hear him exhale loudly and into my neck, in his low, gravelly whisper, "Poppet." I hear the relief in his tone.

I pull back far enough and I kiss him too just for good measure. He opens to me and kisses me back. I'm so happy I'm not standing because this kiss is amazing.

"You really weren't kidding, Zharia," Shawn says, wide eyed.

I end my lip locking with Shadow in time to turn to Shawn. I can tell most of the gunfire has subsided but there's still people yelling though. "Are you coming with us or are you going to let Pete kill you?"

"You're the only survivor at this point, dude. And the only reason you breathe is because my girl deems it," Leo warns him, still pointing a gun at him.

Shawn swallows, bouncing his Adam's apple, and he nods, "Y-Yes, I'll come."

Shadow finishes slinging his gun to his back, and handing Shawn's gun over to Leo, he hefts me up in his arms. On instinct I wrap my legs around him. Balancing a hand on my ass, he says, "Keep your eyes closed, poppet. Don't open them until we say. Hang on to me, don't let go." I feel his chest rumbling through his Kevlar and it's so comforting to me. His scent, the sandalwood and cedar that I've missed so much, be still my heart. I just wrap my arms tighter around his neck and bury my face in his collarbone.

"Ok, Bear," I whisper in his ear as he holds me. He responds with a growl, the contented kind I've missed. I've always loved how he could hold me and carry me in his arms like I weigh nothing, when in fact I know I do weigh something.

"Let me out front," Leo says. I peek and watch him grab Shawn by the vest and haul him out in the hallway ahead of us. As we exit my prison cell, I clamp my eyes closed. I sure as fuck don't want to see the carnage the Devils have left in the wake of their rescue. But then again, maybe I do. These people were indifferent to me, they didn't help, but they didn't hurt me either.

The irony of Shadow carrying me to freedom is not lost on me. I broke his heart for freedom, yet he's one of the ones setting me free today.

Touche, Universe.

My last thought from inside the room, as he marches me through all the death surrounding us in this building is—I can't wait to sleep in my own fucking bed tonight and get some fucking Q-tips.

Chapter 32 – Shadow

Gunney walks with that son of a bitching Saint up ahead of us. The truck is literally right outside the front door. We pulled right up and bailed out.

As Gunney walks beside the little guy, he looks like a big ogre next to that scrawny runt. I have no idea why Zharia's saving his ass but it better be a good reason before Gunney throws him in the truck with us on a three-hour fucking drive back home.

"Open your eyes, baby girl," I tell Zharia once we reach the truck and I ease her down. She leaves her arms around my neck, but I have to pry them off and her look of dejection kills me. "Look, as much as I want your arms around me, and I really, *really* fucking want that, we have to go, poppet. I need you to get in the truck, baby girl, we'll talk at home and I can hold you then."

Her face relaxes and she actually smiles at me. How the fuck this woman so goddamn calm through this ordeal is mystifying to me. She has such strength and composure.

I hope like fuck they didn't drug her.

She's my vicious poppet. She cast a love spell on me so deeply rooted in the very fibers inside my body and stuck her claws into me, sealing my fate. From the first kiss, my life was intertwined with hers permanently. I want her of sound mind and body when she agrees to bring me back into her life.

My poppet, full of magic, full of spark.

Gunney holds the passenger door open for her and she kisses him before she climbs in without any argument. Thank fuck. He runs around to his side while I slide into the seat behind her. Fucknuts is already in the backseat, making sure he knows by one glare: I will fucking kill him if needed.

Dropping the truck into drive, Gunney speeds away and runs over the curb where the opening through vehicles was left for our getaway. We all bounce around in the cab but settle down once we hit the road.

As soon as we do get to the main stretch, my phone starts blaring an alarm very loudly. How could I forget. I pull it out of my vest pocket, only making the shrill noise louder.

"What is that?" Zharia tries to turn her head in her seat.

Gunney's eyes meet mine in the rearview mirror. Zharia can't know about her tracker yet. Not until I've had time to explain. I'll lose her if she finds out right now, like this.

So, I lie.

"It's letting us know it's time to get out of here, our time's up. But we're all good." I lean forward and run my fingertips across her cheek and she sighs and leans into my touch. My heart soars.

Holy fuck.

Gunney's idea might work.

Goddamn, I really, really hope it does. As long as I can be part of her life in some capacity, preferably as a lover and partner, but I will share if it means keeping her.

Just give me a chance to prove it, poppet.

CHAPTER 33 – GUNNEY

There are no words to express how elated I am about her return. My heart is a fountain of emotions, spilling out every time I touch her. I'm not a crying type of guy, but I teared up holding her in that janitor's closet she was kept in. I wanted to drop to my knees and thank every god out there when she was in that room and we found her. My heart slammed into my ribs, clawing its way out to wrap her in our love and protect her.

I still can't believe she's in the truck. We've searched high and low for so long and now she's here. And it doesn't seem like she was hurt, but you can never tell. Physically she looks ok, but how is she mentally.

Zharia is one of the strongest, most resilient women I have ever met. She handles things with grace and dignity and if those motherfuckers laid a hand on her, I will burn down every one of their houses and hideouts.

No sooner than we get Shadow's alarm off, my phone is ringing through the Bluetooth in the truck. I see it's Birdie so I hit accept.

Immediately, Birdie is gushing, "Zharia! Oh my god, say it's true, you have her." You can tell Birdie has been crying and she still continues to sob into the phone.

"I'm here, babes," Zharia says on a sob and then she's crying.

Together they both sob.

"Oh god, thank fuck. I'm so happy to hear your voice. I love you so much." More hiccups. I hear a sniffle from behind me. I guess the kid is moved too. With one hand I reach into the center console and grab some fast-food napkins then hand them to Zhar. Shadow pets her hair from the backseat. I knew this call was going to be an emotional one for both of them.

Unfortunately for Birdie, she has no one there to comfort her seeing as how her husband was left back in Lake Charles. Until she says, "Pierre is here, he's coming into the room now."

"Babes..." Pierre's hoarse voice says, which makes Zhar cry harder. You can tell he's been crying and upset too. I'm glad Zharia's friends love her so much. She's going to need more than us.

I speak up, "Birdie, I swear on my life, once we get Zhar home and she's slept for a few hours, you will be one of the first people to hug her. I'll even let you have a running start to tackle her with."

That gets a soft chuckle from all three of them. It's music to my ears. Their crying gets to me deep down in my soul. Their bond is unbreakable. I've seen it firsthand this past year and a half. They truly are sisters/bro from another mister and they love each other so much. It makes me happy to see them together, along with the other members of the Fab Four, their friendship has been a lifesaver for Zhar.

"I'll let Tally know. She's going to be so happy. I'll call your parents too. Be prepared to have us all over later today. Don't worry about dinner, I got it covered, ok? I'm just so happy all my prayers have been answered by someone, anyone, I'll take it. Thank you Gunney and Shadow for all your tireless efforts." I can tell from Birdie's tone she's not as upset as she has been now after talking to Zharia. Good, that woman's been through enough.

"Yeah, thank you so much, guys. You've been awesome. Sincerely, thank you," Pierre throws in.

"I look forward to seeing you, B and P," even Zharia sounds better. Tired as fuck, but better.

"I love you so much, Z."

"Love you, babes."

After Birdie and Pierre disconnect, Zharia leans her head back against the head rest and sighs. It's the sigh of extreme exhaustion and relief. In a way it's good to hear. I just want to hear every one of her sounds now. I'll take anything. It means she's here. She's alive.

Shadow pulls the pillow from the back seat and tosses it up front, then slides the blanket over the seat. I take the pillow, flip up the center console and lay the pillow propped against my leg. She looks over, weary eyes meet mine.

"We came prepared, poppet. Have a little nap, we have a long drive and you need rest." Shadow continues petting her. She's practically purring.

"Thank you, Bear."

"Before you sleep, are you hungry?" I ask her.

"No, Shawn fed me a very good breakfast."

Shadow growls from the backseat. He's got the same thought I do. What is this guy to her and what's between them? My hands tighten on the steering wheel thinking about another man having my baby.

Well, another man besides Shadow.

Zharia yawns long and hard and says, "Don't worry guys, it's not like that. It was French toast and it was some of the best I've ever had."

I glance over, "Better than mine?"

She grins and her sleepy eyes droop further, "I plead the fifth."

Her head starts lolling around. She's going to pass out any second. I reach for her and pull her down, fluffing the pillow on to my thigh. "Lay down, baby, we'll be home before you know it. I love you." I fan her hair out behind her and gently brush away the tendrils by her face.

"I love you too, Leo," she mumbles before she's knocked out.

I see Shadow turn to this Shawn guy. "You better start explaining yourself. I want your version before she wakes up and tells me hers."

My eyes cut over to Shawn's in the rearview mirror. "It's clear our girl has taken a liking to you or you'd be dead. This better be good," I grumble.

Shawn starts stammering his words, "I couldn't help get her out. I swear. She doesn't know he threatened my family too, he had proof he was threatening my grandma and sister. I was just sworn in two months ago. I go to college to be a chef. I'm just a nineteen-year-old college kid who got a sweet scholarship and was approached by some bikers to join them, man. I thought it would be a great way to get to know people here. I'm from Detroit. I had no idea they were evil and by the time I realized it, it was too late. I was her chef whether I wanted to be or not. I was tasked with feeding her and watching her eat to make sure she does eat. I can assure you, she has been fed well and she still kept her appetite."

"Go on," Shadow prompts him when Shawn pauses too long.

"Zharia tried to pay me a million dollars to call you while I went out to the grocery store. She begged me to let her talk to you but there were signal jammers all around the building. She doesn't know I had my phone checked for calls or texts when I got back from each grocery trip."

I fucking knew it. By the hard set of Shadow's jaw, he knows he hit the nail on the head with that one. By all accounts, that tracker should have worked…up until it didn't. Now we certainly know why with Shawn confirming our suspicions.

"My grandma and sister's lives were not worth a million dollars to me," he says quietly.

I can't blame the kid. If someone threatened all I loved—well actually they did—I would do anything to protect them too. I reckon I can see why he didn't call.

Panhead Pete is turning out to be just as crazy as Grim. How lovely.

"So, let me get this straight, you let them hold our girl hostage and torture her?"

"No, sir!" Shawn is quick to refute, "They did not touch her, no one did. She was strictly off limits. Our doctor, nothing more. I checked on her often, I guess you can say we were friendly and we would talk while she ate. I can tell you; she missed both of you very much. She talked about each of you often. I would often catch her crying and she would only say she missed her men."

His words warm my heart and I feel it in my soul, but damn, do they piss me off. Of all the things I expect this kid to say, that was not it. I wasn't sure how Zhar would feel since she left me for three days after pouring my heart out to her. I know she texted me the night she disappeared to come see her, but I don't know if it was to 'break-up' with me as friends or to take it to the next step. I can't wait to find out answers from her.

Although, her greeting to us kinda solidified my thoughts that she loves us and wants us both. I'll wait until the time is right to spring my idea on her.

I'm just fucking ecstatic she's ok.

Chapter 34 – Shadow

I'm trying really hard not to be pissed at this fucking kid sitting next to me. He keeps fiddling with the hem of his vest. His Lone Star Saints vest.

"Take off the vest and give it to me," I demand.

His wide eyes stare over at me from his seat behind Gunney. "But—"

"No buts, do it."

I see the fight die from his eyes as he starts to awkwardly shift around to get the vest off.

"I spent all my money on this leather vest they said I had to have." He seriously looks like he's pouting.

"I'll buy you a new one if you patch to Southern Devils Society, ok?" Gunney says from up front.

"Ok." Shawn hands over the vest and I hold it away from me like it's a nasty, crusty STD I don't want to catch. I roll down the back window and toss it out on the side of the road as we haul ass back to New Orleans.

I wipe my hands off on my jeans and turn to Shawn, "How old are you again?"

"Nineteen, sir."

"Where did you say you're from?" Gunney asks quietly.

"Originally, I'm from Detroit, Michigan. I moved down to Houston over a year ago when I won a full scholarship to culinary school. Hey, am I going to be allowed to finish school? Am I going back there at all?"

Both Gunney and I say 'No' at the same time.

Shawn turns his head and looks at the window. I wouldn't doubt it if he starts crying. He's a quiet kid, not at all aggressive. I'm starting to see how he wiggled his way into Zharia's good graces. Even in the situation she was in, I think she found a kindred spirit.

Quiet, as not to wake Zhar, Shawn tells us, "She tried to get me to leave, go to New Orleans. Said if I left and ran to Rock he would let me live and Zhar would put me through college here in New Orleans. I was just so scared, ya know, I've never known such terrifying men like those guys. Hell, up until a few weeks ago I thought shit like that happened only in movies. Boy, was I wrong. So fucking wrong. I mean look at me, do you really think I can fight off men your size. It's laughable to even consider it."

I imagine it was shocking to see that kind of life for the first time. I bet this kid realized too late he was in over his head.

"Most likely tomorrow is when we can talk about your future. Right now, no one knows you're gone. By this time tomorrow, I'm sure your absence will be noticed," Gunney lets him know. Shawn just nods his head and continues to bite his nails.

"I'm a traitor, ain't I?" Shawn says softly.

"Yes, you are," I answer him.

"How do you want to do this?" I ask Gunney while we stand in front of Zhar's house by the truck. Shawn stands idlily by awaiting instructions. He will get to come in once she's in. I'm putting him in the downstairs bedrooms.

Zharia is still passed out cold in the passenger seat, laying down. She didn't stir the rest of the way home, not a peep or snore.

I put my hands on my hips and sigh, "One of us needs to carry her inside. I think it should be you. Clearly she's happy to see us both, but I carried her out of the place, you can carry her home." As much as it pains me, I know Zharia would want that. I'm still shocked that she wrapped herself around me willingly. And kissed me!

In the middle of a fire fight, the last thing I expected was to get hard and be aroused.

My mind briefly slips over to the memory of Bam running into the building with his M-16 shooting and shouting, "Your death makes my dick hard." Certifiably crazy.

"Ok, I'll take her in. Do you want to run ahead of me and get her bed ready?"

My gut twists at entering her room. I'm unwelcome there, but how many times have I brought her body to climax, over and over again, hearing her either sigh or scream my name in that room. A pang stabs my heart remembering, that's where he sleeps now.

"Got it. What's the code?"

He snorts. "Like you need one. 0505."

"You're kidding me, right?" I laugh.

Gunney truly looks puzzled, "No, why?"

"That's my birthday, dude."

Gunney starts laughing. "And here she told me she was over you once and for all."

Changing my mind about letting him in, I peer over at Shawn and say, "Come with me." Gunney's still laughing as I walk away grumbling yet smiling to myself. My little poppet is nowhere near over me. I will always be hot in her blood.

Sure enough, the bolt slides open and I enter the house. All the other times I've been here while she's been gone, Gunney opened the door or he was already here and I never had the opportunity to punch the code in.

While I make Shawn sit in the living room, I hastily make my way down the hallway into her room. As soon as the doors open, the smell hits me. Jasmine, amber and vanilla, the sultry scent that makes up my Indian goddess. How my dick can twitch from love and my heart squeeze from hurt at the same time is a mystery to me. My mind is all over the place currently.

I quickly pull her blankets and top sheet down and haul another pillow over to her side. Well, what I assume is still her side. The spot furthest away from the door. I trained her to sleep that way so I could guard the door. If any of my enemies come for us, at least I can cover her body while she grabs the gun under her side of the bed. I know she knows how to shoot it because Danger and I taught her and Birdie back when they were in college.

I come back in time for Gunney to carry her into the house princess style. Her head is on his chest and her lashes flutter on her cheeks. She looks so peaceful in his arms.

"All ready, brother."

He nods and continues to the hallway, his boots clomping on the hardwood.

I swing my gaze back over to Shawn sitting on the edge of the couch, like he might bolt any minute or he's trying to get prepared to fight.

"You can relax; we aren't going to kill you…yet. I'm taking you downstairs to the spare bedrooms, so follow me."

I watch his throat bob up and down as he contemplates following me into the bowels of the house. Everyone knows bad things happen in basements. But this isn't a basement, not how his Northern ass thinks. We don't do basements in New Orleans due to the water but Zhar's basement is above ground. Technically her living quarters are on the second floor of her house.

I get halfway down the steps and I feel him fall in line behind, then hear his footsteps on the stairs cautiously. I think it's safe to say he's scared out of his mind. He's a young kid that's gotten wrapped up in some heavy shit and he doesn't know how to get out of it.

Zharia taught me how to have compassion. Her bleeding heart floods with compassion over stray animals, old people and lost causes. This compassion kicks in when I put my hand on his shoulder at the bottom of the stairs in the other living room.

"Look, I know you're scared. We aren't the bad guys. Give Zhar some time to sleep and realize she's safe again and I'm sure we'll figure out something for you. Give her until tomorrow." I drop my hand, "Take a nap, you look shellshocked and exhausted too. If you need anything, food's in the kitchen, have at it. We'll be upstairs, probably asleep since we've been up all night."

I pull out my wallet and thumb through my bills. I pull a few hundreds out and toss them on the coffee table, then point to the exit, "There's French doors if you decide to leave while we sleep. That should be enough to catch a ride back to Houston." I point behind him, "There's the bathroom and two bedrooms, pick a room, they're both open."

"Th-Thank you, sir."

"Enough with the sir, ok? I'm Shadow. See ya tonight, kid."

After I'm back upstairs and have taken all my gear off, I head down the hall to Zharia's room to check on her and to make my mind believe she's here. I walk in, then stand a few steps from the bed. She's smack dab in the middle of her king size bed, facing the door, sleeping peacefully. Gunney is wrapped up behind her with his arm resting on her hip, face buried in her hair.

I smile down at her and I accept that I will do anything to make her happy, even if she wants me to leave when she wakes up. From everyone filling me in, Gunney more than makes her happy. Birdie told me in confidence that Zharia tends to glow when she's around Gunney, much like she did when she was with me.

That was news to me. I didn't know Zharia radiated her happiness that much to where other people noticed. Of course, Birdie told me she saw it written all over my face too and it all made sense when Zharia finally broke and let it be known how deep she had gotten.

Birdie said I scared Zhar. She fell so hard and so fast, felt so deeply, more than she ever had for someone else. She was afraid of losing herself. I admit it was all-consuming to be with her. I became obsessed with her quickly and when I fell, it was headfirst into her walnut brown eyes and into her heart.

I will never love another woman like I love her.

My heart sees she's ok, I turn to leave and go back to the spare bedroom beside hers that I've been staying in and her soft, silky voice says, "No."

Am I hearing things? Is she having a nightmare?

It stops me in my tracks. I turn back around to see if she's ok. She has her little arm outside the comforter and her hand is held out to me. My heart trips over itself.

"Stay with me." She pulls the blankets back and I look at the empty space next to her. I must look too long because Gunney gives an exasperated sigh.

"Just get in the fucking bed, bro," Gunney mumbles from his spot behind her, still buried in her hair.

Her beautiful bottom lip is caught in her teeth while I walk over to the bed. I don't even need to think if this is a bad idea; I know it is, but I do it anyways.

I have no will power when it comes to her. I can't tell her no. I will give her anything she wants.

Princess treatment.

She looks up at me while I close the distance. I quickly strip off my clothes, leaving my boxer briefs on and slide in next to her. Rolling to my side facing her, I pull up the covers as she slides her hand down the side of my face. I close my eyes and lean into her touch.

Zhar leans towards me and her lips gently brush mine. "Thank you," she quietly says as her breath fans across my lips.

I get shivers down to my toes from this moment. "You're welcome." I reach up and brush her hair off her cheek with my fingertips.

She leans in to kiss me again. Her warm tongue slides into my mouth and my tongue meets hers. It's like coming home. Holy fuck, my chest is tight and I'm losing my head. Angels are weeping in joy.

She wiggles closer and Gunney sleepily says, "Jesus fuck, Zhar, I need you to stop rubbing this sweet ass on my dick before this turns into an X-rated nap. And none of us have the energy for that. Go to sleep."

She giggles and I fucking love that sound. She pulls her hand away but she watches me until she's nestled her way into my chest. Pretty soon her breathing evens out and then I follow her into sweet sleep with a lighter heart than I've had in almost two years.

Before I even open my eyes, I slowly stretch my sore body in a languid cat arch, groaning deep in my gut. I hum my appreciation for my bed. Goddamn I slept so well in my gloriously soft and clean bed—that I will never take for granted ever again—sandwiched between the two men I love. Yeah, I love these fuckers. They saved me, took care of me and now comes the hard part, talking about our relationships. I'm sure they're confused as to my actions and what's really going on. For sure, Shadow is confused.

I roll from my side facing the window, intending to slide out of bed and I'm met with a hard, hot body after I flip over. I stare up at Shadow's sleeping face. He's so beautiful. All his muscles are on display with just a sheet over his sculpted hips. His smooth tan skin, his dark lashes sweeping over his high cheekbones and his long black hair fanning the pillow under him. He lays on his back with one arm, the one closest to me, lifted over his head.

The perfect invitation.

I scooch next to him, sliding my arm over his middle then laying my head on his smooth, hard chest. His smell, god! Just the way I remember it. I can't help the big sigh that leaves my body. I remember what this was like. I have missed this so much.

Being in his energy gives my body happy vibrations and gives me feel goods all over again. I became so addicted to this reaction. Everything always felt like it was more colorful, softer, just more of everything when I was with him. No one has ever made me feel like he does…until Leo.

Accepting that our story isn't done yet, I squeeze him tighter to me and throw my leg over his. I know I shouldn't be doing this but fuck, it's what I want right now.

I deserve this. I deserve to feel safe and loved.

I close my eyes and snuggle down, feeling all of those things all over again and filling the cracks of my heart with renewed happiness and peace. His steady heartbeat thumps under my cheek. I missed this rhythm.

"Poppet," Shadow breathes and his chest rumbles under me. His arms come around me and he holds me to him, just like we used to do.

"Good morning, Bear."

He groans in his sexy way, squeezes me to him and says, "I've missed you so much."

"I missed you too for what seems like forever," I whisper up to him while still nestled on his chest.

The door opens and Leo walks in. I don't bother to move off of Shadow. I thought Leo would be mad but he walks up to the bed and around it to the empty space. He crawls across and kisses my head, "Good morning, my beautiful princess, how did you sleep?"

He rolls me to my back, so he can snuggle into the crook of my neck and kiss me there. It tickles and I end up giggling and then sighing in contentment while he looks at me with a playful grin. I smile lazily at him. "I slept like a baby."

"Good, that's what I like to hear." He takes my hand and laces our fingers together. This is bliss for me. I know it's probably not long lasting, but for this moment, I'm the happiest I've ever been. Who wouldn't be happy with having two fine ass men in their bed, doting on them?

No complaints from me. They are top tier eye candy.

More importantly, they are really good men.

I don't deserve either of them, let alone both.

"You will be receiving guests in the front room, M'lady," Leo says in a haughty, fake British accent with his knockout smile that makes me giggle. "Your parents will be arriving in an hour, with the detective on your case." I quirk an eyebrow at that. "Birdie will be arriving in two hours, madam. I've kept them all away until I couldn't any longer." I smile at that.

I groan, "What time is it? Can I go back to sleep?"

"No, baby, it's already four in the afternoon. You've slept the whole day away. If you don't get up now, you might be up all night."

"Well, don't be surprised if I still am," I snort, "They had my sleeping schedule all fucked up. I never knew what time it was or what day, I stayed locked in that concrete room until I had to patch people up. Shawn was the only person who talked to me like a human being." Suddenly I remember! "Oh! Where's Shawn?" My eyes narrow, "Have you hurt him?"

Leo chuckles and holds our linked hands up, "Simmer down, fighter. Shawn is in the living room. He's showered, fed and I gave him a pair of Shadow's sweats and a t-shirt."

"Hey, dick, what the fuck."

"I couldn't give him any of my stuff 'cause it's in here and I was letting our royal sleeping beauty have her rest." He leans down and kisses the tip of my nose.

"Ok," I whine, "Let me get up and shower. I want to wash their stench off of me."

I see Leo's eyes move over to Shadow and something passes between them. I turn my head back and forth trying to see if I can make out their silent language. I see they have spent quite a bit of time together if they are talking with blinks and eye movements alone.

"What?" I look up into Leo's face and watch him swallow, seeing his throat work with nervousness. "Just say it, Leo," I whisper.

"Did they touch you? Are you ok?"

"No, I wasn't raped." I feel the relief rolling off both of these strong men. I hear their releases of breath and Leo actually sags into the bed. "I was not assaulted by any of them surprisingly, although Pete did backhand me once for telling him I wasn't a fucking miracle worker."

Leo's eyes flash with hardness. I put my hand up to his face and run my palm over his beard, "I swear, Leo, I'm ok, just exhausted."

"I still love you more than anything," he whispers to me then puts his forehead on mine.

"I love you too, Leo."

He smiles and gives me a peck on the lips, "Good. Better than great. Excellent. Now get up, sexy, you have court to hold for your visitors."

Shadow pipes up in his sexy sleepy voice, "And we three need to have a heart to heart after everyone leaves."

I bite my bottom lip, nervous about how they will react to my idea of having them both. It's asking a lot of them, especially for two alpha-holes who think they are the one in charge and both have a vicious possessive streak.

"I agree," Leo says. "After they leave so that means you can't get mad at me for ushering people out after an appropriate visiting time."

"I won't get mad. I look forward to our conversation. I missed you both so much," I tell them. I mean it. I am looking forward to seeing how they want everything to go. They've had plenty enough time to duke it out and figure out a plan for our situationship among themselves. I'm eager to hear what they've come up with.

Walking into the kitchen after my shower—which felt a-may-zing—with clean hair and a fresh blow out, I barely have time to catch the plate Leo is shoving at my chest, ordering me to eat.

I look down and see it's a tuna fish sandwich, made exactly how I love and cut into triangles. See, this is why I love him. I damn near tear up. He is so thoughtful and kind and he truly does love me. He's my dream guy.

"I ran to the store and got cookies 'n cream ice cream for later, but right now, I have your favorite chocolate soy milk."

I do tear up at that.

I feel my bottom lip quiver, "Th-Thank you, Leo," I breathe out.

"You're welcome, baby." He pushes me towards the living room, "Don't cry. Eat. Besides, this is the perfect time to start talking to Shawn." He smacks me on the ass and sends me on my way.

I make my way to the fluffy armchair that's my favorite and get settled. I missed my chair. Shawn watches me with his dark eyes the entire time from the furthest spot away on the couch. He doesn't say anything as I sit down. I look at him over my sandwich as I take my first bite. I groan so deep in my soul, dayum, it's a good sandwich.

"Why am I here, Zharia?"

"I'm glad you asked, Shawn. It seems like you're still here so that's a good sign. Do you not want to be here?"

"It's not that. I appreciate your hospitality, but what am I doing here? My life plan is ruined. I have nowhere to go, no job, no school, no apartment." He sits back into the couch cushions, arms crossed and his bottom lip pushed out while he pouts.

Calming breath! I have to remind myself that he's still a kid, barely legal. It seems like he's had a quiet upbringing from what he's already said in our chats. He told me about his grandma raising him in a Detroit suburb and she made sure he had manners and graduated high school. She helped him get into college and she's still taking care of his younger sister.

And now he's here, not going to college.

His fear and disappointment are understandable.

In my defense, he wasn't going to college back at where I was being held anyways. He was going in Houston, an hour away, so he has already missed a week of school at this point.

"Do you want to go back?" I ask him.

"I don't know what I want. I want to graduate college and get a job so I can build a life. I feel like all that's gone now," Shawn finishes quietly.

"Do you have a phone on you? Did you bring it?"

"Yeah, it was in my pocket. With my wallet thankfully."

"Good. I want you to look up culinary schools in New Orleans."

"Do you have any idea how hard I had to work to get that scholarship to that school? I'm not going to be granted one like that again. Especially since I walked away from this one."

He sits up, elbows resting on knees, he puts his head in his hands and sighs deeply.

"I don't mean to interrupt your pity party, but I'm in the business of finding solutions to problems and fixing them. Do you want to find a solution?" I hear Leo snort in the kitchen.

His weary eyes meet mine and he softly says, "Yeah Zhar. I do. I don't want this mistake to ruin my life."

"Good. While my visitors are here," I get up and move the coffee table in front of the couch. The top lifts and reveals storage space. I pull out a legal pad and pen, handing it to him as I continue, "I want you to write down three colleges you are interested in. I'll look it over tomorrow and we will make a plan of action, ok? Don't worry. We will figure it out."

I feel Shadow and Leo in the entranceway from the hallway, by kitchen. I'm sure they are curious and most likely worried I've lost my damn mind bringing the enemy into my home. But there's something I saw in Shawn—potential.

"How am I going to pay for it?"

"We're going to apply for scholarships and grants and we are going to find a sponsor. We. Will. Figure. It. Out. Ok?"

"Ok," he mumbles.

"Trust me?"

"Yeah. I really have no choice."

I look at my smart watch…that's not there. I can't because those fuckers took it. I can't tell you how many times I've looked at my wrist through all this ordeal. Note to self: Buy a new one ASAP.

"You have fifteen minutes, babe," Shadow answers my question I hadn't asked but wanted to know. I look over with an endearing smile and tell him thank you. He looks so delish leaning up against the wall with his bulging arms crossed. Oh, my my.

Focus, Z.

"Do you still want to be a Lone Star Saint?"

"Fuck no! Those guys were too fucked up for me." Shawn shakes his head and visibly shudders.

"Have you given thought to what we talked about? Patching over to the Devils?"

He blows out a breath. "Yeah. I'd like to talk to some of them though, ya know, before I decide."

Leo comes in and perches on the arm of my chair, smoothing his hand on my still drying hair, "What do you want to know, kid?"

Shadow makes his way to the chaise, and as soon as he lowers himself into it, Sir Waffles jumps onto his lap. My beautiful kitty came and slept with me once Shadow opened the door back up and let him in. I say he slept with me but actually he slept next to Shadow.

Sir Waffles Fluffenstein missed his momma, but by the looks of him right now, he missed Shadow more. He always did love my cat and Sir Waffles adored him. I think it's all the treaties Shadow gave him. It's easy to buy a cat's love through food and treats.

Sitting in my seat smiling over at him like he's the freshest thing on the menu, I let my heart have this moment. He frowns and says, "What? I like this cat more than I like most people."

I cover my mouth with my hand and laugh. Leo says, "You don't like anyone that's not her, and you mildly tolerate me and Danger," he finishes on a laugh.

"It's true. Your attitude is shit to people," I chastise him.

"Excuse you, I'm a ray of fucking sunshine."

"He says with the grumpiest look he can manage," I roll my eyes and still laugh at him while puffing up my chest and scrunching my face to mock him.

Sir Waffles headbutts his chin, wanting pets, "You love me don't you Sir Waffles, at least someone does." Shadow buries his face in Sir Waffle's fur and I swear to god, the cat is smiling.

Shawn points to Shadow and says, "He already told me his name is Shadow," he points at Leo, "So, that must mean you're Leo."

Leo dips his chin and replies, "Only to her I am Leo, to everyone else I'm Gunney."

"Got it." He looks back over to me and says, "Do you guys all live here?"

"It's complicated," Shadow says.

"But you're her boyfriends, right? She told me all about her boyfriends named Shadow and Leo."

"It's complicated," Leo reiterates and I can't help but giggle.

I wave my hand and say, "I only told him about you as people and what I loved about each one of you. I didn't spin us a fairytale."

Shadow just quirks his eyebrow at me. According to Shawn over here, all I did was blab about these guys, which was not the case. Least I don't think I did.

Ehh, maybe I did a little.

"No, she didn't, but she loves you both very much, you can tell."

I try my hardest to stare daggers at Shawn to get him to shut his trap.

Betrayer.

"Take him back to Houston since he's so chatty." Shawn grins at me but all it does is tell me he can feel the sexual tension between us three and is taking the opportunity to raze me. God, it's making me antsy. I can't wait until our talk later. I can tell by the way neither of them has been far from me and the way their eyes track my every move, they are anxiously waiting too.

I can tell they've spent a lot of time together and they seem comfortable with each other showing me affection.

Leo and Shadow start laughing, "No, no Shawn, please continue. What was she saying? Do tell," Leo presses him.

"Yeah, tell us how much she *loves* us," Shadow jokes to him.

Shawn gives me a look and I take my finger and run it across my throat at him. I almost get all the way across before him and the guys crack up at my antics.

There's a knock at the front door and Leo stands, his laughter dying off, "I'll get it." Shawn scampers off to the basement. Shadow stands, grabbing my empty plate and Sir Waffles jumps down to follow him into the kitchen where he's taking it.

Probably to hide from my parents. He's heard the things I've said about them.

Can I come hide in there with you?

I have a million dollars on the first thing my mother says to me is something about how awful I look.

Bet me.

CHAPTER 36 – GUNNEY

Opening the door, I greet Zharia's parents and welcome them in, even though they give me a wary glance. I've never met them, but I've heard plenty about them from her. Zharia is not particularly close to them. I imagine their stay won't be a long one.

Zharia stands up from the chair as her mom shrieks, "Oh my Zharia!" and starts crying and wobbling her hobbit self over to her daughter. From my viewpoint, her mom is genuinely shaken up and is barely keeping it together. Far from the haughty heartless bitch Zhar thinks she is.

Zharia towers over her mother, at least a head taller. But I see her dad is our height and that's where Zhar's height comes from. Our girl is like five-eight and her mom looks like a child standing next to Zhar.

"Mom," Zharia hugs her mom to her. Her dad walks over and puts his arms around her too. He kisses the top of her head and moves her long hair off her shoulders. I think he just wants to touch her; make sure she's here for real.

We're all that way. I can't keep my hands off her, for fuck sure not taking my eyes off her, I'm never letting her out of my sight again.

Her mom pulls back and places her hands on Zhar's cheeks, "You look exhausted, too pale, too thin, but I'm glad you're home and well." Her mom grabs her back up in a hug.

Another knock at the door and I see it's the older detective who's in charge of her case. Fat lot of work they did for us. To say we are impressed with their investigation would be a bold-faced lie.

Her mom lets her go to meet the paunchy detective. He holds his hand out and says, "You're the woman of the hour. Hello, young lady, I am really happy to see you. Damn happy. I'm Detective Scott, lead investigator on your missing person's case."

She shakes his hand, "Pleasure to meet you. Thank you for your assistance."

She knows damn well he didn't do shit.

To be fair, she doesn't know the extent we went to as well.

"I'd like to ask you some questions if that's ok?" Detective Scott asks.

"Absolutely," Zhar agrees.

Birdie, Danger, Rock, and Pierre show up as the detective is finishing up. Zharia's parents and him just left and Zharia is holding Denver tight to her body. It catches in my chest to see her with the baby.

I would love to see her with my kid, but it's solely up to her. I know she's been avoiding the idea for a long time, and that's why she broke up with Shadow for pushing the idea, but you can clearly see the genuine joy on her face when she holds Denver.

Birdie is a crying mess. Danger is trying to console her but she keeps starting over with a fresh wave of tears every five minutes. Even Pierre's eyes are a little misty. I see him smudge his cheek every once in a while.

"I know you just spoke to the police, but their investigation was trash. We need to ask you some questions too because LSS isn't getting away with this. Are you up to this right now?"

"Yeah, sure." Zharia settles back onto the couch. Shawn stayed down in his room to give us all privacy. Shadow is stretched out beside her on the couch, manspreading, and the other side is reserved for me. I head to the kitchen to grab Zhar another cup of tea and a snack when I hear Danger ask her, "Are you ok?"

"Yes, surprisingly they treated me well given the circumstances."

"Did this have anything to do with your affiliation to SDS?" Danger asks.

"No, I don't think so, Linc, not at first. It had everything to do with me being a doctor." I love how she uses his shortened government name on him. Only people super close to him will he allow to use his given name and she appears to be one of them.

"Will you explain that for me, please?"

"Yeah but just know this totally breaks HIPAA law and doctor patient confidentiality and you know I'm not like that, so this has to stay in this room and go no further. There was a man who suffered a gunshot wound. The ER was super busy with flu patients, and those with life threatening injuries, such as gunshots, which we all know this town has a plethora of, were rerouted to my facility. Mr. Matt Callahan is responsible for my abduction. He came in with a gunshot wound and I operated on him. He took a liking to me and arranged for me to be taken after I turned him down when he asked me to come to Houston with him. Pete explained when I got there, they needed a doctor, a war was coming, and they were fighting to take over Lake Charles and more ports along the way. He said they were growing an army and taking over."

Zharia puts her hand to her forehead and holds it there. She takes a deep breath in and lets it out, calming herself. These are details she did not mention to the cop. It doesn't concern him. Even though we are ex-military, we are still leery of police.

"I was taken because I was a skilled doctor. I discharged him and when I left work later that night, they got me in the parking garage."

"Your purse and cell phone were found kicked under your car. The camera that would have had your kidnapping was completely disabled. We had nothing to go on from it," Birdie supplies.

"They drugged me. I woke up disorientated in what I came to refer to as my prison cell. It was a concrete room, like a storage closet. I had the most uncomfortable cot and that was it. Shawn was kind enough to bring me a blanket and pillow and he fed me so well. That's another thing. I brought an LSS member back. Oh! And Pete says you have one of his moles amongst y'all."

All of us guys growl with that revelation. We are gonna have to kill one of our own. But were they really one of us if they're a mole?

I hand her a bowl of her favorite ice cream and she gladly takes it. She needs something to make her happy right now. Talking to her parents and the police made her anxious. I take my seat next to her and lay my hand on her thigh.

Birdie does not miss the move.

Shadow puts his hand on her other thigh.

Birdie definitely didn't miss that one, but she says nothing. She's searching Zhar's face for any reaction, to which Zharia gives nothing away. But I see Birdie's scrutinizing glances.

If all works out according to dreams and wishes, this will be normal for them soon enough. We'll discuss that later.

"Wait, you brought a member back? How the fuck did you two allow this?" Rock is agitated by the news and his jaw is set to anger as he points back and forth between me and Shadow.

Shadow holds up his other hand, "Whoa, we do as the rescued lady says."

"His name is Shawn. He's nineteen, from Detroit, and was in culinary school in Houston. He got mixed up with some very bad people thinking he could make friends and never banked on them being psychos. His family was threatened and he complied to protect them. He's currently downstairs looking up culinary schools in NOLA. I've asked him if he wants to patch over to SDS but he's thinking about it. He's got a bad taste for bikers now, if you can imagine." Zhar levels a look at Rock and continues, "Said he wants to talk to a few of you first. I reckon he wants to make sure he's not signing up for another fuckshow like he just left. He's going to be a hunted man when Pete finds out he's not among the dead and bailed."

Rock and Danger seem to be mulling over this information between them. A look between them is exchanged and Danger nods.

"When we're done talking, we want to speak to him," Rock says.

Zhar narrows her eyes at him, "You will not scare him any further. I won't allow it. He's just a kid. You be nice to him or you answer to me."

Rock's eyebrows raise, seeing the challenge in her words. He holds his hands up and nods at her. Him, nor can the rest of us keep the surprised looks off our faces at her demand of the great and powerful wizard of NOLA. No one ever demands anything of Rock or speaks to him in this tone. Well, except for brave Birdie over there, she gets a pass as his daughter though.

"Ok, I will not scare him, but what are your plans for him?"

Her face softens when she replies, "I wish to see him back in school, graduating, making his grandma proud, having his own place, building a life. He's just a kid who made a bad, uninformed decision to join the Saints. He's sweet and nice, and he was kind to me when I was just as terrified as him. He's my sweet friend."

Nope, don't like her saying another man was sweet. I refrain from growling under my breath. An intense wave of possessiveness churns up the emotions inside of me.

'MINE' chants over and over in my warped head.

Birdie leans forward, "This needs asked, babes. Did they hurt you? Do we need to go to the hospital for a rape kit?"

Both Shadow and I stiffen at Birdie's question. Even though we know the answer already, it still kicks us in the balls to hear the word rape. Especially when it's in the same sentence as our girl.

Any man who rapes a woman deserves a torturous death.

"No, no one hurt me except for Pete. He hit me when I told him I wasn't a miracle worker. Other than that, no one hurt me. I was lonely and afraid and so goddamn exhausted. They ran me ragged."

That man will die for that one. I hope I get to him first. It will be a race between me and Shadow. I want to rip him apart with my bare hands. Maybe pluck his eyes out and wear them as a necklace so he can see me dismember him limb by limb.

Birdie lets out the pent-up breath she was holding. "Oh, thank fuck."

"Yeah, I agree. Although, I was terrified that it was coming at any second but no one ever attempted it. Shawn said Pete told everyone I was off limits and if they did try anything, they would die…which I found rich coming from the flesh peddler himself. Don't get me wrong, I'm immensely grateful for that because let me tell you, there were a few who weren't shy about leering at me every time I left the room. Creepy skeevies. I didn't leave the room without an escort any of the times, but I just never knew if whoever was going to pay a guard to come in at any time."

Shadow does not even attempt to hide his growl. I'm right there with him. Shadow grumbles under his breath a string of curses.

"I'm just exhausted." Zharia lets out a heavy sigh. For the first time since being home, her eyes fill with tears. I've been worried about how she's processing all this. I texted Birdie about it. She's been guarded but happy, almost fluttery. Almost like she's acting like the past nineteen days didn't happen.

Ignoring it isn't a great coping mechanism. She's compartmentalizing her trauma. I make a mental note to ask her about it when everyone leaves and we have our talk.

"I had no idea what time it was, ever, and Shawn was nice enough to tell me what day it was and how long I had been there. I felt like I would just get to sleep and they were banging open the door and dragging me back over to their makeshift treatment and surgery room. It's going to take me a while to get back on schedule. But I was fed well, Shawn made sure of it. I loved being his guinea pig for new recipes he tried." Zharia rubs her belly as she says this. She doesn't look like she was starved while being there, she just looks exhausted.

"How is my hospital?" she tentatively asks.

Birdie is the one to answer. "It's good. Everyone is worried sick about you. Most of them have been showing your pictures around town too. Isolabella really stepped up and has been running things since you we taken. You owe her a hefty bonus. I've been going for a few hours every other day to help her out. Goddamn, you have too much paperwork to do," Birdie chuckles.

Zharia laughs and replies, "You have no idea, sis. It's ridiculous." Zharia blows her a kiss across the table. Birdie snatches the invisible kiss out of the air and leans sideways and puts her hand behind her, to slap it on her ass. Both of them crack up at themselves.

I've seen them do this between them for a while now. I know that's their code for I love you more than life. She told me about a year ago at a club function when I saw them do it. They were tipsy and I had to take Z home. That night when I walked her to bed, tucked her in, I told her goodnight and she blew me a kiss. That's how I knew her feelings were changing. It was the first time she had blew me a kiss. That night I slept in the spare room. I didn't trust my resolve if she tried anything in her drunken state.

Zharia turns to Pierre and blows him a kiss too, "I don't want you to feel left out." Pierre's catch is always different from Birdie's. He grabs at the air and places his open hand on his chest over his heart and nods to her with his own smile and a wink.

"I would have made sure your plants were watered and Sir Waffles was taken care of, but these guys had it the entire time while staying here," Pierre tells her.

Yeah, Pierre offered but we told him since we were here already, there was no need for him to make a special trip. Pierre was satisfied with our reassurance that we weren't going to starve Sir Waffles to death; however we did call on him when we went to Lake Charles.

We kept the house running without our baby.

Her SUV has had an oil change and even the toilets are clean.

Chapter 37 – Shadow

Her teary eyes look over to Rock who's leaning up against the entrance into the small dining room. "Pete told me what he asked you for. First, I have to tell you, I never expected you to trade off a port for me, I'm nobody to you." She almost lets a sob out, "But it still hurt deeply when Pete told me you told him to fuck off."

Christ, an arrow straight to the heart.

Rock clears his throat, staggers against the wall, shifting his weight. He looks like she struck him across the face, he's so moved and instantly upset. He stands up to his full height, "It was never about not trading the port for your return. I was going to do it, Zhar. You're like another daughter to me," Rock pauses to swallow, "of course I was going to negotiate your return, but you popped up on our radar before the deadline came. We knew your approximate location and Travares was whittling it down to the exact spot. That was why I confidently told him to fuck off. We already knew where you were and we were coming for you. I would never have left you there, sweetheart, please know that."

Her tears run down her cheeks and I lean over and wipe a few of them from her face. She leans into my hands and I brush some of her wild hair away from her face.

Rock moves towards her, pulls her up and wraps his arms around her. He smiles sadly, cheek resting on top of her head, "I love you too, Zharia, I was ready to give in to him to get you back. He didn't send the ultimatum until the day before. I had twenty-four hours to decide. I was willing to give him anything he wanted until you showed up on the map."

She pulls away from him and accepts the tissues Birdie is handing her. Zhar blows her nose and sits back down while Rock goes back to his spot on the wall.

"Yeah, about that, how did y'all find me?" Zharia looks around the room at us.

I gulp like a cartoon character. This is the moment she hates me again. This is it. I have to bare my soul and tell her what I did to her…without her consent.

I'm going to lose her all over again.

She will never forgive me.

She looks around to each of us for an answer, but we sit there quietly. They're waiting for me to fess up.

Fuck.

"Please don't get mad." I slip her hand in mine and face her. Deep breath. *Face the music, man.* "When Birdie got taken, I was terrified they would take you next. I was next in line after Danger. I saw how easy it was to find Birdie."

"What did you do, Bear?" she whispers, horrified, her eyes pleading with me. She knows. She's piecing it together.

I take a deep breath and peer into her gorgeous brown eyes, "I implanted a tracker in you while you slept."

She jerks her hand away from me and gasps. She stands up and hisses with venom, "Shadow Theodore! How dare you!"

I stand up too and reach for her and she jerks back. That pisses me off. "That tracker saved your ass, Zhar. We would have found you sooner if they had not had a jammer on the entire building. You left to a blood bank and came online. So be pissed at me all you want, but without that, we would never have found you. And don't think for one second Pete would have given you back when he got his way. He had no intention of giving you up. I did what I did without your consent because I loved you so much and I couldn't bear to lose you."

Her face is fuming. Her chest is heaving in her anger.

"You had no right," she yells at me.

I stare into her angry eyes, "You're right, but I don't regret it. Not one bit. It brought you home. It worked like it was meant to. I know I should have asked but I knew you wouldn't agree to it. I couldn't take the chance of losing you," I finish and try to reach for her hand again. This time she lets me take it and hold it. I lace our fingers and pull her to me, I speak to her in a soothing low tone, I have to earn her forgiveness, "I was terrified they'd take you, poppet. I did what I did out of love. I'd do it again if I knew it would bring you home again. I won't apologize for trying to keep you safe by any means necessary." My hand cups her face and I pull her chin up to look at me.

Her eyes overflow with tears as she stares up at me, her lips tremble and her chin wobbles, "I love you, Zhar, so fucking much. I regret a lot between us, but that is not one of them. I will never stop protecting you. It brought you home."

Her shoulders shake as she finally lets loose crying, fingers gripping the front of my shirt. I crush her to my chest and let her cry, soaking my shirt where she grabs. Great, wracking sobs shake her beautiful body. I keep my arms wrapped around her, helping hold her up, my cheek resting on top of her head.

I look at Gunney over on the couch and he nods with approval. By her ear, I whisper how much I love her.

I swing my gaze to everyone else in the room. Birdie wipes tears away as she watches Zharia sob. Danger and Rock are standing with their arms crossed as they watch us, one of them sniffing the air, like there's not onions under their noses. You can tell by their eyes Zharia's tears are hurting their hearts too.

Hearing Zharia hiccup and cry is killing me.

At one time Danger could have kept his face unreadable, but not now, not after being a man openly in love. His lips press into a thin line and his head bobs up and down.

During all of our meetings while searching for her, none of them had gotten mad at me for the tracker. Birdie was a little bit miffed, but she soon relented when Danger reminded her of her own tracker and how it saved her life. Then Birdie became just as hopeful as the rest of us.

She had absolute faith in us that we would find her and bring her home. Her unwavering support meant the world to us.

Since I texted Danger and then Birdie, the small audience here knows Zhar hasn't processed or dealt with the emotions or experience yet. She's pushed it aside and feigned a calm, cool attitude. When seriously, all of us knew she was going to have a breakdown at some point. I'm just glad she's having one at all.

They also know, this thing between me and her, it's not over, far from it and she's processing that too. There's a lot dumped on her shoulders right now, burdening her heart, and part of this breakdown—totally predictable.

Wrapping my arms around her, I pick her up and sit back down with her cradled in my lap, head tucked in the crook of my arm, cheek on my chest. We let her cry into my shirt as much and as long as she needs. We feed her tissues and take the full ones for the trash.

Gunney scoots over and caresses his fingertips down the side of her head, from her forehead down to her chin, and combs his fingers through her hair with the other hand. He rains down kisses on her eyes and forehead. He murmurs something in her ear and she nods and sighs into me, finally relaxing her body. I dip my chin and kiss her forehead too as I slightly rock her like a baby. Her body jerks with a hiccup every once in a while as her meltdown subsides.

Both Gunney and I look up to see everyone gawking at us. Gunney shrugs and I simply say, "It's complicated."

Birdie can't stop the smile spreading across her face. And I can't stop the slow smile spreading across mine too as I look into her twinkling eyes across the coffee table, rocking my vicious little poppet in my lap. A bestie approval. I'll take it. The strongest woman I know and love is going to be mine again.

Well, partly mine.

There's this other guy too.

CHAPTER 38 – ZHARIA

Birdie and the crew left about twenty minutes ago. She had plenty of pizzas delivered and we invited Shawn up to eat with us. Afterwards, the guys took him out on the back porch to talk to him. They were nice to him, or so Shawn says.

I will beat up those bikers if they are mean to him, I swear to fucking god I will.

Even though Shawn was too afraid to help me, I still want to give him a fighting chance in life. I don't know, something just compels me to help him. I feel protective of him now for some reason. Maybe it's trauma bonding and becoming friends despite the age difference and servitude we were both forced into.

"So…"

Shadow comes into the living room after helping Leo clean up in only a pair of gray sweats slung low on his hips. He sits down in the chaise and makes kissy noises while he watches me. In the blink of an eye, Sir Waffles is in his lap, head held high, wanting pets and purring like a Harley motor. Of course.

Leo follows him wearing only basketball shorts looking like some kind of biker god.

Why don't these boys have shirts on? This is like torture. They both look mouthwatering delicious. It makes my pussy throb thinking about taking both of them on at the same time. It was my number one fantasy while locked up.

It's like they're trying to be irresistible.

They're winning at it. It's totally working.

I will give them whatever they want if at least one of them will fuck me within an inch of my life.

I squirm in my corner of the couch and look at both of them. I can see they're both nervous. I'm about to either fuck all this up or get everything I dreamed of.

"Ok, first, thank you so much for looking for me." Everyone told me how diligent these two were and they never gave up, pushing themselves past the brink of exhaustion. I wipe away a few tears that spill over. I wave my hand in front of me, "Don't worry, happy tears," I smile at them. "I am so grateful for both of you. I don't know what I did to deserve two such loyal men as yourselves. But I appreciate you."

They both nod at me. "Anytime, poppet."

"We would have never stopped."

This is why I love them. They really would have kept going. I clasp my hands and hold them to my heart.

"Second, I've done a shit ton of thinking, lots of soul searching, and taken accountability for all my red flag behaviors. I've looked at my core and who I am. I realize I'm the problem most of the time. So, I'll just come out and say it, I love both of you very much. I want both of you and I'm not going to pick between you two, ever, so you can learn to share or get nothing at all."

By the astonished looks on their faces, I've surprised them. I'm surprising myself here so at least we are all on the same confusing page. I would never have gone for being shared like this before. But sitting for hours in your own silence and twisted mind lets you really take a good, close-up look inside yourself and why you were against it in the first place.

Leo and Shadow look at each other and then back at me. Shadow steeples his fingers with that feral grin of his and Leo licks his lips and says, "Well, funny you should say that, princess, because we've talked, uh, Shadow and I," this is the moment I realize how nervous he is, "and we…that's the plan we wanted to present to you. We're both onboard and I kinda think the past twenty-four hours has proven we can work well together and take care of each other."

Shadow sits in the chaise and begins to stroke Sir Waffles's silky fur with one hand and nods his head while looking at me. He props his head up with the other hand and gives me a devilish look.

I look at Leo's face and he has his cute boyish grin going. The one he has when he's excited or happy.

Dear fuck, they really are serious. I never thought they would go for this.

"Really? For real, not joking? I'm talking like a real poly relationship not just fucking." I supply.

Leo smiles and his eyes crinkle at the corners, "Not joking in the slightest. See, Shadow and I were already brothers, but we've grown closer in our mutual pursuit to get our woman back. Topics come up, ya know, we're good, baby, all in. All that's needed is to decide whose house we're all going to live in."

I feel my mouth drop open. What? Holy fuck. It's happening! My dreams are coming true.

I look over at Shadow and sit up a bit, "And you're ok with this?" He's the one I worry about most.

"I've realized if I want love, I'm going to have to learn how to change. I need to handle you better. I need more compassion, calmness, patience. Less aggression when I don't get my way. But I promise my communication skills will get much better going forward. As proven, I will do anything to make you happy and keep you that way. I'm still full of the love you want so badly, the love you miss. I'm still the man who's deeply in love with you. If sharing you means I get to stay in your life and kiss you every day, then I will share. But only with Gunney. No one else, ever."

I'm so shocked I could be knocked over by a feather.

I land my gaze on Leo, "And you?" I know now that he's bisexual, so does this mean he and Shadow have been?...

"Same, babes. If the only way to keep you is share you, then considered yourself communal property," he says with a wide grin. Sobering up a little, "I can see the wheels moving inside there. No, there's nothing between me and Shadow. I think he'd rather cut my dick off than let me fuck him."

Shadow scoffs and says, "As if I would be bottom. Good luck topping from the bottom, *bro.*"

Leo and I both laugh because we both know there's no way Shadow would ever be submissive. He may bend and concede to me, spoiling me, but in the act of sex, I'm all his to bend and break. He's the only man to make me want to feel that submissive. His praise is the best when I just submit and let myself go.

Leo leans from his end of the couch to the middle cushion looking up at me, "Absolutely ok with it, if you'll have me, because I want you so fucking bad." I watch his eyes darken and it makes my heart speed up. Wet heat gathers inside me.

"So, we're really going to do this?" I ask while I bite my thumbnail. I don't know why I'm nervous for their confirmations but a jolt of adrenaline courses through my veins. The excitement at the possibility of having both of them rocks my pussy's core and my walls clench tight in anticipation. Two dicks. The butterflies in my chest explode when they answer. Two gorgeous and perfect men.

"All in, poppet."

"I'm most definitely in, baby."

"What about you? Are you ok with this?" Shadow asks me. He's a hard man to get a read on, but not for me, I see the nervousness lining his eyes.

"I'm good," I say softly with a smile. "It was my favorite fantasy while locked away in my mind for hours on end."

Gunney flashes me his eyebrows and a huge smile, "Oh yeah?" He reaches over and drags me across the couch to straddle him on the other side, "Do tell, baby."

He starts kissing on my neck, moving my hair away from my collarbone. His hands roam over my ribs and back down my spine. I angle my head down to look him in the eyes. All I see is love there.

He grips the back of my head and crushes his lips to mine. I immediately part my lips and give him access. His tongue comes in hot and sweet to tangle with mine. I lose my breath as he squeezes my left boob. Leo swallows up all the moans he's pulling out of me. I feel him getting harder beneath me and it excites the shit outta me.

I hear Shadow get out of the chair behind me and pad over to stand at my back. While Gunney nibbles my chest and neck, kneading my breasts through my shirt, he's intent on making me shiver with goosebumps. Shadow tilts my head back with one finger under my chin. About that time Leo sucks a nipple into his mouth. My mouth pops open on a sharp inhale of air.

They've awakened what's beneath. My body's on fire.

The top of my head rests on Shadow's hard stomach, lips parted and my breath coming in pants now, I look up at him from this angle. Fucking hell, my clit throbs, he's so beautiful.

They're going to make every one of my dreams come true. I just know it.

Fuck Yes!

"Were you a bad girl while you were away? Did you finger yourself to fantasies of us fucking you together?"

His filthy mouth always gets my blood pumping harder and harder and for each beat it shudders in my chest.

"Yes," I whisper.

"Oh, poppet. That's my dirty girl." My heart flutters at being his dirty, filthy girl again. "Tell me where you went to make yourself come thinking about us making you feel really good."

Leo pops off my nipple, "Oh, she liked it, brother. I just felt her pussy clench on top of my dick."

Tattletale.

Leo's hands expertly pull my tank top off and his thumbs brush across my nipples through my lacy bra. Now I'm really happy I planned ahead for this when I got dressed after my shower earlier. This panty set is gorgeous and so sexy.

"Oh my fuck, just beautiful," Leo whispers as I answer Shadow quietly, "The shower."

Leo growls into my neck and nips it a little harder. Shadow grinds his hard cock into my back. Both of their hands on my body is driving me crazy. I know I'm getting so wet. I can literally feel it dripping out of me into these pajama shorts.

Shadow smiles and tsks at me, "Such a naughty girl."

Leo groans and says, "Fuck, I love naughty girls. They make the best good girls."

"What do you think, Gunney? Should we take her to bed and worship her? Show her how much we missed her?"

My breath comes in ragged pants waiting for his response. I still haven't taken my gaze off Shadow. His eyes are almost completely black with desire.

"Please," I softly plead.

I'm so turned on even my toes are vibrating. My hips have started moving on their own accord. My hands grip Leo's head to my bosom therefore when he talks I feel his breath flutter across my delicate skin, "I say let's do it, bro. Let's make her ours. But I'm claiming this pussy, you've already been in it."

Shadow chuckles then leans down to kiss me upside-down, "That's ok, I love her ass just as much," he whispers across my lips. He looks into my eyes again, "You're so beautiful between us." He runs his hand down the back of my arm and pulls at my hand, "Come here, poppet. We're going to make your dreams come true."

Through my lust haze I have enough decency to ask, "What if Shawn hears us?"

Shadow frowns at me for even thinking about this right now. "He has a shiny new PS5 and Grand Theft Auto with a headset. Trust me, he's busy for the rest of the week."

Ok then. Seems they thought of everything. They really were planning this. Mission: Seduction—complete.

"Now come on, baby girl," Shadow pulls me off of Leo's lap and leads me down the hallway to my bedroom. Leo is quick to follow. Shadow enters before me but when his broad shoulders move out of the way I see they have numerous candles lit around the room casting a romantic glow.

Yep. They really did plan to seduce me.

It worked. Like a charm.

It settles in my core; I made the right decision. Finally.

Leo puts his thumbs in my waistband and slowly tugs my cotton shorts down, taking my panties with them. I feel the chill in the air settle on my skin. I feel the wetness pooled at the apex of my lower lips.

Shadow takes my bra off, I'm not sure if my hard nips are from the chill of the room or from excitement. I'm going to say a little of both.

"Zharia you are just as beautiful as I remember," Shadow breathes out in awe.

I smile at him, still not believing we are at this point.

Gunney leans out from behind me, he stands almost in front of me by Shadow's side and says, "I had to see for myself. Goddamn, you're gorgeous. I can't tell you how many times I've wanted to see this very sight."

Both of their attention makes me blush. Instead of being coy, I put my hands on my hips, baring my full breasts to them in a flirty way.

Gunney sucks in a breath while Shadow growls in appreciation. That's the effect I was going for.

"Fuck, I can't wait to be inside you again." Shadow strips off his sweatpants and grips his pierced cock in his hands, stroking slowly. "Have you missed me, baby?"

"Yes," I whisper.

"Who's your shadow daddy?"

"You are," my breathy voice answers like the dirty girl I am. Shadow drags his fingertips down the front of my chest to the tip of my hardened nipple where he pinches it into a stiffer peak.

"So beautiful."

Leo looks over and says, "No fucking way, you're pierced and you never said anything this entire time."

"They feel wonderful too." That's my truth. It's amazeballs.

Shadow chuckles and says, "I just didn't think it was important to bring up. We never talked about dick size, *bro* but I got one of these barbells for every inch."

"That thing looks like a monster, Shadow. I'm being honest, dude, but I'm not counting those barbells under there."

"Well then, there will be no confusion on who's big dick in charge, huh?"

I can't help but laugh at these two. I fucking love it. But I came into this room to fuck and they are veering off the path.

"Umm guys, can we get back to the plan? Mainly dicks inside me, regardless of size." I ask.

This gets their attention and hungry eyes back on me.

Leo drops his shorts and I finally get to see what that nice bulge in his pants looks like up close and personal. He's perfect. I can't wait to taste him. He's built not so different than Shadow. I don't know why he's playing with Shadow like that; they both have great cocks. The sight of them standing in front of me naked and hard makes more wetness drip from me.

"Please. Hurry," my voice breathy with arousal.

"Does our precious baby want stuffed full of our cocks that bad?" Leo asks me as he spreads his precum over the crown of his cock. It shines in the candlelight and I lick my lips.

Goddamn. It's almost my undoing when Leo brings his cum glistened thumb up to his mouth and licks it off. Shit, that's hot. I catch myself opening my mouth for it.

Leo doesn't miss it though.

Shadow neither, "Do you want to suck our cocks, Zhar? Do you want on your knees for us?"

"Yes," I moan. "Please."

My clit's a steady drum, beating to a rhythm old as time. The heavy throb demands release. Shadow is a master at edging. I'm fucked.

Shadow reaches and grabs a pillow, throwing it on the hardwood floor in front of them. He crooks a finger and beckons me to the floor. I go down to my knees very willingly. Fuck yeah, I can't wait to taste them. I love sucking cock.

"That's it, surrender to us baby. Let us take care of you."

I wrap a hand around each one of their cocks. They hiss in unison at the contact and I smile. This is going to be so much fun. The butterflies in my stomach answer my whimper by opening up the floodgates and taking flight.

"Are you sure this is what you want?" Shadow asks.

Closing my eyes, I sigh in contentment before taking my time to lick them up their rods from balls to tip.

I look up at them through my lashes, "I'm tired of fighting it, this is what I want." I slip Leo into my mouth and roll my tongue over his tip and seal my lips around him.

I love the groan that vibrates out of him, "Oh god, Zhar." His breath catches in his chest. He grabs my hair, "Fuck. You look so beautiful with me in your mouth."

Shadow pulls my hair over my shoulder on my other side, "You suck cock like a goddess, Zharia, and you look so fucking sexy doing it. Your lips are made to wrap around a dick."

Leo's hand strokes my cheek and I pop off of him and look up into his adoring eyes. He smiles and says, "Better than imagined."

That makes me smile, damn straight it is.

I lean over in front of Shadow and he's got a shit-eating grin, "How you want it, poppet?"

The wicked smile unfurls across my lips, "Disrespectfully."

"Let's show Leo what our girl's capable of."

"Be a good boy and put that cock in my mouth," I tell him.

I know my role, I put my hands on his thighs, then I open and stick my tongue out.

"I swear to fucking god, you and that mouth," he groans as he slides his dick into my mouth. The pulse of electricity between us reignites and explodes in my chest. I wrap my tongue and lips around him and hang on.

This is where I'm supposed to be. Stuffed full of their dicks.

It's official. They are mine.

Mine.

Chapter 39 – Shadow

One thing you should know, Zharia loves oral—giving and receiving. One of her favorite things is a Sixty-Nine. She loves road head, elevator head, anywhere head where she can fit time in for sucking a cock. And by the gods, she is incredible at it too. Expert level. You will never see me pass up a chance at a Zharia blowie.

Real soon now, Gunney's going to be really happy he's got a truck with a bench seat.

Fuck her mouth feels amazing. I've got her hair threaded through my fingers, pulling that hot mouth deeper on me.

"Ready?"

She nods while bobbing on my rod. Putting my hands on the sides of her head, I fuck her mouth in earnest, hitting that thingy thang in the back of her throat.

Her hot tongue swirls all over me as she moans around my dick. She pays attention to that little spot I love some much.

"Goddamn. Lips like sugar, and so addicting. I love the way you suck cock. I fucking missed you so much, Zharia," I groan breathlessly as I move in and out of her mouth while she moans deep in her throat. Her ragged breathing is filling up the room. "You take me so well. You love sucking dick, don't you?"

She whimpers, but when I say, "Are you ready for the good part, poppet?" she groans loudly and hums, "Uh-huh."

My grip on her head tightens and I start fucking her face fast and hard. She gags and I pull out, she's breathing heavy, drooling on the floor, coughing a few times, "Want more?"

At her nod, I push back in, hitting the deep back of her throat, a few times making her gag again. Her eyes tear up and I look over at Gunney with a smirk and silently let him know, Zharia can handle anything we dish out to her. "She loves it, Leo and she can never get enough cock. You've hit the jackpot, brother. Look how beautiful she is."

I pull my dick out of her mouth. Her lips are swollen and there's spit running down her chin. "More?"

She nods and says, "Yes, please."

"Good. Suck his cock now. Fuck her face, Gunney."

She's so obedient. I love that about her. She knows anything I tell her to do will benefit her also.

Her lips wrap around Gunney again and he exhales, "Fuck, baby."

As I stroke my hard as steel dick, slick with her saliva, I gaze at her lovingly, "She's so needy. That greedy little pussy says one dick isn't enough. You have to have two of us fuck that tight pussy and plump ass."

"Christ, Shadow. You're gonna make me come with your fucking mouth," Gunney pants.

"Get used to it. Zharia loves it, don't you babe? Let me check." I crouch down beside her and run a finger over her pussy lips, her very wet pussy and brush my fingertips over her clit. A guttural moan rumbles deep in her chest. "Oh, yes, she's ready. You want fucked, poppet?"

I push my finger in, feeling her tight wetness around me. Just as heavenly as I remember.

I'm right by her ear when I let my voice wash over her, "You're so wet, baby girl, so very greedy. That pussy just sucked my finger right in. You want filled up, poppet?"

Her eyes slide over to me as I stand back up, never once taking my eyes off of her. She watches me with her big brown eyes, bedroom begging eyes. As I lift my hand to Gunney's mouth, he opens his lips and sucks my fingers into his mouth.

Zharia growls her arousal around his cock, like a primal animal in heat. She starts breathing heavy through her nose. He pulls out with a hiss and a groan.

She takes a deep breath and pants, "Please, god yes. I want you inside me," she looks over to Gunney, "both of you. Please."

"On the bed it is then," Gunney says as he helps her stand up. She hops on the big bed and crawls to the middle. Fuck, it's a glorious sight, her ass up in the air, everything in view. I throw my arm out to halt Gunney and I gesture to her most succulent, most rounded, curvaceous ass I've ever saw and whisper to him, "Now would you ever give that up?"

Zharia reaches the middle and turns around sitting back on her calves with her legs spread. Her beautiful wet pussy's on display in the candlelight. Her puffy pussy lips and upper thighs glisten and I know she's more than ready.

"Never brother, fucking never. I get it now."

CHAPTER 40 – GUNNEY

Goddamn, I've died.

This is heaven. Nothing feels better than this.

My cock throbs at the sight of her luscious ass swaying to the bed in front of me, but it didn't top the sight of her turning and putting her pussy on display for us. Jesus fuck. It's beautiful. The most beautiful sight I've ever seen.

I stretch out beside her and as soon as I'm laying down, she's already on me, leaning over and kissing me. I love how vocal she is and all the noises she's been making, they're driving me crazy with need. I can't wait to see her unravel.

I roll to my back and pull her up my body. She wants to stop at my hips but I keep pulling, I break our steamy kiss and tell her, "Com'mere baby, sit on my face. Let me practice eating pussy."

She bites her lip and whimpers. I don't think it'll take her long to detonate. I know how long it's been for her. I've been through it all right beside her, yearning for this moment.

Zharia settles her thighs on the sides of my head and I immediately wrap my hands around them and yank her down to my mouth. Two swipes of my tongue and I'm hooked. I longed for good, sweet pussy, the kind I've always heard stories about, and Zharia's sweet taste is everything I ever dreamed it would be. Better because it's her.

I'm a full believer that I had just never found the right pussy for me. The desire was there all along but I was waiting for her.

All the others from my teens to my early twenties were just practice for her.

Her hips work over top of me as she chases her orgasm. I push one finger into her and understand Shadow a little more. Two fingers go in and her noises get louder. I don't think I've ever been with a woman so tight.

"Leo," her beautiful mouth says.

Her pussy walls are trembling and her pants above me sound beautiful. She needs to be pushed over the edge, tipped in a way that will shatter her.

Curling up my fingers like all the diagrams online told me to do, I find her sensitive g-spot tucked back in there. I'm just happy to remember in a time like this where it's sorta important. I know the minute she feels it, because she jerks, drops her head back. Her channel gets super tight and her hips buck.

"Leo, oh god, Leo, don't stop, please."

I pull her clit into my mouth, sucking it and caressing it with my tongue and that's what sets her off. Noted.

With a few good rubs of her magic spot and a couple good swirls of my tongue, a rush of wet heat floods my chin and chest as she comes on my tongue. I think my girl just squirted all over my chin because I feel it running down my neck. Damn, her pussy is tightening on my fingers to the point they feel like they're going to break.

Zhar bucks her hips as her cum dribbles down my fingers to my hand, down my chin to my chest. Hell fucking yeah. I've only read about this good stuff.

Proof that female ejaculation is not a myth. I'm forever changed. That was hot as fuck. I've never been with a girl who squirts but I am fucking here for it. I love it!

She sits back on my chest, catching her breath. "That was incredible," she pants.

"Goddamn, that was amazing," I say breathlessly when I finally take my mouth off of her. "Best fucking thing ever."

Shadow appears beside the bed. He tangles his hand in her hair, using it to pull Zhar over to kiss her deeply. When he pulls away he murmurs, "You look stunning riding his face. So fucking gorgeous, poppet. Now show me how well you ride his cock. I wanna see you fuck him real good."

She gets a beautiful smile across her serene face and starts sliding down the front of me. I have to say, Shadow directing this is hot as fuck. His filthy ass mouth was something I wasn't expecting. I sure as hell wasn't expecting it to turn me on quite so much.

Zharia moves herself over my cock. I feel her warm, wet center sliding over me. I wrack my brain for condoms. I don't ever remember her having them in these drawers but I know there's some in my bag.

Shadow stands there whispering in her ear and she giggles. This woman is giggling like a schoolgirl, I tell ya.

"Shadow get in my bag would ya and get the condoms out of the pocket."

He looks at me and smiles, "Only because that was one of the best shows I've ever seen." He moves off towards my bag on the floor by the dresser and she grabs his arm and says, "No."

What?

He steps back to her and wraps an arm around her waist while he nuzzles in her neck, "You gonna let your good boys fuck you bare? Nothin' in between us?"

Her head falls back and she whispers, "Yes. I trust you."

Holy fuck.

"I've never fucked anyone bare." That might be a stupid thing to admit.

"Zharia is the only person I've ever fucked bare and I'm clean. Just tested at Christmas."

"Shadow's my only." She reaches back and cups my balls, "As you remember my test from a long time ago and I've been with no one after that. It's ok to say no. We'll get your condoms for you."

"No. I'm all in, forever. I trust you. I'm clean. I had my test when you did Zhar." I hesitate, "I've not been with anyone else either."

Her eyes get big as saucers. She grins and it's adorable. "You waited that long for me?"

"Yes, baby, I did."

"I trust you too, bro," Shadow says. "You get first dibs man, but don't come. I know this is your first time with her and I want you to feel her come on your cock." He strokes down her neck with his hand and rubs her boob with this other hand, "It's an out of this world experience when she comes on you. Enjoy the ride, baby girl. Then I'm going to fuck that luscious ass while he fucks your pussy good. We're gonna fill you with so much cum." He slaps her ass cheek and I feel the jiggle clear down on my balls. God, I love her ass.

I can tell it excites Zharia because her breathing changes. Shadow's hands slide off her body and he says, "Get to it, love. Fuck him within an inch of his life."

"Yes, sir." She lifts herself up and positions me at her hot entrance. We lock eyes as she works her way up and down my shaft. Holy fuck, she's hot as hell.

I don't remember it feeling quite like this.

This is everything my dreams are made of.

Zhar lets out a ragged breath on a moan when she fully seats herself on my cock. Nothing's better than this. Absolutely nothing.

I understand how Shadow became so obsessed.

It's all so clear now.

All has been revealed. I believe.

I could never leave her and walk away.

Nothing could keep me away.

"Fuck me, Zharia, you feel so good. I missed you so fucking much, baby."

She whimpers and breathes, "I missed you too, Leo."

I grab her hips and buck up into her making her gasp and arch her back. "Fuck me, Zhar. Take what you need and ride me, baby."

Her hips start circling, making magic happen. She glides her hands up her belly, over her ribs and breast, up her neck and into her hair. Sexy ass move. She holds her hair up as she bounces on my cock, shaking her titties and moaning. She's glorious in the candlelight.

It's damn near my undoing. I bite my lip to keep from grinding my teeth.

She looks like a belly dancer the way she's moving her hips on me. I've never had a woman fuck me like this, with so much passion and need, with absolute submission to her pleasure. I must say, I love this.

Zhar rolls her head back and her long hair tickles my balls and thighs. One of my favorite things about her is her long sexy as fuck hair. I can't wait to wrap it around my fist as I rail into her from behind. I've pictured it every way you can think of.

My hands find their way from her hips to her boobs. I knead and rub them, gently squeezing. They're so plump and make the perfect tear drops.

"So goddamn perfect, you're so beautiful like this, baby. Better than I ever imagined."

I graze my thumbs over her nipples and she falls forward, her hands resting on my chest, her tits pushed out chasing my touch.

Pressing herself into me harder, moaning louder, Zharia grinds her pelvis down on me taking me deeper. Zhar's breath catches in her throat and she groans when I move a different way. Ahh, there's her sweet spot.

"Leo, I'm so close," she whimpers.

"You look beautiful riding me like this. Your pussy's so good, baby, I'm addicted already." I lift my hips up, grinding my teeth to keep from coming. "Come for me, Zhar. Let go, just let go. Come on my cock, beautiful, I want to feel you," I rasp.

This spurs her on, and a few seconds later I'm rewarded with her wet heat powerfully clamping down on my dick as she starts coming, scratching up my chest with her nails. The room fills up with her cries.

"LEO! Oh god, Leo." That's the most beautiful thing I've ever heard. I can't help but smile.

Zharia is loud!

"F-ff-f-uck, god it's so hard not to come." I grit my teeth to keep from coming. From some far away land I hear Shadow chuckling.

Don't come, Leo!

It's so hard, pun intended. "Yes, baby, that's it," I say as she's losing her mind on top of me.

As her orgasm ebbs, I reach up and pull her down to me and seal her lips with a fiery, full of desire, full of love kiss. Her hair curtains around us so I don't see Shadow come around to the nightstand. When I look through her hair, I see him grab the lube and head back towards the end of the bed.

Suddenly Zharia halts all movement and I know that's the moment he touches her asshole. I can only imagine the sight Shadow's getting to see right now. Fucking glorious. I'm jealous.

"Hey Shadow, how's that look back there?"

"Ohh, brother, it's the best sight in the world, I tell ya."

"You should take a pic so I can see."

Zharia gasps and says, "Wait…"

"If you don't want us taking pics of you like this, say so and we won't do it," I tell her gently.

"You promise to never use them against me?"

I reach up to cradle her face, "Baby, we're not going anywhere and do you really think we would do that to you? Never."

"Ok. Ok then, take a pic for Leo."

He sticks his thumb in her ass, making her yelp, and then there's a bright as fuck flash. He brings it up for me to see. My cock jumps inside her causing her to moan. "Oh goddamn," I say in awe. "That's…that's the best thing I've ever seen." I'm speechless.

Zharia jumps again and I know he's back to fingering her ass, getting her ready.

"Come down here," I prod her.

She leans down and starts kissing me. Fuck, her kisses are so sweet. Her tongue pushes into my mouth and she has total control over this. My hands slide down to her ass cheeks and I help spread her apart for Shadow. Zhar slowly rotates her hips on my hard dick while he fingers her ass from behind. I don't mind one bit.

Zharia moans into my mouth and I feel her pussy fluttering.

"You're doing so good, my dirty girl. She loves her ass played with, doesn't she?"

Zhar whimpers into my mouth and her hips apply more pressure.

"My filthy girl wants cock in her ass. You want your ass fucked raw, don't you, poppet?"

I'm pretty sure she loves his filthy talk.

Goddamn. I know I do.

She's chasing his touch and I can feel her backing up to meet his fingers harder.

She breaks our kiss and breathlessly tells Shadow, no begs him, "Please Shadow, fuck my ass. Fuck me, Bear, I need you in my ass."

Holy fuck. She's just as bad as him. They're both going to be the death of me.

"I'm gonna stuff my cock in this sweet ass. I'm going to stretch you so good. Are you ready, Zhar?"

She throws her head back, panting, "Please, Shadow, please fuck me. I want to feel both of you inside me, now, please." It's so cute how she growls out the 'now please,' like that will make us go faster.

However, I reply, "Say no more beautiful. It's time, Shadow. Let's fill our girl with cum."

CHAPTER 41 – ZHARIA

I groan so deep in my body from Shadow's fingers in my ass that I'm positive I vibrated the solar system. It feels so damn good.

I'm no stranger to anal, not even a stranger to anal with Shadow, but man, it's been such a long time. The stretch feels good at first, but when he adds a second finger, the stretch starts the delicious burn, that pleasure burn we love to hate. But we always want more of it.

He's scissoring his fingers inside me, preparing me, but it's his sexy fucking potty mouth that really sets me on fire. Each and every time. He can give me one of his smoldering looks and my knees get weak and my pussy walls clench from just a look.

"Your ass feels so good like this, Zhar, the perfect ass on display for me. I can't wait to put my dick in here." He pumps three fingers with every word. "To feel you squeeze me while you come on both our cocks, goddamn, it's a dream come true. Tell us how much you want it, poppet."

I push back on his fingers, seeking more depth, more pressure, just more everything. I whimper and tell them, "I want so stuffed I feel cock tickling my intestines. Fill me up, boys."

Leo chuckles and says, "We aren't quite that long but I'll try for you." He pulls me down for a kiss and Shadow removes his fingers from me.

"I'll never get enough of this sweet ass on display for me," he murmurs as he squeezes my cheeks.

I hear the squelchy sounds of lube slickening his cock and pretty soon he rubs his lubed fingers over my backdoor, spreading lube all over my hole. I've never had a threesome in all the things I've done sexually. Never had double penetration. I'm so happy these guys are my first. I know they will try everything in their power to not make it hurt.

So far, I'm loving it.

"Got her, Gunney?" Leo snakes a hand between us so his fingers stroke my clit.

"Yeah. Slow down, baby, let Shadow line up." Leo stills my movements but keeps moving his fingers. Shadow presses the crown of his cock at my entrance then slowly pushes into my back hole. "Slow and easy, Zhar. Take a breath for me," Shadow grits out.

As I take a breath, Leo grabs my ass and pulls me further apart, he looks into my eyes as I lean over top of him, "You're doing so good, baby. How do you feel?"

"I feel like I'm on fire. I want to come so bad." I wiggle my hips and Shadow hisses. I can't wait to feel those metal barbells pop in one by one. It feels amazing.

Once the head pops through the tight ring, Shadow slowly slides in inch by inch, barbell by barbell, "This is what you need. Goddamn, your body is made for us, poppet."

"Fuck yes it is," Leo agrees.

Tired of fucking around, I slam my hips back against Shadow and take him to the base of his cock and moan so loud my teeth rattle. This also takes Leo into my pussy deeper and makes him groan loudly.

"Goddamn," Shadow breathes, "That's it, all the way in, babe. Let us know when we can move."

I nod, biting my lip. The burn is intense now. "Move! Please move," I beg of them.

It's not like Shadow is a small man. Thank fuck he isn't huge. Both of my men are the perfect size for me. They hit all the good spots and I feel full; that's all that matters to me.

They begin moving in tandem at first. My body shakes from pleasure and pain. My mind and body needs this so bad. My heart needs this connection with them.

"You look so beautiful taking us both, so fucking beautiful," Leo says in his low, sexy voice over my skin, giving me shivers just as he pulls me down to him further. He whispers, "Fuck me, baby, ride my cock, Zhar," right before his lips crush against mine and his fingers speed up. Sweeping his tongue in, dancing with mine, he captures my moans. Another light sheen of sweat breaks out on my body. I feel it in the coolness of the air and it adds to the sensations.

Shadow leans over the back of me and kisses my spine, "So beautiful, Zharia. I love fucking you. You're doing so good, babe."

"Please," I whimper across Leo's lips.

"You're such a good girl for us, so good," Leo lovingly says. It makes my heart skip a beat. So, maybe I have a little praise kink.

"The fuck she is, she's such a bad girl, dirty little slut for us, needy little pussy swallowing us up, but begging for more, aren't you?"

"Yes! Yes! I want more!"

"You crave more of this, taking two cocks at once, you dirty little girl. You want to be our dirty girl, getting her ass and pussy fucked at the same time, don't you?"

All I can do is blubber out incoherent whimpers. Shadow definitely knows how to make my pussy clench and drip. I feel a huge hit of heat in my loins making my head spin as I climb higher.

"Jesus, Shadow," Leo groans.

"You like that too, bad boy? I got more where that came from. We about to get real nasty together. Fuck her good, Leo, I'm coming in this ass soon, I can't hold out much longer. Ready to fuck that pussy hard?"

"Yeah," Leo breathlessly replies. I don't think Leo is going to last much longer either.

"Do it, please do it, oh god, do it," I pant.

Both my guys feel amazing inside of me but my clit aches to come.

"Fucking this ass is going to become our full-time job. So tight, so hot it could melt my dick. But you want more, don't you? You can't get enough."

They find a good rhythm and their groans and grunts fuel my desire. "Harder," I cry.

They mind so well. Shadow grabs my long hair and wraps it around his fist, pulling my head back. Leo kneads my breast and plays with my nipple.

It's too much. It's all mind blowing, "I-I'm going to co—"

My orgasm hits me like a freight train: strong, detonating, ruthless, blazing a path inside my body. I barely can hear

Shadow and Leo over my keening and moaning and the blood whooshing through my veins. I see stars and fireworks and the light of the universe. It feels like an out of body experience like they said.

"Holy fuck! Oh god," I yell through my orgasm induced haze, "Come inside me, please, I need it so much," I beg them to give me their cum while I have the wildest orgasm of my life.

"Fuck, Zhar, oh god," Leo moves his hands from my boob and grips my hips, slamming up inside me, hard. "Baby, your pussy is drowning me," he grunts out. Leo swells inside of me, it feels amazing, and he topples over the edge with his own moans, chanting my name over and over. Goddamn, they sound so sexy. Loud lovers are my jam.

Shadow is pounding my ass behind me and I feel his control slipping. "I feel you coming inside her, Leo, right up against my dick through her walls. It's going to make me come."

"Oh god," Leo cries.

A few thrusts and Shadow is roaring out, "Fuck! Zharia, fuck, it's so good," as I feel him jerking inside me, spilling his seed deep in my ass.

"I fucking feel you, Shadow, oh fuck," Leo pants.

There's no way Shawn didn't hear all that. Fucking hell, Mrs. Fontenot next door had to have heard it. Raul at the corner store heard all this.

I fucking love it!

All of us out of breath lay in a heap on the bed, stacked on top of each other. Shadow is the first to move, and warns me, "I have to pull out, babe."

I nod my head in understanding because I don't know if I trust myself to speak. I believe I'm drooling on Leo's shoulder. "Ok," is my weak mumbled response.

He pulls his softening cock slowly out of my ass and when he's out, I feel so empty. Like our connection is broken. But I know it's still there, only the moment is drifting away, not the bond.

Next, Leo rolls me to his side, onto my back in the middle of the bed, slipping out of me too. "Don't move baby, we'll get you cleaned up."

He slides out of bed and meets Shadow in the ensuite. I hear them talking together, murmuring mostly, until Leo lets out a laugh and tells Shadow, "Next time, bud," while walking back to the bed with a big smile, his pearly whites on display.

"Here we go, Zhar." Leo spreads my legs and gently wipes me off with a warm washcloth, making sure to be careful with my behind. I appreciate that. It's going to be difficult to sit down for a day or so. But it was so, so worth every bit of pain.

Finally breathing normal, when Shadow gets beside the bed and puts a pair of sweats on, I tell them both, "That was amazing. I loved it. Thank you."

Leo cocks a brow at me. "Uhh, I had fun too, no need to thank us for fucking our girl right. It's kinda our job, our honor bound duty to make sure you are taken care of properly, princess," Leo says with a wink as he slides into the bed next to me, rolling on his side to run his fingers over my skin, making my skin goosebump.

Shadow comes around to the other side of the bed, closest to the window, Leo has the door side—I guess this is how we're all sleeping from now on—and gets in but pulls the covers up over us before settling on his side facing me. He cups my chin and pulls my face to look at him. He's so gentle and loving, a far cry from how he was treating me not ten minutes ago.

I love both sides of him though.

His thumb traces my bottom lip, "I love you. More than anything, for infinity, Zhar," Shadow chokes up with emotions, "I'm so glad you're home and I can be a part of your life again. I missed you so fucking much, my *pihi*, my heart." A tear does slip from his eye then, sliding to the pillow beneath him, and I know in this vulnerable moment, just how much Shadow trusts Leo. To see a grown man cry is utterly heartbreaking, such an intimately private thing. This is twice now Shadow has cried with me. It's not lost on me.

It amazes me I evoke such a response from him, such strong emotions. The sheer magnitude of love this man has for me is unfathomable.

My hand comes to rest on his cheek, my own tears slipping out, "I love you too. I thought I would never see you again to tell you how much I love you, and that I never stopped, I couldn't. I'm so sorry I ruined us. I don't deserve your devotion, but I'm happy I have it." I have to stop here or I'm going to all out ugly cry, I'm so emotional.

"Shh, no more of that guilt and sadness. This is our future," Shadow hugs my head and kisses my forehead then settles back onto his pillow.

I feel Leo stir behind me, his hand rubbing across my stomach area. How could I forget my Leo.

I half roll towards him so I can put my hand on his cheek now, "I don't know what I did to deserve a best friend like you, but I'm happy to be blessed with someone like you. Thank you for telling me, thank you for giving me time. I love you, Leo, and I have for a long time but I was terrified you'd laugh at me or never even entertain the idea of a woman for you. I love you so, so much. I'm very happy we had our time together before this new journey. Falling for you was so easy, there's nothing I don't love about you."

"Ride or die, baby. I love you too."

I slump onto my back and just breathe. I take a deep breath and try to hold the flood of emotions in. I look between them both, back and forth, "Th-Thank you both for searching for m-me, and not g-giving up." Both of them put their arms around me, caressing me, holding me, making me feel safe and loved.

I can't help it, the tears start flowing, the sobs escape. My body shakes with the feeling of completeness, the wholeness of my life, the happiness I'm bestowed. Peace settles over me with the departure of my sadness; this cleansing that's been going on with me has paid off tenfold. I'm beyond blessed.

As my eyes drift shut and my body relaxes into their auras, I think to myself: They are home to me—safe, loved, cherished, comforted—each of them is my home. And I never want to leave their arms ever again.

Chapter 42 – Shadow

I flip the pancake and return the pan to the burner when all of a sudden I hear the keypad on the front door beeping. Then the door is opening. Someone is walking in at seven thirty in the morning.

I grab my gun off the counter, quickly push the pan over to the back burner, and level it at the man's head who's walking in like he owns the place.

"Who the fuck are you?" I boom.

The man actually screams. Like a girl. He keeps screaming. And screaming more. Jesus.

"Shut up!" I yell at him.

Can't blame him really, he does have a loaded weapon pointed at his face. "Oh my god," he cries, "I-I live here! Well, sorta, I mean I used to but I don't anymore."

Zharia comes barreling out of the bedroom with Gunney hot on her tail.

She comes to a sudden stop when she sees what's happening, "Shadow, no! Put the gun away." She runs over to this guy and hugs him.

He literally cries into her hair. "Thank god you're here! Thank you. I'm so glad you're back."

Zharia releases him then turns around and gives me a scathing look. "This is my husband, Raj."

Leo is there on the chair and gesturing for this guy to sit down. When 'Raj' or The-Man-Who-Stole-My-Woman walks by, he shakes Gunney's hand while Gunney says, "Hey, Raj. Good to see ya, again."

So, Gunney knew who he was. And is on friendly terms with the woman stealer.

This is the first time I've seen him. It reminds me of the conversation I had with Danger:

Danger: I'm sorry, bud, you're just the wrong kind of Indian.
Me: Do you even hear how ridiculous you sound right now. Besides, my people are called Native Americans, dumbass, get with the times.

He thought that was the greatest Dad joke once the dust had settled and he thought I could joke around about mine and Zharia's break up. It was not the time. It was never the time to joke about it.

"Raj, this is Shadow."

The man looks at me wide eyed, turns to her and whisper-yells, "*The* Shadow?"

That makes my lips twitch. So, he *has* heard of me.

"We don't pull guns on your girlfriend's husband," Zharia admonishes me. *Nice try.*

"Girlfriend?" he squeaks out.

"Forgive me, my vicious little poppet, I thought he was an intruder so early in the fucking morning," I say with a hint of sarcasm. Zhar still gives me a glare but I know she sees the reasoning. Her anger is ebbing away because she knows I'm right.

After the wife thief left, we pulled the trundle out from under the couch to make a queen bed. We piled onto it with blankets and pillows and we've been watching movies all morning, with Shawn walking up and down the stairs. Mainly to the kitchen for snacks. He's really enjoying the PS5 games down there.

Without warning, nearly to the end of the movie, Zharia sits up and announces she wants to go to her facility. To see her people, she says.

Ehh, wait a minute.

"You want to go where you were kidnapped from?" Gunney asks her.

She nods her head.

"Is this going to be triggering for you? If it is, we aren't doing it yet," I supply.

"Yes, I want to go. No, it won't be triggering, but if it is I have you guys to calm me down. I'm going to have to get used to it at some point, I have to go back to work eventually."

As much as I clench my jaw at the thought of her in that parking garage again…my fists curl to take some of the heat I feel about that shit.

"Please don't, Shadow. Please don't fight me on this."

"My love, I'm not fighting, I'm asking if you'll be ok." I run my fingers through her tresses, tucking a strand behind her ear. "I don't mind going with you. You aren't leaving our sight right now. There's a target on you, also on that guy you insisted on saving downstairs; you're both wanted. This is the first place he's coming. Oh, that reminds me, you have an entirely new security system, which I can see we forgot to set last night." I catch Leo's eye beside me. Both of us forgot. That could have ended really badly.

"Whatever you want, princess," Leo says diverting her attention from that mishap. Of course he says that; he's pussy whipped too much now to tell her no about anything. I am too but nobody needs to know that shit.

It's complicated.

As the final credits roll on our movie, I pat her thigh and lift up to kiss her, "Go get ready, babe."

She smiles really big and hops off the makeshift bed, her bare feet falling on the floor and padding off.

Once she's out of the room, I turn to Gunney and slap is chest, "Bro, what the fuck? We forgot to set the fucking alarm we paid a fortune for. First fucking night, man."

"I know, goddamn it, we fucked up." Leo sits shaking his head.

"We can't fuck up again. He's probably coming back for her. From now on, we have to tell the other if we've set it, ok?"

"Yeah, right, ok, hold each other accountable. I like that."

"Come on, bro, let's get this over with."

I throw on some jeans and a teal colored, form fitting light sweater. I toss on a pair of ankle boots with a small heel. Today is chilly and uncommonly cold so I grab my short leather jacket off the hanger.

I leave my hair down and put on some mascara and lip gloss. This is about as good as it's going to get. It's a far cry from what they are used to but I seriously doubt any one of them is going to judge me on how I look, especially since it's my second day home after the ordeal.

I come out to the kitchen where both my guys are waiting and they look positively ravishing. Holy shit, how did I get so lucky to have both of these fine as fuck men fall in love with me? Me, of all people.

"You look nice, baby," Leo says to me.

"Thank you," I say softly, slightly taken aback. I'm still getting used to the 'baby' part. I love it, don't get me wrong, I'm just not used to it coming from him with the intention behind it.

"Smokin' hot, Zhar," Shadow eye fucks me with a lethal look.

"Thank you." I smile at both of them, but it falls when I ask, "So hey, guys? I don't know where my purse is. Was it stolen? I hope not, it's my favorite one. I thought you guys had it though."

"Your purse is here; it's in your closet. Everything was still in there. Good idea kicking it under the car like that," Leo says as he leaves the room, headed for my bedroom. Wait, I guess it's our bedroom now. This is going to be a lot to figure out.

Oh god. Am I ready to have them live here with me? Would Shadow give up his high-rise apartment he just bought? What if Leo doesn't want to give up his modern townhouse? And what the fuck am I going to do with Shawn?

One crisis at a time, Zharia.

Shadow pulls a box out of the side table's drawer. He strides across the living room to hand it to me.

"We bought you a new phone. All your old information has been transferred to this one. Your other one is toast. It didn't survive the fall."

I look up at him as he sets the box in my hand, "Thank you Bear. That's really sweet. Is there a tracker on this thing too?" I finish with a smirk, teasing him.

"As a matter of fact, smartass, there is. You won't be able to delete it either." He taps the end of my nose with his finger and winks at me. I know he's not joking. I guarantee there's a tracker in it, on my car, in my hair, hell, one's already inside me.

I should have known he would track me every way he can given what they went through. Honestly, it makes me feel safer and loved that much more considering what I've been through. I've come to accept Shadow loved me enough to always be able to find me. He knew I would refuse but he did it anyways because he listened to his intuition.

His intuition that saved me.

I can't stay mad about it. I mean I should. I really should. He violated so many privacy rules. It's stalking at its finest smothered under the guise of love.

No matter how infuriating it is to me, I'm grateful he did it. Without that, I may never have been found. I like to think I'd have worn down Shawn but there weren't good odds for that working out in my favor.

However, it gave me a chance to brush up on my flirting.

I raise up to my tip toes, hooking my arms around his neck and I kiss him. Slow, sensual, timeless. I love surrendering control to him and he doesn't miss an opportunity to take charge.

Shadow runs his hands down my body to cup my ass and squeeze. He growls into my mouth as he takes over. He presses his hard cock into me. Just a few layers of clothes stand between us and it feels like it's too much. My body answers back with some pressing of my own. I want to rip off my clothes right now and bend over for them all over again. Soreness be damned.

He pulls away and whispers, "Be careful, poppet, you're playing with fire."

"Mmm, I've always liked to play with fire." Then I bite his lip.

"Do you want to leave this house or go back to bed?" Leo says with a snicker as he enters the room with my purse.

"Later," Shadow promises me before he lets me go with a swat on my ass.

"Leave the house," I answer.

Leo hands me my purse and I rummage through it. He's right, everything's in there, right down to the spilled breath mints rolling around at the bottom clanging against some change and a thankfully unbroken perfume roll-on.

Playfully I say, "Ok, let's roll, buttholes," and cackle at their faces.

I'm happy today. Happier than I've been in two years.

Sure, I may have just survived a kidnapping and hostage situation but I'm safe now. Nothing painful happened to me, unless you count the slap and the exhaustion. The danger is still out there, but I have two warriors protecting me. I'm golden. My fantasies are coming true and life is great. I'd say I'm real happy.

"Ma'am." Leo shakes his head and walks to the front door, a smile on his face. He opens the door and with a flourish of his arm he gestures me out the door.

Shadow brings up the rear. Just as I reach the front entrance, Shadow slaps my ass, hard enough to make it sting, "Go ahead and call me a butthole again, poppet, see where that gets ya."

His tone makes me shiver with anticipation. Note to self: For a good time, be more childish and get creative with names that Shadow won't like.

As I'm walking down the steps a sudden thought occurs to me, "Wait, did anyone tell Shawn he will be here alone?"

"Yes, baby, it's all set. He'll be fine. He's not a child." Leo steers me to my SUV and opens the passenger door for me. I slide in and Shadow gets into the back. Pretty soon Leo is getting behind the wheel.

"Thank you for bringing my car home," I tell them.

"You're welcome."

It's as if they thought of every way to take care of me. Maybe this will work out after all. I just need to sit back and let them.

I try not to depend on anyone because that's where disappointment grows.

But I'm prepared to let them take care of me how they see fit. I'm excited for us to plan this new relationship we've got going. I can't wait to see where it takes us.

CHAPTER 44 – GUNNEY

Every single one of Zharia's staff members tears up or starts ugly crying upon seeing her. A few just sobbed incoherently for a solid five minutes. Couldn't understand a word they said through their snot.

It was nice to see so many people care for our girl. She gave each one a hug back and more started showing up as word spread throughout the facility. Isolabella, Zhar's right hand woman, came screaming down the hallway, arms out, excited to see Zharia.

She's probably excited she doesn't have to run this facility by herself now. Even with Birdie's help, I imagine it's a lot. I don't know how Zharia oversees everything she does. Maybe it's time I talked to her about hiring more managers and maybe make up some director positions. She can't keep working at the pace she has been.

Anything to make her job less stressful and give her more free time. The woman is a goddamn workaholic and I'm hoping now that we've established this threesome she will want to spend more time with us. She's going to have to give up some of her control and work in order to have more free time to build a relationship to maintain this level of happiness.

While the excited chatter and tears subside from the crowd that's gathered, Shadow and I settle into the nurses' station while we get eye fucked from the nursing staff.

In no way am I complaining, I love the attention, but Zharia is the center of attention right now. We are merely a nice-looking supporting role, manspreading in office chairs in tight jeans, watching Zharia's sweet ass fill out those pants. And those shapely legs. The thick thighs I want to wear as headgear again.

Christ.

Shadow sits up and leans over to me, where only I can hear, slaps my bicep and says, "Stop fucking drooling, ya maniac. You're giving the staff heated thoughts." He gets closer to my ear, "I know you're watching the same thing as I am. It's fine as fuck. Tonight, I'd like to be balls deep in her pussy and you can take the backdoor. I can't wait to be in that tight pussy again."

I smile and nod to myself thinking about tapping that cute ass of hers. Fuck, I'm getting a stiffy right here. When it starts, I shoot Shadow a glare and he knows exactly what he's doing and what's happening.

"Dr. Davish, who are these guys? Do you have a security detail now?" One of the older nurses asks. She's been giving us nervous eyes compared to the looks of the other people standing around.

That blond over there though, I wouldn't be surprised if she tries to slip us her number before she leaves.

I'm rather curious how we are getting introduced to people. Namely her colleagues, the people who call her boss. The people she guards her personal life from. Are we friends of hers? Does she say we are the bodyguards?

She turns to us with a huge smile, "Everyone, this is Shadow," he waves nonchalant like, "and this is Leo." I lift my hand, "They're my boyfriends." I smile and dip my chin at them.

Warm fuzzies spread across my chest. *Right answer, princess.* A few eyebrows raise, a few recover quicker than some. There's more than one curious glance our way.

Blondie's shoulders sag in defeat.

Everyone is shocked by her answer. Zharia's normally a private person and doesn't share very much of herself with her co-workers, but a poly relationship with their boss is news to them. I'm sure this is a total shock for some of them. Especially the people who are against poly lifestyles.

Shadow-the-Instigator knows this, that's why he gets up, saunter overs to Zhar and wraps her up in his arms from behind and softly tells her, "Introduce me to your friends."

Man, he just can't stop trying to fluster her. I think it's cute. She gets all flush and tongue tied when she's trying to introduce everyone to Shadow. She looks around Shadow's big, bulky body and gestures me to come over.

I stand and walk to her, taking her offered hand and lacing our fingers together. I lean in to nuzzle her neck and kiss her cheek. I catch her small sigh of relief and contentment with both of us touching her. I can tell this has been overwhelming for her and that's exactly what we were worried about.

"Well, it's been nice seeing everyone, but I'd like to go back home now," Zharia tells her staff with a tight smile, "I can't say for sure when I'll be back but give me a few days."

"Dr. Davish, you take as long as you need. We'll be fine. We can manage for another week. Take the week off and come back fresh, actually I insist, take two weeks," Isolabella says.

"Are you putting me on involuntary leave?" Zhar grins at her.

"You betcha, boss. Gentlemen, thank you for bringing her to us today, but please keep her away for another two weeks, maybe three." Isolabella winks at us and spins on her heel and sashays back down the hall. I like her.

"You heard the lady, let's go, poppet. Tell the good people goodbye."

Shadow releases her and she hugs everyone again, and of course, she sheds a fresh round of tears, but eventually we get her back out to the SUV. Just as she collapses into the passenger seat with a big, bone weary puff of air and weakly says, "I'm tired."

Shadow starts up the car and looks at her before pulling off and asks, "Do you want to go home, or would you like to go somewhere else?"

I go to argue with Shadow, but he catches my eye in the rearview mirror. I see what he's done, he's giving her the option but also knows what the outcome will be already. She's going to be too tired to go anywhere else, but the important part for her is that she was given the choice.

I just sit back and let this play out.

She puts her hand over her eyes and props her arm on the door. "I'd like to go home and figure out my life, please."

Welp. That sounds ominous.

Setting her plate in front of her, I pull back her hair and kiss her cheek, "You ok, sweetness?"

We are sitting down to dinner, Shawn joining us three. It's a good thing she has a four-seater table.

She seems distant and quite frankly, a little spacey since we came back from her surgery center. She may think she's ok, but Shadow and I talked while she napped this afternoon and we both are in agreeance, she needs this week off. Her mind and body need the rest. She's still in survival mode and every time a door opens, she jumps or flinches.

Our goal is to help her relax as much as possible and to love on her as much as she will allow. I don't know about his plan, but mine is to suffocate her with love. There's an abundance of love at her fingertips and we are here for her. There's no other place we want to be.

We spent so much time and energy looking for her; it's like living in a surreal parallel time space that could burst at any minute, making her disappear again. I've had to remind myself on more than one occasion that she's actually home and she's staying.

"I just feel off."

"Talk to us. What's off?" Shadow rubs her thigh under the table.

She glances at Shawn before looking back at her plate, picking at her food. I know there has to be a lot of things swirling in her mind. We are taking this one minute at a time but Zharia's a planner. She's been knocked off her axis for the past month. She missed so much and I know that's made her sad.

She shrugs. "I don't know. I know I just don't feel the same as I did before I got taken."

I place my hand on her forearm, "That's trauma, baby. We will help you deal with it. With anything that comes our way. First, you have to tell us what's going on inside you."

I don't want to push her but she needs to deal with the trauma and the overload of feelings that cross her face all the time. I know she's struggling…we all know.

"Would it help if we called Birdie to come over and talk with you?" Shadow's concerned face looks at me over the table. He's on edge too. We hate watching her struggle, bouncing between the brave woman she is, to the scared, meek woman bad things happened to. We are at a loss on what to do.

She shrugs again.

I scoot my chair back and pick her up and put her on my lap, cradling her to my chest. "Talk to us, baby."

She starts crying into my shirt. I don't mind one bit. I'm not going to be a dick and say I like seeing her cry, but for this bullshit happening, I like seeing her process emotions and release what needs cleansed from her soul. It was a pretty harrowing experience and we only know bits and pieces so far. She's not come out and told us everything but we have talked to Shawn while she's been asleep or bathing.

I can't imagine being locked in a concrete room for days on end, not knowing if you were going to be raped or hurt every time the door opens. No wonder she freaks out when a door opens.

She sniffles and quietly says, "It's all a lot. I don't know where to begin."

"Start at any place, beautiful. We can always circle back." Shadow continues eating while he waits on her to begin. I should have known nothing would keep him from a meal. When he does eventually eat during the day, he packs away enough to make Dr. Nowzaradan shit a brick and shake his head.

"I don't know what I'm supposed to do now. I've never been in a lasting and serious relationship. I got a taste of one with Shadow two years ago, but other than that, I'm not sure how I'm supposed to act, what I'm supposed to say. I'm worried everyone will be mad at me because I didn't try harder to get away. I'm worried about the patient I left behind in that massacre. I'm weirdly concerned about my lack of drive to go immediately back to work. I just want to stay here, cuddled up with you two, watching movies or sleeping. I'm so fucking tired," she ends on a whisper.

"OK, babe, let's tackle us." Shadow circles between us with his fork, "we are not going anywhere. We are here to stay. I realize you might not want to talk about us in front of Shawn, and we can respect that and make time to sit for however long you need to hash out our future. I understand it needs to be done and we are on your timeline. You set the pace, babe. We are at your mercy; we are here to serve you with anything you need."

I grin over her head at Shadow, "Yeah, what he said."

"I think I would like to spend some time with Birdie. Is it Wednesday?"

"Yes baby, all day long."

"I'd like to go to Wine Wednesday then."

"Ok. We can do that. I'll text them and see if it can still happen." It's still early evening and they don't normally meet until seven anyways.

The text confirmation I got from Birdie for Wine Wednesday with her best friends seems to cheer her up quite a bit. She ends up finishing half her dinner then insists on taking another shower. She keeps saying she doesn't feel clean. I can understand that. I saw the conditions she was being held in. If she wants to lay around and take bubble baths all day, then that's what she can do. We will towel dry her off when she gets out and rub her down with lotion.

Once I hear the water running I call Birdie from the living room with Shadow listening in.

"Hello, Gunney! Everything ok?"

"Hey, Birdie. That's what we are calling about."

"We?"

"Yes Shadow's here. Zhar is in the shower. She needs to come to Wine Wednesday. Can y'all swing that tonight? Look, she has her moments and it's to be expected, but she really needs to talk to someone about how she's feeling and how she's processing this trauma. She needs her friends right now and we aim to make that happen for her. Thank you for pulling a Wine Wednesday out of your ass tonight on such short notice."

"Well, it's arranged, even if it's just me. She still hasn't opened up?"

"No, but we are also not trying to push her, just give her the time and space, ya know."

"One thing I've learned about Zhar is you have to push her to get a genuine response. She's used to hiding a lot and bottling it up. I mean fuck, I didn't know about Shadow for months and here my best friend was head over heels in love. I'll get her to open up, we'll set up some time tonight. I'll call Pierre and Tally when I get off the phone."

"Thank you, Birdie," Shadow interjects.

"Don't thank me yet, she can be a tough cookie to crack."

CHAPTER 45 – ZHARIA

After I kissed Leo goodbye in the car, with the promise of
calling when I'm ready to come home, I find myself in the
middle of a Fab Four get together in my honor. They still had
Wine Wednesdays but it consisted of staying sober and
pouring over maps and leads. They did research and handed
it over to the guys to help find me. They worked hard
alongside the Devils to find me.

I have no words. Nothing strong enough. I'm so blessed to
be so loved. It chokes me up at times. My cup runneth over.

Tally is on the TV screen on video chat. She's a blubbering
mess again. I had video chatted her the night I got back

while Birdie was at the house. Tally is planning on coming to New Orleans this weekend to see me. She said it would make her feel better. How can I tell her no. Plus, she gave me pouty face when I tried to say no because I didn't want to inconvenience her.

I should have known better.

She'll be here this weekend, and that's final. She told me to shut my piehole and she will take care of me when she wants.

Alrighty then.

Pierre sat behind me brushing my hair and saying soothing words to me as I talked to the three of them and cried. Birdie gave me a pedicure and she's currently sitting in front of me painting my nails pink as I pour out my heart.

The hot topic of the minute is my new threesome…and how conflicted I am.

This can't possibly work, can it? Surely one of them will get jealous of the other. What if I spent too much time with one and the other doesn't like it? What if one gets bored with me and the other doesn't want to stick around either? Then I'm devastated.

"I think you are overthinking all of this with your big doctor brain," Tally professes from the TV screen.

"I have to agree with her, babes," Birdie says from in front of me.

Birdie shakes her head while she paints, "It's obvious they love you very much. Girl, they didn't rest until they found you. Leo was out of his mind the night you went missing. It was everything me and Linx could do to keep him calm. I was at your house when the initial plans were being made and it gave him something productive to do." Birdie looks up into my eyes with a serious expression. Oh shit, this is where the deep end starts, "I was there in the garage, at your car, when Gunney dropped to his knees and roared, fucking roared like a lion, sis. That man bellowed and shook the beams with his heartache. He loves you. More than you realize, I believe."

My chest erupts in warmth at her words. He does love me more than I realize. I needed confirmation I suppose. It makes me feel bad that his words weren't enough. I trust Leo, I honestly do, but part of me still has doubts…or else I wouldn't be here crying and drinking wine.

Birdie uses the hot stones on my calves, and it feels like heaven. Pierre is behind me rubbing Argon oil into my tresses. I'm being pampered. Tally says my treat will be coming this weekend in the form of a massage.

"They called Shadow back early. He made it in less than two hours. He arrived at your house and walked in the house, straight up to Gunney and hugged him. Stand up move. Shadow gained some of my respect back with that action."

Pierre jumps in with his comments, "Fuck yeah, he did. I thought for sure they would have beef considering the last interaction, and we would have to referee a fight. Both said fuck that and became thick as thieves, true brothers in their pursuit of you. Shadow was right there on the front lines, in the trenches right next to Gunney the whole time. They've been living at your house since you disappeared, ya know in case you came home."

Pierre pulls my hair away from my face as he leans around me. I look at him, my heart full of the love I see in his eyes. "They found you together, never giving up, never stopping until they found you. I imagine it's that same energy they love you with and Zhar, that's so powerful, so pure. Hold on to it, babes, accept it and live your best life. I want this for you, we all want this for you, you deserve it, you need this, so allow yourself to be happy. Let something happen organically for once, no planning, no anxiety, no self-doubts, no forecasting the future, running numbers, analyzing statistics; just love and be loved in return. Live in the now."

Pierre softly kisses my cheek when he's done talking. He is one of the sweetest men I've ever met. Wise beyond his years. He really strikes a nerve inside me, the one riddled with self-doubt, the nerve I listen to too much when it comes to planning my life. I want to be loved. I think between watching Pierre for years be married to Seven and be happy, and now seeing Birdie and Danger together, I don't want to be alone anymore. I want love like they have; I want it all.

Most specifically, I want to spend my time in my men's company, being loved by them.

Shadow scared me two years ago. He offered me the world and I was too afraid to take it. I can't let fear hold me back from this. I just can't.

"I want to build a life with them, both of them. I don't want to be without them ever again." I put my hands in my lap, squeezing them to stop fidgeting. "I love them," I whisper before big, fat, hot tears slide down my cheeks. "but I'm scared. What if I fuck it up? What if I get cold feet again? What if I'm not enough? I don't want to self-sabotage it again." I believe I'm tipsy and it's bringing out all the worrying, sappy feelings I have about all of this.

God, I hope Leo doesn't think bad of me because I drank. This is one of the very few times I've drank around him. I shouldn't have done that. Now I feel awful.

Being sober so long has made me a lightweight. I haven't drank that much tonight. I feel anxious even with the wine.

Birdie grabs my hands in her warm ones, Pierre hugs me tighter from behind, Tally lets out a tiny sob. "Honey, that's the risk you have to take to be loved, to love someone with abandonment in the face of uncertainty." Birdie wipes a tear off my cheek while giving me a watery, compassionate smile of her own. "The fear will always be there. It's what you decide to do despite it."

Pierre's soft voice washes over me, "Nothing is guaranteed long term. We just love like we've never been hurt, live in the moment and work towards being our best self for our partners. Open, honest communication is going to be mandatory in your relationships with them. The guys are going to have to communicate between themselves too." Pierre comes around to sit in front of me with Birdie, kneeling on the ground on one knee, "They love you and will do anything for you, let them in, babes, let them love you how they desperately want to. I'd swear on my soul if I had one, that those guys will never leave your side." He puts his hands over Birdie's, "Death won't even keep them away. You're gonna have to get a psychic medium out there to shoo their ghosts away," he ends with a wide grin. He wins. It makes me smile.

"Probably." And then I chuckle thinking about them fighting together, teasing the other. All the pranks. "I'm just picturing them fighting the other's ghost if one of them dies and Shadow smacking Leo's ass or Leo tripping Shadow every chance he got."

This makes them laugh too.

"Or Leo pulling Shadow's hair while he's on top of you," Birdie giggles.

"Wait," Tally says between laughs, "or Shadow trying to stick his thumb in Leo's ass during sex."

"Or one of them pulling ass hairs, ouch," Pierre adds. This brings on a fresh set of giggles with some tears. Happy tears, at least.

God, I love my friends.

Once we settle down from our laughing spell, I take a deep breath and blow it out. "Ok, so just go with the flow. Let it form its own path. Go against everything I've ever done. Got it."

I grab my wine glass and lift it up. What glass was this? It's close to ten PM. I've been here three hours already. "Here's to best friends and boyfriends, may I never lack either one." Hearty gulp and I feel better about my life.

My friends are right; I just want to be loved. I need to allow it.

After Leo picked me up at Birdie's he took me to get beignets at my favorite spot where he told me Shadow was at a meeting and didn't know when he would be home.
Home.
"Our home?" It's our home now.
"Well, your home. I'm not sure if it's ours yet. We haven't had that talk yet. But it feels like home to us. Soon though we are going to need to figure that part out."
I just stare at the powdered sugar on my fingers, on the table, it's everywhere. I've got a good buzz, drunken buzz for sure and the powdered sugar in the air fascinates me as does the melodic sound of his voice. I know I'm looking at him with some lovestruck expression by his grin and twinkle, but I can't stop. I'm really happy right now. I can't keep the smile off my face. All is right in the world when I'm with one of them. "I think I'd like you both living with me," I say solidly without one slur. Look at me go! Right now it sounds like a splendid idea.
Live with two incredibly hot guys? Yes, please.
Am I ready? Ready as I'll ever be I suppose. Git 'er done! *Just jump in, dive into the deep end and live a little, girl.*
Yes, listen to the vagina more, she knows what's up.
"That can definitely be arranged, princess. Let's go home." His response gives me tingles.

I dust the powder off my hands and down the front of me, well, as much as I can get anyways. I look like I dipped headfirst into a pile of cocaine.

Leo had said I needed something to soak up the bottle of wine I had drunk and sugar is always a perfect idea. Pierre told him I hadn't eaten since dinner at five and refused all the snacks. Tattletale. Teller of fables that guy, I ate a cupcake. I protested but Leo won when he mentioned beignets, deep fried powdered donuts are always the right answer. That's all it took to convince me to eat something.

Me and Leo laughed about wearing more powdered sugar than we actually ate while we sat at the little iron table. It's always like this. I have yet to see one person who can eat a beignet and stay clean. It's impossible. That's part of the charm.

As I walk into the house, half tipsy, covered in white powder like Tony Montana, Shawn's coming out of the kitchen with more snacky snacks but stands in the living room with an eyebrow cocked at us. Good for him. Good for everybody.

We're all good. Goody good, great.

Sir Waffles comes running up to me and I bend over to pet my welcoming committee, "It's all good. There were no cute firemen or kittens. We are alllll gooood."

I sang that last part for you. You're welcome.

Shit. I may be drunker than I originally thought, and the beignets are not helping all of a sudden. I might be diabetic now from all the sugar or I'm going to throw up on my white rug, very unladylike.

Glancing up I see the boy I've come to care for, "Shawn!" I run up to him and throw my arms around him, pressing my body against him in a tight hug. Behind me lickity split is Leo slipping his arm around my middle, pulling me off Shawn with a gruff, "At-At no, princess."

His possessiveness makes me shiver and I feel my nipples harden at his tone. "Oh, big guy wants a hug too," I hiccup and giggle because that came out all Marilyn Monroe style and I crack myself up.

Actually, through my alcohol sloshed brain the thought surfaces, I should consider this possessiveness toxic behavior from a boyfriend and be upset. But I understand my guys. I get it, even through the wine haze. It excites me if I'm honest.

"We'll talk tomorrow, Shawney Boy," I hunker further into Leo's arms, wiggling around. I wink at Shawn and say, "Soon you'll have a shiny new life, buddy." I may have sung that too. Terribly off key.

Hey, I said I was smart, not talented.

"Is she drunk?" Shawn looks at me with a perplexed smile. I can only smile like a loon at this point. Wine is hitting me hard right now. I should not have downed two glasses right before Leo arrived. But it was sooolalalaaaa gooood.

Everything sounds so much better as a song right now.

"Yes, slightly more than I originally thought and getting worse," Leo sounds amused as he says it, still holding me tightly against the front of him. I sigh, melting into him as much as possible.

"I'm a cat woman myself," I say to no one in particular.

"What?"

"Me too, big guy," I reply dreamily reaching up to pat Leo's chest. "You know, I love your boobies too." I just want to lay down.

Shawney Boy and Leo laugh as Leo grabs my hand from pinching his nipple through his shirt.

"I don't think we should be putting tomatoes or peppermint in gumbo, Shawn. Yikes, toothpaste sausage guacamole." I say directly to Shawn, who looks dumbfounded.

Leo hauls me up princess style and I pat his chest, listening to it rumble as he tells me, "Ok, sweetness, time for you to go to bed."

"I'll see you tomorrow Shawney, we need to talk about school, buddy boy. I haven't forgotten about you." Leo and Shawn both snort and I settle in Leo's strong arms, ready to be carted off to my own bubble of happiness—my bed.

"Our bed of love," I mumble.

"Yes, baby, our bed of love."

"There's been a hurricane of thoughts in my head all day but right now, I feel like I'm off the carousel."

Leo chuckles in response. "Ok, baby, go to sleep."

"Licks and kisses, Leo, I love you." Goddamn, I'm so sleepy. It's been an emotional day for me. The darkness claims me almost immediately.

Chapter 46 – Shadow

Zharia's been home a few days now and we are no closer to finding Panhead than we were the day we rescued her. The piece of shit has gone underground to recoup. Unfortunately, he was not among the dead at the scene.

"We know his wife was admitted to the hospital the day we saved Zhar since we called EMS. We know she is still there. We also know there have been no visitors," Danger fills us in at the debriefing. Info I will relay to Gunney once I get home tonight. He stayed behind so Zharia could have her Fab Four night.

His absence at this mandatory meeting was excused by Rock personally, given the circumstances. We've let a select few know Zhar is having a hard time and is super clingy right now.

"What a douchebag move. The bastard hasn't even visited his wife in the hospital," Slim says grumbling.

A few other grumbles of agreement float in the room.

Gunney and I have been relieved of some of the search duties so we can see to acclimating Zharia back into life and taking care of her. She's been doing a lot of sleeping and watching her murder documentaries and reality trash shows in bed. We've sat through so much On The Case With Paula Zahn, and she can't make it through two episodes of True Blood before she climbs on top of one of us either wanting snuggles or wanting to be fucked. Blood and vampires fucking at lightning speed gets our girl going. We are more than happy to let her use us.

We even go one step further and feed her ice cream in bed, making sure it's her favorite.

Anything for our girl.

She gets pampered with princess treatment.

Our princess.

Gunney's right, she's our royal brat.

I can't wait to get home and see her. She's like a drug to me and I need my hit. It makes my skin crawl and itch to be away from her, even for a few hours.

Yeah, that's how far I'm wrapped up in her.

I'm not sure how this is going to work out when she goes back to work and I have to do my duties to the organization.

For now, I'm trying to concentrate on this meeting and I'm failing. All I can think about is Zharia under me, legs wrapped around me, my tongue on her—

"Is that ok, Shadow?"

I shake myself out of my train of thought and jerk back into reality. "I apologize. Run that by me again."

Danger stands there with a shit-eating grin on his pretty boy face, that I'd like to punch in those all-knowing eyes. He can see right through me and knows exactly where my thoughts were. "I asked if you were ok leaving her for a few days so we can go scout out Lake Charles and remind them who the fuck is in charge."

My heart thunders in my chest. Leave her?

"For how long?"

"A week."

I blink. I don't want to do this. But it's my job.

"Hey man, no one's expecting you to run right back out there and leave your old lady at home. We know you just got her back a few days ago. You guys have spent weeks searching. We understand if you don't want to go right now. Catch the next one." Rock finishes.

He's being awfully nice. I think Zharia getting kidnapped hurt him too. Not to mention it wasn't that long ago his own daughter was kidnapped by the same rival biker gang. I think Rock's heart got cracked.

Travares stands up and says, "I'll go in Shadow's place. I'll join the hunt." IT boy is going out on a job for me? He's usually behind a laptop and a wall of screens doing his thing. Rarely is he on the front lines or in trenches. It's been known to happen, but not a lot. Gotta protect his big brain.

This surprises me. Enough to raise an eyebrow at him. Travares turns, looking at the back of the room where I sit.

"Stay here and take care of Zhar, she needs you both."

"Thanks, brother," I tell him and mean it. I wasn't sure how I was going to break it to Zhar that I was going back to Lake Charles for a week. Her separation anxiety has been heightened, like through the roof at times. Like I said, she's been super clingy to both of us since she's been back. We are definitely not complaining about it.

I love letting her crawl onto my lap, tucking her under my chin, running my hands on her supple body, smelling her hair and just being enveloped in everything that's her. These are the times I cherish. The moments I missed with her. All the long nights without her in my arms.

Do not dwell on the times without her. We are here and now.

"You're welcome. Just buy me a tattoo and we're even," Travares jokes and winks at me.

"You're on," I tell him, knowing damn well the guy has somehow managed to have only two tattoos on his body. I doubt he takes me up on payment.

"Alright, that's settled. Travares there's a meeting tomorrow at eleven to leave by three. Be here," Danger says.

"Got it. I'll be here."

The search party is about ten men, including Slim, T-Bone, Joker, Dobby, and now Travares. They have enough muscle and manpower to take on a few bar brawls if needed.

The circle of trust is getting smaller by the day since Zhar confirmed there's a traitor in our midst.

Travares looks at me and nods. I dip my chin back to him, signaling my appreciation. He didn't have to do it, but I am grateful he stepped up in my place. He's one of the best guys I know, even if he is a quiet man sometimes. When he finally lets you in, he's a character. I feel honored he calls me a close friend and I got to know him outside of club business.

"Next order of business, we are already planning the events for the coming year. Our first fundraiser for the Greater Louisiana Children's Society, our group homes, is set to happen for Valentine's Day. I know that's like a month away, but I have a sign-up sheet for y'all to pick a duty. As a reminder, you are obligated within the vows you took to volunteer for at least three fundraising events for the year. We have an event every month and keep track of who volunteers."

Rock steps up and says, "The GLCS organization we support is our organization buried under an umbrella, untraceable back to us. No one really knows it's a bunch of cranky bikers killing guys and saving hundreds of people. They just know it's bikers giving away money to children's homes. They don't need to know that those safe houses are ours. With your help and the corporate donations we received last year, we raised over two hundred thousand dollars for all of our human trafficking rescue efforts and safe houses. We solely support them and it's imperative we keep them operating. Last year you all saved over fifteen hundred women and children and set them up for recovery and success. That's a fantastic job! I'm really proud of y'all. Take a bow, gentlemen."

The room erupts in applause, whistles, and hoots and hollers. Our guys work really hard all year to support this cause. We are sworn under oath not to divulge our missions and charity. So far so good. No one has told our secrets. But then again, no one's ever left our organization.

I check my tactical watch and see it's close to ten-thirty. Danger will be wrapping this up soon and that's the sooner I can get home to my baby girl.

Fuck. It feels good to call her mine again.

When I arrive home, Gunney is sitting on the couch watching TV.

Alone.

"Hey bud, how did it go?" he asks when I walk in and sit in the chair by him.

"Went well. They tried to get me to leave tomorrow for a mission over to Lake Charles again. Just to go throw some weight around and to sniff out some intel. Travares is going in my place. They're going to be gone a week and I don't want to leave this situation we got going on here for a week. Not when we just got her back."

"Understandable."

"How she doing?"

Gunney chuckles to himself, "Ah man, so I took her to Wine Wednesday, right. She proceeded to refuse all food, and they said she drank a whole bottle of wine herself. She's sloshed, bro."

I'm sure my shocked face is comical. "Wait, she's drunk as a skunk right now? Where is she?"

"In our bed passed the fuck out, drooling. I carried her in there right when we got home, after she gibbered nonsense, but not before she plastered herself against Shawn and called him Shawney boy." I know I have the surprised getting-hot-tea face going on but I can't stop it, this is good shit, "I made her a grilled cheese sandwich, and she woke up long enough to eat it, watch ten minutes of True Blood and mumble about hot vampire sex, then she drank some water before she was out cold."

"Damn, I'm happy she had a good time. She's going to feel that tomorrow though," I chuckle to myself. Oh boy, she gets some doozey hangovers from wine. She should know better.

"Good thing she doesn't have to work tomorrow."

I nod absently. "Hey, before I forget, Rock released the numbers from last year's missions." After we talked about that for a while, I see movement out of the corner of my eye near the stairs. Shawn appears and stops when he sees us sitting in the living room.

I'm still not sure about this kid.

"Hey guys," he offers tentatively.

"Hey, what's up?" Gunney asks him.

"I was wondering if I'm allowed to leave. Not to escape or anything, but am I allowed to go to the store? Am I allowed to go to the French Quarter since we are so close? I've never been."

Gunney and I exchange a look. I'm sure by now the Saints realize he's missing. It's possible Panhead Pete is looking for him. He may even realize we've taken him. Shawn did say he was the person who spent the most time with Zhar while she was there.

They might have connected the dots.

"I was also wondering if I could go back and get my belongings."

"What do you have there that can't be replaced?" I ask.

Shawn stands there and thinks for a minute. "I guess nothing. I have clothes and my book bag with my books and school supplies. I reckon I don't need my books anymore." He looks away and I swear he's trying not to cry. "I know she's been busy and she's trying to recover from trauma and all, but I feel useless."

"Ok. Give her tonight to sleep it off. Even drunk she hasn't forgotten about you if tonight was any indication with her flirty ways," Gunney supplies.

I cock an eyebrow at that remark. What the hell happened earlier?

"Yeah, I suppose you're right. She did say we'll talk tomorrow." He offers a wary expression.

"Look, we know this has been strange and uncomfortable for you. Tomorrow sounds like a great time to go over details. Did you do the homework she assigned? Have you picked out three schools? I have a feeling you already have a sponsor for school." I watch him as I say all this and he seems even more nervous and downtrodden tonight.

"Yeah right. Who in their right mind is going to give me a full scholarship to become a chef?" he scoffs.

"Let's work on your positivity. You must not know enough about Zhar. This will all work out. Trust her. She's a doer, she gets shit done. Fuck, she built her own empire with sacrifices that damn near killed her," Gunney's eyes flick over to mine before he continues, "so you can give her until tomorrow."

　"Ok, tomorrow then." Shawn heads to the kitchen. I swear that kid can eat his weight in snacks. He better watch or he'll be as big as this house before too long. Wait, he's young; he'll be fine.

Goddamn, it's been a rough morning. Bleh. Fuck hangovers and fuck that bottle of wine. Who the fuck authorized me to drink that much?

Fuck everything.

My tongue feels like dirty shag carpet.

I vaguely remember coming home and Leo feeding me grilled cheese. It was the best fucking grilled cheese I've ever eaten. I almost cried over it.

I don't remember them coming to bed with me but they were there when I woke up. I vaguely remember being held in someone's arms all night. I do remember the smell of them in close proximity to me. I tried to wake up so I could seduce at least one of them but that was a no go for me. I slept so soundly with no nightmares, no bad thoughts, no dark rooms made of concrete sucking the life out of me.

However, everything's so loud right now. I hear the air moving through the house. Whooshhh. I hear the dust settling in this room and it's cracking my skull open. Maybe I really am dying. Maybe I'm exaggerating.

Maybe I'm just extra and dramatic.

Bahh. Once again, here I am swearing off alcohol. I should possibly take up smoking weed instead. I've never woken up feeling like I'm dying when I've only smoked. Stupid ass drug tests.

I roll out of bed and stumble to the bathroom. Time to get a new life. I turn on the shower and step into bliss. Ahh.

Holy fuck balls. That shower was heaven.

"Hey baby, how you doing?" Leo says as he sits on the couch next to the chair I'm melting into. God, he's so loud. I just rub my hand over my forehead and breathe. I can smell his soap and cologne so he must have just gotten out of the shower. I tried very hard to walk out here fresh and sober.

I'm failing. I might still be drunk, I don't have a clue, but at least I'm fresh and clean. It's a start.

And I brushed my hairy teeth. That's important.

I'm perched in my favorite oversized chair, sipping on some black tea with honey. I didn't think I should chance coffee sitting on my stomach like lead, churning. I may love coffee, but sometimes it's my frenemy. Can't ever trust it during a hangover. Never trust a hangover fart and coffee together. Hard lessons were learned, that's all you need to know. Go ahead and laugh, I give you permission. Picture the worst and you won't even come close to reality.

Shuddering at that embarrassing memory. Mor-ti-fied.

Oh, right, Leo's waiting for my answer as I blink at him like a zombie. I don't really know if zombies blink but this one does.

"Hi. I feel like dog shit."

"I figured as much. Is there anything I can do for you?" He blows on his own mug, which smells like coffee and his tons of French Vanilla creamer, his girly drink. I guarantee he put caramel in it too.

"I know I need to eat but I haven't brought myself to do it yet."

"I picked up one of your favorites. Do you want me to fix you a blueberry bagel with lots of creamy-creamy?" Oh god, fuck yes. I love how thoughtful he is, and that he remembers what I eat.

"God, I'd love a bagel," I gush out. I'm not sure how cream cheese will sit on my stomach but I think I'll feel better with something on my belly and a creamy-creamy bagel sounds stellar.

"As my princess wishes." Leo gets up and goes to the kitchen as Shadow comes into the kitchen from our bedroom. His hair is wet and he's shirtless. Lords above, he is mouthwatering. My guys fist bump and go about their business.

While I watch them, I think to myself, *this could actually work.*

Shadow, ever the tease, comes strolling into the living room wearing a pair of low-slung joggers like a goddamn supermodel. Now this fucker knows that makes me drool, so he's just taunting me in my fragile state.

"How's my poppet? I didn't get to see you last night before you passed out. Did you have a good time, babe?" He looks very concerned as he leans down and kisses my forehead. I imagine I look a fright so his expression is valid. I feel like used sandpaper is rubbing across my brain.

For the hundredth time this morning, I ask myself why I put myself through this.

Oh right, I was having a pity party.

"I missed you too," I croak, while trying to watch him through one eye. Why is the fucking air so loud in here? The daylight is too bright too. "I feel like hell."

"Well, you're still beautiful even if you feel like hell."

"Don't. I know I look like trash garbage."

"There's no teasing there. You truly look beautiful this morning, like you do every second of the day."

"Thank you, but I think you're trying to kiss my ass for something," I point out.

He laughs, "Nope, not at all. I'm merely making an observation and a true statement. Not everything I say is dickish." He grins at me and makes me produce a small smile. He is a dick a lot of the time. Not to me, but to everyone else. I'm special.

Ok, I totally feel like I did get a new life. Between the bagel, the shower and the ibuprofen Leo gave me, I'm feeling much better. Can't forget the three gallons of water they keep pushing on me to drink.

No amount of me insisting that tea is just brown water stops them from shoving water at me every time I turn around.

I'm sitting here with Shawn discussing his future. And I have my handy dandy emotional support thermal cup Leo handed me so I can suck down this ocean. I grudgingly admit, it does make me feel better. I missed my cup.

If you have a favorite tumbler, you know.

"What kind of chef do you want to be?" Shadow asks him while he's hauled me half on his lap in my overstuffed chaise lounger. With his arms wrapped around me and his warm body pressed up against one side of my back, I'm content and wonder why I ever gave this up. Nothing could have been more important than this happiness. I was a fool.

Back to business, no time for mind wandering.

I have a surprise for Shawn.

"I want to do everything, but I really have a passion for food and pairing ingredients. Cooking in general. I look at it like science and it fascinates me. The ability to create so many different things," he raises his hands to his head excitedly, "it's mind-blowing the combinations. I want to know them all." He drops his arms and smiles.

That's the kind of enthusiasm I was looking for. My surprise is a good idea then. I feel good about this.

"What schools did you come up with, bud?" Leo asks from Shawn's side sitting next to him on the couch.

"I have three like you asked," Shawn hands me a legal pad with his notes on it. "Two are in New Orleans and one is in Baton Rouge."

I read over them and he has the amount of time he will have to go to the school and the total price for the year. It's going to take him a few years for this schooling but the place I'm thinking of is a four-year degree, possibly shorter with all the credits he's earned already.

"What kind of commitment are you looking at here? Two years? Four-year degrees?" I ask him.

"I had a full scholarship for a two-year degree," he answers. I slowly nod my head in thought at his admission. I chew on my thumbnail picking through his schools, trying to see what drew him to them.

Two-year degree, hmm. So, this means he basically has almost two years of training and learning thus far. This fits in good.

"Can you do a four-year degree? Do you have it in you to stay in school that long?" The place I'm looking at will take his credits from the other school and apply to their curriculum, however, they have their very own specialized curriculum.

"Yeah, that shouldn't be a problem as long as I can afford it. I'll have to work somewhere. I can take public transport or walk. I saw one of them is two miles away. I can walk that easily. It's also the cheapest so that's good too." I watch the spark of excitement grow in his eyes. He's truly passionate about his education and that makes me excited for him.

I remember someone else excited about school and knowledge.

Maybe I see myself in Shawn.

I was born privileged. Maybe this is my way of giving back.

Either way, I hope he loves what I'm about to present.

I begin my idea that will very much change his life. "Hear me out, I have an idea, tell me if it interests you. I want to send you to France to go to culinary school at l'art Alimentaire for their degree in French foods, specifically. I want to have you come back here and work in the authentically French restaurant I want to open here in a few years. I want you to help me run it, so l'art Alimentaire's management program would be your minor. I will fund your schooling, housing, food and clothes, in return you will sign a contract to work for me for five years after school at a slightly reduced salary. Enough to live on but after five years, if you sign a new contract, I'll triple your salary. What do you think of that idea?"

Every set of eyes in the room is on me in shock. Leo is the first to recover, "Damn baby, your heart is so big."

Shawn is still there stunned, positively shook. I know it's a lot to take in.

"Shawn, you would be an idiot to not take this deal," Shadow informs him.

"A-Are you sure?" His eyes are excited, guarded and panicked at the same time.

"Absolutely sure. My father owns restaurants in the city but they're Indian or Asian. I want a truly authentic French restaurant, something I feel is lacking here in the city. I need a damn good chef for it. I want one that's as serious and as passionate about cooking food as you are. So, what do you say?"

Shawn looks at Shadow who nods at him with a grin. Then Shawn looks over at Leo and Leo gives him a thumbs up with a smile. It makes my heart happy to see him seek reassurance from the guys. He needs the kind of role models Shadow and Leo are.

Minus the violence and killing though. I'm not stupid, I know they do that.

Outside of these walls, my guys are dangerous and lethal. It's a big turn on for me that they go out and fight evil and stop evil men. I'm whacked in the head, I know.

"I-I don't know what t-to say," he stammers. He looks like he's going to cry. I think I've shocked him to his core. "Why? Why me? I'm just some black kid from the Detroit projects."

"I see something in you. There's a fire inside you and it would be a shame not to stoke it if I have the means. You have no idea how much of a bright light you were to me in that concrete prison. You made my captivity more bearable and I'm eternally grateful to you and our little talks for keeping me sane."

Shawn tries to hide it, but I see the sheen in his eyes forming. He clears his throat, likely clearing the emotions that are clogging his airway. *I have some too, friend.* There's chopped onions around here somewhere. I'm sticking to that excuse.

I dab at the corners of my eyes with my sleeve. Leo slips a tissue out of the box on the side table and hands it to me. I gladly take it because I don't trust myself right now. I'm a loaded gun of feelings and I might start crying any minute.

Shawn says, "I guess I never thought about how important I was to you. You were important to me too. I mean, you still are. I was basically a prisoner there too."

I kick myself in the ass one more time, "I realize that, and I feel bad I've been too wrapped up in my own head to see how you are after your trauma. Are you ok?" I do feel guilty that I've been selfishly ignoring him, processing the huge changes in my life and processing the huge experience we just survived. I brought him here and then stayed locked in my mind. It was immensely unfair to him.

He blows out a breath. "I'm ok. Seriously. I'm glad to be away, I'm grateful I was allowed to live. I'm fortunate you brought me here with you. I made a mistake, a bad call and it almost cost me my life. Thank you, Zhar. I'd be dead without you."

Now he's making me catch a sob, and overflow with tears. I just let them overflow. I have no shame. We survived a horrible situation together. Trauma bonded friends now.

I take a deep, cleansing breath while Shadow rubs his hand across my body from shoulder to thigh. "So, what's it going to be?"

He starts nodding, gets a big smile and proclaims, "Yes! I'll do it!" He looks so damn happy.

I match his smile and so do the guys. I bet this is his first adult choice he's made with no influence from family.

"That's wonderful!" I jump up out of the chair and rush over to hug Shawn. Both my alpha-holes growl at the physical contact.

"Stop it, you two. I can hug people."

"Yeah, no. Your body won't be pressed up against another man's. I don't give a shit if it's a friend. Shake his hand, even then, that's iffy."

"I'm with him, baby girl," Shadow says.

I release Shawn and stand up to look at them. "You two are insufferable. I'm not abiding by that stupid rule."

"Why do you have to hurt other people?" Shadow chides.

"I'm not hurting anyone," I protest.

"If another man lays a finger on you, we will cause him pain. You're ours, not his. Only we get to touch," Shadow supplies in a no nonsense, drop dead serious tone. I do believe he's telling the truth.

Shawn holds his hands up, "Got it. No touchy touchy."

"I'll hug you whenever I want," I scoff. They do not want to make rules like this.

"Have it your way. When Shawn is beat up, you're responsible for it."

"Fuck no you will not gaslight me, you insane fuckers." I stand over them in their seats and then slip by Shadow still lounging on the chaise. "This won't work at all if you try to impose stupid shit like that and try to control me. I won't allow it."

I can't even with these two. I'm mad, and I just need to walk away before I say anything more. Sooo, before I stand here clenching my fists anymore, I snap my mouth shut then turn on my heel and march my angry ass into my room and shut the door. I can't help that it was so forceful it shook the dishes in the cabinets.

I would open it and shut it a dozen more times to take out my frustration and make a point but even I know that's childish. I refrained. But just know, I wanna do it.

Hard.

I breathe in through my nose, out my mouth. Am I being rational here? Probably not.

Why the hell am I so pissed? Stupid macho shit.

Am I being a brat about this? Most definitely.

I know they are possessive assholes, but this is ridiculous.

Perhaps I just need a nap so I stop acting like a two-year-old throwing a temper tantrum.

CHAPTER 48 – GUNNEY

"You might want to go downstairs, shut the door and put your headphones on loud while we go handle our woman," Shadow tells Shawn as he rises from the chaise with a determined look.

I slap my thighs and say, "Yep. She gets loud when we make her see things our way, but she loves it," I finish with my eyebrows wagging. I know he catches my drift, because he jumps up and heads down the stairs in a hurry with our laughter following him.

"You ready?" Shadow asks me.

"Yep."

"Good, 'cause I'm calling pussy tonight."

"I'm good with either," I reply.

She would be astonished to learn we do talk to each other about the things we want to do together with her, or separately. We have the understanding that it won't always be us three all the time and we're cool with that—NO jealousy is allowed. Number one rule—We get it, she has to maintain her relationship with each of us and some of that requires her to spend one-on-one time with each of us.

Our life is a non-negotiable jealousy free zone.

I walk in the room first and Shadow brings up the rear. We see her curvy form under the covers in the middle of the bed, on her side, facing away and we immediately start undressing. At this point, it no longer matters if we are naked together. Our dicks have touched, we're good.

I follow Shadow to the bed with a hum of excitement and a little bit of trepidation. The second she sees us, "Oh no! I'm mad at you two assholes. Go away."

Shadow smirks at her while putting his hair up in a messy bun with his hair tie he always wears on his wrist and gets in bed anyways, laying down whether she likes it or not.

"Poppet."

"Don't you poppet me, you jealous maniac." She's adorable when she's mad.

Shadow leans to bury his face in the crook of her neck, "Tell me, what if a beautiful woman walked up to us and pressed her body to us, boobs to bush, splattered across the front of us, we can feel the softness and outline of her titties, would you be ok with another woman's tits on me?"

"Of course not," she replies with sharp conviction. I know she's remembering her interaction with Dreama while Shadow was here for the Christmas party.

Coming up to the other side of the bed, I crawl over to her and lay on my side facing her, hand on her hip, "So, you want us to be ok with another man feeling your body, your perfect boobs pressing into his chest, arms around you?" I ask her by the shell of her ear.

"You can't just boss me around and act like cavemen," she snaps at us.

Shadow's hand reaches out and grips her chin, lifting her face off the pillow, "Answer the question, love. Tell him you want to slide up against other men."

My eyes dart from Shadow to Zhar and back. Shadow asks her again, "If you aren't ok with a woman on us, why do we have to be ok with your body on another man. The double standard is killing your stance on us being barbarians. Wait, we're maniacs."

"I'm definitely not ok with your arms around another woman…besides family."

"Then we agree, no more hugging men, who's not family of course."

I see the wheels turning in her head. Her gorgeous mind works extremely fast so I know she's already realized she's lost this argument. She's just dragging it on.

Shadow pulls her lips close to his, turning her over partly on her back, staring into her eyes he promises, "I agree to not hold another woman in my arms, if you keep your hands off other men."

He bends his head and licks up the column of her neck. Her body yields to us then. I swoop in and grab her wrists, holding her arms over her head while Shadow gets her on her back.

"Look at these gorgeous tits." He cups them in his hands and rolls the nipples, kneading their plush softness through her shirt. He bounces them in his hands and they look beautiful jiggling like so.

"This needs off now." I help him relieve her of her clothes. He leans forward to run his tongue across a nipple. Staring into her eyes, he tells her, "I'm not ok with these touching another man, through clothes or not. We aren't trying to tell you what to do," another lick, and a few small pinches thrown in there, "we are expressing our wishes."

Damn. Shadow is like a master at handling her sometimes. I know the moment she concedes because her body sags against mine. He sees it too. A wicked smile spreads across his features.

"Ugh. I don't know if I want to kill you or fuck you. You drive me crazy," she pouts.

He grips her chin and pulls her face close to his, "We aren't doing this shit again, poppet. Lose the attitude. Now, tell me who you belong to."

I don't know how anyone can resist Shadow's intense stares but Zhar does it somehow and rolls her eyes. "You," she breathes out, but you can hear her voice drip with arousal.

"You're going to pay for the eye roll," Shadow threatens.

He turns her face to look up at mine, making my stomach summersault, "Do you belong to him too?"

"Yes," she says softly, looking into my eyes. I feel her lust filled eyes looking into my soul, our connection is so deep. Fuck, I love her so much. I'll move heaven and Earth for her. I'll run as fast as the wind to catch her if she ever leaves. I'll beg on my knees for her to stay. I want to rip her clothes off and worship her, proving just how much I love her and how beautiful she is.

I bow at her feet and offer up my life.

Shadow reaches between her legs and gets a devious smirk, "By the feel of your slick pussy, you want to be ours as much as we are yours. Things will be more negotiable this time around, love. We'll fuck, then talk." He sucks his fingers into his mouth and brings them out with a pop and a glint to his eyes as he stares her down. Her breaths are coming faster now.

It's almost too easy to turn her on.

"Wait, I want to be fucked with my other fantasy. Please," she begs in such a sweet little voice. I can't deny her anything when she uses that tone, asking so sweetly, her earlier irritation slipping away. I release her arms then watch her run her hands down his face to cup his jaw.

"Tell us more, poppet."

"I want to hang my head off the bed while my pussy and mouth get fucked." Her eyes dart over to me to see my reaction and I just give her a lazy smile. I'm down for whatever. She knows this.

"That can be done," I answer for the both of us. I can't deny her anything. I'm completely powerless against her. "Lay across the bed, get into position, princess."

Once she's laying with her head slightly off the edge, with me caressing her face, Shadow spreads her legs apart while he situates himself between them bent over breathing her in.

"Zharia, you are beautiful, stunning. Don't ever think we don't want you." Shadow strokes his cock a few times as she tries to close her legs.

He yanks them back open, "You will never try to hide from us. This pussy is ours. This luscious body, this brilliant mind is ours. It's criminal, torturous even, to keep it from us, baby girl."

Shadow drops to his elbows, gripping her thighs and open mouth kisses down the inside of her thigh, half dragging his tongue across her skin, giving little nips here and there, and finally he comes to her opening. I watch him shove his tongue in her entrance and she sighs. The fight has left her; she's putty in our hands.

Finally. The anger is leaving her body.

It's like he's teaching me all the shortcuts to her pleasure. Since he has more experience pleasing her, I take notes from him. I'm not at all mad about it. It's sexy as fuck watching them together.

He brings his mouth up to her clit and lightly swirls his tongue around her bundle of nerves. She bows off the bed then, catching her breath in her throat. Goddamn, it's a purdy sight to witness.

"Our baby loves this." I sensually rub my hands from her head to her belly and back up. My hands are all over her, kneading, gripping, fondling. I caress her breasts and tease her nipples, "She especially loves this," as she bows off the bed, shoving her gorgeous tits into my palms. I pinch the peaks of her nipples and her legs start shaking.

Shadow breaks the seal he has on her clit. "Do you like when I'm on my knees for you, poppet?" Her rapid panting echoes in the room.

She whispers, "Yes. Shadow, please."

"Shadow Daddy is going to make you feel good, baby girl."

Shadow dips his head back between her legs. I continue rubbing on her body as he slips two fingers inside her. I know the moment he hits her magic button. She arches her back and mewls her pleasure.

It's erotic as fuck to watch Shadow's mouth and jaw working while eating her out. His shiny tongue peeks out occasionally as he lathers it on her clit.

Zharia tangles her fingers in his man bun and pulls his face closer. Shadow starts humming and a few moments later Zharia stiffens and her eyes flutter shut.

"No baby, look at me while you come on Shadow's tongue. Eyes up here, beautiful."

Zharia's eyes lock on mine, just in time for her mouth to pop open and sing her orgasm song. It's the best sound in the fucking world. I resist coming like some randy teenager standing right here just watching all of this.

Once her climax has tapered off, Shadow sits up with a wicked grin on his face, face glistening with her juices. He looks thoroughly pleased with himself. He grips his cock while she leans up to watch him situate himself in the cradle of her hips.

"Let me pull her over here more to hang off the bed to suck my cock," I suggest to Shadow.

"Have at it, bad boy." Shadow crawls up her body and leans over her, his hands on each side of her waist. "You want to be our naughty little girl, Zhar? You love being a filthy girl for us. Tell me, do you want to stick his fat cock in your mouth and suck his cum down your throat?"

Him and that fucking mouth. He's going to make me cum before I even get in there.

She nods and whimpers "Yes" as an answer. Good enough for me.

I pull her over to my side of the bed until her head hangs off the edge. She immediately opens her mouth and sticks out her tongue, ready for whatever I'm going to give her.

"Such a good girl for me," I tell her while I make sure her hair is out of the way, and I'm not standing on it, then put the tip of my dick on her tongue and my eyes roll back when her lips close over me.

Shadow scoffs, "Good girl, my ass. She's our dirty little cumslut that loves taking us in every hole."

She pops off of me and almost undoes us both, "Yes, I am, to both. I want to be a good girl and a cumslut," she groans. "Make me be both."

I'm never going to last with these two I swear to fucking god.

After rubbing his flat hand across her pussy, he rubs her juices up and down his cock to get it wet. I can hear how wet she is from clear over here.

She moans deep in her throat and it causes me to groan, "Goddamn, she's excited," I try my hardest, against every instinct, to hold back from just going hard as a motherfucker and fucking her mouth too hard.

But fuck all, man, I want to choke the shit out of her with my cock. Shove it in as deep as it will go, then push it a little past that point just for good measure.

We are trying to take it slow and easy right now. Please dick, don't embarrass me. As long as Shadow keeps his dirty mouth shut, I should be good.

"I can't wait to be in this pussy again," he lines up to her entrance.

I breathe through my nose while she swirls her tongue over me, concentrating on lasting but watching the best porn I've ever seen. *Don't come* chants through my head. Goddamn she gives good head. Baby ducks in a row. Peanut butter and jelly sandwich. Disney on Ice. Cute kittens playing with yarn.

Shadow rubs his large hand up her torso to her neck as he pushes in and she groans, vibrating my cock in her throat. He encircles the delicate column at the base of her throat. He doesn't squeeze, it's there more as a weight, a reminder of who's in charge. Zharia whimpers again and lifts her hips, seeking him out.

"There's my needy whore. Always willing to spread her legs for us. She's ours. All ours. She's addicted to us, Leo." Shadow starts slowly pushing in and out of her. Her body writhing under him. He pulls her legs to hook around his hips. He leans over and grabs a pillow, lifting her ass and shoving it under her ass.

Oh god.

I grit my teeth before I answer. "Fuck yeah, she is. I'm just as addicted to her," in my husky tone. "I need to watch her come with my cock choking her."

"Yesss," Shadow hisses. "I'm utterly obsessed with you, Zhar, as if you couldn't tell," his dark chuckle rumbles in his chest. He teases her clit with his fingers.

I love the moans she's making around my dick. They're so fucking sexy. She continues to cup my balls and tease me with her tongue.

Shadow looks across the bed, "I'm going to fuck you so hard, poppet, you're going to choke on his dick, remember to squeeze his legs if it's too much. You're going to love it, because you belong to us and want to please us, you want to be our beautiful whore, giving it up to us how we want. We own you, Zharia."

Fuck. He makes my dick throb.

"Please. Fuck me. I need fucked hard."

"Shit. I don't know how long I'm going to last between you two."

Her lips wrap around me again with a deep moan starting in her chest, rumbling up her throat, and vibrating my cock letting us know she's in total agreement with everything he says. I fucking know I am, Jesus, he gets me unbelievably hard when he starts talking like that.

"Be our whore, Zhar, be ours, babe," Shadow groans out as he pushes into her harder, bottoming out.

Zhar answers him with a growl, so possessive, so rough, so aroused. Fuck, it's amazing to hear her claim us too. She spreads her legs as wide as she can in invitation while I play with her nipples and squeeze her boobs.

He pulls back and slams into her balls deep, pushing her further up, right onto my dick making her take it deeper. She opens her throat. Shadow gives her a few short strokes and then bends her legs up to her chest. "Get ready, love."

She gives him a thumbs up.

He proceeds to fuck the shit out of her. Goddamn. That's a fucking.

Her moans turn to muffled screams as her body shakes.

It's a beautiful sight. This is by far the best experience of my life.

She's hanging in there longer than I thought she would. She's getting a straight dirty fucking from Shadow. I don't even have to move that's how good it is. Suddenly she pinches my thighs. I quickly pull back out of her mouth. I was so close.

She's sobbing when she says, "Please Shadow, please let me come. Leo, please."

He wraps her thighs around his hips and grinds into her, rubbing her clit with his body. "Here? Right here, Zhar?"

Her loud moans fill the room. I fucking love it.

"Yes! Yes! Just like that. Don't stop, fuck me harder," she yells.

Zharia drops her head back off the bed and reaches for my dick like a thirsty woman in the desert who needs water to live. Ravenous. She guides me to her hot, open mouth and I about lose my shit when her tongue wraps around me. I watch her tongue smear the precum I had running down my length all over my cock. It's fucking hot.

I resume playing with her nipples. Her mouth works harder on me as her body shakes and she's practically growling. My baby is lost in primal need and it's one of the most beautiful things I've ever seen.

"Fuck, Zhar," I hiss.

"Come for me, poppet. Give us what belongs to us." Shadow's hips work into her and you can tell the second the orgasm hits her. It's like a force of nature slams into her and her back bows and she throws her arms out on the bed. She screams around my dick. Garbled screams and sobs that send me over the edge.

"Zhar, fuck, I'm coming.."

She seals her lush lips around me and sucks hard. I come so hard, my soul leaves my body, like a tidal wave rushes through me, forceful, ripping at my body. I barely stay standing as her mouth works me over.

Shadow stiffens and slams into her one last time, "Zharia, fuck," he groans loudly as he empties into her.

As I pull out of her mouth, I run my fingers over her black hair, smoothing it off her sweaty forehead, trying to catch my breath. "Shit. I think I've died and gone to heaven." I lean back against the window behind me, bracing myself and working to catch my breath.

She takes a few deep breaths and loudly declares, "Holy fuck!" Her thighs fall to the wayside on the bed with a soft thud. I hurry to help her sit up and get her head on the bed. She sits up and rolls to the middle of the bed, her face red and a ripe flush to her neck and chest. Shadow and I fall beside her on the bed.

"I'm pretty sure if you hadn't have had a dick stuffed in your throat, Mrs. Fontenot would have called the police."

This only makes her smile and snort.

"Yeah, I love when she's loud. That's our good girl," I say as I roll over and rub my hand on her stomach. "Our perfect girl."

EPILOGUE — ZHARIA

Ok, we survived our first lover's spat two weeks ago. They more than made up for it since then.

If they didn't act like possessive barbarians I wouldn't have to throw a tizzy fit.

We did negotiate and there is a *very* short list of men I'm allowed to hug. I mean, small, small list. Them, Danger, Rock, Pierre, my dad and brother, and maybe Shawn. That's it.

I hated to admit I went off half-cocked, like the old me would have, and I didn't give them a chance to explain their reasonings and feelings. Lesson learned. I get it now. Communication, but first take a deep breath. Practice the pause.

Hesitating with my words when I'm angry is now my new goal. Don't let my temper override my brain, short circuit it and cause us drama. No one needs my dramatic ass being even more extra right now.

Trust me. I get sick of my own drama sometimes.

I do love to run my mouth but I'm learning these two pick and choose when they cave to me. For the most part they give me whatever I want and treat me like a queen.

I admitted defeat and then compromised with the short list. It was a small victory for both sides. My mistake last time was not hearing Shadow out, not listening to his side, and well, being a selfish brat. I like to think I've grown in the past two years and changed how I handle things.

But I'll be damned if I let these two control me.

Ok, so I mean outside the bedroom. Eh, let's not go overboard. They can do whatever they want to me in there and wherever else they want to bend me over at. All the good things that make me blush and scream in ecstasy are allowed. I blush now just thinking about it.

It's been a wild ride since I've gotten back. Literally. I've rode so much dick my head is spinning all the time. There's no shortage of orgasms around here. And they refuse to stop at just one for me.

Shadow and Leo have been gone mostly during the day here lately. They've installed a state-of-the-art security system. Shadow tested it since he had a bad habit of breaking and entering here. It kept him out.

I've taken Shawn shopping…with Travares as security detail. There was zero compromise on that front. We went shopping for everything he will need for school in France. He was accepted, like I knew he would be. He screamed and danced when he got the acceptance email. He immediately called his grandma.

He starts in two weeks and since he tested so high and with all his earned credits, he's estimated to only do two years of a four-year degree. But while he's waiting to leave, he's going to Detroit to spend time with his family, then leaving for France from Detroit.

We had our goodbyes yesterday when we dropped him at the airport.

I was allowed a Shawn hug then.

And I was more self-conscience about pressing my boobies up against him than the last time I hugged him. Damn them for that. Assholes. I could have happily lived without these thoughts.

It was agreed by all involved that I would take a couple more weeks off work. I admitted I needed it in a bad way. My mind is still coping with the bad things. I get to go back this Monday. I'm excited.

Every once in a while I have a nightmare where I'm trapped in that concrete room and something bad always happens to me in there when the door opens. I wake up arms flailing or yelling in my sleep. One of the guys always holds me afterwards, whispering soothing words to me as I drift back to sleep. They've been really understanding. I don't deserve them and their patience.

It's also been agreed upon by everyone in this relationship that we would live in my house. Leo's lease is up next month anyways. He's moved in all his belongings already. We're just going to have one whole wall of dressers in the bedroom I suppose. To each their own chest of drawers.

They refuse to have their own rooms, so we share the master bedroom and one king bed, and one bathroom…that thankfully has two sinks. Guys are slobs.

By guys, I mean Shadow.

I didn't like the idea of them having their own rooms either. They said no. Their word was final.

I don't want them to be far away from me anyways, so I'm good with their plan.

Shadow owns his apartment…which he just bought upon his return…he plans on putting it on the market here soon. He said it was no hardship for him; he's been waiting for this day for far too long and he doesn't give two shits and a fuck about that apartment.

Ok then.

I can't help but worry. Am I rushing into this? Maybe. Could this possibly blow up in my face? Sure, but I'm trying hard to live more in-the-now and not fret about the future so much.

Sometimes I have imposter syndrome and I don't really believe this is how my life is turning out. I mean, everything I've ever wanted is happening.

We even talked about kids. After working with plenty of moms and seeing how they balance life, I'm lessening up on my refusal to have kids.

Plus it doesn't help that little baby Denver makes my ovaries pant with want. Baby fever is too real when he's around, y'all. I hold him and think to myself, *Yeah, you can do this, Zhar* but I know the day he starts running around being a terror, I'll switch back to *Fuck that.* Birdie said I'm not getting any younger so I need to shit or get off the pot when deciding about a future family. She was terrified it would never happen to her.

The difference is she wanted to be a mom. Nowadays I'm not sure if I want that. I mean if it happens, it happens but I'm on birth control for a reason and it better hold up strong. It has twice the cum coming at it now.

I just don't know how to balance a kid with work or having to vie for the attention of my men. It's not something we are looking at doing right away anyways. I have time.

While I'm contemplating life, Leo walks through the front door. He spots me in my favorite chair, "Hey baby," he says while he drops his keys in the dish and toes his riding boots off.

"Hey," I reply. Looking at him will never be a hardship for me. Fuck me, he is fine. I don't know how I got so lucky. My men are beautiful, sexy, smart, and everything I've ever wanted.

"Whatcha doing sitting all alone, pretty baby?" He makes his way over to the chair and drops a kiss on my lips before sliding down the side of the chair with me until I'm forced to move and accept him. He pulls me on top of his lap and I lay my head on his shoulder.

"Just thinking," I shrug.

He runs his fingers over my forearm causing goosebumps. Jesus, I can't think when they are near, especially when one of them is touching me.

"Oh yeah? What's got you in a mood?"

I snuggle into his neck and take a big whiff of his essence. He smells like the sunshine infused air from riding his bike, but I can smell his spicy cologne still on him. I love how they smell when they get in from riding their bikes.

"I just realized I'm never going to have a wedding that I want, that I wasn't coerced into. You know, weddings like every little girl dreams of."

He moves me to sit up and look at him. As he holds my face cupped in his hands, searching my eyes, he asks, "Do you want a wedding?" He asks with such seriousness too. Like this is no joke to him. Like if I said yes, would he marry me tomorrow? Is this a trick question?

"I won't pick between you two," I say softly. "You know this."

His eyes bore into mine, searching my soul, like he can see the truth written in the abyss of my eyes.

"That's not what I asked. What if you could have it all? You could marry us both? Would that be enough to fulfill the dream the little girl inside you has?"

"Yes," I whisper. He gives me hope he can find a way to give this to me. Leo's my bleeding romantic. If anyone can find a solution, he's it for the job. I'm too blessed to be ungrateful, so I'll let him give me what I dream of on his own timeline. If he says it will happen, it will happen.

He rubs his thumbs under my eyes, catching a lone tear, "Hey, none of this crying. I love you. I will give you anything I can give. I'll be the light in your darkness, I want to be your everything. I want to make all your dreams come true, anything to make you happy. Don't be sad, princess."

"I want that too. I love you, Leo," I reply softly.

"I think you'll get your dream, baby, when the moment is perfect you'll get your dream proposal. You just won't know when it will happen and I promise it will happen, but you can have anything you want. Start a journal, a vision board, a photo album, whatever, just show us all your dreams so we can make them come true. I would pluck every star from the sky if you wanted them." He pulls my face down to kiss me. It's so sweet and soft at first. I sigh into the kiss and that's when he slips his tongue into my mouth.

God, I love kissing them. It's like an out-of-body experience. It makes my toes curl and I simper like a blushing teenager. The taste of their lips is my idea of paradise.

I moan and start to wiggle my ass on his hard length under me. I didn't mean for this to happen, but come on, it always happens when one of them is near me.

It's definitely lifting my spirits.

However, I'm onto their games. Seducing her into a better mood is the name of the game. Sometimes I play along. I'll be upset later but for right now I'm giving up control and just feeling him love me.

I relax into him and rest my hands on his rock-hard abs. As soon as he breaks away from me for air, I beg, "Please, Leo. I want you inside me, now. Please."

"Ok, baby, lift up here," he taps my thigh so he can undo his belt and pull out his hard dick. "Pull your panties over or I can rip them off of you like the last time."

"Umm, no, I'll just kindly take these off. I like them. There's a great panty shortage going on and I suspect Shadow is hoarding them in one of his drawers." He laughs while he helps me get them off with some wrangling and I straddle his lap. He tucks my bohemian skirt into the waistband behind me. He lines up to my slick entrance and mixes his precum with my juices, smearing it all over. It sends a shiver of excitement through me. I'm so impatient I whine.

"I know, baby, I'm getting there."

The quick amount of time it takes for me to be ready for one of them is alarming. Jesus, I really am a whore for them. That thought makes me tilt my chin and bask in the sunlight of their love.

"Sit down here, baby, slide down my cock, Zhar. That's it baby, you're taking me so good." He guides my hips down and back up, deeper each time. I gasp at the feeling of being so full. I love Leo's slight upward curve. I loll my head back and breathe out any stress in my body as I welcome one of the loves of my life into my sacred temple. I feel him bottom out right up next to my cervix so sweetly and I begin to move my hips.

God, it feels so good.

I'm not wearing a bra under this light sweater and his hands soon learn this. He lifts it over my breasts, over my head and tosses it on the couch. Leo takes a peaked nipple into his mouth and gently sucks. I jerk in response from the sensation, my pussy clenching hard at the contact. I moan and circle my hips on him faster.

"Good girl, that's my perfect princess. Fuck me, Zhar."

Leo moves to the other breast and gives it the same delicious treatment. It really sets off my juices and I feel that familiar rush of heat inside me. His arms are locked around me, holding me to him, driving me crazy with need. I feel myself getting closer. Dangerously close to the edge.

I move like a belly dancer, I keep dancing along to the rhythm, undulating on his cock. I tell him as my hands cover his on my breasts, "You know I'll be yours always, I just want to be worth it. I want everything you can give me, Leo, I'm yours." I clench him inside me and it feels amazing. He hisses around my nipple.

Leo sucks off my bud and looks up at me riding him, "That's it, baby, take what you need from me. I'll give you anything, pretty girl. I love you so much, Zhar, my perfect girl."

"Leo…" I breathe, my body stiffening, blood rushing through my body like a freight train. Flames shoot through my veins as I explode from my center and come on him hard as fuck. My mouth opens and his name shouts from it.

He's gripped my body so hard, having pulled me down harder on top of him, his bucking takes him deeper into me if possible. He grits out, "There's my good girl. All for me, Zharia, good girl." Leo tightens his arms one last time and unleashes inside of me, pulsating and shooting his seed in me with a ragged cry, "Fuck, Zhar! Oh god, baby."

I love feeling them coming inside of me. I like carrying a piece of them around with me everywhere I go.

I want the whole cumslut experience twenty-four-seven. I want to walk around leaking their cum.

We collapse back into the chair, me against his chest, and we try to catch our breaths. Leo recovers first, "Do you feel better now, princess?" He rubs circles into my back and it feels so good.

"Yes, thank you, Leo," I say into the crook of his neck that I'm nuzzled up into. Ahh yes, peace. "Yes, exactly what I needed."

"Let's go get you cleaned up, so we can do it all over again. Shadow should be home soon to join the fun."

There's a rhythmic buzzing, like tapping on a bongo drum that vibrates. Oh good, I'm going to be swept away to an exotic island in this dream. Do-da-do-da-dum. It's a happy little tune. I can't wait to lie on the beach under palm trees. *Bring it on.*

I hear it through my sleep. Least I think I'm asleep. I'm trying to pry my eyes open when I hear Shadow's gruff, sleepy voice say "Hello" while he's rolling towards me. "Yeah Pierre, here she is."

Shadow props the phone on my ear, my groggy voice croaks out, "Hey Pierre, is everything ok, babes?"

This is a dream, right? Pierre never calls me at this hour. I start waking up some more. Something is very wrong. Damn my fucking sleeping pill the doctor put me on.

Pierre sobs. I immediately gasp awake and sit up. "Pierre, talk to me. What's wrong, honey?"

My heart pounds out of my chest waiting on Pierre's next words.

"Pierre," I whisper, on the verge of tears.

Shadow and Leo are both sitting up beside me now, catching the drift that something's wrong.

Pierre heaves a breath in, "Seven left me. He left, Zhar," Pierre's voice cracks in a heartbreakingly haunting way. "He's gone. Everything's packed up, just gone, all of his things," another sob. "What am I going to do, Zhar? I feel like I'm dying." Pierre sobs some more and it destroys my heart.

Very few times have I seen him cry. He's not usually very emotional like this. This is shocking to me. I've never heard him like this. But I can understand the current situation. His husband of ten years has left him.

I'm already moving out of bed as he explains all this, I speak, "I'll be right over. I'm getting ready right now, ok, I'll be there. I love you, Pierre, I'm coming. I love you, wait for me, promise me you'll wait." I'm already throwing on a pair of sweats and a T-shirt, most likely one of their motorcycle shirts when the guys start moving. I'm not bothering with a bra or panties. This is DEFCON 1 level.

Pierre gives me a weak promise then disconnects, and for the first time I actually fear for my best friend. He suffers from depression and I fear for his life right now. He's had bad thoughts before. Dark thoughts. Admitted to hospital thoughts.

Shadow and Leo both drag themselves out of bed quickly and start dressing. "You don't have to come, it'll be ok. I can do this."

"Maybe we want to come. Pierre's our family too," Shadow growls.

He stills and then sighs. "Look, I didn't mean that any sort of twisted way. Just saying, we want to come." He leans forward and kisses me, "I'll warm up the car." He moves off towards the door.

I put my hand out, my fingers grasping for his big bicep, pulling him back to me. I put my arms around his neck, "I love you, Shadow. I didn't take it any kinda way." I hold my hand out for Leo to join. He puts his arm around my hips.

"Promise me you won't ever leave me like this. I won't survive it. I can't do it again." I barely hide the sob in my throat. "Speak my love language, I need words of affirmation right now, before I head into this."

Shadow lifts his hand and extends his pinky. I put my digit around his.

"I promise I am never leaving you. I know what it's like to be without you. I know darkness. I will never stop loving you. I can't live a day where you aren't in it. My sun, my moon and stars, my universe, my everything. My life means nothing without you. You're the light in my darkness. I'm here for eternity. Every breath and heartbeat inside me is yours. I promise, poppet." He lightly kisses my lips. I sink into pure happiness at his words.

Leo holds his pinky out. I move my finger over to his outstretched digit and he squeezes. "I'm not leaving. I'm here for infinity. I'll always find you in every lifetime. You're the very air I breathe, the blood that runs through me. I am forever yours. You've got nothing to worry about, baby." He kisses me on my forehead.

God, I love them so much.

"Don't let the emotions of your best friend sabotage how you feel about us. We're good, baby girl. Let's go take care of our bestie," Shadow finishes, pulling on my hand to lead me out of the door. I reach back for Leo and he grips my hand tightly, hurrying along after us. I give Leo a goofy smile as Shadow drags me out of the room.

I ask them, "So, we're practically married now with those vows, right?"

I am right where I'm supposed to be, smack dab in the middle. Inescapable, as TayTay said, I'm not even gonna try and if I get burned, at least we were electrified.

I never want to leave.

This was meant to be.

It's about time I found out what home truly is.

The End.

Follow the third book in the Southern Devils Society series, The Ink King, with Pierre's story. He's heart broken, his life shattered, what's a man to do? Zharia's advice: Get under someone new and forget Seven. Will he take her advice?

THANK YOU!

Thank YOU so much for reading my stories. It means so much to me. I really appreciate it. I already have ideas for books 3, 4, & 5 swirling in my head.

Thank you to my husband who is my ride or die, always my hype man, my biggest fan. Thanks for being you, babe. Ilu

Thank you to myself for coming up with this. Just seeing if you're reading this LOL

I'm super grateful for all the Spotify playlists I'm constantly listening to.

Thank you so very much to Bethany for her kind words, friendship and expertise in the English language when my brain fails me. Thank you for your invaluable edits.

Thank you to my ARC readers, Kim, Laura, Bethany, Amanda and Sarah. I'm honored to have you read my book.

Last but not least, thank you to Count-Chunkula-hybrid. IFKYK.